THE ONE WITHOUT FLAME

MICHELLE MASSIE

The Mirri Series

Book 1: *A Magic Evermore*

Book 2: *A Secret Nevermore*

For my two best friends.

Best. Family. Ever.

Anatomy of a Female Svari

25 % bigger than male, would give their lives for their Queen

Why no males?

Majestic and grand, the Queen Svari is a gentle giant. Since their arrival during the Upheaval of Havelock, (see pg. 3) these female dragonsA have proven to be an interesting, although mysterious study.

Female dragons, respectfully referred to as "Queens," can grow as tall as sixteen feet into the air. Their grand size makes their muscle mass immense, suggesting they would be excellent candidates for hauling extreme weight, such as another smaller, injured dragon. The weight of the largest Svari is nearly 11,000 pounds, which is as heavy as four to six Blue Gavel Sharks. One could understand why, at one time, these creatures would have been the most feared in the wild.

The wing span of a female Svari reaches as wide as seventy-five feet, which is one reason these dragons would not fly deep into the mountains. It is reasonable to assume Svaris lived and bred in low-lying areas worldwide.

Female Svaris are not born with the proper ingredients in their chemical makeup for harnessing flame. After extensive research, it is believed that the females have the tube running down their trachea needed to produce flames. However, due to hormone levels in females, they do not produce enough of the chemical Vroulik, a chemical that creates fire when mixed with oxygen.

FIRE OF A MALE CONTAINS "SUITSU" FOR FERTILIZING DRAGON EGGS

Svari queens-aka "the one
with the spotted underbelly"
** Article 3 section 4 **
Wingspan: 65-75 feet
14-16 foot
Prime age for
pregnany-400-500
years
Tail-vital orga-
near underbelly
Weight-between 10,000-11,000 lbs
Length-between 90-100 feet

CHAPTER 1

Quinn

It was the first time I had the opportunity and rage to bring my knee up between a man's legs.

But I didn't.

I had seen what he had done. I had watched from afar as he stood in front of Selyse with that remote in his hand. Then I watched her fall.

"You bastard!" I screamed, flinging open the cold metal gate of the Keep and running toward the uniformed man. "What are you *doing* to her?" I ran to Selyse's side, hopping over her large front claw, closer than anyone else would get to the dragons, and peered into her enormous eye. She fell to the ground right outside the pond, where the dragons would cool themselves after flight.

Her leathery skin moved up and down slowly. "Are you all right? What happened?" It was only loud enough for her to hear.

She simply shook her gigantic head, bringing up a cloud of dust. Then she closed her eyes. No colors flowed from her eyes. No lovely swirls around her face. Just dust.

My mouth hanging open, I turned and marched toward the uniformed man.

"What did you do to her?" I asked slowly. My insides burned, and my hands clenched at my sides.

He rolled his eyes. "Doing my job, little lady. I'd expect a girl like you would want me to."

I narrowed my eyes at his remark, knowing exactly what he was referring to. "What I want is none of your business. Give me the remote." I held my hand out, throwing my brown hair across my back, displaying my scarred face. My scar didn't change a thing. And I wasn't ashamed of it.

"No," he sneered. "Now get outta here."

"Give me it."

He ignored me and held it up to his face, humming. His greasy blonde hair hung out of the front of his cap, which was perched sideways on his head, and he gave me a devilish smile. Without warning, he flipped a switch, making Veseria—a small but mighty Svari—jump from her position, and roll her long green neck in pain.

"Stop it!" I screamed. I jumped on the man before I could think, reaching for the remote, grabbing his unbuttoned collar by the gold snap, and knocking him on his ass.

He grunted as I pushed his chubby face sideways into the dirt. I cried out as he grabbed me by the back of my long hair, the stench of his armpit enough to make me gag. He threw the remote backward, little glints of silver hopping across the field. The sun glared off the metal device, illuminating its position perfectly. He grabbed my shoe as I scrambled off of him, trying to retrieve the metal object capable of downing even the most magnificent of creatures. My nose landed hard on the ground and I kicked at him furiously, spitting out the grimy dirt, my foot still in his grasp.

"What is going on here?" A familiar voice thundered.

The sloppily dressed man and I both froze. He sat on his rear in a field with his hand wrapped around my skinny ankle. I was mid-kick, my foot high in the air, on my hands and knees in the middle of the Keep. He dropped my leg, and I righted myself, standing and pulling my skirt right.

Luther strode to us with his nose in the air, his gray handlebar mustache perfectly combed. Though not really in charge of anything in Port Tarrith, he treated his job as a delicate flower and still gave off the impression he was a man to be feared. But only to those who didn't know better.

"And what is going on here?" Luther asked, cocking his head.

My face warmed when I imagined what that scene must have looked like. Oh, well. What Luther thought of me was hardly worth caring about.

The blonde man stood up quickly, dusting off his blue pants and running a hand over his greasy hair, replacing his cap. "Nothing, sir," he muttered, more red in the face than I was.

I pointed at him. "He was shocking the dragons with that thing. I saw Selyse fall." I doubted it would do any good to tattle. The head of the Union of the Protection of Dragons cared very little about protecting dragons. He only cared about the amused looks he got behind his back for heading a ridiculous organization that existed solely for tax purposes.

Luther raised his bushy eyebrows. "And you thought it best to tackle him, Quinn?"

I glared at the guard then turned back to Luther. "Yes."

Luther sighed dramatically and put his hands in the pocket of his ridiculous blue suit. "I suppose it's time to go see Sir Ambrose."

"Yes," I said. "I think it is." I put my hands out equally dramatically to the uniformed man.

Sloppy-man paled slightly and looked at Luther for confirmation.

"No, Quinn," Luther said. "It is time for you and I to go."

"That piece of filth was shocking the dragons for sport, and Luther didn't even care. I watched him, Father." I leaned on my father's desk, my face burning. "He didn't even care."

Father sighed and removed his glasses, tossing them on the mountain of paper-work spread on the desk. He leaned back in his brown chair. "It was not for sport, Quinn. The dragon collars will be tested every day for the sake of the riders. It is a new protocol."

I stared, open-mouthed. "New protocol? To hurt them?" I slammed my fist on his desk so hard papers flew and my hand ached. "Every goddamn day?"

Father stood up, walking around his desk. "Quinn—"

I dropped my hand, gazing numbly at the lovely wooden shelves, packed with folders and books, and the maroon drapes behind him, things that once brought me comfort in this great room. "How could you let him do this?" I whispered. "How could you let him disregard every rule, everything in place to protect them?"

He closed his eyes and rubbed at his wrinkled forehead. "Because I believe it is necessary to protect the Flyers. There will be daily tests on the collars before each flight. It is for the safety of the riders, dear. And the doctor agrees that these tests pose no harm to the dragons themselves."

I shook my head, tears threatening. My own father. Signing off on the torment of the dragons. My friends. It made me physically ill. Luther's smirk, the one I knew he was giving me behind my back, filled the room. It positively smothered me.

I put my hands to either side of my face. "No, Father—you don't understand. It hurts them. More than you know! It puts them in pain, exhausts them, and then they are expected to haul Tarrith Rock all over the country?"

"It hurts them, Ms. Ambrose? And how would you know that?" Luther asked, leaning on the window frame. "Well?"

I bit my inner cheek, bristling at his question. I knew because dragons spoke to me. Plain as day. Did Luther know? Some days, I thought he might. Even if he did, it changed nothing. No one could know. No one.

Powers, or gifts, were scoffed at around here, especially by those of any high standing. The word 'magic' was flat-out taboo. Now and then, a story will float through the Port, or you will hear whispers around town, about someone with a gift, then their tragic death or disappearance. Who knows what they would do to the daughter of the leader of Port Tarrith?

But I was not about to be stopped. "You feed them *cattle*, Luther. The excess iron hurts their teeth, causes their fangs to crack. Imagine if someone forced you to eat a diet that destroyed your teeth—"

"Yes, you have told me all about this repeatedly," Luther snapped.

Father cleared his throat, lifting his eyebrows.

Luther straightened his tie, his cheeks reddening. "Yes, Ms. Ambrose. I recall this information. Thank you for reminding me of it again."

I jumped at the opportunity. "And the fail-safe? You said you would look into it by the end of last month." I stood with my hands on my hips.

The reddening of his face deepened. He straightened his shoulders. "I assure you, the fail-safe around the Keep is completely within code, Ms. Ambrose. It does not violate the Protection of Dragons clause."

"It completely violates it!" I could have slapped the man across the face. "If you think having an electric current fry your brain is nothing more than an inconvenience, I think you've got your head up your—"

"Quinn," my father said, standing up. "I think you've made your point."

"But—"

He held his hands up, interrupting my rant, signaling the side he was taking.

My hands fell to my side. The fail-safe method around the Keep was a degrading and horrendous insult to the dragons. Installed just last month. I argued it went against the Protection of Dragons clause, a contract that I took seriously. The collars they wore could send an electric shock through their bodies, rendering them immobile with the flip of a switch. It was unspeakable.

I stood with my arms crossed, trying not to let my bottom lip tremble.

Luther gave me a sympathetic nod. "I am truly sorry, Ms. Ambrose. Perhaps your unfortunate incident with the dragons has caused you to feel something not truly there."

I held my breath. Every time someone mentioned my 'unfortunate incident' or my scar, they thought it proved something. All it did was prove my point. The same point I had been trying to make for years.

Turning back to my father, I let out my breath slowly. "The dragons were never meant to be our slaves, Father. What you are doing to them is nothing less than torture."

He walked around his desk with a sigh. The lines by his eyes had deepened in the last few months, along with the wrinkles on his forehead. But I couldn't let this go. It was too much.

"Quinn, we have been through this. Without the dragons, Tarrith would be back in the slums. You know this. It is the reason our economy flourishes. The reason we have an economy at all." He gave me a tired smile. "How can we settle this?"

"Change the protocol." I crossed my arms in front of me. "Stop testing the collars."

He pinched the bridge of his nose.

A loud knock came from his office door. Martha opened the door and smiled tightly. "Sir? Minister Farrow is waiting."

Father nodded. "Thank you, Martha." He grabbed his jacket off of the coat rack. "Luther? Perhaps you would like to tell Quinn about the replenishment program we have put into place for the dragons."

"Of course, Arden," Luther replied, nodding.

Father nodded and left the room, leaving me and one of the most putrid, loathsome men in the country standing two feet from one another.

Just as I was about to flounce out of the room, Luther stepped in my way.

Glaring at him, I crossed my arms. "I would like to leave now."

He smiled and put his hands in his pockets. Instead of moving out of my way, he stepped toward me, forcing me to step back.

"Please," I said through clenched teeth. "I need to leave."

But he simply stared.

I swallowed, determined not to look nervous, wedged between him and an overgrown house plant. The heat of his body crept up my neck, making me turn my head at the scent of his overpriced cologne. A fake, loathsome smell. It reminded me of a disgusting ale Father would bring out for parties—like one that had sat out in the sun for far too long. Bitter. Nauseating.

"You know, it truly impresses me the lengths you go to for these beasts, my dear."

I clenched my teeth until it hurt. Both at the fact he called the dragons 'beasts' and his term of endearment. He had no right to either.

"We were a dying country, Quinn. Now, we flourish. You would not want to return to the old times, would you? The poverty? Illness? Crime rampant?"

Of course. Tarrith—such a flourishing city. The envy of every other city in this province. Financially sound, unified as the leading producer of Tarrith Crystal, and the pet that the President of Havelock favored in every sense.

Frankly, I thought the cost was too great.

He used his rough finger to brush a stray hair off my cheek, pushing it behind my ear. My breath halted as he grazed the scar that started underneath my eye. "After all that has happened to you, I'm surprised you defend them like you do."

The nausea cartwheeling in my stomach was mixing with grays and blacks—swirling in my mind as he spoke. I shook my head, a moment too long probably, but he took his hand away from my face. Turning my head, I tried to concentrate on this broad-leaf plant, its sad white flowers wilting, and not on Luther's true colors.

He was the only human that evoked colors in me. Dragons, yes, but humans? Only Luther Grimbley could make the grays and blacks swirl. It made me shudder to think why, of all people, my mind would choose to see these colors seeping out of this one man.

"You remind me so much of your mother, my dear."

My brain snapped, my usual disgust with the man turning into a deepening rage. I wiped my palm over my cheek, trying to rid my skin of the feel of his sandpaper touch.

"The dragons should be set free, Mr. Grimbley. They are not our slaves." My voice came out soaked with a seeping hatred, a hatred that appeared whenever he dared to speak of my mother.

He leaned toward me, almost close enough for his gray mustache to graze my cheek.

"I'm afraid they are, Quinn. And there is nothing you and your dragons can do about it."

CHAPTER 2

Tess

I grinded against him, breathing hard, leaving nail marks up and down his biceps. At the moment, I could see nothing but red. Anger. He moaned underneath me, and I leaned over and bit his chest, hard enough to make him yelp and throw me back onto the handmade mattress. He climbed back on top of me as the red in my brain settled, giving me the relief I had been praying for. I ached for a drink of cool water as I licked my dry lips, trying to ignore the taste of his sweaty skin in my mouth.

He rocked back and forth on top of me, his energy lasting much longer than I would have liked. I wiped at my sweaty forehead, ready for this to be over. The colors had stopped. Finally. I stared at the ceiling in the room, waiting for him to be finished as he bit at my neck, dragging his tongue over my ear.

The smell of sex hung in the air all around us, almost sour, and it made my stomach turn. I rubbed my forehead, wishing he would hurry it up already.

Lights flashed all around us, like some little messenger from above, sent straight to the bunk room to relieve me of the man huffing and puffing above my body. He stopped mid-thrust, raised his muscular body off mine, and looked around. "What the hell is that?"

"Code Green." I took the opportunity to slide underneath him, off the pile of worn and dirty blankets, and away from his sweaty body. I grasped at the cracked concrete floor for the green pants that I had discarded wildly several minutes before, not long after the reds commenced a swirling in my brain. The rest of my clothes were somewhere in this room, camouflaged pieces mocking my absence as the flashing lights continued. Dammit, I should be there. Dammit, dammit. I shoved my bare feet into my boots, the strings still dragging along the floor.

"Hey!" Loic said, running a hand through his blonde hair. "What the hell—"

I pulled the wrinkled shirt down and ran out into the hallway, leaving my naked bedmate looking dazed and confused. He hadn't been here quite two weeks yet. This was probably his first code.

To warn others of a Code Green, one would go to the electrical box in the building's front near the floor and flip the switch on and off. A silent warning of what a team member thought they spied flying through the sky, fangs baring, spouting fire wherever it saw a weakness in the mountain.

The odds of this being a genuine emergency? Not likely.

Pushing past the people hurrying in the opposite direction, all following orders of a Code Green, I made my way to the front of the base. I stopped at the exit, still sweaty and breathless from my prior activities. Two of my team stood at the door, peeking through the small window, one gauge weapon between the two of them.

"Let me see."

Hash, the only member of my team who managed to brush and clean his hair every day, turned to me with an intense gaze. He paused, eyebrows raised, as his eyes ran up and down my person.

I tugged at the collar of my shirt, noticing the tag that stuck out at the top. I gave him a sigh and pursed my lips, giving him a silent, *Yeah, so what?*

He opened the door and stepped back without a word.

I reached back for the knife that should have been sheathed at my waistband. My fingers grazed the air. Shit. These weren't even my damn pants. The problem with wearing militia uniforms—everyone's clothes looked exactly the same.

I stepped out of the door, making sure it creaked closed behind me. My eyes went directly into the late afternoon sky, scanning the green peaks of the treetops first, then higher into the warm and cool curves of the mountain range. The krekels cawed louder than I could scream in those trees, unaware of the concern of the humans below. But I took their annoying cadence as a good sign. Apparently, the obnoxious birds who once stole a week's worth of ashami fruit had spotted nothing worth worrying about.

Arik crouched behind Benny's tree. It was the only tree in the meadow surrounding the base, a giant Mangway tree. Using the stained sheet hanging off a low branch as cover, he pointed his gauge at the sky. The slow and steady movements of his rifle told me he had seen nothing concrete, but concern still kept the weapon in the air. I hoped Benny had tucked himself up tight in his tent, out of sight.

I kept my eyes up, letting my hands brush the tops of the tall grass as I crept to Arik and kneeled down. "Anything?" I stared up into the sky, following his line of vision.

He shook his head. "Hash tripped the alarm. Swears he saw a Svari patrolling the area. Or maybe a Redwing."

I winced at the mention of a Redwing. Kings, I hoped not. We hadn't seen Redwings this far south in years, maybe ever, but since word of the weapon had leaked out, we expected more patrols, even in our remote area of the woods. Still . . . part of me knew it was only a matter of time.

"Which direction?"

"North."

I bit my lip. Not including the false alarm by Finch a few weeks ago, it was the third possible dragon sighting this month. But usually, team members saw trees flutter or a large shadow cast over the ground and assumed the worst. I wasn't sure if people were getting overly cautious or if there were dragons searching the mountains. Either way, it was a problem.

"Probably another false alarm. A Svari couldn't get up this far," I said, more to myself than Arik.

"But a Redwing could." He handed me the gauge. "Check it out, up there on the highest ridge."

I took the weapon and peered up through the scope, using my fingers to adjust the vision. I saw what he was referring to. A blackened tree burned to a crisp, a ringlet of smoke wafting up from its dead branches. I gulped.

"Maybe it was just a Svari," I whispered, still looking through the scope.

"No way a Svari could hit that tree at that angle, this high up."

My heart sank as I knew he was right. "Shit."

We both jumped as the sheet in front of us moved. The bushy gray beard poked out of the tent, and the back of Benny's head swung up to the north. I immediately regretted talking about the Redwing this close to the old man. I had forgotten he was even there.

"It's okay, Benny," Arik said. "Why don't you come and sleep inside tonight?"

Benny answered us by turning and staring with those shockingly blue eyes. He shook his head, his long hair and beard flying, and ducked back inside.

I stood, tapping on the dingy sheet. "Benny, I think you should stay inside tonight. Please?"

Nothing.

I sighed, running a hand through my short hair. "Fine. C'mon. Let's go back in. I'll send Finch out to keep watch for a while."

Arik stood and looked at Benny's tent, then back at me.

I sighed, throwing my arms up. "What do you want me to do? I can't knock him out and drag him in there."

Arik sighed and threw the gauge over his shoulders, heading back toward the entrance to the squat one-story building. I followed closely, glancing back at the dirty sheet. Benny had been in town almost as long as we had, a silent guest who just… hung around. He picked up trash and random pieces of earth, and the only speaking I had ever heard from him was the conversations he had with himself. We left food for him when we had extra, which didn't happen often, but we did what we could. The sheet he slept under every night came from my own bed, one I had given him almost four years ago.

Hash let us back in the main door, and Arik handed over the gauge to Finch. "Go hang by Benny. Best vantage point," Arik instructed. "Keep an eye on the north ridge." Arik's eye caught mine. No point in mentioning the Redwing at the moment. No need to worry everyone for no reason. We left Hash at the front door to stand watch and headed to the room at the end of the only hallway in the building, where everyone would be waiting, as per Code Green protocol. We called it the war room—no windows or cracks in the ceiling. The most secure area on the base.

"What I would give for that radio now," I said as we walked down the narrow hall, referring to the radio Arik and I used to spend hours fiddling with as children, down in the basement of my building.

"Ha." Arik scoffed. "As if we'd be able to hear anything on it."

"We almost did. Once."

He rolled his eyes. "Yeah, very helpful."

We spent countless hours in that basement, wrapped in blankets, our fingers blue from the cold. But that didn't stop us from turning those knobs back and forth. Ignoring the scurrying mice and water continuously dripping from pipes, we sat on the freezing concrete, desperate for news from the militia. We were sure we could find secret war reports, maybe hear pilots screaming as they flew in battle. Hear about all the dragon fights, or maybe find out how many soldiers had perished in a single day. Every year, the age for drafting sank a little lower. We needed to be prepared. After a year or so, we finally gave up.

We stopped at the door as Arik glanced down at my front. "Nice pants."

I ignored him and shoved my way into the room. Arik had the bad habit of noticing everything.

People stood in groups and leaned against the brick walls. Loic stood at the back, his arms crossed and a scowl on his face. We kept this room open and empty for these Code Greens. Our emergency bunker, should the need arise. A few people looked up as we entered, but most people remained indifferent, hands in their pockets and a bored look on their faces. Code Greens just didn't evoke the same sense of urgency as they once did.

Harlen approached me, arms wrapped around her waist. The issued shirt she wore was a few sizes too big, but she would never complain. "What was it?" She was a younger, newer member of the base. She still took these codes seriously.

I shook my head. "We're not sure. Might have been a Svari." I stopped. "Might not."

"Svaris don't come this deep into the mountains," Harlen said, gnawing on her nails. "So, was it anything?" Every time she chewed on her fingernails, my eyes trailed to the freckles that still covered her face. She was so young.

I hitched up my sagging pants, avoiding my team's gaze. "Don't know. We'll keep watch overnight." I turned to the right. "Kemp, you'll relieve Finch in a couple hours."

He nodded and left the room, but I saw his eyes narrow. Kemp came from Mylar, a northern country we didn't hear a lot about—territory of Redwings. He came to Tarrith with his grandfather right before the wars. Swears he saw a Redwing or two in his lifetime, when he was a boy, but I wasn't sure if anyone believed him. Redwings are supposed to be fierce and crave the taste of human flesh—they leave no survivors.

"Let's shut the place down this evening, guys. No lights. Everybody gets to the bunk room. Let's stay quiet and dark the rest of the night."

If anyone found this odd, they didn't mention it. Code Greens rarely ended in the entire team being quarantined in the bunk room this soon after the evening meal. Code Greens usually meant we patrolled the area for an hour or two, kept eyes on the sky, and then called it off. Svaris were poor hunters, with poor eyesight and hearing, and wings that stretched too wide to fly deep in the mountains. But I was determined to always be ready.

And I had a bad feeling.

I stepped out of the exit, trying to quiet the creaking door, the sound practically bouncing off the mountain range in the distance. I knew right where Arik would be. He leaned against the building, right at the corner, with a cigarette in his mouth, staring up at the sky. I wrinkled my nose as I leaned against the brick next to him.

"I told you to get rid of those. They're not worth trading for."

He smiled darkly. "Oh, no, I got this one for free."

I rolled my eyes. "Of course you did."

Kemp stood positioned with the gauge right behind the tree, eyes in the sky. If anyone believed in a threat, it was Kemp. I knew he wouldn't be falling asleep on the job. He was easily the tallest guy here—and one of the best guards.

"Planning on getting any sleep tonight?" I settled down on the ground against the base.

"Nope." He shook his head, putting the cigarette to his lips. "You?'

"Can't sleep now."

I thought of all the nights Arik and I had spent awake, staring up at the night sky. Ironic that we did that now, for a very different reason. We used to count the stars. Lying on the roof of my building, we would point out constellations, giggling at our success in breaking the rules.

But it wasn't all simply to be obnoxious. Once we had shoved sticks with shirts tied around the ends inside our nightclothes, made it to the roof, and then soaked them in kerosene. Our plan was to bring the Fire Goddess, Vatra, back to the world, right from the roof of my building. Vatra had the power of the flame in her hand, and the legend tells of a story in which Vatra stole fire from the devil to gift it to her people. Who better to defeat the dragons than the Goddess of Fire?

Indivar, a wrinkled, toothless old man who lived in the woods, sold us the incantation to summon her for two bronze coins. It had taken three tries and one beating to my bare ass to get those coins. All for nothing. Vatra did not show up to save our city as we had planned.

Arik lived beyond the walls of the military compound, but his family's farmland kept them in good graces with the militia. He was afforded more leniency than others who lived beyond the compound. No one whipped or beat him for being found sneaking around inside the gates. Usually, the Praetorian guards—who we so lovingly called Prats—dragged him out by his ear. They couldn't injure him too badly. Arik's participation in the dragon's favorite sport kept the Svaris entertained and got his mother the medicine she needed.

"Everything quiet in there?" he asked.

"Yup. Locked up tight."

"Wouldn't help much if a Redwing was out there," he murmured, looking up.

"Well, you standing in front of the building smoking wouldn't exactly help either, dumb ass."

If stories were true, a Redwing could smell a human's scent from miles away. They saw best at night, the time they preferred to hunt. When they were bloodthirsty. Even worse, because of their compact size, Redwings could navigate and fly as they pleased, especially through the mountains where they were bred. They were mountain dragons.

Something occurred to me. "You think a Redwing could be the weapon?"

Arik shook his head. "No, the weapon is supposed to control dragons. Why would it be a Redwing?"

I thought about it. True. Though it would be just like my father to pull some kind of stunt like that. Spread the rumor, making everyone chase their tails, searching and hoping to find some object to one day take their land back. And the whole time, it would be a dragon. An enemy dragon.

"Wouldn't surprise me." I lowered my voice. "Especially if my father had something to do with it." I coughed as smoke wafted in my direction, burning my nose with the scent of rancid tar. I slapped him on the leg.

Arik stayed silent, looking thoughtful. "Maybe. But he'd actually have to get his hands on one."

"And use it on the Svari. A Redwing could probably take them out."

"Nah, not an entire fleet of Svaris." Svaris might have been poor hunters, but they were intense fighters.

"But it would totally make sense," I said, covering my nose as I looked up at him. "This horrible weapon, with the power to control dragons and abolish Dragon Rule, suddenly comes into play? What if it's a Redwing?"

He put the cigarette butt out on his rubber sole. "And how would one Redwing abolish Dragon Rule?"

"Maybe it's a whole flock of them." My stomach turned at the thought.

"No way. If it was a whole flock, we would know. Everyone would. There would be no people left."

I watched him rub his arm up by his elbow, a nervous tick of his. I don't even think he realized he did it. A long scar ran from his bicep to his forearm, one that he wouldn't speak about, a scar he received during a fighting match. I had asked about the Fights many times, but he always refused to speak of them. I don't think I wanted to know, anyway.

After being lost in the forest for days, near death, we stumbled out of the forest into this meadow, which contained a locked-down base and an ancient chapel. We spent two nights sleeping in the dilapidated church under wooden benches, freezing our asses off, staring up at the gaping hole in the roof, seeing the constellations but not mentioning them. Vatra had let us down when we were children. We couldn't bear the thought of her letting us down again. At least I couldn't.

"What do we do about the weapon?"

Arik startled me out of my memory. "What about it?"

"What if that's the big deal going on at the port tomorrow? Maybe that's why the Svaris are flying around down there."

We had been keeping an eye on the port. If you walked about a half mile from the back door of the base, through the thick layer of trees, and around a corner, you had a decent view of ships, as well as the Svaris. Another reason we assumed this building had once been a military base of some sort. Those trees had been planted in a keen location to spy on the port, in the days it was used regularly.

I bit my lower lip, wondering if it would be worth taking a trip down to the docks tomorrow. We hadn't raided a container in weeks. When the war was going badly, shipments were rare, if nonexistent. Just the fact that a ship was arriving was out of the ordinary. And it would be worth it to see the weapon. Just maybe.

We sneaked a peek at each other. He raised his eyebrows. After eleven years side by side, we could read each other's thoughts.

I let out a slow smile. "I like what you're thinking."

Chapter 3

Quinn

As the sun sank lower in the sky that evening, I wandered down the long gravel trail that led to the Dragon Keep. A long walk, especially in my flats, but one I tried to make every evening. Lately, with my course load, it had just not been feasible. The Svaris slept, ate, and lived their lives in this bare, confined field—anytime they were not being forced to haul freight across the continent for Tarrith's profit.

I used to ask Selyse what it was like to fly. She would only sigh and say she could not remember what it felt like to really fly. It made my heart heavy to see the shine in her eyes fade away when she spoke like that. Like it dampened her spirit—as if it hurt her heart as much as it hurt mine.

The Svaris gathered by the pond, slurping and dipping their faces in the water, trying to get enough nourishment to reward their worn and tired bodies. Svaris were enormous dragons. I didn't even stand as tall as Selyse's front leg. I'd never understood why people found these creatures so frightening. To me, they were beautiful. Truly amazing.

Most of the Flyers were okay, I guess. I had never heard of them using the collars to shock a Svari or behave poorly toward them. Some even called the dragons by their names. But in the end, just a bunch of guys who had a job to do, I suppose. Fly the crystal all over the world. "Tarrith Rock," they called it. And countries paid handsomely for it.

I lifted the latch of the eighteen-foot gate and entered the Keep, nodding at the group of Flyers removing their gear. Miles waved, an older gentleman who had known my father for years. Father even invited him to dinner occasionally. Miles always spoke kindly of the dragons, and I never once heard him refer to them as commodities or beasts. So I waved back. I spoke little to the rest of the group, and they didn't care to speak to me. They referred to me as Sir Ambrose's daughter, the strange girl in the long skirt who came to the Dragon Keep every night after the day's runs and talked to herself. "A dragon lover," one had called me when they thought I wasn't listening. To them, I was the only person dumb enough to sit next to a dragon.

What did they expect? I had grown up in the house on the hill, next to the Keep, and watched dragons my whole life. My father ran all things related to dragons, the Keep, etcetera, so it seemed only natural I would be interested. The Union of Protection for Dragons, on the other hand, existed solely for the president's placation on the matter, soothing his fears and keeping his ass out of hot water when it came time for foreign deliberations about the six Svari.

I strolled through the field in the Keep, letting my fingers graze the long grass. I kicked at the same rock the entire way, if only to lengthen the time until I had to tell my friend the new protocols that were being put in place. Protocols that pained her, and one more thing to keep the female Svari dragons housed here as prisoners. These majestic, wise, and kind creatures. In the hands of petty humans. It was too much.

The woody scent of ambrosia mixed with ginger floated through the air, always heaviest when the dragons returned from flight. Their sweat pores practically leaked the scent out of them. A comforting smell, especially when I was younger, but now it only angered me. Too heavy a smell meant the dragons were over-worked. Exhausted.

By the time I reached out to rub her face, her eyes were already closed, her chin resting in the watering pond. The collar attached around her long neck blinked red, situated up by her chin, where it would never come off. The thirty-four years of slavery had not been easy on her body. By now, her green scales reflected more of a brown color, probably the most obvious sign of aging. She was thicker than the other dragons, therefore expected to be the strongest, the most productive. Selyse always flew the heaviest load, and it angered me. I studied her scales, noticing they looked even darker than the last time I was here. I frowned. They felt much too dry, as well.

Fenwick, her Flyer, stood to the side, working the water pump up and down furiously to fill the pond as full as possible. I smiled. Fenwick had my vote of approval. He was a Flyer, yes, but only because his father made him. And he didn't have to work that water pump. There was a guard who did the job twice a day. But I appreciated it nevertheless. I had a feeling if he didn't ride Selyse six days out of the week, he would be on my side a bit more.

Selyse turned when I got close enough, her tired eyes brightening. I patted her long tail as I walked closer, dropping on the edge of the pond, pulling my skirt underneath my short legs. I swirled the dirt around with my finger as she drank. Putting my chin on my knees, I watched Fenwick struggle with the lever, wiping his chin with his arm.

I gazed around at the rest of the dragons. The labored breathing, sweating scales, the exhaustion in their eyes. Too tired for their usual colors to swirl. By now, each dragon in the Keep had specific colors I recognized, hues that were a part of them.

"Hey, Quinn!" Fenwick hurried over, wiping his hands on his leather vest.

I said nothing but laid my head against her leg.

"Quinn!" he waved again and stopped, not wanting to invade the space that Selyse and I had.

She nudged me, and I raised my head. "Hey, Fenwick."

Selyse respected Fenwick immensely, and respect with dragons does not come easily. So I made myself stand and walk over to him, smiling as he waved so hard I thought he would fall over. "How did Selyse do today?"

"Pretty good. She had some trouble over the Ridge, but we kept it in line. Didn't we, Selyse?" He smiled up at her proudly.

Selyse smiled back down at him, but I'm not sure if Fenwick knew she was smiling. Small ribbons of orange and red usually flowed out of Selyse's eyes when she looked at her Flyer—but not tonight.

"Do you want me to walk you back home?" Fenwick asked, running a hand through his short hair.

Per usual. He was the only male I knew who wasn't afraid of my father. Probably because he had nothing to be afraid of. Fenwick had no ill intentions and hadn't disrespected a female in his life. Father had mentioned his name more than once, and had even asked if I would like to invite him to tea. But I had skipped the subject fairly quickly. There was nothing wrong with Fenwick, really, just sort of . . . tall and lanky. He wasn't my type. If I even had one.

"Uh, no thanks. I'm gonna stay here for a while," I said, putting my hair behind my ear. "Rough day."

His shoulders fell. "Okay."

I gave a silent sigh as his green eyes cast downward. Kind eyes. When he smiled, his left eye was darker than the right eye. But then I always caused his eyes to fall to the ground. I'm still not sure why he insisted on asking.

He turned and trudged toward the gate to exit the Keep, his saddle draped over his arm.

I waited for the usual disapproval from Selyse of my turning Fenwick down, as always, but she stayed quiet.

I settled down in the dirt, near her eyes, waiting for the colors that always flowed when she spoke to me. But nothing came.

Frowning, I elbowed her in the cheek. "You asleep already or something?" But that would be ridiculous. Dragons didn't sleep during the daylight, no matter how exhausted they were. I hadn't been to the Keep as often as I would have liked in the past few weeks. I wondered if she was mad at me.

Her long lashes fluttered. She made a sort of huff, blinking and blowing dust into the pond. No, she wasn't sleeping. Just thinking, maybe? So why hadn't she spoken to me?

I narrowed my eyes. "What's wrong?" Leaning in closer, I took in a breath. The ambrosia. Still strong. I stood up, confused. "Selyse? If something is wrong with you and you don't tell me what—"

I am fine.

I jumped at the low growl. Selyse never spoke that way to me. My heart pounded. I reached out, if only just to comfort myself, but she pulled away. The red blinking moved with her, like some devil attached to her skin.

The collar.

"Show me." I called to her. "Now!"

There is nothing to see. The voice snapped in my mind. *I would suggest returning home.*

I put my hands to my face. "Oh, God. What did they do to you?" I whispered.

Turning, I looked for the rest of the females. They, too, all were lying with their heads on the ground and eyes closed. Why weren't they drinking the cool water, or speaking with one another?

"Selyse!" I cried. "You will tell me what is going on or I will keep screaming until you do!"

Tell her, Selyse, Veseria mumbled. *So we may get some rest.*

"Thank you, Veseria," I said, turning toward her. I stopped. Her colors. They were gone. Veseria usually produced a light blue and yellow swirl from the top of her head. I always thought it matched her personality.

Slowly, I turned. "It's . . . the collars, isn't it? It's what they've been doing to you, isn't it?"

Selyse sighed. *It's been going on much longer than you knew, Quinn. And I believe it is aging us prematurely.*

"Aging you? Why haven't you told me? How long have they been doing this to you?" My hands shook, and my eyes filled with tears. I had no idea if these tears were from anger or pure horror.

Selyse remained quiet. I turned to face the other queens.

Six months, Veseria said. *Six long months.*

My stomach began doing backflips, threatening to produce my last meal. I shook my head, trying to clear the confusion and the anger, to separate the two. I squeezed my eyes shut and leaned forward, taking a deep breath.

"Selyse!" I cried. "Why wouldn't you tell me? For six months, you have lied to me! I could have helped, I could have done something! Now look at you!" The tears running down my face burned. Tears of betrayal. Tears of anger. Then just some tears.

There was nothing you could have done, Quinn. I was trying to protect you. Her voice was husky, as if keeping in tears herself. She had once told me dragons could not cry. I wondered if she had lied about that as well.

Standing straight, I stared into the eye of my best friend, in pain and aging. I wiped at my face, even though hot tears continued to fall. "There is something we can do, Selyse. Something we have to do."

It had always been in the back of my mind. A last resort. I think we had reached that point.

She only sighed again.

"We have to get you pregnant." My voice was still thick with tears but now also full of determination.

Selyse's enormous eye turned toward me.

I stared into the brilliant colors, biting my lower lip. "If you were pregnant, they would have to free you. It's dragon law. Article Three, Section Four of the Acceptable Use of Dragons statute." I knew the thing by heart. Had memorized it when I was thirteen.

You are chasing fairy tales. There is no way to get a male's fire I know of. That law was made because it is not possible for a female dragon to become pregnant.

Oh, I knew that. They thought by putting this law in the statute, they showed compassion to dragons. They knew without male dragons, a female could not produce young. There would be no way to free a dragon.

Unless I knew something they didn't.

"All we need is a male." I leaned in closer. "Or his fire."

I paused, waiting for her to raise her great head, look interested, or something. But she only stared, giving me a look of complete indifference. She could have been sleeping with her eyes open.

"Selyse!" I hissed. "Are you even listening? All we need is a male's fire, and you could get the hell out of here. And then you could free the rest of them. If you had fire, you could do—anything!"

Female Svaris weren't capable of producing fire, unless they were with young. And if the research was accurate, the older the dragon, the easier to impregnate. Selyse was the obvious choice.

Taking a deep breath, I wiped my nose. "I'm going to the Axis."

That got her attention. She snapped her head up and looked around at the other sleeping dragons. *What?*

I gasped. "It exists, doesn't it? He was right, wasn't he? Where all the dragons came from. If I can get there, I can do it. I know I can."

Selyse turned her head toward me, her eyes set in a grim glare. *No, you may not. It is a silly story. One I don't care to discuss.*

"No, no, you have to," I said, falling over myself to get closer to her face. "Don't you get it? It's the only way to get you all out of here. Corben was right the whole time. Is that why he disappeared? Because he knew? No one could ever explain his disappearance—they killed him, didn't they?" By now, my heart was beating triple what it should have. I gnawed on my fingers, my mind whirling with thoughts.

I had received Corben Willoughby's text on Dragon histology over nine years ago, and as far as I knew, it was the only copy. A former scientist turned dragonologist, his amazement of these beautiful creatures matched my own. As far as I know, the only dragonologist there had ever been.

The day after my tenth birthday, I had written him a lengthy letter. Begging him to help me free the dragons. Asking him to help me, to tell me where the dragons came from, why only these six Svari appeared. He called the day the dragons appeared the Upheaval—a day that technology mixed with forces we didn't understand. Forces only dragons were meant to experience. The day the earth spun out of Axis, he said. The day everything changed.

In response, about six weeks later, I received a package in the mail. Thankfully, Father hadn't seen or he would have insisted on opening the brown packing paper himself. I remember holding the book in my hands, looking at it for the first time, completely forgetting to breathe. *Dragons Among Us.* I ran my fingers over the beautiful Svari dragon sketched on the cover. It was a beautiful, 209-page textbook describing his theories and all his research on Svari dragons. My most prized possession. But even the book could still not answer all my questions. Or his. He spent the last years of his life trying to unravel the mystery of the dragon's appearance on that dreary, stormy day sixteen years before I came into this world.

I put a hand to her dry scales. "Selyse. I have to get to the Axis. But I need a dragon's help. Corben said the only way to get there was through a dragon. Something happened during the Upheaval, something that altered your chemistry, so—"

I know perfectly well his teachings, Quinn. That book is far too dangerous in the hands of a young woman with foolish hopes.

I stared at her, agape. "What?" I demanded. "A foolish quest? You are the one that is always telling me to stand up for myself! To go for it! That I can be more than Sir Ambrose's daughter! That I *am* more than just his daughter! And now you are telling me to quit?"

By now, the other Svaris had heard our argument, and several dragon heads raised from their slumber. Selyse looked around at the other female dragons and then back at me.

It is not quitting if it is an unwinnable situation. She turned her head away.

The other dragons had moved in, crowding around me and Selyse, blocking out any of the remaining sunset, towering over me.

She's right, Selyse. If any human deserves to know, it is Quinn.

I looked up at Veseria. Six months ago, she was a spry green Svari in excellent health. Now, her scales had taken on a brown hue, and the light in her eyes had dulled. Why had I not noticed? I swallowed. "Thank you, Veseria."

Selyse raised her head to glare at Veseria, a look that would make any normal human cower in fear. I tensed, glancing up at Selyse. They were all queens, of their own factions, of course, but their males had been gone since the Upheaval. But Selyse was no doubt the biggest. And most stubborn.

Selyse dropped back to the ground as if just raising her head was strenuous exercise.

The other dragons murmured their agreement.

I am only trying to protect you, Quinn. She huffed again, glaring at the other dragons.

Stepping toward her, I looked up with my mouth set in a firm line. "I do not need your protection. There is no other choice. It is why I am here, on this earth." I had believed nothing stronger. "If you choose not to help me, I will ask another dragon."

Selyse stared out at the fading sun. At this angle, my neck ached to stare up at her. She creased her forehead and sighed, laying her enormous head on the ground.

There is only one way to the Axis. And you must have the protection of a dragon to get there. She spoke with her eyes closed. Maybe she was hoping it was all a dream.

My heart rate quickened as I nodded wildly. Finally. There was hope.

But. Her gigantic greenish-brown head raised up to me. *Getting there will not be the only problem. How do you plan on bringing back a male's fire?*

"All I need is a male dragon, and I'll take care of the rest. Just get me there." A bit of a fib on my part. But I must have concealed it well, because Selyse didn't comment. All I knew was what Corben had written. "You must accept a dragon's fire, as you are the vessel." It was possible. Most likely, I would bring back a male. They would do anything for their queens, the book said so. If I could convince Selyse, I knew I could convince a male.

It is not that easy. To return, you would need access to a completely different location, an untouched area of staphonite. After an area has been linked once, it will not work again. How would you even get back?

"Staphonite? Tarrith is filled with staphonite! Do I need to remind you how they make Tarrith rock?"

Selyse's giant eyes stared at me, her head on the ground. *I have not been in the Axis for a long time, Quinn. What if you were to be hurt? What if . . .* Her words trailed away, and she stood roughly, shaking her enormous head.

"Selyse," I whispered, following her. "I can't stand by and watch you in pain. Any of you. I refuse to let you suffer at the hands of man. Please. I have to do this." More tears started, dang it, and I shook my head. I straightened my shoulders and lifted my chin. "To make a change, we must take the risk. And I know you would do the same for me."

Her glassy golden eyes turned toward me. I stared into those enormous eyes, feeling the hot breath flowing out of her nostrils. Dragon eyes always amazed me—golden slits surrounded by a smattering of brilliant colors.

"Corben sent me that book for a reason, Selyse. I know he did. And this is why. He knew one day I would need it. To get to the Axis. To make a difference."

Her long, delicate eyelashes fluttered to the ground as her giant eyes closed. *You are an amazing woman, Quinn Ambrose. With the spark of a young Svari.*

Wiping at my eyes, I gave a small laugh. "Maybe someone up there made me wrong, huh?"

Her eyes became glassy, and she smiled, just a small smile. The whites of her teeth barely showed, but I smiled back.

No, my dear. You were made perfectly.

CHAPTER 4

Tess

We gathered around the sloppily placed logs and thick branches that served as a handmade wooden table behind the school just inside of the forest line, the seven of us. The sun seemed to complain, though not as much as the rest of the team, slow to stretch its rays through the forest. I rubbed my hands together, ignoring the goosebumps that covered my arms. There had been an overflow of grumbling when I woke the team members out of bed this morning, even though I promised them first dibs on the breakfast supply. We needed this meeting to remain clear of the ears of the other team members, and the best time to do that was before Arik woke everyone up.

To me, early mornings provided relief, solace, and a place to clear my head after dream-filled nights. After four years in this place, I found that sitting back here during sunrise, with the forest silent around me and the aroma of tall, majestic pines with a touch of salt water was much more enjoyable than being inside the twelve-room, single-hallway base. Freedom. I reveled in it, though Arik's snoring often interrupted my quiet mornings. He slept outside most nights on a hammock we had constructed out of a rug a few years back, using the back of the building and a large post. Said he couldn't sleep inside anymore.

I pretended not to notice that two of the team members were ones I had been naked with in the last few months. Perhaps I shouldn't have left Arik in charge of assembling the team. Not sure exactly what point he was trying to make, but I shouldered the annoyance. We had bigger things to worry about right now.

"Okay, guys, shut up for a minute. Let's get serious." I took a deep breath. "We've had a development."

All mouths immediately snapped shut while continuing to gnaw on their bruised horse apples. Loic took a bite of dried squirrel meat. The heat from his stare was making me regret our encounter yesterday. I kept my eyes far away from his, wishing he would stop undressing me in his mind. Or maybe he was doing something much worse in his mind. I didn't know him well enough yet to decide.

Arik and I had discussed it, and we agreed that with our dominant group, we needed to be completely transparent. They needed to know the danger they were walking into. It was only fair.

"Last night. The Code Green. There is a chance it wasn't a Svari but something else." I looked around at the faces of my team. "There is a chance it was a Redwing."

Silence. Harlen went rigid beside me. I requested Harlen personally because of her gift. She had amazing hearing, and as long as she had a visual, she could hear what was being said, no matter the distance. Her skills were incredibly important to our cause, especially on a mission depending mainly on spying. I had spent extra time with her, practicing her hand-to-hand combat and weapon skills in her last few months, my personal requirement before anyone could go with us on a mission. At only seventeen, she was one of the younger rebels of the group, from a village she said was too small to even have a name. I had grown fairly close to her over the last year. I tried not to get too attached to anyone—except Arik. I had to remind myself this was a rebellion, not some outdoor camping excursion.

"As you all know, Redwings mean dirty business. Redwings mean human hunting."

"What can we possibly do against a Redwing?" Harlen whispered.

There was a murmur of agreement throughout the group.

I put my hands up. "Relax. We are not planning to interact with a Redwing. We need to find out what is going on at the docks today. But I wanted everyone to know what we may, and I stress *may*, run into today."

Arik handed me the rolled-up parchment, and together we spread it on the table, running our hands over the soft wrinkles in the faded and aged paper. The map of the ocean port, showing the area where ships docked and unloaded cargo, was drawn here. These maps were damn near priceless, if only for the sheer luck at finding them. Another reason we suspected the building's first intent had been some sort of military base. We spent a long time arguing and studying over these drawings. After four years, there were still several we had not deciphered, but the aerial view of the tall building around a landing field, with a road leading to the port, was obvious. Port Tarrith.

We all leaned over the table, staring at the map in front of us. Our lookout spot was near the containers. The map also specified the length of the docks, the number of feet between each one, and the approximate length and width of the beach, given each time of year. A minor road led through the forest on the other side, running to the main road to the city. Symbols and calculations we still didn't understand decorated all four sides of the map. For nearly a year, we guessed at what these symbols could mean. By now, I had filed them in the back of my memory, ready if I ever saw them. To date, they simply remained a mystery.

I put my finger on the drawing of the docks, tracing the way up to the tree line, muttering to myself. The tree line was where we stayed, never going too near the water. Too much of a risk. Nowhere to hide down there. I chewed on a ragged fingernail as the wet crunching of breakfast continued all around me.

We weren't seeing anything I didn't already know by heart. We had made raids on ship cargo before, but only after it was unloaded and dragged up the hill to the containers by the pulley and two guards. Up the hill ran right into the start of the forest, with plenty of places to wait patiently, sneak out, and quietly empty valuables. We tried to keep a very low profile so we didn't risk my father sending someone to search for some crew that sabotaged shipments.

But this was different. We weren't raiding cargo containers. The weapon could arrive at this location. The weapon that could control dragons. The weapon that could potentially change our lives. In four years, we had never had an opportunity like the one we had now.

"What do you think?" I murmured to Arik.

He had his eyes narrowed, studying the map with his arms crossed in front of him. He looked at me with one finger, tapping his chin. "No place for a ground assault."

"Okay, so we wait. They'll have to actually transport the weapons. We hide in the trees like usual—"

"No good," Arik cut me off. "Do you realize how heavily guarded that thing is going to be? There will probably be Svaris on the ground for this."

I chewed on the inside of my lip. I had thought of that already. "Then we launch a silent attack like we always do. Best bet would be to get on the ship before it docks. We won't have enough time if we wait till it docks."

"And how are we supposed to get on the boat before it docks?" Loic gave me a look.

I ignored him. My hasty departure last night obviously tarnished his ego. He wouldn't be the first.

Arik pointed at the map in front of us, further into the water. "Right there." We all stared.

I glanced back up at him. "Why there?"

"That's where the ship will slow. They'll reduce the engines and cut back to about forty jutes. Best to board the ship sometime between here and the dock. Probably give us about ten minutes to get on, grab what we need, and hop off right before it docks." Arik nodded to himself, still staring at the map.

Loic scoffed. "And how do we board the ship? Float around in the water and hope we don't get incinerated by the engines?"

I glared at him. I did not appreciate the tone, especially at a meeting as important as this.

Just as I was about to throw his ass back on base, Arik spoke up. "What about Oof?"

"Very funny," I said, still glaring at Loic. "Anyone who doesn't think they are *man* enough to complete this one can leave now." I leaned onto the table.

Loic scoffed, shoving his hands into his pockets and looking away. That's what I thought.

I put my hands on my hips. "Okay. We need to get on—"

Arik cleared his throat. "I was serious. About Oof."

I stared at him for a moment. Oof was an overweight fifty-year-old man who hung around the base, folding and washing laundry when needed. Stared at you blankly as you spoke. He had been with us for over a year now. Not the type of team member I invited to mission meetings. Because of his age and slightly . . . strange demeanor, we could assume only one thing. He had escaped from the Rule.

"How in the world could Oof help us board a ship? In the middle of the ocean?"

Arik shrugged. "Kick up some waves. Raise some fog. We've seen him mess with the water before."

I laughed out loud. "He moved water in a bowl. Far cry from raising waves."

"You could at least give him a chance. Why not?"

I shook my head. "No way. He'd never make it. What if a fight broke out? How could that man defend himself?"

"You don't even want to ask him?"

"No. We need a solid plan, not lunatic ideas." I turned back to the group, shoving Arik behind me. "Any ideas?"

"Yeah, we could go ask Oof," Arik said loudly.

My eyes rolled up in my head, and I gritted my teeth. I hated it when Arik did this. Spoke over me. In front of everyone. This should have been a private conversation, not a way to embarrass me in front of previous bedmates. "If you think for one second—"

"It might work." The small voice came from beside me.

I looked to my side. Harlen peeked up at me, swallowing thickly. She cleared her throat. "I've seen Oof use his gift. He might do it."

There was a murmur of consent around the table. Nods and raised eyebrows.

I looked around the table, aghast. "But he's old and can't fight and what if he gets hurt?" I sputtered. "He can't defend himself out there!"

"How about you let him decide?" Arik said from behind me. "He knows exactly what will happen if he goes down there. We all know the risks, right?" More nods. "Maybe it is something he would think is worth it."

I cleared my throat and crossed my arms, staring at the map in front of me. Talk about mutiny. I fought the urge to punch Arik in the face and instead used my calm, leadership voice. "Fine. We'll ask Oof." I fumbled with the map off the table and ended up folding it hastily, not bothering to roll it like I usually did. Shoving it under my arm, I turned and walked off, leaving the team standing around the table. "Meeting adjourned," I called over my shoulder, my fists still clenched at my sides.

I flipped the threadbare blanket in the air, whipping it down on the bunk, tucking it down in the metal bar, ignoring the scraping sound of metal against concrete. Bending to the bed underneath, I repeated the process with the discolored sheet covering. I punched the pillow lying bunched up against the wall, leaving my fist imprint in the lumpy filling. Having a pillow around here was a privilege. They should take better care of the damn thing.

With every flip of a blanket or sheet, the aroma of swamp water and sweaty feet filled the air, not to mention the spattering of dirt and litter hitting the floor. First thing tomorrow, we were washing every one of these damn beds.

"Enjoying yourself?"

I ignored Arik and stepped to the next "bed," which was actually several layers of towels, blankets, and even an oversized shirt bunched up on the floor. When

Arik and I first searched this building, we were overjoyed to find six metal bunks in this large room. Twelve beds. But only two mattresses. There was a third, but a small furry creature with claws and fangs had already claimed it as its own, clawing out most of the stuffing to make room for her bald, large-eyed babies. We had to get very creative when making bed padding, but we managed. The newer team members had to design their own "bed," usually somewhere along the wall of the large room. Most of the bedding found in this room Arik and I had pilfered from the large house on the hill, but there was only so much to go around. We dragged down three more mattresses as well, but none that fit in the small bunks.

I didn't come into this room often. As the leader, it seemed I should sleep apart from the group. If I ever slept, I did it in the room down the hall, the one I'd taken as my own. A lumpy blue couch sat under the window, but it worked for getting a few hours of shuteye now and then, if I didn't mind my clothes reeking of piss and stale cigarettes. My neck still ached every day after I slept—another reason I slept so little.

"Someone has to do it," I grumbled, straightening the towels into a tight pile.

"Sure, sure." Arik came in and lay on the bottom bunk I made, stretching out and putting his hands behind his head. "I know how important it is to you to have the beds made."

I stopped and stared at him with my hands on my hips. "Do you mind?" I kicked his feet off the blanket I had just straightened. "I'm a little busy."

"Making beds?"

"Yes." I heaved a pillow at him and moved to another lumpy mattress.

"It had to be done, Tess." He sighed.

I ignored him but continued shoving blankets under mattress edges and punching lumpy pillows. I had to do something. My mind was running red. My heart was practically beating out of my chest. There wasn't a man here to screw, a man I could shove against a wall and tear his clothes off. So I was making beds.

"Hey." He grabbed me by the elbow and pulled me to him, stopping me inches from his face. I lowered my eyes, struggling against him, knowing exactly what he was thinking. He raised his eyebrows, stuffing his hand in the pocket of my pants.

I wrenched out of his grasp as he held up the multicolored, over-sized marble in my face.

"I told you not to carry this. You know how you get."

Glaring at him, I snatched it out of his hand, wrapping my fingers around the smooth surface. Light as air in my palm. Yet it felt thicker than steel. When you studied it, you could see the thin, golden slit in the center of all the spots and dabs of colors.

"Since when do I listen to you, anyway?" I shoved the ball into my shirt pocket. I didn't even have a good reason for carrying it anymore. It had a perfectly safe hiding spot, one Arik and I had found years ago. But I needed it within reach.

"Get rid of it, Tess. I told you not to carry that thing around."

I ignored him and moved to another bed, grabbing the corner of a fraying blanket.

Arik grabbed my arm. "You need to cool it, ya hear? We don't have time for your little tantrum. So punch me or whatever. Or go find some *other* man to screw. Whatever you need to do, just do it." He stuck his hand in my breast pocket and snatched the ball out. "Without this."

I opened my mouth to reply, but he shoved me away. He strode out of the room, throwing the door open so hard it slammed the wall behind it.

Glaring at the open door, I rubbed my arm where he grabbed me. Fine. Maybe I would.

CHAPTER 5

Quinn

I banged on the wooden door of the small white, one-story house. A lantern burned brightly next to the porch, illuminating the shaking of my hands. Hurry. Hurry, I thought. The sun had already set. The lights up and down the street shone brightly, and a chill cut right through my thin blouse. My father would kill me if he knew I had hopped on the train and into the city this late at night. But I had no choice. There was no other way.

I jumped when the heavy door whooshed open.

"Quinn?" Mr. Seals opened the door, squinting in the darkness, a confused look on his face. I couldn't quite blame him. I had never banged on his front door at eight-thirty in the evening. Curfew was in a half hour, and I was pushing it. Not to mention the fact that I lived a good twenty-minute train ride away. Sir Ambrose's daughter was surely the last person he expected on the other side of his door.

I put on my brightest smile. "Hi, Mr. Seals! Could I, uh, talk to Fenwick for a moment?"

He stared at me for a moment. "Is everything all right?"

I pushed my hair behind my ear. "Yes, I'm so sorry for the late hour. I, uh, need to ask him something." Plastering another innocent smile on my face, I cleared my throat instead and pushed my hair back, trying to look anywhere but the bewildered stare behind his wire-rimmed glasses.

"Sure. I'll go get him." He nodded and left me standing alone on the porch. I blew out the nervous breath I had been holding, rubbing my upper arms. The temperature was no lower than it had been all week. But for some reason, I couldn't stop shivering. And truthfully, I had no idea what I needed to ask Fenwick. But he was a Flyer. Flew every day. And I needed to fly Selyse out of here. As soon as possible.

Fenwick appeared at the door, not wearing the leather suit I usually saw him in, but white pants and a light blue polo that showed off his light skin. He wore a similar look of confusion, much like his father's, but recovered nicely.

"Hi, Quinn. What's going on?" He stepped out onto the porch with his hands in his pockets.

I swallowed, forcing my arms to relax at my sides. "Can I ask you something?"

He nodded, shrugging. "Sure."

Here goes. "Would it be all right if I went on your ride with you tomorrow?" I blurted out.

He stared at me. In the many years Fenwick had been offering to take me for a ride on Selyse, I had never thought he was serious. Why would he be? I was not a Flyer and not trained to be on a dragon. All things Fenwick knew well. To take me on a joyride on Selyse with freight attached would require some kind of intervention from my father, I presumed. All things I would worry about after I spoke to Fenwick.

The silence stretched on. Even the damn birds that cawed throughout the night had shut up to witness my humiliation. I looked down at my feet, chewing on my bottom lip. I never should have come here. But now that I stood here, in front of him, I didn't know how to excuse myself or make him un-hear what I had just asked.

He opened his mouth and closed it again. Then he ran his hand through his short brown hair. "You, uh, want to go on a ride with me? Tomorrow?"

"Yes," I said weakly, still staring at my white flats.

He stepped past me, studying the fading paint on the porch. He leaned against the railing, looking back at me with a cocked head. "Why?"

I swallowed. "Uh, just . . . because. I just do," I said with a small, desperately fake laugh. I sighed when I saw the amused look on his face. My shoulders sagged when I realized this plan was ultimately going to fail, just like so many other plans I had attempted. I crossed my arms in front of myself and shook my head. "Never mind," I whispered. I walked past him down the steps, feeling the weight of my continued failure.

"Okay."

I froze. I took a deep breath before turning to give him the same startled look he had given me not so many moments before. "What?"

"I'll take you," he said.

"You'll—What?"

"You can come with me tomorrow."

"Oh. Uh, thanks. Yeah, okay," I said, trying to calm my racing heart. My head spun with confusion, and I tried to make sense of his words. Instead, I conjured up another fake smile and turned, eager to get away from the calm look on his face.

"But it'll never work," he called.

I stopped again. "I don't know what you're talking about." The moment the words slipped out of my mouth, I cringed. Probably the guiltiest I had ever sounded.

He sighed and stepped down off the porch. "Quinn, the tracking collars will never let Selyse stray off path. She'll be shocked, or worse, the second she veers off course."

I opened my mouth to argue but closed it to chew on my bottom lip. "Well, fine. You must know how to disable them. Your father designed them."

He shook his head. "That's how I know they won't fail. There is no way those trackers won't pick up on her the second she heads for the Axis."

My face burned in the light shining above us. He must have been listening the entire time. Hearing it said out loud by another human being confirmed my worst fear. It sounded ridiculous. The Axis? The myth the psycho-dragonologist based his career on? It was the reason he disappeared, the reason the government had to shut him up. I felt like a foolish ten-year-old, staring at the crisp, clean pages of that textbook, my mouth hanging open in awe and wonderment.

I flopped down on the sidewalk, pulling my skirt under my legs. He was right. Of course, he was right. I just didn't know what else to do.

"I'm not sure why I thought I could make a difference, anyway," I muttered into my knees. Staring across the street, I watched the woman across the street sweep a broom across her front porch—a white porch, just like Fenwick's. These houses were all quite small compared to my house on the hill, but they had a certain feel about them. Lived in. Real. Family. A place where you might see children playing in the street and neighbors waving to each other from their front doors.

Too bad I didn't come to Fenwick's house more often.

Fenwick came and stood next to me. Slowly, he settled down in the grass, pulling his knees up to his chest.

"I think you do make a difference, actually."

I snorted. "Oh, yeah. Big difference."

"You at least try," he offered. "I couldn't do that."

My shoulders stiffened at the thought of tackling the guard. How ridiculous I must have looked, rolling on the ground on top of that greasy-haired man. And a lot of good it did.

"Yeah." I turned my head to fiddle with my skirt, relieved that Fenwick didn't know of my rolling around in the grass with that man. Or did he? "Stupid, huh?"

For a moment, he stayed silent. My face reddened even more, horrified at the idea that he actually *did* think it was stupid, and was searching for a nice way to tell me.

"Maybe you can't change everything all at once. But I bet at least one person listens."

"Yeah, right. Like who?" I said to the street. I couldn't look at him and wanted to get up and run away.

"My father, for one. But you actually convinced him two years ago. When you stood up in front of the U.P.D. and gave that speech."

My sagging shoulders lifted. Just a touch. I glanced at him and smiled. "Really?"

He smiled back. "Yeah. Really." His smile reached his green eyes this time. His cheeks even went pink. Scratching the back of his neck, he took a breath. "I have an idea. About the dragons."

My heart leaped. "Really?"

He spoke slowly at first. "There's a dead zone. Right over the Delmar Ridge. The mountains there are filled with some foreign mineral that cuts out the radio signal. But only for about two seconds," he rushed on, seeing the look on my face. "If we could cause some sort of disturbance or brawl right there, Selyse might be able to get away without them noticing. If she could get high enough into the Savage Lands before things would calm down, her signal . . . might get kind of, well, lost."

"The Savage Lands?" I squeaked, seeing images of the jagged black, sweating rocks and peaks that make up the tightly packed mountain range. It was called the Savage Lands for a reason. Uninhabitable terrain that adventure seekers had wasted their lives and life savings trying to cross. Rocks that could explode at the slightest touch. Air that would scar your lungs if inhaled for too long. Selyse was a dragon with a fifty-foot wingspan. I rubbed my forehead. "Svaris can't fly through those tight peaks. If we hit the wrong place . . ."

"Yeah, I know." His eyes met mine. "But it's the only way to free them."

"You ready for this?" Fenwick murmured as we watched the other members of the Flying team walk through the open gate. Yawns and thermoses accompanied them, for Flyers had to leave before sunrise. I tried to keep my composure at the looks of surprise I was getting.

I squirmed uncomfortably in the leather outfit I wore. The sweat dripping down the back of my neck and pooling at my collarbone made me keep tugging at the tight neck of my costume. I cringed as my slimy skin stuck to the inside of the leather, down by the small of my back. The morning breeze cooled my dripping brow and shaking hands, though it could not cut through the layers I wore around the rest of my skin. My hand kept sneaking up to put my hair behind my ear, even though I had pulled it into a tight, low bun that morning. Fenwick had given me one warning when I asked what I needed to do to prepare: wear my hair back.

We had worked out a fairly reasonable story to tell my father that night. And I thought I handled it well. I left Fenwick's porch and caught the last train back up the hill, sneaking into the house at 9:03. As luck would have it, Father had been on an important call with President Havelock for over an hour, discussing logistics and project costs. He had no reason to suspect I wasn't in my room or down at the Keep, lying next to Selyse.

I paced around my room for at least thirty minutes, running my bare toes through the soft shag rug, trying to think of the best way to approach my father. I silently repeated the words of betrayal I would spew to him, chewing my thumb. Even with the metallic taste of blood filling my mouth, I gnawed on that finger, trying to pound down the guilt building in my brain to a tiny, justifiable lump.

Finally, I turned and threw my bedroom door open, shaking the family portrait that hung on the wall. I strode down the hall barefoot and rapped on the door with a shaking hand, repeating silent words of encouragement I knew Selyse would give at this exact moment.

I entered slowly, trying to play the part of an innocent daughter. If I knew anything by now, it was that I was a terrible actress.

"What are you still doing up, Quinn?" Father took off his reading glasses and rubbed his face. His dark eyes were tired, and the lines creased over his forehead. Until that moment, I had never truly realized how tired my father looked. So handsome, yet so aged. His salt-and-pepper hair, normally combed straight back with a bit of shine, fell to the side. The tie around his neck hung loosely, probably because of the mountain of paperwork scattered on his desk.

I settled myself in my favorite chair in front of his desk. I glanced at the flowered bench that sat against the wall with the false top. I could always find a teddy bear inside or one of my blankets. I smiled as I thought of the days when I was younger, sitting with a picture book on that bench, listening to him on the phone, or hearing the swishing of parchment as he leafed through piles of documents. For weeks after my mother had died, I refused to leave his side. The idea of losing him as well was just too much for my child's brain.

"What's on your mind, dear?" he asked, rubbing his face and settling back in his chair.

I took a deep breath, concentrating on the relaxing scent of leather and parchment. "I would like to go on a dragon flight. With Fenwick Seals," I added. Then I waited for what seemed like several minutes. I kept my eyes level with his as Father stared at me. Just stared.

Finally, he nodded. "Fine. May I ask why?"

My breath caught in my throat. He had just said fine, hadn't he? He was agreeing? I forced myself to look at his face instead of staring at my hands.

"It's something I think I should do."

He nodded again. "That's quite diplomatic of you, Quinn."

I gave a small, fake laugh. "Yes." What?

"I appreciate the fact that you are willing to see this side of the argument. How important dragons are to our culture. To this city."

I straightened my shoulders. "Yes, I am."

He turned in his chair, speaking to the thick drapes. "I remember what life was like before the dragons, Quinn. Working all day for a few coins, just to put a few bites of food in front of my sister and mother." He sighed. "If not for the dragons, I never would have considered having children. A wife."

I nodded, having heard this story before. But I let him continue.

"And now." He gestured out the window. "Look at us. This town. Our city. We may never understand why it happened, but I am so glad it did. It gave me the chance to meet you. My daughter." He smiled, turning to face me. "I know how you feel about those Svaris, Quinn. It's one of the things I love about you."

The weight of the story Fenwick and I had rehearsed suddenly seemed so much heavier. "I love you too," I whispered, looking at my hands.

"Well, then." He clapped his hands together. "When would you like to go?"

"Tomorrow."

He raised his eyebrows. "Tomorrow?"

The heat began creeping up my neck. "Yes. Fenwick offered. I told him about today, uh, you know." I cleared my throat. "He offered." I put on my best downcast face.

"Facing your fears, are you, Quinn?"

I forced a smile. "I suppose."

"All right, I'll make the arrangements." He smiled again. "I'm very proud of you, Quinn."

The guilt stabbed me in the soul like a weapon of war, then wrenched around in my heart for a bit. I did not like lying to my father and rarely did so. *But this was important*, I argued to my inner self. This was the only way.

"Guess we'll need to get you a riding outfit, hmm?" He picked up the receiver and began dialing. "I'll get Martha to take care of it tonight. I'll take care of everything, Quinn."

As I stood in the field the next morning, trying to hold my stomach in one piece, I could not erase the smile on my father's face from my mind. While tugging at the leather around my neck, I instead focused on the dragon that stood in front of me—towered in front of me. In all my years in this Keep with Selyse, she had never seemed so enormous. For years, I had stared at these dragons, seeing only magnificent creatures with souls of pure gold. These female dragons didn't have an evil bone in their body. But now, staring up at her with a dry mouth and a dizzying sense of fear, I saw what others must see when they pass by the Keep.

I had to climb on a sixteen-foot dragon and fly into the sunrise. The nausea rose into my throat as I looked up at Selyse. She gave me a comforting look and most likely said something, but in my state of hyper-stress, I never would have been able to understand her. I gave her a small nod and swallowed thickly, trying to act casual as my body begged for a reprieve from the suffocating suit.

Fenwick had walked over to the Keep House to get the saddle, and as I watched him walking back with the thick, black saddle draped over his shoulder, my head spun. At the look on his face, I put a hand on my forehead. I must have looked as bad as I felt.

"You gonna be able to do this?"

I nodded fiercely and put a hand on my stomach. "I just . . . uh . . ." Before I could continue, I put a hand to my mouth and dove for the watering pond behind us, falling down on my knees in the grass and retching up the fruit blend I had consumed earlier that morning. I heaved and lurched until, finally, I could take a shaky breath.

I stood shakily, wiping the spit and vomit from my face. The tears that leaked out over the pond cooled my face slightly in the breeze, but I wiped them away before anyone noticed. Luckily, Selyse had pulled her tail around my slackened body to hide me retching into the water she would later consume. I put a hand to her tail and patted her gratefully.

Taking a deep breath, I stepped around Selyse, keeping my eyes glued to the heavy black boots that rubbed the sides of my big toes whenever I moved. There were no snickers, no laughs at the girl who had just thrown up into a dragon pond. I cleared my throat, ignoring the taste of bile, and walked toward Fenwick with my shoulders back, praying no one else had noticed.

He took my hand and squeezed it. "It'll be okay."

My instinct would have been to pull my hand away, but I squeezed it back, surprising us both. "Okay."

"Let's get saddled up," Fenwick said, leading me over toward Selyse's right wing.

I clenched his hand, glancing up at Selyse's neck. She lowered her great wing to be nearly flat to the ground as Fenwick stepped up onto the thick of her wing. I hesitated, terrified the two of us together would cause her pain.

"It's okay," he assured me instantly. "Feel it." He put his hand down to her wing and rubbed the surface. "See how thick they are?"

I knew exactly what a dragon wing felt like. I had grown up with Selyse—given her hugs. She had even covered me with these wings for protection from rain or lightning on more than one occasion. But to stand on her? It seemed so disrespectful.

It's okay, Quinn, her soothing voice said. *To lift the two of you in the sky together would be a great honor.*

I took a slow breath, her words having the usual calming effect on my frazzled brain. I grabbed Fenwick's outstretched hand. He pulled me up as I wobbled on Selyse's slanted surface, just for a second. One slow step, then another. I could do this. I took another step. My foot slipped down the smooth slant of her wing. Fenwick grabbed me around the waist.

I gasped and grabbed at his shoulders, squeezing my eyes shut. He was so strong, so brave. I let him hold me tight, just long enough to slow my thumping heart. Selyse stretched her long neck around, watching me intently.

"I'm okay," I murmured, pulling back and speaking to them both.

He began making the steep ascent up her thick wing, holding my right hand in his. I followed shakily, forcing my eyes to remain on Selyse's.

Fenwick went to work on the saddle while I held his upper arm, moving with him. I peeked downward before I could stop myself. The ground below was so far . . . I could not do this. The fear clawed up my stomach like black, evil insects, swarming through my chest, and squeezing my overworked heart.

You can do this, child. Sit down and let Fenwick take care of you. We will protect you.

I gave a faint nod and let Fenwick position me into the seat and pull a strap that ran from my left shoulder to my right hip. I forgot to blush as the back of his hand made contact with the front of my leather suit, my flat chest hiding behind it.

He squatted next to me, balancing on Selyse's back. "Ready? I, uh, added this strap in last night. It will help keep you balanced. But hold on tight, okay?"

I nodded again, looking to the front of me. Then to the sides. My body took up the only seat in the saddle. "Where—where do you sit? You can't leave, y-you—"

"I am going to sit right in front of you. Here." He pointed in front of the saddle, where Selyse's neck thinned.

I swallowed. "Will it hurt?" I squeaked, looking in horror at the spikes running up and down her neck.

"Nope," he said, patting my shoulder. "Her spikes are flexible." He ran his hand down her neck, demonstrating the flexibility of the dark-colored spikes. "I fit right here." He settled himself between two of the spikes directly in front of me. "She'll be fine."

I bit my lip and would have smiled if I hadn't been near tears. I had been worried it would hurt him, actually, not the two-ton dragon we were sitting on. Keeping my eyes forward, I placed my hands on either side of the saddle, letting the warmth of Selyse's skin spread through my fingers.

"You ready for this?" he called over his shoulder.

No.

No, I was not.

CHAPTER 6

Tess

Harlen and Arik lead Oof past me out the back door, the loose screw jingling as the door slammed shut. I stood with my arms crossed, leaning against the door to the kitchen, staring at the closed door.

Well, fine. I stood there for a while, Arik's words from earlier echoing inside my brain. After a few minutes, growing bored with my pout, I wandered down the silent hall, trying to keep the red blotches in my mind at bay. By now, they had settled into more of a hazy, transparent color, giving me enough room to breathe. The haziness meant more of a dull headache, which I could manage. Not even Arik knew of my problem with the reds. The suffocating, blinding color that started behind my eyes when anger or frustration became too great.

It had been only luck in finding out the remedy to the swirling, blood-red attack in my mind. Last year, during a horrible freeze that left my team stuck inside for six days, a male knocked on the metal door to the room I slept in. I had thrown him on the couch before he had a chance to deny me. We had a romp on my stained blue sofa, fast and rough, ripping off clothes and gasping for breath, the smell of pine cones fresh on his skin. He had pulled up his pants and left me half-naked on the couch, but my mind was blissfully silent and calm.

To this day, I still wasn't sure exactly which of my male team members it was. Forced sterilization had its benefits, I supposed. Any woman my age who lived in the Tarrith would have been sterilized, thanks to the medical requirements of all military children. Overpopulation was a concern for the city, they said, so every third year, women between the ages of sixteen and twenty-four were given "the treatment." I was one of the lucky ones. Or unlucky. Not quite sure yet.

I ran a hand through my greasy hair. The silence in this place was worse than a headache. Turning, I marched to the back exit. Time to see what was going on for myself.

I had never personally seen Oof use his powers and only heard rumors of his days in the service to the Dragon Rule. You didn't end up in the Dragon Rule without being able to do something amazing. But as well, you didn't leave the Dragon Rule either, so it makes a person wonder exactly what happened.

He came to us a little over a year ago, seeking sanctuary. In truth, I wasn't even sure how he got as far deep inside the mountain as he did. Must've taken him days, along with a strong desire to live. The guy barely talked but was okay, I guessed. Helped where he could. The look in his eyes was always distant, and he would never look right at a person. We assumed a type of punishment damaged him somehow. Probably some form of torture fried his brain or carved out his soul were a few guesses. No one really knew. After someone was forced into Dragon Rule, it was rare to see them again.

The three of them sat near the cliff, right over the ocean. A risky spot to be in the mornings, out of the protection of the tree line and right over the ocean, close enough to breathe in the saltwater.

I spied on them from the edge of the woods as Harlen crouched down next to Oof's chair, pointing out at the ocean. "Can you make waves for me, Oof? Can you?"

Sort of how you would talk a toddler into eating limp vegetables. I stood there, frowning. They were treating him like some sort of invalid, some idiot who wasn't once part of the Dragon Rule.

Not that people were lining up to be a part of it. Most tried to conceal their power so as not to attract attention. But there were always those idiots who wanted to showcase themselves, get special treatment, and ensure their family's protection. But once you were in the Dragon Rule, you were done for. In for life. A piece of property. Used against other humans, made to do horrible things to others. Things dragons didn't want to waste their time on. How Oof escaped? I doubt he even knew.

Watching them, I almost reached into my pocket but stopped when I remembered Arik had taken away the Dragon Eye. I tried to push away the resentment tugging at my brain, threatening with those damn reds. Why did I carry it? I used to tell myself it was to protect it. Keep it safe. But it was more than that, and Arik knew it. Holding it made me feel powerful, alive, like I could take any fear or misgivings I had of life and toss them into the ocean. Like I could look a dragon in the eye and laugh at them, mocking their fire and scaly skin, and scream out my real thoughts on the Svari.

Dragon magic, I reminded myself. I didn't need it.

Arik put his hand on Oof's shoulder. "Can you do anything with the water, buddy? Show us you can do something." Oof stared out at the crashing waves, then back up at Arik.

Shaking my head, I turned back around. I stomped back to base and shoved open the door, heading straight for the kitchen, or what we called the kitchen. It consisted of a sink and a lot of empty counter space. I found a dirty plastic bucket stowed in a cabinet and marched over to the sink. Praying, I turned the knob. Nothing. Didn't think so. It was a rare and joyous day when we had running water in this place.

Grabbing the bucket, I headed back out the door and around the base. I plodded through the yellow meadow, searching around the side of Benny's tree. There. The stench assaulted my nose even before I laid my eyes on it. The puddle Benny soaked his feet in every morning. I sniffed, then blew the air back out. Like decomposing animal carcass mixed with Loic's undershirt. I kneeled down and scooped up the dark water, grimacing at the foul stench as I filled the bucket as full as possible. I wiped my hands on my pants and headed for the cliff.

Harlen was patting Oof him on the back and smiling at him. Arik had his hand on the large shoulder, leaning down to speak to him. Part of me wanted to wait just to say I was right. But the other part of me wanted to rub the two's noses in this plastic bucket of disgusting filth. *That* part of me wanted Oof to succeed.

"Here." I dropped the bucket of water at Oof's feet, sloshing dirty water all over. I pointed at it. "Now do something."

Oof looked up at me with a question mark on his face. Then he pulled his large body forward, tipping the chair out from underneath him. He fell to the ground, landing on his hands and knees.

"Oof!" Harlen cried, immediately coming to his aid.

"No." I grabbed her elbow and pulled her back. "Stay right here."

She looked at me as if I had struck her. "Tess, let me help—"

"No. Stop treating this man like a child and let him be a man. For once."

She struggled against my grip and looked helplessly at Arik, who now stood leaning against a tree, observing. He gave her a nod. She stopped fighting me and yanked her arm away, giving me a wounded look.

I turned back to Oof on the ground. "Do it, Oof."

The large man looked up at me through long wisps of dark hair, then down at the bucket. Reaching out slowly, still on his knees, he touched the muddy water. He jumped back, wincing, and put a hand to his chest. He looked up at me with a hesitant smile and nodded, his chubby cheeks pink from the sunlight.

"No, Oof. Use the water. Do something."

Oof shook his head slowly and reached a hand out toward me.

"No," I said stubbornly. "You are not getting up until you do something with that water. Now."

He put a thick finger on the bucket and pushed it over, spilling the muddy water out into a small brown puddle.

I took a deep breath and clenched my teeth together. Wasn't this what I wanted? To prove that he couldn't do it? To prove that this overweight, sad, mute man wasn't strong enough? No. It wasn't what I wanted.

Kicking the bucket away, I put my hand on the back of his thick neck and turned his head. "Look at the damn water. You will not move from this position until you do something with it."

He whimpered beneath me, pulling his arms around himself.

"Let him go, Tess," Harlen said in a trembling voice.

"Not a chance." I turned and looked at her. "You were the one who said he could do something amazing. Now he will do it."

"Not like this!" she cried shrilly, grabbing my shoulder. "You are going to hurt him!"

"He is a man, Harlen, not a child." I shoved her away.

She stumbled backward but corrected quickly and stepped back up to be nose-to-nose with me. "Don't be a bitch, Tess!" She placed both hands on my chest and shoved me back with little reward. "You can't treat him like this!"

"Treating him like a stupid kid will not help him summon a power that got him into the Dragon Rule, a power that no one else had. You act as if he is an infant to be coddled, not a man that—"

"Look."

We both swung our heads at Arik, who had remained cautiously silent the whole time. He nodded at the ground where Oof still kneeled.

Harlen gasped. A small wave of fog curled up from the puddle, meeting Oof's outstretched fingers. He looked at it curiously, then wiggled his fingers, making the line of fog wiggle as well. He reached both hands down toward the puddle. We watched in silence as the water lifted off the ground. One large puddle floated through the air, depositing itself back into the bucket. The bucket slowly righted itself, sloshing the muddy water inside.

Oof looked up at me with a satisfied smile.

Smiling back, I offered him my hand and helped the man stand. He stood easily, surprisingly easily, in fact, and squeezed my hand.

"Thank you," he murmured.

His eyes shone a bright blue—a strong, brilliant blue I didn't remember being there before. I stared at his face as he turned to look out at the sky in front of us. The lines on his face had faded. His double chin was gone. In its place, a strong jaw with an easy smile as he gazed out at the water. He closed his eyes and breathed in deeply, trying to imprint on every one of his senses what lay before him. The smell of freedom, perhaps. The taste of it. Maybe the beauty in those white, crisp waves crashing against the rock.

He turned and strode back toward the base without his usual limp, holding up the large pants we had mended to fit him by the waist.

Harlen turned to look at me, tears shining brightly in her eyes. "He changed."

I looked at Arik, and he gave me that crooked smile that he hadn't given me in so long.

"Yeah, he did."

We finally came to an agreement. Attacking the ship was not feasible right now, especially if this wasn't the delivery of the weapon. This was going to be a reconnaissance mission. Gather info. That was all. No use trying to take down the entire militia on a whim. If it was the delivery of the weapon, well, we would have to come up with a different plan. I recalled four members of the original mission team and ordered them to stay on base and do something useful.

Arik, Harlen, Oof, and I climbed through the thick and stabbing woods, reaching our landmark—a tree that curved to the forest floor, bigger around than Arik and I could reach. We had made this clearing ourselves, large enough to fit several team members but still enclosed and out of view. It took thinning down several overgrown Moss trees, removing a shit ton of vines, shrubs, and concealed evil brier bushes—which caused nasty rashes, keeping several team members down for days— but it was worth it. We designed a small trail that led directly from the oversized tree to our clearing, where we had views of the port and docks.

Oof, who we found out actually went by Vic, had the most powerful gift I had seen. We had the entire team outside earlier, watching him push and pull water, and bring it up damn near close enough to touch. We all stood on the cliff in plain view, gazing like dummies out at the ocean, enjoying Vic's show. What the man could do with the water kept us wide-eyed and not caring for at least a half hour. Arik finally let sense take over and ordered us all back behind the tree line.

I grilled Vic for information on the Dragon Rule, but after over an hour of questions, phrased and rephrased, asked and re-asked, it was clear his brain had been wiped of any information that would have proved useful. Whatever the dragons had done to him, whatever punishment he had received, the Svaris didn't want him telling anyone. It only made me more curious and increasingly more frustrated.

At least he still had most of his memories of his family. Vic told me of his home, a little shack near the creek he and his father would fish in. His mother, a lovely woman with a heavy Marcuth accent, would sell herself to the guards in Ogala, a miserable slum area that only stood because of its military supply warehouse. Marcuth women were highly sought after by guards of any city in our province. Their thick accents and large chests were something of a trigger for perverted men carrying gauge weapons.

I wanted to ask if he knew what became of his parents after his screening. After a person's magic was established, the family sort of . . . disappeared. Fell between the cracks. The family of a person with a gift was a liability. A danger to the dragons. No one knew exactly what happened to these people, but I had a bad feeling my father and his Praetorian guards had something to do with it.

Harlen, on the other hand, knew about her gift as a child and told no one. No one, not even her parents, had known about the girl who could hear from miles away. She left her home the day before her sixteenth birthday. At seventeen, they would have pulled her to be screened. The only way to save herself and her family was to leave. Quietly.

I led the way through the crusty brush, grimacing every time someone stepped on a pile of crunchy leaves. The sound seemed to reverberate through the forest, and I was sure every member of the armed forces heard it from where they were probably standing, guarding the port. Half the militia was probably on alert by now.

After several minutes of traipsing over the crispy terrain, the branches and trees opened up, giving us a wide enough berth to breathe and group together.

I looked at Vic and Arik. "You guys stay here. C'mon, Harlen." Arik was still on my shit list, and I wanted him to know it. And the less noise we made as we got closer to the docks, the better.

Harlen and I crept closer toward the waves, underneath the brush, on our hands and knees. Things had chilled considerably between the two of us since our encounter with Oof. Perhaps she has seen me for the person I really was. Whatever the reason, I still needed her. I needed her to get her eyes on that weapon.

We settled on our stomachs, the scent of salt water strong with the ocean in view. Resting my chin on the forest floor, I took a mental survey, noting the emptiest areas on the beach, how many dragons flew over the water, and where troops stood in relation to our position.

Two Svaris hovered over the ocean, large wings flapping, causing quite a disturbance in the water. They hung fairly close to the waves. I tucked that bit of info into my back pocket for later. Might come in handy with Vic around. Troops lined the port, red-faced and sweating. A few even had weapons resting on the ground, leaning against their leg.

"Some battalion," I muttered, swatting at the leaves sticking to my cheek.

I moved to the side to allow Harlen a view of the scene. She settled on her stomach, resting her face on her hands. Taking a deep breath, she stared. I poked at the bushes in front of me, trying to pry the branches open enough to see through.

"Hear anything?"

"The ship should have arrived by now. Was supposed to be here hours ago."

"Hours ago?" I hissed. "I thought it wasn't due until this evening?"

"You probably heard exactly what they wanted you to hear."

I wanted to smack myself in the face. Of course, they would spread the misinformation. My contact usually had better intel than that. I had no reason to doubt her information, but dealing with the weapon, I should have taken extra precautions.

"There's your father," Arik whispered in my ear.

I jumped, nearly screaming and giving away our reconnaissance mission and killing us all. "I told you to wait back there," I said through gritted teeth.

"When was the last time I listened?" he murmured, leaning over me to get a better view. "So, the ship is late, huh? Were we duped?"

I shook my head. "No way. She wouldn't do that."

"But your father might." He spoke quietly, turning away from the others.

I paused. Had he found out? Did he know what she was doing? I bit my bottom lip.

"They're hanging out pretty close to the water. I could totally soak those scale heads," Vic commented, peering through the foliage.

"Don't even think about it," I said.

"Something is going on," Harlen whispered.

"The ship?"

"I-I don't know. I need those guys to turn around." She rested her head on her hands, still on her stomach. "We might be here a while."

Fine. We would wait all night if we had to.

Chapter 7

Quinn

I was going to die. That much I knew. As I clenched to the saddle for dear life, the vicious wind tearing through the bare flesh on my body, thoughts flashed through my brain. They were thoughts I wish I had before I climbed onto a sixteen-foot dragon's back. My father's face . . . thanking Martha for breakfast . . . thanking Fenwick for breaking every rule he ever knew . . .

He sat directly in front of me. Forget humility—my arms were wrapped around his waist, squeezing the life out of him. I was busy concentrating on staying alive. He rode Selyse with ease, whooping and calling out to her, congratulating her on strong turns or shouting chants of encouragement.

The collar she wore high on her neck was blinking, and even in my fear, I noticed the change of color. It blinked blue one second, then red. With a sick feeling, I realized that was what must have been leading her to our destination. Was it shocking her? Sending a painful jolt of electricity through her neck every time we needed to make a turn?

I buried my face in Fenwick's back, not able to tell if I cried tears of pain or horror. The wind up this high burned my face and made me wish the suffocating leather covered my face and hands, too. I shakily breathed in the scent of the earthiness and musk on his back. Deep breaths helped the nausea stay down, and as long as I kept my eyes closed, I could survive this. I hoped.

The load Selyse carried must have been heavy. Her body quivered underneath my legs as we flew. Her back moved up and down awkwardly as if she was gasping for breath, and I could sense her exhaustion. It never entered my mind to even ask what we were hauling. I assumed the crystal. At this point, I didn't care. Selyse's pain bounced all over my brain, making the tears fall for a different reason. Her aged and tired body should never have to be forced to carry thousands of pounds across the sky, over the ocean, and into rough winds.

"Okay," Fenwick called. "We just crossed over the Black Raven. Just ahead is where the others will start."

I only nodded into his back, the nausea creeping up my throat. Our plan was coming, happening sooner than I wanted, but too late to stop it now. To successfully get away, we needed the other dragons to create a distraction right over the Dreadmore Sea. They would get into a dragon fight.

I'd never seen the dragons fight—never even heard of it happening. Female dragons were calm, friendly creatures. It was my firm belief that queen dragons were more like mothers than anything. More prone to stopping disagreements than starting them.

The part I feared wasn't the dragon fight. It was the punishment they would receive.

Fenwick reached up awkwardly toward the collar around Selyse's neck. The vibration would stop for about two seconds when we entered the dead space. He would signal, and we would fly away. Far, far away, to leave the other dragons to the repercussions of the humans controlling them. I squeezed Fenwick tighter, wishing I could see into Selyse's eyes.

Do not worry, child. They are ready for this to end. They know exactly what will happen.

I nodded miserably, letting my tears get as far as Fenwick's leather back before they blew away. Her voice shook as she spoke, even though she tried to hide it. What if she couldn't make it to the Axis? We had no backup plan, nothing to do if everything went wrong—

"Now!" Fenwick screamed, raising himself onto his knees, pulling me with him. The homemade strap Fenwick put on the saddle flew away, slapping me in the face as it swirled through the wind and disappeared.

I screamed as Selyse made a sharp right turn and went into an immediate nosedive. She flew low, next to the ocean, so low that freezing water stung my face. I wanted to turn around and check on the dragons, but I fought for my life as they were fighting for theirs, practically strangling Fenwick. I peeked over his shoulder, seeing the rocky mountain we were nearing.

"What— Selyse! No!" I screamed as we almost came face to face with the side of the black rock.

In the last second, she shot straight upward, throwing me backward in the saddle, flying like a young Svari, up and down, around sharp curves, twirling in the damn air. I should have been amazed or relieved at her amazing flying skills, but my brain became fuzzy. My head started to pulse. My grip on Fenwick's waist slackened as I fought to keep my mind alert.

"Selyse . . ." I muttered, trying to keep my head up. I was losing the fight, and I was losing fast.

Quinn!

I could vaguely see Selyse's head whip back as my arms fell to my sides. A thundering roar made me blink, still dazed, and I saw the look on Fenwick's face as he turned, reaching out.

"Quinn! Hold on!"

Then I was all the way back in the saddle, my arms splayed out to the sides. The strap that Fenwick tightened around my body was long gone, leaving me here, light as a feather . . . To do whatever the rough winds commanded of me. I felt my body being lifted, which seemed wrong at that moment, taking my arms with it and trying to rip them from the sockets. I was light as air, and could simply float away . . . Far, far away.

I gasped as my back hit something hard, coughing and blinking madly. I stared up into the dirty and bleeding face of Fenwick, unaware that he had me under the armpits, dragging me across a hard surface.

"Quinn!" He gasped as he fell down beside me.

I groggily reached up to his face, wondering what in the world could have caused the gash that ran along his cheekbone.

And then I remembered.

I sat up so fast we knocked foreheads, both gasping and putting a hand to our already pounding heads. At least mine was.

"Where— What—" I gazed around slowly, not even realizing I was holding my breath. Darkness hung heavy in the air, along with a slow, creeping mist that seemed to hover, almost whispering in the dark. It prickled at my bare skin enjoying the scent of my terror. Black, shining rock stretched as far as I could see. Hills of black rock, deep gouges of black rock—like the color black exploded, then froze after mere seconds, trapped in motion.

I turned my pounding head and gasped. The dark figure lying in the distance was motionless with her left wing at an unnatural angle. The freight cart Selyse had been hauling was further back, split in two.

"Selyse!" Struggling to my feet, I ran toward her, ignoring the pain that shot up through my right leg with every step. I fell over large wooden crates, splintered and shattered, and tripped over white stone strewn everywhere. Collapsing next to her, I touched her dark scales softly, right above her closed eyes. Nothing.

"Selyse!" I screamed shrilly, loud enough to echo off the black rock walls surrounding us.

I'm still here, Quinn. I-I just need a moment.

The tears had already started in free-flowing, gasping sobs. I fell over her neck, wrapping my arms around her. I nodded into her sweating skin, the scent of ambrosia practically thick enough to grasp. "Okay."

"You can talk to her," Fenwick said from behind me. "Can't you?"

I sat up on my knees, wiping at my nose. "Yeah."

He fell on his knees beside me. "Is she all right?"

It was only at that moment I remembered Selyse was important to Fenwick, too. He had been her Flyer for over two years now. The only Flyer I had ever seen her smile at.

"I don't know," I whispered, stroking her neck. "What happened?"

He shook his head. "One second, we were fine. The next, she roared like I have never heard. You almost fell out of the saddle. She must have lost control. Then we crashed here."

I clapped a hand over my mouth. Oh, God. She roared as I passed out. I could hear her weak voice screaming in my mind. I remember being startled but too woozy to care. She tried to save me. I must have called to her.

"Oh, God," I moaned again, putting both hands to my face. "It's my fault. If I hadn't lost it— If I could have held it together, she never would have turned, she never would have—"

I stopped as I looked down at the neon green substance that covered the ground in front of my knees. Dragon blood.

"Selyse . . ." Fenwick moaned.

I reached out, desperate to touch her, to make sure she was still with me. "Selyse—"

Stay back, child. Please stay back.

Fenwick stopped and stared. "I heard her."

"Yes," I sobbed into my hands. "She's hurt, and there is nothing we can do."

He fell to the ground and took me in his arms. We kneeled on the rock, in the alien, prickling fog, holding each other, my tears now dripping down his face. Or maybe they were his tears.

"Where are we?" he whispered into my hair.

We have made it to the link to the Axis, Fenwick. We made it.

He gasped as Selyse's words entered his mind, along with mine. "This is the Axis?" he whispered.

This is the link to the Axis. She took a large breath, and I gripped Fenwick's shoulder as I heard her gasp in pain.

"Selyse?" I murmured.

We have little time, Quinn.

As if on cue, a crack appeared beneath our feet. It started small, just a tiny complaint from an entire mountain range. Nothing to be alarmed at, Fenwick's wide eyes spoke to me. Then, the complaining grew louder and more vicious, spreading under Selyse's enormous body.

Fenwick grabbed me back as the ground below us shifted, creating an awkward stair step in the surface we stood on and expelling clouds of white dust, reeking of sulfur. We watched in horror as the rock under Selyse's giant body shifted. Her back legs and tail jerked downward—then stopped. My mouth froze open in a silent scream, my lungs too afraid to move.

She lay at a horrible angle, the stair step crack going down at least four or five feet. I ran for her as Fenwick grabbed me and whipped me back toward him.

"Be careful! This is Dead Rock. I'd bet my life on it."

"What is Dead Rock?" I asked, glancing around at our feet.

"It's staphonite—aged staphonite. Unstable, crumbling. The whole place is made of it. Just take it easy, okay?" His usually calm face had beads of perspiration inching their way down his brow, and his fingernails dug into the palm of my hand.

I stared around, too afraid to breathe. We were on a mountain of crumbling stone?

We inched our way toward Selyse. Fenwick gripped my right hand, and his other was on the small of my back. Another crack sounded, this one further away, but loud enough to make us both freeze. After several moments of holding my breath, Fenwick nodded. I squeezed his hand and swallowed hard, setting my foot down as lightly as possible. We crept through the mist, along the black rock, imagining ourselves light as air.

Selyse lay still.

"Selyse!" I put my hands to her face, right under her closed eye. "Tell us how to get to the Axis! Then you have to fly away! Selyse?"

Her eyelids fluttered. *To . . . to enter the link, you must walk through my life source. It will carry you to the Axis. You must walk through . . . me.* She groaned in pain, her long lashes fluttering closed.

"Your life source? What does that even mean? What . . ." My voice suddenly became small. "What will happen to you? Selyse?" I grabbed at her face again, determined to make her open her eyes.

I cannot go with you, Quinn. You must take the journey alone.

"You didn't answer my question," I whispered. The tears stung in my eyes. "What will happen to you?"

I watched her eyes, the soulful, deep eyes with the golden center, close slowly.

My time is up, Quinn. I am not leaving this place. A large, scalding drop ran down her pained face, falling at my knees, sending a curl of steam into the air. *I will miss you dearly, Quinn.*

She had known. She had known the whole time. A dragon could not make it to the Axis. They were only there to open the link.

"Why didn't you tell me?" I whispered. "I can't—"

Another rift opened in the ground to the side of us, leading to another, then another. The cracks echoed all around us, faster and faster, until I had no idea what direction they came from. Fenwick grabbed my arms as spider webs of crevices formed all around us, widening, spilling rock down below, pulling the mist down with them.

You must go now! There is no time! You do this for all dragon kind!

"I do not want you to die!" I screamed over the earth-splitting noises. In the distance, the black rock structures began to fall, giant black boulders crashing to the surface and creating gouges in the hard black stone.

"We have to go, Quinn," Fenwick yelled. "Don't make this all for nothing!"

Now! You must go now!

I was speechless, with no idea what to do, when I felt the tugging at my arm. "Look!" Fenwick cried, pointing toward Selyse.

The green blood pooling from her back shimmered and glared as if some invisible light was being aimed at it from above. It formed a perfect circle on the rock, shining up through the mist.

I gasped. "Her life source. We have to walk through her blood?"

He pulled me to my feet, and we held each other, staring at the pool of blood in front of us. The world around us was crumbling, the shaking making me dizzy, but the blood . . . I stepped toward it, grasping Fenwick's hand.

You must go now!

I took a tearful nod and gripped Fenwick's hand.

"You want me to go with you?" he asked, his eyes wide.

I put my hand on top of his. "Yes. Please."

Hurry.

I stepped toward her shimmering blood, feeling Fenwick close behind. Looking around one last time, I grasped the reality of what I was about to do. I closed my eyes and took a breath. At the same time, a jarring crack knocked me to the side and almost off my feet. I looked down at the spreading ground, then back at Fenwick. The earth split right between us, losing our grip on each other. Time seemed to freeze, that moment, with Selyse dying at my feet.

"Fenwick!"

Our eyes met. Then he dove. Almost as if he meant to tackle me, to land on top of me, but I only felt his hands on my chest. He shoved me backward, knocking me toward Selyse. I fell hard on my side in her pool of blood, reaching out for his hand, but only grasping at the mist.

The last thing I remember seeing was him falling . . . falling . . .

Chapter 8

Tess

We stared as dragons flew in circles, up and down, roaring so loud Harlen threw her hands over her ears. Arik and I shared a wide-eyed look of astonishment. We shoved each other aside, fighting for the best view of the chaos happening at the bay. Vic finally reached into the row of shrubs and pulled out a bush, roots, and all, leaving the wall to our hiding spot wide open. At the moment, I forgot to care. We huddled around the small opening over Harlen, still lying on the ground.

Black and gray clouds swirled in the sky, swallowing the afternoon whole. The bright afternoon disappeared, plunging the bay into a strange darkness—a darkness that chilled me to the bone. Or perhaps it was the silence that stretched throughout the forest and over the ocean. A gigantic blanket seemed to stretch over this entire scenario, cutting off everything I could see and hear from the real, loud, bright world. I reached down and grabbed Arik's hand, holding my breath and staring at the sky. Waiting. Waiting for whatever was coming. We stared, waiting for the blanket to fall.

The militia held their weapons toward the sky, then down at the ground, waving them in confusion. The wind came up next. We ducked as branches whipped through the air, blowing up dirt and leaves. The cracking sounded throughout the forest as every part of our cover cowered in response. I gasped as something hit me in the face, throwing my hand to my cheek.

"Harlen, get up!"

Arik and I grabbed her under the arms and pulled her to her feet, just before the ground began to rumble.

"What the hell is this?" I yelled at Vic.

"I don't know. Get out of here!" He pointed toward the beach.

Another loud clap sounded over my head. Before I could look up, I pushed Harlen out of the way and fell to the ground, covering my head. Arik rolled directly on top of me, momentarily cutting off my air supply.

"Watch out!" he cried into my ear.

I screamed as the tree fell, causing us to knock heads.

"Get it . . . off," he gasped, speaking into my hair.

I struggled underneath him, as my chest threatened to explode. I kicked my legs desperately, able to get my left foot on the log.

Vic struggled with the fallen tree. He wrapped his arms around the trunk as I pushed upward, fighting the monster tree with all I was. With a primal cry, he pulled the tree off of us, falling over it as he dropped to the ground. Arik grimaced in pain as I helped him stand. I leaned on my knees and took a deep breath, rubbing my sore ribs.

Panting, I looked up. "The weapon."

Harlen gasped, her hand clutching my arm. Could this be the weapon? Could this mass destruction somehow be linked to the thing we were here to find? The one thing said to control dragons, the only thing to give humans a fighting chance?

Another tree cracked and shifted as I grabbed Harlen's wrist and pulled her close. "Get to the beach!"

We fought our way through the tumbling trees, whipping branches, and flying brush to fall out in a pile on the sand. We stared up at the sky as the troops ran around us, oblivious to the four strangers lying bruised and battered in front of them. In the distance, I could see my father screaming orders, pointing, and running as well, though his yells were drowned out by the howling wind.

I looked up, shading my eyes from the stinging sand. "Look!" I cried, pointing upward. A crack appeared in the sky, some sort of fissure snaking out of the swirling gray clouds. Arik and I stood, frozen to the sandy ground, gripping each other's hands, forgetting about the failing world all around us.

Things moved in slow motion. Something fought its way through the clouds, falling but not falling, fighting to stay in the sky. At first, a speck of dark, then a small piece. The dragons spotted it at the same time. They flew in from the west, low and determined, surely planning to catch whatever was falling in their jaws.

"Vic!" Arik yelled. "Waves!"

Vic appeared next to us, immediately understanding what Arik needed. He put his hands up toward the flying dragons, against the howling wind, and gave a flick of his wrists. He fought to hold control against the ripping wind that pulled at his shirt and blew sand in his eyes. But it worked. Large tumulus waves appeared, chasing the speeding dragons, drenching and pulling them into the water.

Arik ran out to the beach into the midst of confused troops still pointing their weapons into the sky.

I yelled his name as the guns went off. We all ducked as the ripple of thundering gunshots filled the area.

And then she was there. In a mess of brown hair, whipping in all directions, falling from the sky, directly into Arik's arms. He crashed into the sand with her in his arms. The sound they made hitting the sand was enough to make me gasp.

I stared in shock. Then looked back up. Then back down. Stuck to the ground where I stood, agape at what had just happened. A girl had just fallen from the sky.

Harlen and Vic ran out onto the beach toward Arik, dragging him and the lifeless woman from the middle of the troops, many who stood around dumbly, with a similar look of confusion. It took only a second for several to recover. Men with guns began running toward them.

I watched, helplessly stuck, as Harlen and Vic dragged Arik to his feet with the girl and ducked as a blast went off near the water.

"Attack!" the familiar voice rang out further down the beach. The general had regained his thought process, and the dragons gave another roar.

Vic and Arik ran, carrying a small body with hair dragging on the sand. Fire rained out on the beach, narrowly missing my teammates, but incinerating several of the troops.

Arik, Vic, and Harlen stumbled toward me as Arik and Vic dove into the destroyed forest. A stream of fire followed them in as I turned and ran behind them., feeling the heat at my heels.

"Run!" I screamed. Then I stopped. "Harlen!"

I turned to see the blonde-haired girl lying face down on the sand, her fingertips only inches from the forest. I dove for her and grabbed her limp hand, dragging her back to our spot of destroyed cover as troops advanced full force. Fire rained down next to me. I cried out in pain as the wave of heat flew over my back.

The scent of burned flesh assaulted my senses. "Harlen!" I coughed as I pulled her small body. When she did not respond, I struggled to throw her over my shoulder, somehow made it to my feet, and ran.

"What the hell were you thinking?"

We traipsed through the fallen trees and disturbed forest at a slow pace. The three of us carried two bodies, dead weight, though I was praying to my soul that Harlen was not dead. She couldn't be. We needed her. I needed her.

Arik grunted in response, still carrying the strange girl awkwardly. Vic had her legs, and they ran sideways. We made it to the small path that led to the base, but I knew with a sinking heart, we'd be climbing through the forest for hours. The only thing keeping me going was getting Harlen home. Back to where she belonged.

"I was thinking this girl might be important," he panted.

"Important enough to get us all killed?" I gasped as we trudged up the hill. "This was a recon mission, nothing more!"

"Let's take the creek! Screw the road!" Vic turned to the left. The path up to the base was the way to get there on a normal day. This was not a normal day.

"She fell from the freakin' sky, Tess!" he yelled back. "I'd say that's pretty damn important!"

"Could you two call it quits for an hour?" Vic said breathlessly. We fought our way through the trees and stared down at the creek below.

Vic wasted no time. He jumped to the creek below, probably a good twelve feet. He landed with his hands and feet in the ankle-deep water, standing and turning to look up.

"Slide her down!" he cried. "I'll catch her!"

Arik dropped the girl's feet down the dirt wall and let her slide down, Vic catching her. He sat her down, sitting against the wall as we struggled to slide Harlen down, putting her face against the ground. I hadn't looked, but her back was badly burned. That was all I needed to know.

We scrambled through the shallow creek, most of the time tripping over loose rock, making it damn near impossible to move faster than a hurried walk. The bottom half of me was drenched, probably adding another ten pounds to my weight. By the time we reached the wall to climb up, we had to stop and lean against it, gasping for air.

I stood much too soon, hefting Harlen in my arms as gently as I could. We stared up. Brown roots stuck out all over this part of the wall from the trees above. Arik and I had climbed it many times when we needed to cut time. I knew it was doable. But to do it without causing Harlen pain? I gritted my teeth at the thought.

"Leave Harlen here. We'll come back down for her," Arik said, grunting as he hefted the woman over his shoulder.

My heart hurt to do it. But I knew we had little choice. "C'mon, Harlen," I said, panting. "You can do it, babe." I lowered her onto the ground as gently as possible, sitting her close to the dirt wall. I squatted in front of her, holding her chin. Frowning, I wiped the soot off her forehead. My breath hitched as the soot refused to budge, more stubborn than I was. Dipping my hand in the creek, I put my thumb back on her forehead, determined to see her light skin underneath.

Her head lolled to the side. I shook my head, wiped my eyes, and stood to look up at the cliff.

"I'll be right back for you." Drying my hands on my pants, I reached for a protruding root, ignoring the aching in my chest.

Vic hefted the girl's legs into Arik's arms. The steepness of the hill made the climb difficult, but the roots created a sort of ladder—a grimy, mud-caked ladder, with rungs that poked and shifted as you tugged on them. I fell over the top of the hill, spitting out dirt and leaves, breathing in the scent of clean air.

I reached back to grab a limp wrist. Groaning, I got to my feet and tugged her back, grinding my nails into her sleeve. The slippery leather suit this girl wore only made things more difficult. What could she have possibly needed this ridiculous outfit for?

Dragging her awkwardly through the dirt, I dropped the stranger's arm and began immediately crawling back down, trying to ignore the fear threatening to take over. The crunch that came from under my feet sent me tumbling, landing on my face next to Harlen, who lay peacefully in the leaves. She could have been sleeping.

I leaned against the wall, trying to catch my breath, as Arik jumped down beside me. Together, we hefted Harlen up as Vic leaned down and grabbed her hand.

By the time we had made it up the cliff with both girls, we all fell on our knees, breathless. "C'mon," I panted. "W-we have to get Harlen back." I stood as Vic helped me lift Harlen.

We fought our way through the trees. The aching in my chest was now more like a thick, dirty rope being pulled tighter and tighter around my ribs. I carried Harlen as you would carry an infant, rocking her to sleep. Her arms fell to the sides, and her head hung back as she moved back and forth with my staggering steps. My heart grew heavier with each step, with each sway of her neck. *Almost there,* I told myself. *Almost home.*

I tried to ignore the smell that now surrounded me, the smell that came from the girl I carried in my arms. Like burned, rancid meat that had sat on the fire for twenty-four extra hours. Forgotten. Destroyed. Mutilated.

It hung in the back of my throat, making me want to bend over and puke.

The meadow came into view—the sweet, sweet meadow—the yellow grass waving in the wind made me want to stop and sob. Hope was in view. Finally.

Vic took off at a slow run. "I'll get Astrid!" he wheezed.

Arik and I staggered out of the forest, now running on fumes alone. I needed to get up. I had to get up. But I was having trouble standing with Harlen in my arms.

Hash and Loic raced to us as we struggled through the tall grass. Hash lifted Harlen out of my arms without question.

"Careful!" I gasped as he turned and ran toward the base with Harlen, jostling her lifeless body against his own.

Loic took the stranger from Arik, throwing her over his shoulder.

They ran back to the base with the women without question as Arik helped me to my feet. Together, we limped to the entrance and staggered in, ignoring the questions and looks of surprise.

I shoved my way into the infirmary, which was actually a room with a single bed, but we had used it before when people needed stitches or bandages. But never something like this.

Coughing into my elbow, I followed the sickening aroma down the hallway. I paused in the doorway, taking a shaky breath.

Harlen was lying on the bed with her lips parted and her eyes closed. Her white skin stood out harshly against the torn green shirt she wore and the soot that stained her face. Matted, blonde hair covered her forehead and stuck to her cheekbone.

Hash looked up at me as we entered. He held Harlen's small hand in his own, patting it and whispering to her. He said nothing to me as I stared. But the look in his eyes said enough.

I put a hand on her forehead and pulled back her hair gently. I swallowed and concentrated on Harlen's small face. "Harlen, I know you can hear me. Please."

Her heart was still beating. I was almost sure. Where the hell was Astrid? I turned and found the first face staring into the room. "Get Astrid! Now!" I yelled at a young man whose eyes went wide, and he disappeared from the doorway.

Sounds of yelling, then something crashing, came from the hallway. I grimaced as I gripped Harlen's small hand. It was cold. Too cold.

"It's okay. Everything will be okay. But you have to open your eyes for me, babe. You have to look at me," I pleaded.

"Everybody move," a voice called from the hallway.

Astrid shoved her way through the door, pulling her black hair into a ponytail. Her hands immediately went to Harlen's throat. "She's got a pulse. Help me turn her," she said.

Slowly, we rolled the limp body over. I gasped as we held her on her side. The back of her clothing was gone. Only burned, red flesh covered her bones, a red so familiar my head throbbed. White pustules bubbled up and down her back, leaking some type of thick, white ooze. I looked away, pressing my lips together.

"Oh, Harlen," Astrid murmured, covering her mouth with her hand. She looked at me with watering eyes. "I-I don't know . . ." Her hands trembled as he looked away.

I shook my head. "No!" I grabbed her arms, squeezing them only because I had to squeeze something. "Do something. You have to do something!"

She closed her eyes and took a breath, grabbing my upper arms as well. "Okay. Okay." We stared at each other for a moment, all words between us lost.

Astrid turned, chewing on her long fingernails. "Okay. Burns, burns, burns," she murmured to herself as she rubbed her face with both hands. "Okay. Prulettu." She looked at me. "Do you know what a Prulettu tree looks like?"

"Uh, yeah, sure." By hell, I would find out.

"Okay." She took a deep breath. "Take a container, get to a Prulettu, and scrape away the bark until you get to the sap. Bring me back that sap. As much as you can."

"Okay, okay, I'll be right back." I turned to leave, but stopped. "Don't leave her."

She shook her head, still holding Harlen on her side. "Never."

I ran from the room and straight into the kitchen, opening and slamming empty cupboards, looking for something, anything, to use. A small, smashed tin can sat on the floor, shoved in a corner, shining like an angel. I silently thanked Arik for trading cigarettes, which people collected and stacked in these cheap tins.

Grabbing it, I ran out of the room, pushing through groups of people wanting news on Harlen. I flew through the exit, stopping only when I heard Astrid's voice. "Tess! Look by water!"

The only water I knew was the creek. I ran down the hill, praying I could get there before the dying sunlight. Prulettu, Prulettu . . . I bit my lip, looking as I ran. Did I know what a Prulettu tree looked like? I didn't but refused to admit it to myself.

"What are we looking for?" Arik appeared at my side.

I glared at him. I opened my mouth to hit him with a nasty insult but decided now was not the time. "A Prulettu tree."

He nodded. "Over here."

We made our way into the forest, trampling over brush and around trees, following the creek. After several minutes, we stopped. "Here." He wiped his face. "I think this is one. They have white bark."

Fighting my way through the long, arched branches, I made it to the light-colored trunk and whipped my knife out.

"How is she?" Arik murmured while I worked.

I ignored him, grinding into the bark harder. It took several minutes and a great deal of sweating before I saw the bit of shine. I nearly cried in relief, digging harder. Finally, I reached the brown sap. I tilted the can toward the sap, having to work my knife back and forth, again and again, just to get a few drips. When I could wait no longer, I turned to run back as Arik grabbed my arm.

"Tess—"

I shoved him back. "I don't have time for this." Harlen was dying. Because Arik had to be a hero.

I made it back to the base and into the infirmary as the sun was setting. Gritting my teeth, Astrid and I spread what we could on Harlen's burned and raw skin. The sap covered about two square inches of her back.

I wanted to pull the hair out of my head. Instead, I grabbed the can. "I'll be back with more."

"Tess—"

I was out of the room before she could finish. "Hash!" I yelled at him at the entrance. "Grab a can!"

I was out the door before he could ask what the hell I was talking about. I flew toward the woods, twisting my ankle in Benny's ditch, with Hash hot on my heels. Apparently, he had understood. The sap was much harder to get to in the dark, not to mention finding the tree to begin with. We were back to the base in an hour, only to have another few inches of Harlen's back covered.

By the next time we burst out the door for more sap, Loic and Arik were there, ready with their cans. By the time we made it back to the base, ignoring the crowd of onlookers standing outside the base, Astrid had tears running down her face. I handed her the can, ignoring her eyes, and headed out of the room, grabbing an empty can out of her hand.

"Tess!" she called after me.

But I ignored her. I ran back to the Prulettu tree in the dark, time and time again, each time avoiding Astrid's eyes. Each time bringing less and less sap. By now, I was the only one running back and forth to the tree. But I didn't care. I wouldn't stop.

I made it back to the infirmary, sweat and tears mixing with tree sap on my face, with only a few drops in the container. Arik was there, his arm around Astrid.

He turned as I ran in. I stared, breathing in deep gasps, refusing to let myself believe what they were about to tell me. He shook his head and looked back down at the girl, the young girl with burns up and down her beautiful back, the young girl who had tried to help when I had failed.

"No!" I threw the can down on the floor. "No! Do something! It's not too late!" I screamed.

Arik grabbed my shoulders. "She's gone, Tess. She's gone."

He pulled me into an embrace, though my arms hung limply at my sides. I pushed him away and walked out of the room.

Chapter 9

Quinn

I put a shaking hand to my head and took a deep breath. Pain stabbed my brain from all sides, but I forced my heavy eyes open. I peered around the dark room I lay in, too afraid to move. Small rays of light fought their way through a window across the room. I couldn't tell, but from my position, it looked to be boarded up. Why would a window be boarded up? My mind flashed with horrible thoughts of what went on in this room with the creaking bed. Things they didn't want the world to see.

My back ached from the thin, lumpy bed I woke up on. It smelled like dirty feet. Maybe sweaty socks. The dang thing creaked with every breath I took. My eyes searched the dim room, seeing outlines of more bunks and piles of blankets all over the floor. I let my head fall back on the limp pillow. At least I was alone. I wiped at the beads of sweat dripping down the side of my face. The skin on my body was aching to take a breath, to be released from the prison of my riding outfit.

I let my fingers curl around my back, letting my fingers feel the hard cover. My back would be permanently bruised from sleeping on it, but just holding it made me feel better. I hadn't even told Fenwick. I couldn't leave without it.

Wait. I sat up, my heart thumping, the bed creaking loudly. *Fenwick*. Where was he? He was coming with me. I had asked him to come. I know I had. My eyes moved around the bunks, searching the empty beds for a sleeping body.

I grabbed at the bricked wall behind me and stood shakily, all the blood rushing to my head. I immediately sat back down. Fenwick . . . He . . . He had fallen. I closed my eyes, seeing his face. Seeing his hand reaching out for me as the ground separated and swallowed him whole. Oh, God. He was gone. He was gone because I had lived. He saved my life. And I would never get to say thank you. For everything. Never.

I wrapped my arms around myself and let the tears slip down my cheeks. Selyse. Selyse was gone. Her blood probably still stuck to the bottom of my boots, her last words to me floating in my mind. *My time is up. You must make this journey alone.* She died so I could get here. For her friends. Because I told her I could save them.

Fenwick and Selyse were both gone, and I lay here alone in a boarded-up room, with no way to get back. Because I wanted to play the hero.

I put my head in my hands and sobbed. Sobbed for myself, for Fenwick, for Selyse. They were dead. Because of me.

I jumped when the door opened. Light filled the room, and a tall figure stood in the doorway. I stood and plastered myself against the wall, trying not to scream.

"No, it's okay." A man put his hands up. "I'm not going to hurt you." He stepped in and closed the door, swallowing us in darkness again.

I felt the fear turn to nausea, and the tears started running again. "Please . . . I didn't do . . . I didn't . . . please," I stuttered, moving along the wall. What would this man do? I had heard horrible stories of men disrobing virgins, abusing them, having their way with them. Was that what he wanted of me?

The figure stopped and put his hands in his pockets. "Whoa, calm down. I'm not going to do anything to you."

"Then what do you want?" I replied shrilly. "Where am I?"

"You're at our base. I carried you from the port. Do you remember what happened?"

The port. I was at the port? That made no sense. I was supposed to be in the Axis. Maybe there was a port in the Axis. I swallowed, trying to decide what to tell the man.

"All I remember was Selyse. And my friend. He . . . died. And then I was here," I whispered.

The young man leaned back against the wall and nodded. "Sure. Okay. You got a name?"

"Do you?" I shot back, surprising myself.

He gave a laugh. "Arik."

I relaxed ever so slightly. "Quinn."

He cocked his head. "Quinn?" He stood and crossed the room toward me, coming into what little light peeked in from the window. He studied me for a moment as I stared at the ground, wrapping my arms around myself.

"Strange," he murmured.

I shrank back against the wall as he came closer. I squeezed my eyes closed and held my breath as rough fingers picked up my chin from my chest. Oh, God. This was it.

He dropped my chin. "That's some scar you've got. Svari?"

I opened my eyes, shocked. How the hell did he know that? He stood a few feet away, hands still in his pockets. He had a kind face. A familiar face. With kind, green eyes. One darker than the other. Wavy brown hair that hung down to his chin, but I could easily imagine it close-cropped against his head.

I stared at him, disbelieving what stood in the room with me. "What was your name?" I squeaked.

"Arik." He looked at me with raised eyebrows. "You know me or something?"

But those eyes." Y-you remind me of s-someone," I stammered. It couldn't be. There was no way. Was I losing my mind? Seeing dead people?

He smiled. A smile that could put anyone at ease. He ran his hand through his hair. "Funny. You remind me of someone, too."

My head began to spin. The way he ran his hand through his hair. I-I knew that. I had seen it. Almost every time we spoke. "Where—"

The door opened, and a large man walked in, making me shrink back against the wall again. They turned and spoke in quiet voices. Arik put his hand on his shoulder. The large man turned and left.

Arik turned back, his face looking pained. "I've got to go up front and keep watch. Are you all right alone?"

I swallowed again, imaging lying in this dark room with boarded-up windows. No. No, I was not. With a teary nod, I sniffed. "Yeah."

He turned to leave and stopped. "You could come with. Wanna help keep watch?"

"Okay. Yeah." Whatever keeping watch meant, it sounded infinitely better than sitting around alone in this dark and creepy room.

I followed him out of the room into a narrow hall. As my eyes adjusted, I stared at the people standing in tight-knit groups, with creased brows and worried eyes. Many had shining tracks up and down their faces. Something bad happened here. The many pairs of narrow eyes glancing my way made me swallow hard. What else could I have done?

I turned and hurried after the familiar stride, keeping my head down. *Impossible,* I told myself, watching him walk. Wasn't it? This man couldn't be who I thought he was.

I stopped in my tracks as he picked up a large weapon against the door. I looked back over my shoulder, wondering if I should run away from him instead of following.

"Relax." He threw the long weapon over his shoulder and stepped outside, holding the door open for me. My brain immediately calmed, relieved to see the blue sky shining through. "You always this nervous?"

Yes, I was. But instead of telling him, I stepped out the door and gazed at my surroundings. Trees. Grass. Mountains in the distance. A salty, fresh scent fluttered into my senses quickly, and just as fast was gone. I took another whiff. The ocean. Well, of course. He mentioned a port. I swallowed, staring at the clearing we stood in, the dense woods not fifty feet away. A lone tree sat in the middle of the meadow with a dirty sheet hanging from a branch, blowing in the breeze.

A church stood across from us, practically close enough to touch, gray and weathered, with a door that hung awkwardly off the hinges. A small steeple sat on the roof, with a miniature cross perched on the top.

I turned to look back at the building behind me. Plain brick, a sort of brownish color. One story. Boarded-up windows. Hidden out here in the middle of nowhere.

"What is this place?"

"Our base. Not much to look at, is it?" He put a leg up on the tree with the sheet and studied the weapon, pulling something open with a loud click.

"No, I . . . How long have you been here?" A base. A military base? In the middle of the Axis?

"'Bout four years. Found this place deserted after we escaped. Too hard of a trek to get up this high. Probably why it was deserted."

"You escaped? From where?"

He raised his eyebrows. "Not from around here, are you?"

He had no idea. I shrugged and avoided his eyes. "No, I'm not."

He nodded at the two men who stepped out of the building. Everyone around here was wearing the same green shirts and pants. Strange. They spoke to him for a moment in hushed voices. He nodded, sighed, and turned back to me. "Sorry. Bad situation going on." He ran his hand through his hair again. "We just lost someone."

I could hear the pain in his voice. My heart hurt for him, even though he was trying to act tough. He looked at the rifle in his hands, but I could see his knuckles turning white, squeezing it.

I bit my lip. "I'm so sorry. Is there anything I can do?"

"Nope," he said as he pulled something back on the weapon and it slid into place. "Not a damn thing." He stared stonily off, his mouth set in a firm glare at the surrounding woods.

Time to change the subject. "Where did you, uh, escape from?"

"The compound."

I frowned. "What compound?"

"Tarrith. Now, you tell me where you came from."

Tarrith? I stopped, wondering if I heard him correctly. How could I be in Tarrith? My heart began to pound again, and I clasped my hands together to hide them shaking. I was supposed to be in the Axis . . . Did that mean something went wrong? I swallowed, pushing my hair behind my ear.

Arik peered at me, his eyes narrowing.

I cleared my throat, my body shaking against the leather. "Uh, what?"

"Where did you come from?" he asked slowly.

"Outside the—compound. Why did you escape?"

He shrugged. "Same reason we all did. Tired of war. Tired of starving." He stared up at the sky. "Done with being a Svari slave."

My pounding heart skipped a beat. "What does that mean?"

He looked at me, a hard look in those green eyes. "I couldn't do it anymore. Watch men die for nothing. Their lives ended for nothing more than a dragon's meal. Limbs ripped from bodies while we watched. Would you enjoy that?"

My knees wobbled. I put a hand to my forehead, wondering if this meant what I thought it meant.

"Arik! They're looking for you!"

"Be right back," he muttered and ran back into the building, leaving me with my mouth hanging open, more confused now than I had been when I woke up.

A horrible feeling swirled around in my gut. I put my hands on my stomach and bent over, trying to take a slow breath. This was not right. Dragons eating people? Limbs pulled off? None of the dragons I knew would ever dream of doing something so horrible. What was this place? I ran my hands through my hair, wishing I had a way to pull it back in that same tight bun to get it off my sweating neck.

I stared at the forest, my chest rising too high and falling too fast. Should I leave? Where would I even go? What the hell was I supposed to do? Go find a military compound I have never heard of and ask a murderous dragon for his fire? I squeezed my fists and bit back the scream building inside my body. Instead, I kicked the dirt in front of me, spraying it toward the dilapidated church. Then again. I rubbed my face until it hurt, trying to form a plan in my weak and pathetic brain. Think. Think. This had to be the Axis. There was no other explanation. God, I needed Selyse right now. To calm me. To speak sense into my brain. My eyes stung with hot tears. I slapped the tears away so hard my cheek stung.

Think. I took a deep breath, closing my eyes. Then another. First, I needed to find out where I was. Yes, that was what I needed to do. Arik said Tarrith. I had just left Tarrith. Ridiculous ideas began running through my brain. Could I be in the future? Was this what my life would look like soon if we freed the dragons? Or worse, if we kept them locked up. Perhaps . . . they rebelled against us. Took everything over. I bit at my thumb nail until I tasted blood. Wiping it on the black leather, I took a deep breath. No. My dragons would never do such a thing. Even to their enemies.

I glanced around, studying the surroundings. Right behind the church was a steep hill, leading up to a better vantage point. If I could make it up that hill, it was possible I could see the surrounding area. Was I in Tarrith? The Tarrith I had come from? I needed to see it. Maybe I would see the ocean and be able to tell how far Tarrith was. With my own eyes.

Keeping my eyes low, I hurried away from the base and passed the church. I stopped in front of the hill, which seemed more like a wall now that I stood in front of it. I bit my lip. A bit taller than I had thought. But what did I care? I had ridden a dragon. Over the seas. I could climb a damn wall. Grabbing a root weaving itself in and out of the vertical ground, I started up, glad for once for the ridiculous getup I wore. And the boots proved much more useful than the simple flats I wore on a normal day. My ankle throbbed as I climbed, but I pressed on, feeling that I was at least doing something.

As long as I kept my eyes in front of me, or up, it wasn't so bad. Twice, my sweaty hand slipped, and both times, I got a mouthful of dirt and rocks in order to keep myself against the wall. And for a few extra steps, I had to climb sideways instead of up, just to find a foothold.

Finally, I threw a leg up on the grass, pulling my sweaty self up the rest of the way. I rested on my back for a moment, staring at the blue sky, giving myself a silent pat on the back. Selyse would have been proud. I sat up, gazing down at the base I had woken up in.

Hmm. Nicely concealed. Now I understood why they used that dirty-looking stone. If you were far enough away, I bet you wouldn't even see the squat, one-story building. I wondered how they had found it in the first place. I turned and looked up at another large hill—at least this one was covered in green. My eyes zeroed in on the large house perched on top of the hill, a suitable location to oversee everything. A light color, at one time, would have been white, with a large tree in the front yard. I swept my eyes to the side, studying the large black fence. That was strange. It almost looked like . . .

"What the hell do you think you're doing? Get your ass down here!"

I grimaced at the voice. Maybe leaving to climb up a hill was the wrong thing to do.

"Okay, okay," I called down. The trip down the cliff took half the time and energy, but also partly because I lost my grip and ended up falling, landing on my rear.

I picked myself up, trying not to scream at the returning pain in my leg. I kept my eyes on the ground and brushed myself off so the red of my face would not be so obvious. Pushing my hair back, I glanced up.

A group of people stared at me with accusatory glares, a few with hands on hips. Arik stood off to the side, his hands in his pockets.

"What?" I asked innocently, looking around at the group of people.

The woman in front grabbed the front of my suit and shoved me back against the hill, dirt and rock flying everywhere. I cried out as my head slammed into the wall.

"What are you— I'm sorry!" I sputtered, not knowing what to say.

"Where is the weapon?" she seethed. With her face so close to mine, I could see the whites of her eyes clearly and smell the scent of dried meat on her breath.

"What weapon?" I asked, clawing at her hands.

"Where the hell did you come from?" Her voice shook with anger. She pulled me from the hill and slammed me back again.

"I don't—I don't know what you're talking about!" I cried. "Get your hands off me!" I kicked at her with my boot, landing squarely at her shin.

She staggered back, rubbing at her leg, muttering something incomprehensible.

Her voice. What was it about her voice? That shaking, the way it got high-pitched at the same time. I stared at her face. Her squared-off jaw with a single mole on her cheek. The way her short hair had that wave to it as it fell over her eyes. I always hated that about my hair. That stupid wave.

No. It couldn't be. There was no way. "Wh-what's your name?" I choked out, still against the wall.

"Why the hell should you care?" That look, her eyes—I would swear she was trying to burn holes in my flesh.

"Who are you?" I repeated shrilly, staring at the women who tried to throttle me.

Arik stepped up. "Tess. Her name is Quinn."

For a moment, my eyes met Arik's. Then they slowly slid to the woman in front of me. Tess. Her name was Tess. For a second, her glare softened to one of confusion, and our brown eyes met. We stared at each other, searching each other's faces. Her eyes slid to my cheek then snapped back to my eyes.

The softened look didn't last. "Get rid of her." She turned and stalked off, back toward the base.

I stilled, breathing hard.

She didn't know my full name. And I wasn't sure she would have wanted to know.

Quintessa, the first.

CHAPTER 10

TESS

I sat with my feet propped up on Vic's bucket, staring out at the dark sky. Closing my eyes, I concentrated on the sound of the waves crashing against each other, each one bigger than the last. I hoped somehow it would help, a source of relaxation in this ever-horrific day. Since Arik had taken the Dragon Eye back, I had to stop myself from reaching into my pocket to feel the cool stone I so desperately needed right now.

Ironic, that something like that could help me feel in control. I still didn't understand why. Or maybe that is what I told myself. I had seen what it could do. The pain and devastation. The same thing my father used to bring pain upon an individual. I hated myself for missing its cool surface and the weight of it in my hand.

I had only seen him use it once. But once was enough.

I pulled the cigarette up to my lips and took a drag, the colors of hate and anger spilling out in front of me. I held my breath as long as possible, letting my lungs burn, letting the acrid taste of tobacco rot on my tongue. Slowly, I blew it out, letting my head rest against the tree.

Normally, this would have been my time to find a partner, some male team member taller and thicker than me, who didn't mind rough sex. Didn't mind nail and teeth marks running down his chest. Maybe a black eye.

But tonight was different.

There was a heaviness in the air. A grief, a sadness, had washed over my little rebel base. We had seen people die before. Just last month, an older gentleman developed an illness that made him cough up blood. He couldn't shake it, and Astrid blamed herself for not knowing how to help. So she sat with him for three days, holding cool rags to his forehead and wiping away the blood.

Last year, a woman named Mel had passed away. We just couldn't rouse her from her bed one morning. But she was old and tired, and no one was terribly shocked to learn she had passed on.

But to sit and watch a young girl be taken by dragon fire, a young woman who had so much to offer, so innocent and beautiful. That was something entirely different. She had been murdered trying to help save another. What I should have been doing. Then it could be me, not her.

His footsteps came up behind me. He always scuffed his feet—couldn't pick up the soles of his boots. On recon missions, I always complained he'd alert everyone within five miles that some overly lazy person was approaching.

"Can I have one?" he asked.

I held the pack up to him without a word. They were his, anyway.

"See anything out there tonight?"

"Nope." Wouldn't have been able to see anything if I tried. The reds that bounced loudly in front of my eyes refused to go away. They kind of melded with the night scenery in front of me. Made for one hell of a headache. But pain was good. Pain helped. Kept me focused.

"I'm sorry, Tess. About Harlen."

I took another drag on the cigarette. "Little late for that, isn't it?" I replied, leaning my head back against the tree. "It's done."

"Guess so."

He took a deep inhale of his cigarette and blew it out. I tried to focus on the sounds of the water instead of the heat of him right behind me. It was who he was, I reminded myself. The hero.

Arik sighed and stamped his cigarette out on the ground. He turned and shuffled his feet back toward the base.

"So who is she?" I asked with my eyes still closed.

He paused and shuffled back toward me. "She's not really saying. I get the feeling she has no idea what's going on."

"Probably some sissy from under the Dragon Rule. Couldn't be a rebel if her life depended on it."

Arik squatted down beside me. "I think she's important enough to keep around. She fell from the sky. Put the dragons in a panic. What if she's the weapon?"

I opened my eyes and stared out at the sky. "She's strange."

"She looks like you."

I scoffed, throwing my cigarette over the cliff at the crashing waves below. "Hardly." But something tugged at my brain. She did look like me, and it was unsettling. She had my eyes. And I didn't like strange women falling from the sky with my eyes.

"What if she's your sister?" he asked quietly.

I shrugged. "No surprise there. Just means ol' daddy couldn't keep it in his pants, even that long ago."

"The scar on her face was from a dragon. What if she actually fought a dragon? She might have powers and be afraid to tell us."

I crossed my arms over my chest. He was right. I didn't want him to be, but he was. "Fine. We'll keep her. But keep an eye on her."

"Okay."

He stood and offered me his hand. I looked up at him and finally took it. He pulled me up. "If you need to talk about Harlen," he whispered, squeezing my shoulders. "I'm still here."

My jaw clenched. I turned to leave without a word when the colors started again.

"Arik?" I called with my back to him.

"Yeah?"

I turned and my clenched fist connected with his nose. It made a satisfying pop as he stumbled backward, tripping over my bucket and falling on his ass.

"That was for Harlen."

The dark colors finally began to settle.

The group stood around in the mist the next morning, the silence heavy around us. We picked a spot further up the mountain, still deep in the woods where there would be no chance of a Svari flying.

Hash and I found the spot earlier that morning. Took us a while to find a decent area, a place big enough to hold a grave but still under adequate tree cover. We found a small, open area surrounded by smaller trees filled with tiny orange blossoms that smelled of fresh rainwater. I knew it was the right spot the moment I saw them.

Took us about three hours to dig a deep enough grave. We didn't have any sort of digging tools, just used axes and blades, and I scooped dirt with Vic's bucket. Digging graves was always the worst part about living out here. Tomorrow, I would be sore as hell.

But I didn't care. I owed it to her. And I knew she'd insist on doing the same for me.

One good thing about living as a rebel: we could bury our dead. Where I came from, the dead would never be wasted to rot in the ground. The dragons would feed on them or pick them up in their mouths and carry them to wherever they stored them for later. Then they would feed. Some days, the smell of blood ran throughout the city.

We gathered around the newly dug grave, all twenty-eight of us, and grasped hands. Made a circle around the fresh hole and waited as Arik and Vic stepped up, each holding the ends of the heavy blanket. Astrid had combed Harlen's hair the best she could and placed a ring of wildflowers around her head.

Arik and Vic stepped into the hole and lowered Harlen in. The group stepped forward, made a ring of clasped hands around Harlen's grave, and stood in silence.

Astrid sobbed quietly next to me. I squeezed her hand, wishing I could give her the comfort she needed. But I was too selfish, too weak, and too consumed in my own grief to be what these people needed.

We stood and let tears fall over the beautiful girl lying in the shallow grave. Arik stood across from me, his head down. I wondered if he felt the guilt I was feeling myself.

I couldn't cry. Instead of tears came an emptiness, an aching that replaced a small part of my insides every time a team member left us. But this aching was different. This aching was filled with something different. Something that made me physically ill when I thought about it.

That Quinn girl stood off to the side near Arik, out of our circle. She stood with her hands clasped tightly in front of her. I watched as she wiped her face, leaving shiny tear marks down her dragon scar.

Just the sight of her angered me. As if she had any right to show emotion at Harlen's burial. It was because of her we all stood here today, crying over the innocent seventeen-year-old. A young woman so eager to learn, so determined to train, and one of my friends.

I didn't realize how hard I was grasping Astrid's hand until she tugged at my palm. Pressing my lips in a thin line, I relaxed my grip, but the anger remained. I took a deep breath, forcing the reds back down to the pit of my soul, just like the small pit a young woman lay in. Deep down.

I stepped out of the circle after a few moments and stepped to the head of the grave with Arik and Hash. The three of us began shoveling soil back into the grave. Dirt, lying on top of a beautiful young woman. Dirtying her already dirty clothes. Dirt, mussing her lovely blonde hair and her wildflower crown. Just throwing dirt over a human being. I had never been able to find the humility in this. But it had to be done.

We worked for hours. The circle of mourners remained a hand-held ring while we worked. A silent group of her friends, her family, waiting patiently while we laid her to rest. The sun finally stretched through the clouds at some point during the day. I let the sweat leak into my eyes, tasting the saltiness in my mouth. That only made me work harder.

The sun was shining from the opposite side of the forest by the time we were done. Astrid placed another flower on top of the tightly packed soil, whispered something, and walked away. We took turns stepping beside the mound of soil to say our goodbyes. Some would leave things, like more flowers or random strange things that, to the rest of us, had no significance. But to Harlen, they were important.

The last person to stand at the grave was Arik. I stood off to the side, staring at what was once Harlen, waiting for his token goodbye. He laid a hand where her head would have lain. He closed his eyes and murmured something I could not hear, turned, and left without a word.

I stood. Just stood. I was not sure for how long. I closed my eyes and let the cool breeze ruffle my hair. On a normal day, this could have been such a wonderful little space in the woods. The sweet scent of flowers. Birds singing in the trees. I swallowed and looked up at the darkening sky, not wanting to leave her here alone. How could I just leave her?

Footsteps behind me made me jump. Benny limped into the small clearing, wearing his long brown overcoat and holding something small in his hands. He stopped at the edge of Harlen's grave and tried to reach the center, where the small stack of items had been placed on the dirt.

He grunted and leaned as I stepped over and caught his arm. "Let me help."

He looked at me and nodded, his long gray beard blowing in the wind. He used me as a crutch as he stepped up onto the mound and laid a small braided bracelet of sticks on top of the pile. I smiled sadly. Harlen had been wearing a bracelet of braided twigs the first day she came to us. Benny was the one who brought her to us. I don't know where he found her. She had been helping him walk, much as I was doing right now, and he led her to the front door of our base. A cold, frightened girl who had escaped the clutches of the Dragon Rule.

Only to be murdered by them a year and a half later.

He settled himself down at the edge of her grave, pulling out a dirty handkerchief. He wiped at his nose, mumbling something. I turned and left, figuring he needed his time to say goodbye as well.

I turned and walked out of the clearing, running my hands over the delicate orange blossoms one last time.

She was gone. And she was never coming back.

Chapter 11

Quinn

I huddled in the corner of the dark room, the leather suit squeaking every time I moved. By now, I wasn't sure if the foul stench was my sweaty, disgusting self, or just how this room smelled. I sniffed and wiped my nose again, ignoring the pain that wiping a raw nose caused. That poor girl. She was so pretty, so young. I didn't even know how she died.

I had only ever been to one funeral before. My mother's. Years ago. And it was quite different from the one I just witnessed in my church, with people talking, singing, and more people talking. Hard to remember. The one I just attended was so much more moving, so much more heartfelt. And it made my heart ache to watch the people holding hands around her grave in silence. Remembering. Thinking.

It was painfully obvious by now that because of me, because of something that happened when I arrived, a young girl laid in a shallow grave. The hatred in Tess's eyes, the way Arik brushed the question aside when I tried to ask him. Another person was gone because I wanted to journey to the Axis. I could feel it. If I had not chosen to risk mine, Fenwick's, and Selyse's lives, none of this would have happened. Harlen would be alive. Fenwick would be alive. Selyse would be alive. What had I done?

Wiping my eyes, I stretched my legs against the cool concrete and rested my head back. I sneaked into the first empty room I found when we returned from the burial. People walked in together, arms around each other, pointing at me.

I felt like such an outsider, such an intruder in their beautiful and sad moment. Why was I even still here? The one who had killed their friend? I needed to leave. This was not the place to be. I would leave as soon as possible. Alone. In a world I didn't understand.

I stilled as the door creaked open and light stretched in. I stood, smoothing my hair and clearing my throat.

Arik stood in the doorway. "Thought you'd left us for a minute."

"Maybe it would be better if I did," I replied, my voice thick with tears. I crossed my arms and stared at the floor.

Arik sighed and stepped into the room, closing the door behind him, letting the darkness return. He walked over to the wall I faced and leaned back.

"Did I kill that girl?"

He shook his head and stared at me. "No. A dragon did. She was killed while trying to save you."

I swallowed. "So it's my fault."

"Actually, Tess thinks it's her fault." He was silent for a moment. "It's strange, huh?"

"What?"

"When something bad happens, everyone is so quick to blame themselves. Why?"

"Maybe it's just the way we deal with bad things in life," I said, wiping my cheeks.

"It's not your fault. Or anyone's. It was the dragon who knocked her down. Not you, or me, or Tess."

"So you blame yourself, too?"

Arik stopped. He cleared his throat. "Yeah. I guess."

"My father always said it's hardest to take your own advice." I scrubbed at my face with my leather sleeve, wishing for once I could stop crying.

He nodded. "Guess so."

We stood for a few minutes in silence. I leaned my head back against the wall and thought of the girl we had put in the ground. The flower crown that sat on top of her head. I gritted my teeth and wished I could get her face out of my head.

"You got a good father?"

I opened my eyes. Seemed like an odd question. But I nodded. "Yes, I do." I wrapped my arms around my stomach. "But I have the feeling I'll never see him again."

"What about your mother?"

I smiled and looked down at my thick boots. "Don't remember her. She died when I was young. But I know she was beautiful."

"What was her name?"

I paused. He was fishing for information. I guess in his place, I couldn't blame him. A complete stranger who fell from the sky.

I shrugged. "You first. Tell me something about you."

He gave me a wry smile. "Not much to tell. Grew up outside Tarrith with my mom. Dad died in the wars."

"Your mom?" His mother? I had never thought to ask Fenwick what happened to his mother.

He looked away. "She died the day Tess and I left."

Oh. "What about Tess?" I couldn't help but ask.

He crossed a foot over another while he leaned back, studying me. "She would have been headed for the military. Her father is the general." He leaned his head back. "The guy in charge of destroying everyone's life."

My heart sank. Her father? "Why?" I asked after a moment.

"Why what?"

"What did he do?" I tensed, not sure I wanted to find out.

He shrugged. "Does whatever the dragons tell him to do. Raid villages, fighting matches. Find men and children for dragons to eat."

My breath caught in my throat. Eating people? I rubbed my forehead. That could not be my father. I wouldn't believe it.

"Maybe he doesn't have a choice?" I asked weakly.

He scoffed. "Oh, he has a choice. Lives up in the fancy building while the rest of us starve to death. Yeah, I'd say he has a choice."

I squeezed my eyes shut, determined not to cry again. "Oh." I chewed on my bottom lip. "The dragons . . . What about them?"

Arik shrugged. "You see one, it's safer just to hide."

"Why?" I squeaked.

He looked up at me curiously, like he was trying to decide whether I was serious. "Because they're dragons."

I put a hand to my forehead. The dizziness was taking over. The reality of what I had done was hitting me, creeping up from my stomach into my throat, then forcing its way into my brain.

Dragons ate people. Tess's father let people starve. My father. Tarrith was a militarized zone. The Axis . . . was horrible.

I slid back down against the wall. I needed a male Svari. But how would it be possible to get near a tyrant dragon? I put my face in my hands. What had I done?

Arik squatted down in front of me. "You wanna change out of that thing? Maybe put on some real clothes?"

I nodded, holding back the tears forming again. "Sure. Yeah, I guess."

"C'mon. Let's get you out of that thing." He held his hand out to me.

I wiped my eyes again. Hesitantly, I reached out and took his hand.

He smiled and shook his head when we reached the door. And then he stared. "You remind me so much of her, it's crazy. How she used to be."

I bit my lip, knowing exactly who he was talking about. He reminded me nothing of Fenwick. Even with his hand in mine, this creature was a completely different person. He seemed so tough, so all-knowing, in charge. And he was very, well, attractive. At the thought of Fenwick, a wave of guilt washed over me. I dropped Arik's hand, though hopefully not too fast. The thoughts I was having for this man while Fenwick lay dead somewhere . . .

Because of me.

MICHELLE MASSIE

The night had been uncomfortable, to say the least. Arik found me pants and a button-up shirt, and we fashioned a belt out of strips of a dirty green shirt, now lying in shreds, to hold the pants to my waist. I had to constantly hitch the pants up, but I was grateful for the time Arik spent trying to help.

The good news was the odor I had thought was coming from under my arms had dissipated. My leather suit lay crumpled up in the corner. I hoped I never saw it again. My secret stowaway was stuffed under the mattress. For some reason, I felt I had to keep it out of sight.

Last night, nothing bothered me. Arik led me to the room with the bunks as soon as the sun had set. I had been expecting some sort of meal or another piece of fruit or something. But he simply smiled and told me good night, putting the child to bed without a bedtime story. Luckily, the pure exhaustion of fear and regret took hold of me and allowed my mind a full night's sleep.

So far, this was the second night in my life I had slept with another person in the room. Or several people. Every time a bed creaked or metal scraped across the floor, I jumped. I counted six metal bunks, but most of the people slept on the floor on piles of blankets.

I stared up at the sagging springs above my head, wondering who slept above me. Glancing down, I stared at the outlines of still bodies lying on the floor. Someone had been forced to give up their bed to the stranger. Surely, just one more person I'd inconvenienced in the short time I'd been here. I peered around in the darkness, trying to see if Arik lay anywhere. He was the only person who had spoken to me here, besides Tess screaming in my face.

I let my head fall back onto the mattress. There had been a flat pillow for me, but I gave it to a young woman who was sleeping in the corner on a limp green blanket. I deserved no special treatment from these people. My cheeks warmed in the darkness as the thought crossed my mind I should have given her my bed. I cursed myself for not thinking of it sooner.

The man sleeping in the bed to the left of me snored loudly. I gave up on sleep and instead stared at the bunk above me. My stomach growled loudly, and I thought back to my last actual meal. The one I had vomited up. Arik had offered me a few pieces of what looked like chewed-up fruit throughout the day yesterday, but they were a far cry from anything substantial. They were all busy planning a funeral.

Sighing, I finally sat up and leaned against the wall, pulling my knees to my chest. I wished I could look out a window, but Arik told me they kept every window boarded up to keep up the facade of an abandoned base.

Just when I was about to get up and see if I could find something to eat, the door slammed open. I hit my head against the concrete wall as moans and groans filled the room.

Arik stood at the entrance. "Morning meal in ten, guys."

He nodded to me, and I hurried to stand, eager to be next to someone I knew. I wasn't sure if these people hated me, liked me, or were afraid of me. And sleeping in the same room with them did not solve that problem.

I stopped in front of him, suddenly unsure of myself.

"Sleep okay?" he asked with one hand still on the door.

I gave him a small smile and pushed my hair behind my ear. "Not really."

He smiled. "Yeah, didn't think so. Hungry?"

As if on cue, my stomach gave a loud rumble. "Yes, please."

We walked out the front door and toward the church. The sun was just lifting, painting the most beautiful peach and pink sunrise.

We stepped up the steps into the church. Arik held the crooked door open for me, and I stepped in, staring at the rows of wooden benches. At the front of the small room a table sat, more of the same yellow fruit sparsely placed with a bucket of water and other things I couldn't quite identify—but prayed they were edible. This was supposed to feed everyone?

The early morning sky was visible through a gaping hole in the ceiling. People began filing in behind us, hurrying to the table with what little food there was, and reaching around Arik and me to snatch up bits of fruit and the dark strips. I smiled nervously and stepped back, unsure of how impolite it would look to reach down and steal their precious food. Arik reached over a shorter girl and grabbed a few strips of what I assumed was meat.

"You gotta be fast around here. Have a couple of these. This stuff fills you up better."

I gave him a smile and took one, wishing I hadn't sniffed it first. It smelled sort of like burned wood. I took a hesitant bite, chewing the tough meat, trying to break my way through the leathery texture. Finally, I swallowed, relieved it didn't taste too horrible. Sort of bland, actually. Kind of how I imagined a pine tree would taste.

I ripped off another piece with my molars and chewed. "What am I eating?"

He shrugged. "Whatever we get in our traps. We find a lot of ketrie. Maybe a raccoon on a good day."

The church door opened again, and before I could turn, the room quieted. Tess walked up to the table, passing by me without a word. Arik tugged at my sleeve, motioning for me to sit in a pew.

She wasted no time. "Okay, guys, here's the list for the day. Loic and Hash, I need you two to head up to the farm on the west side. This was the last of our food. I need you to see what he's willing to part with and see if he's got anything worth trading. For a day's work, he's usually pretty generous. See if he'd part with a goat."

"Last time he asked for a few more hands," Hash replied.

Tess bit her lip. "Okay, take Finch with you. If he absolutely needs someone else, come get me and I'll go."

Hash cleared his throat. "He'd, uh, like that tree sap. He usually needs medical supplies. You know."

There was an uncomfortable silence after that. I looked around warily, wondering what this tree sap was.

"Fine. Take whatever we got left." She ran a hand through her hair. "We still haven't heard from Forster. We were supposed to have word by now about a shipment of dry supplies coming in." She looked over at a young couple sitting, holding hands. "Can you guys head down around Tarrith? Check with the villagers, and stay away from the compound. We need that shipment."

They nodded.

"Okay, everybody else, stick to the usual. I want everybody out checking our traps and foraging. Watch out for that ivy that Rynnin got tangled up in last week. It's growing wild and we can't eat those berries. Classes start at dusk, and I want every single team member there." She looked around. "Everybody good?"

People nodded and stood, wiping their hands on their pants and licking their fingers.

"One more thing. Stay in the trees. Out of sight. We've had too many Code Greens." She looked at the couple standing up. "Including you guys. You're gonna have to skip the path and go through the woods to get to the city. Take enough supplies for a couple days."

They nodded, the idea of having to camp out in the woods not fazing them at all. I looked around uneasily as people filed out. What would I be expected to do? I couldn't even remember a time I had been in the woods in my nineteen years. And what the hell was foraging?

Arik stood and stepped to Tess. They talked with their heads bent low, Tess eying me. I gulped.

Arik nodded and turned, stepping toward me. "You're gonna stay on base today. You be okay by yourself?"

I stood, my breath already coming in faster than I would have liked. "Uh, okay. Yeah." I ran my hand through my wild mane of hair and followed him out of the church. At the last second, I turned, my hand still on the door.

Tess was staring at me, eyes narrowed. I gulped. I was scared of myself now.

Chapter 12

Tess

I gazed at the Prulettu tree I had massacred the night before while I should have been cleaning fruit. My fingers reached out and touched the jagged cuts, wondering if I ever would have gotten enough sap to ease Harlen's pain. To save her. My hand dropped to my side, and I sighed. Settling down near the water, I continued washing the ashami fruit and bole leaves we had collected. The bole leaves were good to have on hand. Helped with cuts and infections. Might even cheer Astrid up a bit.

The creek was a fair distance away from the base, but the only place that had reasonably clean water. I chewed on the inside of my cheek as I scrubbed the fruit, stacking it in a small pile on a blanket. By now, my hands were numb. One more sign of an approaching winter, when the creek would freeze over. Winter was not an easy time around here. But not much better at the compound, either.

I finished with the ashami and stood, tapping my foot. She was overdue. Very overdue. The reason I had been on edge for the last week, the reason I had a man in my bed while I should have been on watch, and the reason I hadn't slept for three days. Well, one of the reasons. The death of Harlen only added to my insurmountable pile of anxiety. Not to mention a girl in a leather get-up fell from the sky two days ago.

I stood, shaking my hands dry. "Let's head back, guys."

The girl had to be the least frightening person I had ever seen. Naive, overly emotional, and a twig. I could snap her in half if I needed to. But she could climb.

That much I saw. Those boots of hers would come in handy. I tossed around the idea of letting her climb to the ridge and check the trap up the way. Besides, it's not like I had extra hands all around. Truthfully, I should have sent hunters to the south, but right now, I didn't have the men and women to spare. This Quinn would just have to do.

I refused to stray far from the base. I yearned for new information, something, anything that would tell me what had happened to our most important contact. Something was wrong. I could feel it. She had never been this late. My biggest fear was her cover had been blown. I closed my eyes as I imagined what the general would do if he found out. Or the dragons. But the general would do much worse, I had no doubt. His pride would be wounded, his ego tarnished. And nothing angered that man more than looking a fool.

At times like this, I would put my hand in my pocket and grip the Dragon Eye. That was literally all it took, wrapping my fingers around its power, even if just for a second. The smoothness in my hand would help my confidence build back up, and all self-doubt would wither away. My determination to live according to my own rules would return. But I trudged up the hill, heaving the splitting bucket, self-worth at an all-time low, knowing my pocket was empty.

I rolled my shoulders, knowing I should never have carried it in the first place. Arik warned me. Said I became a different person. Said he could tell when I had it. I didn't believe that. It's not like it's that uncommon for me to be a bitch.

The five of us trudged back up the hill carrying the little food we had procured. Some fruits, a bunch of berries to only be eaten as a last resort—they tasted like rotten, berry-flavored eggs—and our traps only turned up one small ketrie.

As we turned the corner, I saw the woman staggering, coming straight at us. She had arrived from the opposite direction, from the direction of the Tarrith.

"Vera!" I dropped the food I was holding and dashed for the limping woman.

"Tess!" she called, pushing back her light brown hair sticking out in all directions.

Throwing my arm around her back, I led her to the church steps—the closest thing to sit on. The rest of the team members followed us, calling her name and offering her food.

They all knew her by now and knew she was the most important contact we had. But they did not know my history with the woman.

"What happened?" I asked, pulling vines out of her hair. "Where have you been?"

"I'm so sorry. Things didn't go as planned. I stayed three days later, then got lost in the woods." She guzzled the cup of dirty water Rynnin handed her.

"Why did you stay three days later?" I asked, narrowing my eyes. Had that man hurt her?

"There was some kind of disagreement. Between the general and the Eldest Dragon. I stayed to see if I could learn anything." She leaned back and wiped the mud off her face. "I didn't learn much."

"Please tell me the dragon ate him." The man had the freedom to do whatever he pleased in Port Tarrith. It was like the dragons actually listened to him. No one knew why. Possibly because he had the gift to speak to them. But I couldn't believe he was the only person in this world that could communicate with a damn Svari.

She shook her head. "No." She sighed. "It wouldn't be that easy."

The dragons were angry. Angry with my father. Was I sad about this? Not in the least. But it was, in a small way, concerning. If the Svaris were ticked, that meant the general was doing something he shouldn't be. Quite impressive that he had the balls to go up against them. I had to give him that. Though quite a shame he hadn't been eaten.

"Is it because of the Redwings?" I asked. "They're getting nervous, aren't they? A little worried they will get their leather asses handed to them?"

"I haven't heard anything about that," she said. "Just your father looking quite stressed and a lot of roars."

Vera was leaning against the counter I sat on. We had found a quiet place to talk, a place to discuss what was really going on behind the scenes. My private talks with Vera were essential. Her true identity on the base remained a secret, and I intended it to stay that way.

We decided long ago no one could ever know who Vera was. She was known throughout the group as a sympathizer from Tarrith, nothing more. We looked nothing alike. She was tall and gorgeous, and I was short and puny. No one could know she was my mother or the wife of the commander of the militia.

Luckily, there were few people on base who came directly from Tarrith. Most came from outlying lands, a prime choice for hungry Svaris. And the wife of a general was not exactly a public figure, anyway.

"Are there really Redwings out there?" I asked quietly, staring at the ceiling.

Vera shook her head. "I haven't seen one yet. They say if there are, they only come out at night. Puny things, anyway," she muttered.

I scoffed. "A Redwing? Puny? Really? I think you've spent too much time with the Svaris." I leaned back against the wall. "What is happening with the villagers?"

"Some have talked about going north, trying to stay under the radar of the dragons. I heard one man is planning to lead a party to the West Sector."

Talk about a death sentence. The West Sector had been demolished years ago, courtesy of my father. Stripped of all natural resources, a barren wasteland, all thanks to the general's missile strikes. I had seen the pictures hanging on his office wall like some kind of damn trophy. Constant war. My father loved war as much as the dragons did. Maybe more.

"So the Svaris want the weapon to use against the Redwings?"

She nodded. "If they could find the weapon, I get the feeling they would take the war to them. Have them under their control."

I rolled my eyes. "That's ridiculous. The weapon controls all dragons, not just Redwings. Have they thought about what it would do to themselves?"

"But." Her eyes were wide. "The Redwings don't know that. At least, that is what I gather. The Svaris want it to threaten them with, not to use it on them."

I ran my hands through my hair. "Okay. We have Svaris, desperate for information and afraid and pissed at their human liaison. Has dragon blood been spilled?"

She shook her head. "No, thank Mercy. Who knows what would happen if there was dragon blood falling from the sky?" She chewed on her bottom lip. "But I have an idea."

I waited for her to go on.

"Who is the girl?" she whispered. "The girl who fell from the sky? You saved her, didn't you? She's here, isn't she?"

I paused. "If you're thinking this girl is the weapon, you're crazy. She's a little fragile thing that cries if she skins her knee. She's a twig," I added.

"No, no, you don't understand. The dragons are afraid of this girl."

Afraid? Of The Twig? "Why?"

"Well, I don't know. But I think it has something to do with the Devil Day."

I raised my eyebrows and slid off the counter. "The day the dragons arrived? What could she have to do with that?"

The term "Devil Day" was well known throughout Tarrith and, I assumed, throughout the entire country. But speaking it usually resulted in a lash across your face or being thrown in a cell for a few days. Or, if a dragon was around, an even worse punishment.

Vera bit her lip. "The day the girl arrived . . . It threw them into a frenzy. They have been at odds with your father since. Maybe she arrived the same way they did."

I laughed. "You mean the dragons fell through the swirling black clouds into Arik's arms? I find that hard to believe."

"I'm serious, Tess." She grabbed my shoulder. "I think you need to hand the girl over. Let me take her back with me. We'll keep the base out of it."

I shook my head. "She's just a girl with a dragon scar down her face. Nothing more."

Vera looked thoughtful. "A dragon scar? That's strange, wouldn't you say?"

"She is strange," I admitted. "Doesn't seem to know the ways around here. Totally clueless."

"I say we give her to him. Hand her over."

"You want to hand over this strange girl to the Svaris and the commander of the militia? If she's what the dragons are afraid of, it would make more sense to keep her." As much as I didn't want to.

She shrugged. "Do you have a better idea?"

"Okay, so what if she is the weapon? I say we find out what she is, and if she is the weapon, we use her. To control the dragons. Take back our freedom. She's got to be good for something."

"I thought you said she's not the weapon," she reminded me.

I paused. "We need Arik."

Vera jumped away from the counter. "Where is he? Let's go find him."

"I sent him to check something. He'll be back soon."

"Fine. Let's go there."

I shook my head. "No, let's wait till he gets back. I can't have anyone seeing where this drop point is."

Arik and I had discussed it, and we decided we needed an alternate location to move to if we were found out. We needed an emergency bunker of sorts. Somewhere we could tell the entire team to meet, regroup, and plan for the next phase. We could think of only one place. Not ideal by any means, but it was well-protected.

She raised her eyebrows. "You mean me?"

I shoved my hands in my pockets. "Well, yeah. You're the wife of a government official. If you were tortured for information or put under the claw, you would have to give it up. I couldn't do that to you."

"You think I would give you up?" She crossed her arms over her chest.

"No," I said, exasperated. "But you wouldn't even know what you'd say. Look, it's already bad enough you know the location of the base, isn't it?"

"Fine. You don't want to tell me. That's just fine." She looked away, her mouth set in a firm line.

I rubbed my forehead. I had never known my mother to act so childish over something like this. Her husband must be stressing her out more than I realized. "Mom, look—"

But she held her hand up, silencing me. "No, don't worry. It's just fine," she snapped. Then she turned and walked out the door, slamming it behind her.

I sighed, knowing I should probably go after her. We were all under pressure. We were all feeling the stress of our pathetic rebellion. Tiredly, I turned and walked out of the kitchen. I stopped in the hallway. Shaking my head, I turned and walked the other way. I had to get out of here. I needed to breathe.

The lookout was crouched on a large piece of firewood. He sat with the gauge weapon, eyes in the sky, doing exactly as he was supposed to be doing.

Trevor had been here a couple of years now. His dark hair had streaks of gray, and I left him out of duties that included heavy climbing and lifting. Walking long distances made him limp badly on his right leg, even though he never complained. All I knew was he was a soldier in the wars. That was enough of an explanation.

We had all heard stories of the Blood Wars. The West Sector had invaded Tarrith, surprising our militia. Seven bloody days of battle passed with defeat imminent, 90 percent of our troops gone, our surrender planned. Tarrith would be handed over. On the seventh day, the Svaris swooped in from the skies, flames shooting from their mouths, destroying the West Sector. The day everything changed. The only reason we stand here today: our saviors, our protectors. It had been drilled into my head so many goddamn times it made me sick.

I walked over to Trevor, gazing at the sky. "Everything looking good up there?"

"Just as it should, Miss Tess."

I shook my head. I continually chided him for calling me "Miss," but he did it, anyway. Said his Grammy wouldn't have it any other way.

I settled down next to him on the log. "You around for the Devil Day? Remember it at all?"

He set the gauge down. "Yeah. I was posted in Tarrith for that day, Miss Tess. Never forget a day like that."

"What was it like?" I asked quietly, staring at the ground.

He was silent for a few moments, staring off into the mountains. I could see the pain in his eyes—the anger before he even spoke. But it was something I had never been told the truth about. No one spoke of that day.

"I wasn't even twenty years old, Miss Tess. I wasn't even a soldier when they ordered me to fight. They pulled me out of the house, gave me a weapon, and threw me in the back of a vehicle with a bunch of other young men, looking as scared as I was. I still remember every one of their faces. Scared to shit." He shook his head with his jaw set tight. "So much blood on that last day. All it was. Blood, everywhere. We hadn't been given orders in days. I wasn't even sure who to fight anymore. Next thing I know, they're screaming at us to run, get back inside the gates. Then I see these giant monsters flying in the sky. They're shooting fire everywhere, picking up men in their teeth. Biggest teeth I ever seen. And claws." He gave a little shudder. "Only the ones who made it back in the gate were safe. A guy got stuck outside the gate, banging at it, begging to be let in. I tried to pry that gate open, Miss Tess, I swear I did." He shook his head, picking up the gauge weapon. "I shook that damn gate till my hands hurt. But they wouldn't open it. Not even a damn inch. I watched that poor chap get torn from the gate by a green monster. Then another landed, and they ate him. I can still hear him screamin'."

I followed his gaze into the mountains, trying to imagine what it would have been like to see a dragon for the first time. A "flying monster," he called them. I couldn't imagine how horrible it would be to watch a friend get eaten when you stood safely behind a barrier, feet away. I'd seen people eaten. But hearing Trevor's voice hardening at parts, then wobbling, made his experience so much more heartbreaking. Witnessing the takeover of his home. The end of Tarrith as he knew it.

He sniffed loudly, wiped at his nose, then settled with the weapon. I stood, knowing that he needed some time. To be alone. Maybe to forget. I was sorry I dredged it up.

I patted him on the shoulder. "Glad you made it to us, Trevor."

He smiled. "I made it, Miss Tess. My Gram always said you never know how tough you are until you have to be."

"Words to live by," I murmured, as I gave his shoulder another pat and headed past the school.

I started up the path to the drop point. Arik was surely there by now. I needed his sarcasm, his sense of humor—maybe a witty insult or something to roll my eyes at. Some days, he seemed like my biggest sense of frustration in life. Other days, it seemed he was the only thing keeping me anchored down.

CHAPTER 13

Quinn

Wiping my forehead with the sleeve of my shirt, I stopped and looked up, wincing in the sunlight. Sweat poured down the side of my face, my limbs ached, but I was almost there. At the moment, the clunky black boots were a life savior.

I kept adjusting and readjusting my waistband, wishing I had an actual belt. That would have definitely made this trek easier. The extra weight I carried at the small of my back wasn't helping.

I looked back down the way I had come. Amazingly, I had never had to make this trek in my world. But then again, we had a road that led right to my front gate from a road that led directly into the city. Was Tess's secret base even around in my world? I scrunched up my face, trying to remember if I had ever been down the hill that was placed so far from my front yard. And what of the forest? Had I never been curious enough to explore the forest that stood at the base of the hill? Though . . . try as I might, I couldn't remember a forest anywhere around my home in my world. The road into the city I had been on many times. An open road, going downhill in a straight shot with farmland all around. No forest at all.

The closer I got to the house, the more discouraged I became. Half the wooden porch was missing, and the rest of it wobbled in the breeze. The window to the right of the door, the same window I would peek through when someone knocked, was spider-web cracked so horribly you couldn't see through it.

My home. Deserted.

I put my hands on the black gate surrounding the front yard. The word "yard" was not quite accurate. Field, more like. Overgrown yellow grass, large bushes with vines trailing out, and a small dirt trail running off toward the side probably made by an animal who enjoyed the comfort of my previous home every night.

To the left, a large section of the gate lay bent, even with the ground. I could have simply climbed over. Instead, I lifted the latch and pushed it open, ignoring the rusted moaning of metal against metal.

I gazed around at my front yard. The tree I often sat under still stood tall. Nothing could take down that beast. I stepped up the creaking stairs of the porch with no railing.

Pressing my lips together, I glanced around. No one to see me. No one to stop me.

I grasped the metal doorknob and pushed. Surprisingly, it opened. I swallowed, looking over my shoulder. I felt like a criminal. Which was ridiculous. This was my house, wasn't it? Regardless, it didn't appear as if anyone cared about it now.

I stepped in before I could change my mind. I gazed around the dim room. Emptiness filled the air, leaving the scent of a musty, deserted space. Of being forgotten. I sighed, running my fingers along the fringe of an antique lampshade, wondering if a family had once lived here. Or maybe just a father and daughter? I gazed around the room, trying not to compare it to what I remembered.

At one time, this could have been a nice room. Faded, blue sofas that once could have been comfortable were now covered in a thick layer of dust, with a dark stain in the middle of a cushion. A small table that once probably held coasters and wine glasses now had a chunk missing from one side and a crack running up the leg. The tall ceilings always made this room seem larger than it was. Now, they were covered in cobwebs so thick Martha would have had a conniption.

Arik had said they had only been in this house once when they first came upon their base. Too high up, he had said. Easier to be spotted by a dragon. Wasn't worth the risk. The reason I loved my old house—high on the hill, overlooking the city. The best place to be. But not anymore. Now, it was the worst place to be.

The flapping of wings interrupted my thoughts. Many wings. Glancing up, I smiled sadly. Maybe at least one family lived here.

I stopped to study a painting that still hung between doorways. Trees and a mountain with a gray sky overhead. Probably the least cheerful painting to be put in a foyer. I passed the stairs and glanced up the winding staircase, wondering who had slept in my room. Didn't much matter to me. I never spent much time there.

The last door at the end of the hallway hung wide open, which made me raise my eyebrows, for only a second. I shook my head, wondering what in the world I was thinking. In my house, it stayed closed since Father was constantly on important calls or having a visitor sitting in with him. But this was not my house.

Glancing around, I stepped in. It was similar—that was for sure. The painting that hung over the wall behind Father's chair was no longer there. Instead, a bright spot stood out against the rest of the wall. Something had been there. Reaching out, I ran a finger across the bumpy wall covered in dust. I used to stare at that painting. Fall asleep underneath it, thinking now she could look down on me all night.

I stood behind the desk, imagining my father there. It had been such a short time ago that I stood there, asking for permission to go on a dragon ride. Again, I could see that proud smile he gave me, assuming I had the best of intentions, offering to help in any way possible, and being a good father. Even though his daughter was lying to him with a smile on her face.

Swallowing thickly, I turned away and sat on the small padded bench underneath the window. It creaked as I sat, and I knocked on the top, a hollow sound coming from inside.

Closing my eyes, I leaned back. If only I had never stepped into his office that night.

I stepped outside, yearning for the wooden rail I would lean against. Instead, I stepped off the porch and made my way to my tree. My bench should have sat right here, underneath it. Another place I liked to sit and wait for Selyse to get back. I would bring my book and could lie there for hours waiting for the familiar sounds of flapping wings. Seeing her enormous body coming up over the horizon made my heart jump every time.

Now it was a field, with a large tree that was too thick to even wrap my arms around. I closed my eyes, leaned against the tree, and stared out at the Keep—or what should have been the Keep.

The black steel fence still stood, with the same majestic gate. But instead of a grassy field inside the gate, there was only dirt, with sporadic bushels of brown grass. The pond now resembled more of a enormous divot in the ground, filled with more weeds.

My heart swelled as I looked to the corner of the pond where Selyse slept. I had gotten in trouble more than once for sneaking out and sleeping by her side. I would always bring my best pillow, but a blanket was never necessary. Dragon's bodies gave off more than enough heat to keep me warm throughout the night.

Wiping the tears from my face, I started down the hill. I tripped a few times on rocks or branches sticking up but made it to the gate, holding the black metal in my hands as tears ran down my face, imagining the dragons landing, their riders dismounting. Fenwick filling the pond. Selyse smiling at him and with her dragon smile.

It was like that last day in the Keep was imprinted on my mind. A forever stamp that was cemented in my memory. This vast void of a fenced field was so empty, so hollow, so . . . nothing.

The gate creaked open. Swallowing thickly, I made my way through the dirt and patches of grass, stepping to the edge of what should have been the pond. Grass grew out of the dry pond at all angles, rocks filling the gaps between. What I would give to see Fenwick there, pumping the well, working so hard for Selyse and the others. He loved the dragons, almost as much as I did. He never flat-out said it, but I could tell. The way he patted Selyse, the way he pumped that well, and the way he smiled when he spoke her name.

I sat at the edge of the empty pond, pulled my knees up to my chest, and watched the sun in the sky, pretending I was waiting for Selyse. It was just a normal day. The tower would recommend I exit the premises before the dragons arrived. Selyse and I would laugh while I told her about the warning that evening while she slurped away at the pond.

Closing my eyes, I took a deep breath. Maybe, just maybe, I could still smell them. Her scent, right before landing. I concentrated deeply, reaching for any one of them, just a hint. That's all I needed.

How ridiculous. I put my head in my hands, shaking my head. I just couldn't help it. The tears would not stop. They free-flowed—trying to fill the empty, sad pond that sat in front of me.

Footsteps behind me made me jump. I scrambled to my feet and turned, seeing Arik walking toward me.

He nodded. "Sorry. Didn't mean to interrupt."

"No, no, you didn't," I said, wiping at my face. I could feel my cheeks burning. I shoved my hands into my pockets, staring at the ground. "Sorry. I shouldn't have left the base."

"Just don't get caught," he said, smiling. He looked out at the sunset I had been watching. "Me and Tess never knew what this place was. Just a big gated-off field."

I nodded, trying to think of something to say. "Yeah."

"You been here awhile?"

I stopped. "Uh, yeah. Just—a nice place to sit, I guess."

He raised his eyebrows and looked around. The dead grass, overgrown brush, pond of rock. "Oh, yeah, nice place."

The look on his face made me laugh out loud, despite the tear tracks on my face. "You wouldn't believe me if I told you."

"Try me," he suggested. "I mean, I believe you fell from the sky and I caught you in my arms. I believe the dragons went nuts when they saw you. Can't get much more crazy than that, can it?"

I smiled, watching the sun. "Yes, it can."

"I have an idea." He stepped next to me. "Just tell me one crazy thing. Just one. Then I'll leave you alone for a couple hours."

I bit my lower lip. "Okay." I took a deep breath, turning to gaze over the Keep that I knew so well. "I watched two friends die to get here."

He stood directly in front of me, close enough for me to see deep in those green eyes. "You must have wanted to get here pretty bad."

I felt my eyes moisten at the thought of Selyse and Fenwick. "I thought I did," I whispered. "But what if I was wrong? What if they died for nothing?" I looked away, wiping my eyes. Good lord, this man had seen me cry more times than I liked to admit.

He reached over and wiped a tear from my face.

I smiled at him again, studying the curve of his jaw, the freckle up by his right eye. Such a handsome, caring face. He would do anything for anyone if it meant doing something right. Why had I never noticed before?

We stood there a moment. His hand stilled on my cheek. I finally looked down and wiped my eyes. "I think you've seen me cry more times than you've seen me not."

He smiled. "That's okay. Better than cold and distant. I prefer my women this way."

There was an awkward silence after his comment, as if he just realized what he had implied. We both looked away, stuck in an uncomfortable hush.

I pushed my hair behind my ear. "Tell me something about yourself," I said, trying to fill the silence.

"Like what?"

I thought for a moment. "You have to tell the truth," I teased him.

He put a hand across his chest. "Red honor."

I had to laugh at the seriousness on his face. "Red honor?"

He smiled. "Something me and Tess used to say. Whenever one of us would dare another to do something stupid, you had to say 'red honor.'"

"Why red?"

He shrugged, looking off. "A way to defy the Svari, I guess. Their greatest enemies are the Redwings. So . . . you know."

"You and Tess used to do some pretty crazy stuff, I'm guessing?"

He scoffed. "Yeah, you could say that. Her father hated me."

My smile faded. Oh. So he must not be much like Fenwick at all. But didn't I already know that?

"So, ask me," he said to the sunset.

"Right. Hmm." I bit my bottom lip. "What was the last thing that made you cry?"

He looked at me with a hint of a smile. "Hmm."

"Red honor," I said warningly.

He nodded. "Right." He settled down where I had been sitting. I took a breath and sat next to him, trying not to sit too close, but still not too far away.

"When I was fourteen, I was in my first fighting match. It was the best way to get coins, and we didn't have any. Mom was sick, and I needed to get her medicine. So I walked over there one night, stepped up, and said I wanted to fight. Must've come at the right time. They shoved me in the ring before I could regret it, then shoved another guy in behind me. Neither of us knew what to do. All these guys stood around yelling and hollering, wanting to see the violence. The guy punched me. I punched him back. It was a really pathetic fight till the Svaris let out this big roar."

"Were they angry?" I asked quietly.

He nodded. "Yeah. Wasn't bloody enough. They wanted a real fight. So this guy jumps on me and starts to choke me. Trying to kill me, like they wanted. If someone dies in a match, they get fed. The Prats threw a couple of knives in, and we fought with those. He got me bad in the arm. I ended up getting him in the gut. It was over when they dragged the guy's body over for the dragons." He stared into the sunset.

I closed my eyes. What was I thinking he'd say? That he had skinned his knee or something? Was I not looking for some horrible reason, bad enough to make a tough rebel who'd left everything he knew to live in the woods, break down?

"I'm so sorry," I whispered. "That's a pretty good reason to cry."

"Nah, that's not when I cried." He shifted on the ground, dropping his knees so his legs were touching mine, and leaned back on his hands. "I got a bag of coins that night. For killing a man." He stared into the sunset.

I looked down, wishing I hadn't started this conversation.

He sat up, fiddling with the lace on his boot. "I took it to his family. A little girl answered the door. Couldn't have been more than two or three. Kings, she looked just like him. The same dimple in one cheek and this mess of dark hair."

Arik stared over the fence, and I knew he was seeing that little girl. Clear as day.

"And here I was, with a bag of coin I got for stabbing her father or her brother or whatever in the gut." He looked up at me with a rueful smile. "Know what that little girl did?"

"What?" I whispered.

"She smiled up at me before I could say anything and handed me a flower." He sighed. "Then I cried."

I stared at him, studying his face. Fenwick's face. That heartbreaking look, the sadness. I had seen that look before.

With Fenwick, the look simply came every time I told him "no." Every time he asked to walk me home. I never gave him the time of day. Every time I watched those green eyes fall. What could have been different if I had said yes? Just once?

Without thinking, I leaned over and kissed Arik on the cheek. He gave me a startled look, and I turned to stare at the sun, putting my chin down on my knees. I closed my eyes for a second, wondering what in the world made me do that.

After a moment of silence, he gave me a playful shove with his shoulder. Smiling into my knees, I gave him one back. Then he threw his arm around my shoulders. I didn't have the courage to look at him. Instead, I laid my head on his shoulder, and we sat, watching the sun sinking over the trees.

CHAPTER 14

Tess

I sat in the church alone on one of the hard benches with my arms crossed over my chest. My feet were propped up on the bench in front of me, making my ass numb. I stared up at the hole in the ceiling. The sun had already sunk into the mountains, leaving dark blues and purples stretching across the sky. Such vibrant and deep colors. They could have been relaxing. But try as I might, I couldn't keep my limbs from shaking. I couldn't keep the red from swirling in and out of my brain. Oh, what I would give to beat the shit out of someone right now.

I had found Arik. Right where he was supposed to be. Almost. He was sitting in the dirt, in the fenced-off field. And he had his arm around her. Quinn. The Twig. The girl with my eyes. My face. The girl who was supposed to be doing what I told her to do and sitting on her ass at the base. I couldn't hear a word they said. But I didn't need to.

I tossed the Dragon's Eye up and caught it with the same hand. Turned it around in my fingers. Studied it for a moment. The mix of colors around the gold. Then I wrapped it tightly in my fist, closed my eyes, held it to my chest, and breathed deeply.

I didn't know what it was. Was it part of my father showing or part of me that yearned for something dark? Or something worse? When I had it in my hand, even in my pocket . . . dragons be damned, I was mighty. Maybe even dangerous.

After leaving Arik and Quinn to finish their little moment, I walked straight back to the chapel. I knew where Arik would have put it. Right where it was supposed to stay, hidden in the cellar where no one else would find it.

Exhaling, I stretched my neck, trying to rid my mind of the pain. I rubbed my eyes, wishing I could shut my damn brain off. These colors, these bright, horrid reds . . . I was sick of these god damn colors. I was sick of the splitting headache piercing the center of my forehead.

Was I jealous? No, not exactly. It's not like I loved Arik, but to see him with another woman was shocking. It hurt. More than it should have. And that it was The Twig made it so much worse. And when he had a job to do, a job I sent him to do. I went to find him because I needed him. But he had other plans— with her. That made it almost unthinkable. I bounced my foot, trying not to think about it.

Tomorrow's schedule. That was what I would think about. Yes. Liv and Sawyer weren't back yet, so we needed to keep an eye out for them. The farmer. We needed more food. Yup, food. Food was good.

The door to the church creaked open. I didn't bother to look up. The shuffling feet came up behind me, and my anger only grew. I told him not to shuffle his damn feet. I shoved the Eye in my pocket.

He didn't say a word, only sat down on the bench next to me. I kept my eyes closed, praying if I ignored him long enough, he would get up and leave. But he wouldn't. I knew he wouldn't.

Had he walked Quinn back to the bunks and kissed her goodnight? Ran his hand through her long mess of hair? Or maybe they had done it right there in the field. Nope. He wouldn't have screwed her already. I knew Arik well enough for that. No, he would want to be a gentleman, court her, romance her. Save the down and dirty for later.

"Just gonna sit here all night?"

My arms folded over my chest tightened. "Yeah."

I heard him stretch out and lie down on the bench. Waiting. He could wait forever. It annoyed the shit out of me.

"How's Vera?"

"Fine."

I stared straight ahead. I refused to look at him. But I knew the look he was giving me. Good. Let him wonder. "How did Quinn do today?" I tried to keep my voice light and easy. But it was very difficult to fool Arik.

"Fine."

"She stay at the base all day?"

"No."

I nodded. At least he didn't lie to me. I hoped he wouldn't go that far. I let myself open my eyes and glance at him. He was lying back with his hands behind his head.

"So she defied my orders? Left the base when I told her not to?"

He shrugged. "Guess so. Can't blame her for being curious."

"What do you have to say about that?" I sat up, glaring at him. "That it's okay to go against orders when you're curious?"

He sighed. "What do you want me to say?"

"She went against my orders. That means punishment."

"Punishment?" He looked at me with an amused look on his face. "What do you want her to do? Make her scrub the floors? Clean up dirty laundry?"

I folded my arms against my chest again and sat back. "We should lock her up until we find out what her real purpose here is. No one knows it. You're just willing to accept that?"

He rolled his eyes. "Accept what? She's someone who needed help. She is alone and scared. We agreed a long time ago that we would take on whoever needed help."

"I never agreed to take on some random woman who fell through the damn sky. You made that choice for us." I glared at him. "Have you ever wondered where the hell she came from? Why she is here? What if she's dangerous? Working for the Redwings?"

He finally sat up. "You think a Redwing would take on a human? Listen to yourself, Tess."

I stood, trying to hide my shaking hands. "Why don't you listen to yourself? You know nothing about this mystery woman who fell from the sky, yet you're all willing to get nice and cozy with her, watching the sunset! We agreed to do whatever was necessary to protect this base, and for all you know, she could be someone dangerous." I turned and ran my hands through my hair, gritting my teeth. "What if my father sent her? What if the Svaris sent her? You ever think about that?"

He was quiet, and for a minute, I thought he was considering my points.

"You followed me," he muttered, shaking his head. "You actually followed me?" He fell back on the bench with his hands on his face. "Mercy, Tess, why don't you open up your eyes?" he muttered.

I felt my mind scramble for a moment. I hadn't meant to let him know that. Damn. "I refuse to let this girl compromise my base. So get rid of her."

He stood, nearly knocking heads with me. "She's not going anywhere. You would really kick someone out of here based on your petty jealousy?"

"Jealousy?" I shoved him away. "I couldn't care less about your love affair with her, Arik. I don't want her putting any of my people in danger, any more than she already has. Look what has happened since she's been here! Look what happened to Harlen! Because of her."

He glared back at me. "You can't keep blaming her for what happened to Harlen."

I turned to stare into his face. "Would you rather I blame you?"

We stood there, nose-to-nose. We stayed that way: my brown eyes locked on his green ones. Maybe he was finally seeing me for who I was. Maybe he was finally fed up.

Finally, I turned my head, feeling my bottom lip quiver. I took a deep breath. I did not cry.

"Am I interrupting?"

Both our heads swung toward the door.

Vera stood there, a tired look on her face. She pushed her curly hair back.

"What?" I snapped.

She raised her eyebrows. "The rest of the base is just curious about the scream-ing match."

I flushed, running a hand through my hair.

Vera sighed and walked in, leaning against the bench. "What's the problem? Let's talk it out."

"We're fine," I said through gritted teeth.

"Your voice echoing through the woods says different. I assume we're talking about the new girl?"

"Yes. I don't trust her."

Arik stood up. "Well, I do. Give her a damn chance. You blame her for Harlen's death. You can't see past it."

I balled my hands into fists at my sides. "I can see just fine. You're the one that can't see past her batting her eyelashes at you and laying her head on your shoulder—"

"Tess," Vera said wearily. "How can we settle this? Have you tried talking to her?"

"No."

"Then how about we start there?"

"Did you really have to have her moved to the shed? Mercy, Tess," he muttered.

"Until I know who she is, I don't care what you think, *Fenwick*."

He gave me a dirty look and pulled the door of the shed open. Quinn sat in the dark corner, small and afraid, practically trembling in fear.

She stood quickly, confusion written all over her face. "What is going on?" she asked in a high-pitched voice.

Arik jumped right in. "I'm sorry, Quinn. Tess wants to ask you a few questions."

"About what?"

I tried not to smile at the shaking in her voice. "First, I would like to know why you defied orders today. Left the base."

She looked to Arik, then down at the ground. "I'm sorry," she mumbled. "I-I had to see the house."

"Why?"

"Just wanted to see it." She kicked at the ground. "Why it was there."

I crossed my arms, nodding my head slowly. "Sure, sure. Why it was there." Like I believed that. "Where did you come from?"

She sighed. "I came through the link. From a long way away. I didn't know I would end up . . . here."

"You came through a link? What in the divine is a 'link?'"

She pushed her hair behind her ear. "A portal. A byway."

"It makes sense, Tess," Arik said quietly next to me. "She fell from the sky."

"Ah," I said, raising my eyebrows. "A lot of these byways around, I imagine? Placed on every corner?"

"This is why I didn't tell you! You don't believe me." She had her face bunched up and her eyes shined.

For Mercy's sake, if this girl cried one more time, I would slap her. "You're damn right I don't believe you. That's the most ridiculous thing I have ever heard."

The door behind us creaked open. "I would like to have a word with her now, Tess."

I gritted my teeth, highly irritated my mother interrupted my interrogation session. "Why?"

"Because I have heard of this byway."

"What?"

Vera stepped into the dim shed and stopped, stared at Quinn, and then stepped closer. "What is your name?"

For a moment, Quinn said nothing. "Quinn," she whispered.

"Quinn," Vera murmured. "You came through the link?"

"Yes."

"How? Where?"

I looked from Quinn to Vera, then back again. They were in some intense staring contest as if one couldn't believe the other stood there.

"My friend helped me to get there," she replied weakly. "Her name was Selyse."

"Where did Selyse take you? How did she know of the byway?" Vera asked.

I stepped between them, holding my hands up. "Whoa, whoa, wait a minute." I did not like being in the dark here. "What is going on? How do you know about some byway?" I asked.

"I'd like to speak to Quinn alone," Vera announced.

"What?" I looked at her incredulously. It was not like her to take over my business.

"Please, Tess? Just for a minute?" Her pleading eyes burned into mine. "Please?"

Arik took my wrist. "Come on, Tess. Give them a minute."

I huffed, looking back and forth between them all. Was this not my base at all? Were these decisions not mine?

I threw open the shed door and stomped off into the dark, Arik right behind.

"Tess! Would you slow down?"

"No." I was furious with Vera, and I didn't care who knew it. For one thing, she actually believed her. For another, she had just kicked me out of my own interrogation.

"Tess!" he called again.

I spun to face him. "You believe her, don't you? She's feeding us some bullshit about link magic, and you are totally buying it."

He threw his hands in the air. "Well, why not?" He grabbed my shoulders. "She fell from the damn *sky*, Tess. That's some type of magic right there, whether you believe it or not. Admit it. You haven't given her a chance. You blame her for Harlen and can't see past it."

I pulled my arms out of his grip. "I want her gone. Tonight."

He took a deep breath and stood back. "No."

I narrowed my eyes. "Either she leaves or I do."

Arik sighed and ran a hand through his hair. "Hand it over, Tess. Now."

"If she doesn't leave—"

"Give me the damn thing!" He backed me into the brick wall. "Now."

Glaring at him with all the might I could muster, I shoved the Dragon Eye into his palm. He pulled away from me, shaking his head.

"Why do you keep doing this to yourself?"

My eyes burned. "Like you care anymore." I shoved him aside, threw open the door, and stepped inside.

Chapter 15

Quinn

I stood with my hand on my cheek, still touching the scar that ran from under my eye to the corner of my mouth. Her hands had been so soft, her touch so warm. I could still see her eyes when she looked at me in the dim light. She was beautiful.

Vera. My mother. Tess's mother. I closed my eyes, wishing she would walk back in the door. I would ask her all the things I never got to ask. I would tell her all the things I never got to tell her. What was her favorite color? What did she like for breakfast? I would tell her when I was younger, I dreamed of us lying together in the Keep, next to Selyse, having a dragon sleepover. But her answers would be very different from the Vera who died when I was young. My eyes welled at the thought, wondering what this Vera was thinking this very moment.

We had only spoken for a moment. Not nearly long enough. She put her hand on my cheek and asked me about the portal. Her voice was so soft . . . I couldn't form the words . . . My brain was stuck, staring at her painting in my father's office.

Then I had blurted it all out—riding the dragon to the link, walking though Selyse's blood to get here, seeing Selyse take her last breath. I had sobbed, and she had taken me in her arms and held me tight. She smelled of fresh flowers, of a spring day, sitting under my tree. She smelled of my father and held me like he would . . . It was like . . . home.

Why couldn't I have just stayed there forever?

I wanted to tell her about my father. I wanted to know if they were happy together, the three of us, like a real family. Did she know the first time she met him he was the one? Or did he have to fight for her attention, asking repeatedly, until finally, she accepted?

But she turned and left before I could ask these questions. Maybe it was too much for her. Maybe she needed time to process everything I said.

Or maybe I was a stranger to her.

I put my fingernail to my mouth and chewed viciously, turning and facing the back wall of the shed. I let my head rest on the wooden surface, wishing I could see her again. Wishing she was standing here looking at me.

When the door opened, I turned with a smile on my face. Then my smile faded.

Tess strode into the shed with a gun slung back on one shoulder. She flopped down on the dirt ground against the wall across from me, set the weapon down next to her, and lit a cigarette.

I eyed her warily, wondering what she was playing at. She said nothing but stretched out on the ground and crossed her ankles.

"So," she said, with the cigarette dangling out of her mouth.

"So," I said back. We simply sat and stared at each other. I took a deep breath, determined not to let her see my confusion. This woman had hated me from the moment she saw me. Was she planning on killing me in this empty, dark shed, away from the others? Away from Arik and Vera? Would they even care?

The silence stretched on. Tess studied me, almost curiously, while smoking the cigarette. I wanted to scream at her, ask her what she wanted from me, to just get it over with, but I held my tongue.

"How did you do it?" she asked conversationally.

"Do what?" I knew what she was talking about. But I didn't feel like volunteering any information at this point.

She shrugged. "Get everyone on base to swoon over you."

I paused. I guess I didn't know what she was talking about. "Excuse me?"

She nodded slowly, pulling the cigarette from her lips. "Arik is usually a bit more controlled. Trying to figure out how you got under his skin."

I tried not to squirm. "What are you talking about?"

"Don't give me that shit. You know exactly what I'm talking about."

I raised my eyebrows and shrugged. "Nope. He's a nice guy."

"Hmm." She nodded. "So, what about Vera? How did you seduce her in the two minutes she stood here?"

So she was jealous. Was I attracting everyone important in her life? Were they taking my side instead of their leader's? I pushed my hair behind my ear. I would have thought I could figure myself out a little better.

"She's important." I looked down at my feet. "I feel like I've met her before." It was all I could think to say, and besides, it was the truth.

Tess gave me that sarcastic nod again. Cocking her head to the side, tucking her lips in, that wave of dark hair falling in her eyes. "Sure."

At least in the dark, she couldn't see my cheeks burning. Every time she nodded like that, my brain flashed. In anger. She was pushing my buttons—buttons I never even knew I had.

"So how'd you get through a magic portal?"

I crossed my arms. "First, I have to know something."

She stared with her arms crossed as well.

"What did I do to you?"

Tess raised her eyebrows. "What?"

"Why do you hate me?"

She stared at me for a long time. Finally, she put her hands behind her head and leaned back against the wood, the cigarette hanging out of her lips.

"Hard for me to trust someone I don't know, I guess. You have to earn my trust. I don't give it freely. The one thing my piece-of shit father taught me."

My heart skipped a beat. "Your father?"

"Yeah."

I pushed my hair behind my ear with a shaking hand. "Do you hate him?"

"My father? Of course, I hate him. And you'd hate him, too, if he was your father." She took a drag on her cigarettes. "Why?"

I swallowed. "Why did you hate him?"

She looked at me curiously. "Let's see. He loves conquering lands only to slaughter people and feed dragons the remains. He hangs photos of his missile strikes and conquests on the wall to admire. Oh, he lets people starve to death and kill each other in fighting matches. He treats my mother and me like pieces of shit. I don't have the time to list everything."

The nausea returned. The same way it had crept up my stomach when Arik told me of the general. Had I not believed him then? A part of me wanted to think he was being dramatic, overly dramatic. Maybe he just didn't care for the man. Somehow, it seemed so much more real when Tess described him. Her father. My father. Slaughtering people? To feed dragons?

"Why would he do that?" I asked, holding my stomach.

She laughed out loud. "I've seen him do worse, lady." Tess continued, almost as if she was enjoying watching me sweat. "You know, have people's intestines ripped out when they didn't perform well in battle. Pick young men to be tossed into a pit to fight to the death for a dragon's enjoyment. Kinda like their religion." She gave me an odd smile over the cigarette.

I pushed down the nausea that was rising in my throat. The acrid smoke coming out of Tess's mouth was purposefully wafting in my direction, making my head throb. "But why?"

She took another long drag on her cigarette and blew the smoke in the air slowly, closing her eyes. "Because he can."

I turned toward the wall with my hand over my mouth. If I gagged, at least she wouldn't have to watch me. I put my hand on the wall to steady myself. Nothing was making sense. I put my forehead to the wall, focusing on the scent of rot and decay instead of cigarette smoke. How could my father do these things? How could my mother let him? What had happened in this god-awful place to turn my father into some monster that even his own daughter hated? And my mother . . . Did she hate him as well?

My shoulders fell in defeat. Why did I come to this place? Why did Selyse not know this place was hell, and why did she agree to my insane plan? I came here to get fire to save dragons. How naïve could I have been? I, Quinn Ambrose, wanted to save the world. I could have laughed at myself, standing here prisoner in a dark and moldy shed, talking to my other self, who wanted to rip my head off.

I took a deep breath and opened my eyes, staring at the dark in front of me. Time to make a decision. I swallowed thickly and turned to face Tess.

"I can speak to dragons. One scarred me when I was young, and I've been able to ever since." I put my hand to my cheek, feeling the edges of the scar. I waited.

She narrowed her eyes, pursing her lips. "You can talk to dragons?"

I nodded.

"So how come you're not dead?"

"What?"

"A dragon attacked you and you survived? Hard to believe."

I shook my head. "No, it was a sick dragon. Sh-she was my friend."

There was silence. "So you are telling me your best bud, a *dragon*, attacked you? My, my. Lucky girl."

I bristled at the tone of her voice. I had just about enough of her patronizing attitude. "Where I come from . . . dragons are not tyrants. We live in peace." I spoke with my jaw clamped shut, breathing hard. I squeezed my eyes shut, rubbing my face.

This was pointless. A shame I was not the type of person who could punch a wall or kick something and simply feel better. It had never occurred to me that my other self might be such a bitch.

"Friendly dragons, you say? That you talk to?" She took another drag on her cigarette. "I'd like to see that," she said, tilting her head back and blowing out a line of smoke. "If you came here looking for friendly dragons, you're wasting your time, lady. No such thing. So I suggest you go back where you came from, and you and your best bud can live happily after all." She stood, dusting her pants off.

That was it. I took two steps toward her, speaking directly into her face, "My best friend, a *dragon*, died to get me here. I watched her bleed to death just so I could come through the link and get what I needed because I promised her I would fix everything. I watched her weep as she lay with a broken wing, in pain, because I couldn't handle something I swore I could handle. I promised her I could free her kind, save everyone, all because I said I could. They are waiting for me, depending on me because I promised them I could do something I don't think I can even do! Now I need your help to get the hell out of here!"

My chest heaved up and down with the pain of the harsh reality. My hand shook as I swatted the tear off my face, glaring at my mirror image. Two of my friends, innocent, wonderful beings, had died for me. Because I thought I was someone special. I was under the insane assumption that my life meant something more than what it did. I wasn't some amazing woman who could assemble an entire rebel force or run a base.

I was just—me. That tiny spark of hope exhausted me, the weight of what I set out to do now lying heavily across my shoulders. Somewhere out there, other dragons—wonderful, kind creatures—were still depending on me. I couldn't let Selyse and Fenwick die for nothing.

I waited for her to say something. To laugh. Mock me. But she put her cigarette out in the dirt and stood, slinging the gun over her shoulder. Then she turned and pulled the shed door open.

"Wait!" I grabbed her arm, then dropped it when I saw her eyes narrow. I took another deep breath. "You have to help me. Just get me to the dragons. Get me to the dragons and I'll prove it."

She put a hand on the strap around her shoulder. "Few problems there. Dragons are not friendly. There is no way to get close to a dragon without being eaten. And people can't talk to dragons."

"What about your father? He talks to dragons, right?"

She scoffed, eyes rolling back into her head. "He was *gifted* that power." She stepped closer to me, practically baring her teeth. "After he tore out a man's chest cavity. "What a gift." She spat the last word out, leaving her saliva on my cheek.

"But you have to let me out!"

She glared at me. "Why?"

"Because I can fix everything!" I cried shrilly. "Put everything back the way it is supposed to be!"

Tess shook her head and opened the shed door. "Sorry, dragon bud. Things are exactly the way they are supposed to be, with you right here in this shed."

I stepped across the shed in one step and slammed the door before she could walk through it. "You have to get me to the dragons. I need to speak to a Svari! You have no idea what is happening!" I stared into her dark eyes, the same dark eyes she was staring into. I pleaded with her, begging her silently. If ever there was a time for this woman to take a chance on someone, it was now. She needed to help herself.

We stood, staring at each other. I wasn't sure for how long.

She finally grabbed the strap around her shoulder and hitched up the rifle. "F ine. Vera leaves tomorrow. Sunrise. She can get you to the city. The rest is up to you."

She shoved past me, pulling the door open and leaving me in the dark, quiet shed.

I stood, shaking, unbelieving what she said. I could go? She was letting me leave? Part of me was uneasy as if she was playing this as a trap, getting me to think I could act only to watch me fail.

I still had one problem. Well, one of many problems. But the biggest at the moment: I had to get dragon fire. Even if I could get close enough, what would I do? My backup plan was to convince a male to come with me to travel through the link. But it seemed these male Svaris were a little more . . . violent than their queens. And probably a little harder to argue with.

I started chewing on my nails again, wondering what the hell I was thinking. This was insane. I felt like I had been slapped in the face with the reality of the situation, and now, part of me wanted to burrow into a little hole and hide there for the rest of my life.

But I had a responsibility. To my world. To the female dragons who still were prisoners in the Dragon Keep. They were depending on me. Selyse and Fenwick had given their lives to get me here. Because they believed I could do something amazing. Because I promised I would.

I closed my eyes and leaned against the flimsy wooden door. It fell open easily, splaying me out on the uneven ground, hurting only my pride. I stood quickly, looking around for anyone who was giggling at the clumsy girl who had just fallen out of a shed. Lucky for me, it was dark enough, the moon still not quite in position, helping conceal my lack of coordination.

Surprisingly, I was alone. No one was guarding my door. Did Tess forget? Or was she implying that she trusted me now? Whatever the reason, I did not care. I ran for the church, the only place in the world I thought I might be safe.

Chapter 16

Tess

"Gather around, guys. We're having a class." I straightened the large, stained piece of parchment on the floor and stepped back, allowing everyone to crowd in around the floor under the lantern we stuck on a pole. We would have help from the moonlight which would be directly over the hole in the roof in a few minutes. I pulled the rolled parchment out of its drawer right before class, thinking it was time for a brief review. The Svari sketched out in pencil stared back up at us, filling most of the paper.

I felt the tension around the large room as people leaned over to study the image. Even this simple drawing evoked fear and made people swallow and glance up, just to make sure. It made them remember. We feared this green monster, the one who had hunted us our entire lives. Picked human beings up in their jaws and tore away precious pieces that made people who they were. Destroyed lives. Destroyed who we used to be. I doubted there would ever be a time when a drawing of one did not evoke fear.

"Given the number of possible sightings we've had this month, I wanted us all to do some extra training. If we ever have to battle these creatures," I looked up, "and I mean *if*, we need to be ready."

We had gone over a week with no class, and I felt the irresponsibility of it. Last week, Astrid had gone over how to apply a tourniquet with no supplies. But the attack on Harlen and the arrival of The Twig had gotten in the way of our training. That would end right now.

Arik sat on a wooden pew in the dark, an unlit cigarette in his mouth. At least he was keeping his mouth shut.

I pulled my knife from the sheath behind me and pointed toward the tail, crouching on the floor. "To attack a dragon, you need to be behind them. Always behind them." I pointed to the lined underbelly of the sketch I had memorized by now. "Here. The underside, near the base of the throat, is the best place to puncture, shoot, or do whatever to injure a dragon. They are most sensitive here, without thick scales and armor."

"Uh, no. That's—not quite right."

All heads swung toward the small voice. Quinn stood at the back of the group. I hadn't even heard her slip in. She left the shed, which I left unguarded, and joined us for training.

"Excuse me?" I asked testily.

Her face was bright red. She bit her upper lip. "That's, uh, not where they are the most sensitive."

I glared at her. Sighing, I threw the knife at the ground, stabbing the sharp tip into the wooden floor and making Hash jump back. "Well, by all means, dragon expert, come and show us how it is done." Crossing my arms over my chest, I stepped back.

The glistening on her forehead shone in the moonlight. "Uh, no, I just mean—"

"Get up here," I growled. "Now!"

Quinn took a tiny step forward, then slowly made her way to my side. She pushed her hair behind her ear and looked at me out of the corner of her eye.

I simply raised my eyebrows at her, then reached down and pulled my knife out of the ground. "Here."

She looked at the knife, then up at me. I expected her to drop to the ground and cower, but she surprised me by taking the knife by the black handle. Tossing her hair behind her head, she kneeled down.

"The underbelly is a sensitive part of the dragons. But here is a section on the underside of the tail that can prove lethal if punctured."

Several team members' heads turned, looking at me as if they needed my permission to believe her.

"And how do you know that?" I asked.

"They have a bundle of nerve endings feeding into their tail. Injury to that area is usually life-threatening. And their necks can't reach the area to clean it. If it doesn't kill them first, they will probably break their necks trying to lick their wounds. The underbelly is still a sensitive area since they have no scales, but given that dragon saliva has incredible regenerative powers, they may be able to repair a wound there. Depending on the dragon" —she pointed toward the stomach with the knife— "the further you can get down on the underbelly, the better. Their major organs are clumped somewhere around here"—she drew a small circle over an area behind their back leg—"so several wounds here would also do significant damage. So," she straightened up, "you want to puncture them in the underbelly under the start of the tail if possible."

Silence. I noticed a few raised eyebrows. How would this girl know these things about dragons? It was odd, to say the least. People didn't get close enough to dragons to know all this shit.

"Okay, dragon expert. How do you suggest we get underneath the tail to kill them?"

Quinn wiped her forehead and pressed her lips together. "Uh, you would have to bait them. Probably with something in a tree, or up high so they would hover."

I took the knife away from her. "Fine. Thank you for your expertise." I stepped back into the center, pushing her away.

"So, now that we have this valuable information, I would like to get back to training." I rolled up the paper of the Svari drawing, then reached under the nearest bench. I cleared my throat as I pulled it out, avoiding the wondering eyes of my teammates.

Rolling it out carefully, I set an empty sheath on one end, and an old boot on the other. I cleared my throat and stood, giving everyone a moment to absorb the drawing. The oversized head and smaller body were obvious, but I wanted to be doubly certain everyone was prepared for a Redwing. Murmurs and a few accusatory glances shifted in my direction. No one but Arik and I had seen this drawing.

"How long have you had this?" Hash asked, motioning toward the floor.

"Not long," I said, speaking to the drawing. I didn't want him to see the truth written all over my face. Arik and I had found this drawing along with the other rolls of parchments, the many maps, and the picture of the Svari. I wasn't sure why I hadn't told anyone. I told myself I was protecting them. Hiding it, so it wouldn't fill their nightmares, as it filled mine. But was I?

Guilt filled my mind, making me want to bite at my own fingernails. The look on Hash's face was one I didn't see often. The glare he gave made me squirm. Hash had been with us almost since the beginning. I depended on him a great deal, and I considered him next in charge, after Arik and myself. I didn't enjoy lying to him.

Forcing a sarcastic smile, I looked up at Quinn. "I assume the dragon expert can tell us all about Redwings?"

She shook her head but kept her eyes on mine. The look she gave me made me look away as if the narrowing of her eyes told me she knew I was lying. I quickly adjusted, reminding myself who I was talking to.

"Here's what we know about Redwings." I announced, trying to shake the shivers Quinn just gave me. "First, they are man-killers, hunters. Second, they are extraordinary fliers, given their small size, and can navigate through any trees and mountains. Third, their sense of smell and vision is intense. They are fast, lethal, and ruthless. If they are in hunting mode, the rumor is they can smell humans from a mile away."

All facts everyone knew.

"So, how do we kill them?" Loic asked.

I shook my head. "You don't. You hide. Or run for your life."

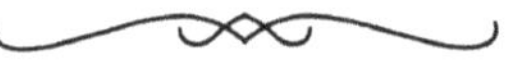

I dismissed the class with express instructions to head back into the base. Curfew was about to be tightened. I had a feeling. Was it simply because we sat and discussed how to kill flying green monsters? How to run away from Redwings? Possibly. Nevertheless, several people hurried back to base, obviously eager to be inside the safety of our brick building, out of sight.

I headed to the back of our one-story base, aiming for the rusty metal ladder attached to the side of the building. The roof stayed off-limits. Our enemy flew in the air. But it was the same place Vera and I met every night she stayed on base. We could speak in private, quietly, and without fear of being overheard.

I grabbed the ladder and glanced around, double-checking once again. These meetings remained secret for a few reasons. Swinging up on the bars, I made it to the top and stepped onto the rough surface. Vera was sitting with her legs hanging off the side. I went and sat next to her, stretching out and lying on my back. The stars shone brightly this evening, almost making things peaceful.

"How was class?"

I shrugged. "Fine." But my blood still ran hot. Colors in my brain still threatened but hadn't reached their full potential yet. For many reasons on this clear night, I closed my eyes and put my hands to my forehead, not looking forward to when they went front and center.

"You're angry." She looked down, her golden brown hair falling over her eyes.

I sighed. "Yes."

"Angry with me?"

I sat up and put my hands down on the edge. "Eh, not so much anymore."

She chuckled. "Why, thank you, Quintessa." She reached over and tousled my hair.

I groaned. "Please don't call me that." I hated my full name. It was just two names, squished together, two names that didn't go together at all. Quinn and Tess. Quinn and Tess . . . I shivered despite the warm weather. Time to change the subject. "So what does he think you are doing right now?"

She shrugged. "They sent him into Holonar before I left. More negotiations," she said quietly. "He'll be back by the end of the week."

"Or if all goes bad, he won't come back at all," I said brightly.

Negotiations meant pissed-off Svaris. Dealing with Svaris from Holonar had always put Tarrith on full alert. From what we had gathered over the last few years, they demanded more troops, and we were unwilling to hand them over. To get there, you had to travel far east by boat. As far as I knew, Holonar was the only other country we dealt with on a neutral basis.

She pressed her lips together and shook her head. "You don't mean that, Tess." She looked down at her hands. "He saved us. And he deserves our respect."

I scoffed. "Respect? After what he has done? That man will never get my respect."

"Sometimes, you have to sacrifice to save someone."

I turned to stare at her in shock. "That's how it should be? You don't abandon your people to rise to the top. If he was such a tough guy, such a great guy, he should have helped the people. It makes me sick to be his child."

We sat in a stony silence. I gripped the edge of the bricked building until it hurt. I turned my head away and stared at the mountains in the distance. Their silhouettes were magnificent, tall, and filled with our enemy. Vera's demeanor and attitude toward my father shocked me. Sticking up for the man. Explaining away his actions. I chewed on the inner of my cheek, wondering how much longer she could keep up the facade of slipping away for days at a time. Not knowing where I was. Completely blind to the rebel base that hid in the woods. It hurt to think that maybe it was time to sever ties with my mother. Maybe it was too much for her.

"I need you to get Quinn to the city tomorrow." My voice came out stiff and hollow.

She looked at me in surprise. "You're letting her go? Why?"

Scratching the back of my head, I shook my head. "Don't know." I put my chin on my elbow. "I think I'm sick of looking at a woman with my chin," I joked.

Vera smiled. "You know, she reminds me of someone."

I looked at my mother with raised eyebrows. "Who?"

"You. Years ago, before you ran a rebel base. Before you had the lives of people in your hands."

I scoffed. "I don't think I cried every time I got nervous. And I think I have a little more meat on my bones.

She stared at me. "She doesn't remind you of you at all? Just a bit? Even back then?"

I shrugged. Tried to remember. Life before our little rebellion base. The long, mousy hair. The wide, fearful eyes. She chewed on the inside of her cheek. That annoyed me. Because I did the same thing.

"Why are you sending her into the city?"

I hadn't let myself dwell on that question. "She says she can change things. Says she can talk to dragons." I shook my head, annoyed with myself for thinking foolish things like I was thinking. "There is just . . . something. I don't know what." I didn't want to admit it. Maybe part of me wanted her away from Arik. Away from my base. Her little speech in the shed got to me. And her eyes. How that woman could give me a look and send shivers up my spine was beyond me. Did I think she could end Dragon Rule? No. But could she do something? Maybe. Just maybe.

And if not, at least she would be gone.

CHAPTER 17

Quinn

I peeked out the door of the bunk room. Empty. Slipping out quietly, I hurried toward the front entrance, eyeing the large man leaning against the wall next to the door.

His head leaned back against the wall with the gun next to him. He turned to me as I walked up.

Light brown hair, the only person with a shirt tucked in. "Hash, right?" I said, pushing my hair behind my ear.

He yawned into his hand, rubbing his eyes. "Yeah."

"Do you think I could talk to Arik?" I was under the assumption that Arik would be outside, standing guard with his weapon.

Hash gave me a tight smile. "I don't think Tess would like that. It's past curfew."

Impressive. Even this man, who could toss me up a tree, took orders from Tess.

I wrung my hands together. "I'm, uh, actually leaving tomorrow. Just wanted to say goodbye."

The door creaked open. Arik stood there, weapon on his shoulder. "Let her out, Hash. I'll keep an eye on her."

I rolled my eyes. Being treated like a prisoner was getting old. But at least Tess let me sleep inside, not in that horrible shed.

Hash moved aside, and I stepped out next to Arik. Instead of the tree he usually leaned against, he walked toward a pile of neatly stacked firewood and settled down in front of it.

After a moment, I followed him, rubbing my arms. I pushed my hair behind my ears, trying to work out what I wanted to say to Arik. After tonight, I might never see him again. Ever. I wanted him to know . . . who I was. And I didn't want to make the same mistake with him I had made with Fenwick. It was almost as if I had been given a second chance in some bizarre way, and I owed him that. I owed Fenwick. And I owed Arik.

I stopped in front of him before I sat down. He had his head leaning back against the logs. The hair he wore down to his shoulders blew in the breeze, framing his handsome face. I liked it, which surprised me. Dirty black boots, his week-old stubble, and a stained button-up shirt were not things I ever would have found appealing. Or maybe I had simply never encountered it before. My father never would have approved of shoulder-length hair. The stubble around his chin made him appear older than he was. In almost every way, he was the exact opposite of Fenwick.

"What?" he asked, looking up at me.

I shook my head and settled next to him. We stared up at the sky in silence. The stars shone brighter than I had ever seen. It would be wonderful to just sit out here and stare at the stars. No worries, no troubles. Just us and the stars.

A horrible cawing noise came from the forest, a sound I had heard often over the past few days. I shook my head. That could put a dent in the relaxing, starry night. "Do you do this every night?"

He nodded. "The only place I can relax."

I shivered in the light breeze. "You mean alone?"

"Guess so."

I let the silence rest between us, a comfortable silence. "Who is that guy?" I asked, nodding toward the hunched-over man, picking at the leaves on the trees near the church. I had seen him a few times, but only from a distance, and never as a part of the group.

"That's Benny. Been with us for a while now. He made his way to us and just never left. Weird guy, but the Rule did that to a lot of people."

How sad. I wondered if the man had a family once. Or if he had ever enjoyed life without fearing for it. Arik and I sat with our heads back while I played with the button on the cuff of my shirt.

"How long have you known Tess?"

He shifted on the ground. "Since we were kids. I lived outside the compound, but they used our farmland for food. Kinda looked the other way when Tess and I would run around."

Swallowing, I glanced at the impassive look on his face. "You two were always just friends?"

"Yup."

I sensed a bitterness in his voice. "Do you love her?" I looked down at my hands.

He paused. "Why?" he asked, speaking up to the star-lit sky.

"I guess I-I want to know. Just because." I could think of no better answer.

He gave a slow nod and set the weapon down in the dirt. "Maybe I loved her. A long time ago. When she needed me. She doesn't need anything now. At least nothing I can give her."

I nodded. A small rush of relief rushed through my brain. "Yeah, that seems like you."

"Oh? Know me well?"

I flushed and looked down at the ground, playing with the hem of my pants. My heart beat in a flutter I couldn't control. Being alone with him under the stars. I glanced at his hand, sitting on his leg. Maybe I should grab it. I shifted on the ground, biting my lip. How I wanted to tell him. That I did know him. A part of him. The part of him that would still be here if I had shoved *him* in that pool of blood and he was still an innocent young man, so eager to please. A man who had feelings for me—feelings I didn't even try to understand.

He turned toward me. His shoulder brushed against mine, making my stomach turn. Hesitating, I leaned into him—just a bit.

"I remember when we would climb to the roof of her building at night. She is scared to death of heights, but would never admit it—even to me," he said, turning toward me.

I fell back against the pile of wood, dismayed. Wrong moment. "So, why would she do it?" I wanted to look up, but was nervous about the proximity of his face to mine.

"I would dare her. I think I wanted her to ask for my help. But she never did. Not once." He shook his head.

When I listened to him talk about Tess, my heart ached. He would die for her, too. Just as Fenwick died for me. She disappointed and hurt him. Just like I did with Fenwick. Maybe we weren't as different as I thought.

Staring at my hands, I squeezed my eyes shut. "I need to tell you something. But I'm afraid you won't believe me." I swallowed. "About who I really am."

"I know exactly who you are," he murmured.

I looked up and took a breath, either surprised or nervous. Those dark eyes studied me, making my cheeks warm. I knew what he was thinking. I could feel it in the goosebumps on my skin.

He smiled and took my chin. "You're the woman who fell in my arms. A woman I never expected to meet." He dropped his hand, looking away. "And you remind me of her so much it hurts."

My stomach did a slow backflip. All tension and heart flickering left my body, leaving me a lonely, disappointed shell of a woman. So it was true. It was Tess he wanted. Not me. I turned away from his dark eyes, my cheeks burning. "Yeah. Sorry about that."

"No." He took my hand and squeezed it. "You were everything I needed her to be. And nothing she was. It wasn't Tess. I just didn't know it until you showed up."

My eyes met his. I saw Fenwick, the young man who smiled every time he saw me. The young man who I turned down every time he offered to do something for me. The man who gave his life for me. My eyes welled with tears when I thought of how I treated him. Every time I told him no instead of saying yes. The one who saved my life. I never even thanked him for what he did.

He ran his fingers through mine. "Do you believe in second chances?" His face was close enough to feel his warm breath on my skin.

I swallowed, trying to slow my racing heartbeat. "I hope so." God, I hoped so. "Thank you for saving my life," I whispered.

Arik reached out and wiped a tear away, holding my face in his calloused hand. "Tell me what you are thinking about. Right now."

"I'm thinking about you." It came out before I could stop it. All the things I should have done. Things I should have told him. Arik was tougher, more handsome, and shouldered more pain. But he was still Fenwick. Through and through.

And then he pulled my face to his. I gasped as his lips met mine, amazed at how soft they felt. At first, I let him kiss me, not knowing where to put my hands or what to do. He tasted like the woods—like a mix of pine trees and campfire. Slowly, I joined him in the strange new dance I only dreamed about. Holding his rough face in my small hands, I kissed him back, running my fingers up and down the stubble on his face. I poured everything into that kiss—my sorrow, my guilt.

He pressed back against my lips hungrily. He told me of every ounce of his pain and grief through those lips. Years of heartache, of giving, with no return. My hands ran up and down his cheeks, feeling the tears running down his face. I had never been kissed before or had another human being's body this close to mine, running his hands through my hair. And yet he felt so familiar. It felt so normal, so right, to have my mouth on his.

I let him wrap his arms around my waist. Our tears stained each other's cheeks with a mixing of emotions I could no longer describe. We needed each other. We had been searching for each other, and for once, I felt I found something I had been missing. That this was what I was supposed to be doing, who I was made for, and the reason I was in this world. The reason I rode a dragon over oceans and rock, the reason Fenwick convinced me to do it. For him. For Arik. I pressed against him harder, wanting this moment to continue, reveling in the warmth his body provided.

The sound of footsteps made me gasp and pull back. Benny stood under his tree, muttering to himself and making a small pile of forest treasures. I looked away bashfully, my face turning red, but already missing my lips on his.

I glanced up at Arik with my hand over my mouth. A brief laugh escaped my lips, exhilaration and embarrassment catching up to my brain. I smiled and looked down, touching my lips. I pushed my hair behind my ears and nibbled on my nail, trying to figure out what to say. What should you say after something like that?

"I—"

But he had my face in his hands again, and his lips on mine. This time, I put my shaking hands up behind his neck and wrapped my arms around him, breathing in the musky scent of a lonely man lost in the woods.

His second chance.

My second chance.

I told him. Lying in his lap, staring at his swollen lips, his dark eyes, the sideburns I had held in my hands. I told him. Almost everything.

Selyse and the Dead Rock. My plan to free the dragons. Nearly dying on the way there. Watching my best friend take her last breaths. I spilled out my entire soul, lying right there in his lap.

But I kept the name Fenwick and Quintessa to myself.

He stayed silent while I spoke, wiping away the tears of frustration leaking down my cheeks. I finished and waited for him to laugh or roll his eyes. Maybe even question my sanity, as I had been doing the last two days.

"Do you believe me?" I whispered, looking up at him.

He brushed the hair out of my face. "Yes."

Did he know, deep down, who I really was? That I was Tess in another life? The woman he had loved for so many years, who refused to give him a second look? I think he did. But neither of us said it, and I don't think we planned on it. Instead, he pulled me up next to him and wrapped his arms around me. I laid against him, closing my eyes and listening to his heartbeat. The taste of his kiss lingered in my mouth, and I breathed in deeply, biting on my lower lip. If only we could have stayed that way forever. If only I had forever.

"I don't want to leave you."

He sighed and put his head against mine. "I guess we're not meant to get what we want in this life. It just doesn't work that way."

I closed my eyes. What a depressing take on life. Why work hard? Why live at all if not meant to get what you want? What you deserved? As if we were forced to treat life as nothing more than a job, day in and day out. I sighed as I realized I could never understand his life, the things he had been through, and he would never understand mine.

"I'm scared," I whispered. "Why was I so sure I could do this?"

He ran his finger down the scar on my cheek. "I think you can do it. And I think I can help."

As we lay under the stars, he told me the story of the Dragon Eye. He didn't know where the stone came from, had only seen it work once, and never hoped to see it work again.

Years ago, while making their plans to leave the compound, Arik and Tess had been on top of her building, late at night. The only place they could ensure total privacy and the only place that had a view of the entire compound.

In the woods, outside the fence, the general stood over a man, in the dark, with no witnesses that he knew of. From their position, they couldn't hear what was said. They could only watch as a man kneeled in front of Tess's father. Loud voices, then the man shook his head as his white hair blew in the wind. He didn't struggle. Didn't fight.

They weren't prepared for what happened next. And again, they could only watch as the general reached forward and shot flames from his hand, encasing the old man in flames. They heard the screams from the top of the building.

"It's strange," he said in a hollow voice. "The smell of burning skin is the same, whether from a weapon or a dragon. Like burned meat."

Later that night, they snuck into her father's office, pulled back the painting, and lifted the handle to open the wall. A palm-sized, perfectly smooth and round rock with a gold slit in its center stared back at them. A Dragon Eye. Still warm to the touch.

"And you just took it?" I asked, my mind still reeling from the thought of my father murdering someone with dragon fire.

"No." He shook his head. "I think we were too scared then. But the night we left the compound, we grabbed it. Tess insisted. She said it was a way to stop him from murdering anyone else like that." His voice dropped. His brow furrowed. "But I think she wanted it for a different reason."

"Like what?" By now, I was sitting, chewing my fingernails, begging for this horrible story to be over, but still wanting to know the end.

He shook his head. "I'm not sure. She has some sort of strange attachment to it. But it's dangerous. When she holds it for too long, she gets angry. Violent."

And now, we were on the way to steal the violence, the fire maker, the thing that my father used to murder a man.

Arik had me by the hand, leading me toward the church. I swallowed as we crept by the base, thinking of the sleeping people right inside the boarded-up windows. Tess was inside that building somewhere. Was she sleeping? Was she lying, staring at the ceiling, hating me? I grimaced, thinking how much more she would hate me after this.

"Are you sure about this?" I said, glancing around the quiet base. Even those noisy birds had stopped screeching by now. The night we had talked and kissed through was fading, replaced by swirls of lighter, brighter colors.

Arik opened the door to the church slowly, looking over his shoulder. We slipped in, and he pulled the door shut behind him. Then we stood silently, though the thumping of my heart could surely be heard for miles.

Taking my hand, he tugged me down the aisle between the pews, leading me toward the front of the room, where I had instructed a group of rebels on how to kill a dragon. A sick feeling took over me at the thought, but I quickly pushed it away. These were not my dragons. These were male dragons, with no queen, and I had deduced by now that males without a queen were an entirely different creature. Vicious man-eaters.

I stared up at the brightening sky, looking out the hole in the roof. The pinks and peaches were combining, rolling out a carpet for the main event, the rising of the sun. If only Arik and I could sit, watch in peace, and forget everything he had told me in the last few hours.

"Come on," he called.

I turned, surprised to see a section of the floor lifted and only his head poking out of the floor.

A cellar. Carefully, I stepped down the creaking steps, further and further away from the beautiful sunrise, into darkness. I stood on uneven, hard ground, looking back and forth in the pitch black as Arik shoved aside boxes and other large objects in the corner. I brought my hand to cover my nose. The stench of dead animals hung in the air, though Arik didn't seem to mind.

"Here."

I licked my dry lips and moved deeper into the cellar toward his voice, losing what little light the upper part of the church provided. Wincing in the darkness, I stepped toward him. Arik held a small wooden box, sweeping dirt off the top.

He cracked open the lid and held it toward me. "It's supposed to stay in here."

I glanced at it, my arms wrapped around myself. This felt so wrong. Looking at it, I tried not to wince, tried not to think of it as a murder weapon, but simply as the eye of a dragon long gone. Which, truthfully, also seemed very wrong.

He took it out of the box when he realized I wasn't going to. He turned it in his fingers, the mix of greens and blues brightening the dark cellar. The colors seemed even more vibrant than the white of the iris. Like it was the opposite of darkness. Or a weapon. The gold slit in the center made me pause as if I had trouble peeling my eyes from the round object.

"Quinn?"

I breathed in sharply at the sound of his voice, forcing my eyes up to the darkness, and into his eyes. As he held it to me, I noticed the sweat glistening on his forehead. I reached out slowly, trying not to think about the smell Arik had described. The smell of burning flesh. I held it in my palm with my fingers spread wide. Slowly, I ran a finger over it, then another, feeling the silky soft glass ball. Not a flaming murder weapon.

"This has fire?" I whispered.

Arik set the wooden box on top of another box, running a hand through his hair. "I'm not really sure. We tried to make a fire with it." He looked away, as if ashamed to say it. "But maybe we weren't the right person to do it. Maybe it takes someone . . . who . . . you know." His voice faded away.

I looked back down at it. Maybe it took someone who could speak to dragons. Maybe it took someone who had a dragon scar down her face. Just maybe.

Arik opened his mouth to say something else but stopped. His eyes snapped upward, and before I could ask, he shoved me aside and jumped up the wooden stairs, grabbing at the rope hanging from the cellar door. He yanked it down, catching it right before it could slam against the church floor.

I froze in the darkness, seeing the fear in Arik's eyes. We stared at each other as the creak of the church door sounded. I winced as clouds of dust fell, and a stomping started above us. It was time for breakfast already. Oh, no.

I looked down at the glass ball in my hand. A glow seemed to surround it, even in the pitch black of the cellar. Had it been glowing when Arik held it? A horrible, hollow feeling started in my chest, growing as I stared at the Eye in my hand. I shuddered, wanting to drop the thing, bury it deep in the dirt, and run away screaming.

Taking a deep breath, I squeezed my eyes shut and shoved it in my pocket, out of sight. I shook my head, chiding myself for an overactive imagination. I stepped toward Arik and he put an arm around me as we stood, listening to the stomping and scraping above us.

The air felt different. Like we had to anchor ourselves to the ground, instead of simply standing here. I wanted to ask Arik if he noticed a rippling of something running through his body right now, almost a calming energy. Like something humming through his veins, but at the same time, making him want to explode from underneath the floor.

Instead, I wrapped my arms around his middle, shoving my face in his shirt, pretending I didn't have that horrible feeling deep in my gut.

Like I was now a part of something. A small piece of something large, something powerful.

Something terrifying.

Chapter 18

Tess

I threw out a basket of bruised fruit onto the bench, spilling most of them on the floor. I stomped out of the church, ignoring the few who were up early and followed me in. Fuming, I marched back to the base to bring the rest of what little food we had from yesterday's gatherings back to the church for the morning meal.

The nerve of him. I had gotten over our fight from last night. Mostly. Whatever the case, Arik had not. What a child. When I stepped into the church this morning, expecting to see him setting up the morning meal, my eyes were met with nothing. Emptiness. I slammed the church door shut, scaring off the stray birds that slept under the eaves. The sound of flapping wings carried them out of the hole in the roof.

Fighting with Arik was one thing. But to completely disregard his duties to the base? To our team? I couldn't believe it. For four damn years, this had been his job. I clenched my fists as I strode back into the kitchen. I grabbed the last, smaller bucket of vegetables and marched down the hall, throwing the door to the bunks open.

"Get up!" I yelled into the room, not even stopping, and slammed out the entrance.

I half expected to see him in the church, giving me that cool look he uses to pretend he's not mad. Hash looked up as I flung the door open. He stood, eyebrows raised, but knew better than to say anything.

"Where's Arik?" I asked.

He shook his head. "Haven't seen him."

"You were on watch last night, right?"

He nodded. "Yeah." He opened his mouth to say more but instead turned and picked up a lumpy piece of yellow fruit.

"And?"

He scratched at his throat. "Uh, that new girl, Quinn. She, uh, went out and sat with him last night."

"You let her out of the base? After curfew?" By now, my chest was heaving. The red blocked my vision and was stuck right in the center of my forehead.

"Hey, hey!" He held his hands up in a defensive position. "I told her no, but Arik said to let her!"

I glared the six-foot, four-inch man down into a shriveling pile. "And you thought it best to listen to Arik when I told you no one goes out after curfew?"

He cleared his throat and glanced at the group of people standing at the door, afraid to enter the room.

"Sorry, Tess. How 'bout I go look for him now?" Instead of waiting for my answer, he pocketed the fruit and hurried out of the church.

"Where the hell is everybody?" I snapped at the staring faces. "It's time for the damn meeting, not a day to sleep in."

People looked around nervously. I turned back to the front of the room, closing my eyes and taking a deep breath. It didn't take an expert to tell me there would be another person unaccounted for that morning.

Quinn.

I paced the room in front of uneasy eyes, drilling out commands like my father would have.

"Loic, go find Hash and go back to the farm. Since you didn't bring back any game yesterday, you won't leave until you do."

Loic shrugged. "He didn't have any to give."

"Yet you stayed and did labor for him all day."

"We brought back those blankets and two pairs of boots."

"Yes, and I instructed you to get food. So go back and get me some, or spend the day in the forest 'til you trap me something."

He opened his mouth to retort, but Astrid elbowed him in the ribs. He rolled his eyes. "Yeah, whatever."

"We need to prepare for winter. I need two trees chopped down today. No excuses. Get on it."

Nods. Hesitant nods, but I didn't care. Could they chop down two trees in one day? Of course not. But maybe they'd at least put their backs into it. Instilling fear in your troops was never a bad thing.

"I want at least three new traps set today. Go deeper into the woods. It's the only way we're gonna catch a damn thing. The rest of you, I want fruits, vegetables, water, whatever. Now get to work."

I headed down the aisle, away from intruding eyes.

"What about the shipment?" Loic called.

Oh, shit. My hands rested on the wooden door of the church. The shipment. The dry goods container that was supposed to come in late this afternoon. I needed that shipment.

And Arik was supposed to be leading the team to retrieve it.

"It's still on. Everybody on that team meets here one hour before evening meal." I stepped out of the church, slamming the door behind me.

I headed back to base, trying to rid my vision of the reds floating in front of my eyeballs. Mercy above. I needed to get laid. Unfortunately, I had just sent all the males out to collect food or chop down trees. Picking up an axe, I started chopping at the log we used as a seat while on watch.

"My, my. Bit of a militia commander, are we today?"

I turned and scoffed at my mother. She was standing against the building with her bag around her shoulders.

"Not in the slightest. I need a rebellion, not a damn party place." I swung the axe down again, missing the wood and instead hitting the rocks that surrounded our overgrown fire pit. Watching the rocks fly off over the grass helped, surprisingly. To connect metal to rock, creating a spark. Two things that were never supposed to connect. Running smack into each other.

"It's a bit frightening, you know."

"I am *not* my father." The reds were swirling faster now. I thought about swinging the axe to my forehead. Possibly that would help.

"Hope you didn't frighten any of your team away. Times could get tough."

I stopped, breathing hard. Wiped the sweat from my forehead. "Arik's gone. So's Quinn."

Silence. I stared out at the forest, wondering what had come over me to think I could trust that girl. With a dragon scar. And Arik? Of all people? To just disappear?

"Hey, Tess?"

I heard the hesitancy in Hash's voice. He had bad news. I let the handle of the axe fall from my hand.

"Yeah."

"I, uh, didn't find Arik." He cleared his throat. "But I found the gauge weapon."

I closed my eyes. "Where?"

"Right there, by the firewood."

I rubbed my forehead. So, he had disappeared with Quinn, leaving one of the only weapons we had lying in the middle of the field. Lovely.

"I left it there on purpose," a loud voice rang out.

I turned, seeing Arik standing off to the side of the base. He had his hands in his pockets, doing his best to look indifferent.

"Yeah, I know. Bad timing. Sorry about that, Hash." He strolled over to Hash and took the weapon out of his hands, tossing it over his shoulder like he always did. He kept walking, right past me.

I crossed my arms over my chest as Hash hurried out of the area. He was probably preparing for blood to be spilled. I know I was.

"Where the hell have you been?" I said to Arik's back.

Vera made a discreet exit, opening the back door to the school and stepping in.

Arik turned to stare at me. "We went up the hill away. Thought we saw something flying." He shrugged. "You're the one that told me to keep an eye on her."

I didn't believe him for one damn second. I was the one person in the world Arik could not lie to, and he knew it.

"We were on a *lockdown*. Why the hell was she outside with you in the first place?"

He dropped the weapon point on the ground and leaned on it. "Didn't realize I needed your permission to speak with another human being."

I crossed my arms, trying to ignore the reds whipping an axe into my skull. "You sure as hell need my permission when it's in the middle of a lockdown. You were on watch, not a damn date."

"Was a pretty damn good date," he said, nodding. "You know, she's quite good at being on watch. You might consider that. After all, she is the only one around here who actually knows how to kill a dragon."

I scoffed and gave him a fake smile. "Oh, so that's how it is, hmm?" Taking two giant steps forward, I glared at him and stabbed him in the chest with my finger. "I don't give a shit who you screw around here, as long as it's not on my time."

He glared back. Then he pushed me hard enough to make me stagger back into the pile of firewood, nearly falling on my ass. "I think you do give a shit, Tess. I think you care because it's her. And I don't give a damn anymore."

The sudden shove surprised me, but I did my best not to show it. Arik had never pushed me before, at least not that hard. But the look in his eyes gave me a different story. We stared at each other for a moment, reading each other's thoughts as we had the uncanny ability to do. And what I saw in his eyes made my blood boil.

"What the hell are you thinking?" I put my face in my hands to keep from punching his lights out. "She is using you! A stranger falling from the sky, and you fall in love with her? What the hell is the matter with you? Just because she looks like me does not mean she *is* me!"

His eyes darkened.

I stopped short and looked away, putting my hands on my hips. I'd gone too far. The words fell out of my mouth before I could stop them. But we'd both known it. Known it for years. Arik loved me. Always had. But I had not, not like that, and that was the end. I did not need him to be my long-lost love or protector. I needed my best friend back.

He nodded again with a strange smile on his face. Then he tilted his head back and laughed. A loud laugh, one that made me stop and look around the empty field.

"You know what, Tess? If I were you, I would have thought the same thing," he drawled, his eyes giving me a look I had never seen. "But you know what attracts me to this woman? Do you want to know why, for one second, I might want something more with her?" He was in my face now, speaking in a hushed whisper.

I swallowed. His eyes were scaring me, though I would never admit it.

"Because she is nothing like you." He stared at me again with those hard, cold eyes. And then he turned and walked off.

I watched him walk away, letting his words settle in my brain. He swaggered off, as carefree as ever, with a weapon propped on one shoulder. Like a man who had just had a great night, a man who had just scored, not giving a damn what it had cost him.

Even if it cost him me.

CHAPTER 19

Quinn

Arik and I had sat in the dark cellar for over an hour. The floor above us creaked miserably every time someone stepped in a particular spot upstairs. If I had to guess, I'd say it was near where the breakfast table sat. We gripped hands, listening to Tess's angry voice above us, then the slamming of a door. After that, conversations quieted, but we knew there were still people above us, probably speaking in hushed tones, wondering where Arik was and what Tess was going to do to him when she found out.

I wasn't just stealing some random stone from underneath a church. I was stealing a murder weapon. Something Tess held in her palm. Something she cherished. Something she would come down here to look for and realize it was missing. The longer the stone sat in my pocket, the darker the realization became. Arik had brought me here and showed me where to find it. Dug the damn box out of the dirt for me. And then he hid underneath the church with me, like a common thief, waiting over an hour until we could sneak out.

I hadn't just stolen the Dragon Eye while we hid in the church. I had stolen Arik.

By now, my nerves returned to full strength. My empty stomach didn't help matters. The growling taking place in my stomach could rival one of Tess's tantrums. Arik had found me a sore-looking apple, but the faint taste of mold lingering on my tongue made me think he probably pulled it from under a bench in the church.

I paced outside the base, waiting for Vera. I didn't realize I was grasping the Dragon Eye until I pulled my hand from my pocket. Gasping, I shoved my clenched fist back in, feeling my face warming. I glanced around, sure Tess would have seen me holding it.

Once I realized I was alone, I took a breath, still holding the Eye. I would swear it pulsed in my hand, and I pushed down the nagging desire to hold it up where I could study it. Holding it tighter, I let it beat in my hand until I could feel the pulsing through my entire body. Faster and faster. The feeling swirled in my chest, almost as if I could take that hand and rip a tree from the ground, roots and all. My eyes widened at the thought. I looked up at the tree I stood next to, wincing, confused by this sudden burst of could-be strength.

A bird screeched in the distance. I jumped, pulling my hand out of my pocket guiltily. I rubbed my hands together, chewing on my upper lip. Ridiculous. Glancing up at the tree, I scoffed at myself, wondering what in the world would make me think these thoughts. Dark magic, Arik called it. My chest tightened at the thought. Selyse did not have dark magic. Of course, she didn't. Rubbing my hands together, I stepped away from the tree. I fidgeted under the sun, wishing we could get a move on. The longer I stood stationary, the further my mind wandered. And I couldn't ignore the desire to wrap my hand around the Dragon Eye again.

I hoped Arik knew what to tell Tess. As we listened to her from the cellar, I could understand why she had the authority she had around here. I never should have let Arik do it. At the mention of her name, I should have called Arik crazy and turned away. *But he took you there,* my inner voice argued. He wanted you to have it. Wanted to help. I put the heel of my hand to my forehead. It was too late to regret it now.

I smiled tightly as people began filing out of the building, heading for the woods in pairs and groups, some by themselves, carrying rope and buckets. I positioned myself behind the fluttering sheet hanging in the tree, trying to avoid Tess, wherever she was. With my luck, she would sense that I was hiding something and have me strip-searched.

"Hiding back there?"

I jumped away from the tree, tripping over my too-long pants and landing on my butt.

Vera smiled and gave me a hand to help me up. My face burned as I let her pull me to my feet, shaking my head.

"I was trying to avoid Tess," I admitted, dusting my pants off and hitching them up. "She doesn't like me very much." I smiled as we stood next to each other. It was silly, but I liked just standing here, looking up at my mother. Her brown eyes were so warm and happy, and even more beautiful when she smiled. Exactly as I remembered them.

"Well, your plan worked. I already said goodbye, so she should assume you're leaving, anyway. Anyone else you need to say goodbye to?" She raised her eyebrows.

I blushed again. "Uh, no. I already said goodbye to Arik. And everyone," I rushed on. I put my forehead in my hands.

She laughed, the most beautiful sound I'd ever heard. "Come on, give me that stuff. We'll stow it in my bag."

At the last moment, I had ran into the bunk room and grabbed the leather outfit I arrived in. Might come in handy if I was going to be facing male dragons who liked to eat people. I had considered going up to the house on the hill but pushed that idea down. I didn't want to risk Vera leaving without me. Things would just have to remain where they were.

We headed down the path, toward the woods, and away from the base. The idea of leaving this place made my heart heavy. I had no idea why. Little food, even less water. Uncomfortable beds. A version of myself that was out for my blood. And Arik. The idea of staying had come across my confused and tired brain. More than once. But I had responsibilities. Fenwick and Selyse had given their lives for me to do this. I could never let myself forget that.

I wondered if I would ever see Arik again. Would he miss me? Pine away for me? I hoped. God, I hoped. The night we spent together, lying under the stars, his soft touch brushing the sides of my face . . . It was a night like no other. Simply to stare up at his face while he spoke in the moonlight, seeing his crooked smile looking down on me . . . I swallowed thickly as I thought of his lips pressed against mine. And how I would never feel that again.

At the last second, I glanced back over my shoulder, wishing I could see him leaning against his tree, his rifle slung over his shoulder, his dark hair blowing in the wind. But all that met my eyes was a dirty white sheet blowing in the wind. I whispered a silent goodbye as I stepped down the hill, and the base disappeared from my view.

We walked in silence until Vera veered off the trail, ducking under a branch. "Sorry," she explained. "If Redwings are around, it's always better to stay off the trail."

I smiled. "I don't mind."

She smiled back at me and mussed my hair. I couldn't suppress the grin on my face as I strolled next to her. To walk and laugh with my mother, for her to tease me about a young man, to play with my hair, it felt so . . . normal. Every time she ran a hand through her hair, I could smell something sweet—like lilacs. Was this what it felt like to have a mother? My mother and I were together, taking a stroll in the woods.

"Sorry about Tess," she said as we walked, maneuvering our way around through the tall brush. "She has a hard time sometimes. Feels the weight of the world on her shoulders, I suppose."

"Understandable." I nodded, eager to stop talking about Tess. I wanted to talk about real things. Things women talked about with their mothers.

Vera didn't waste any time. "Where did you get your scar? Was it really from a dragon?"

I nodded. "A sick dragon. She was hallucinating. It was my fault, actually."

"Your fault? Why?"

I sighed. "My father told me to stay away from her. She had been sick for days, in and out of consciousness. But I was too worried. I snuck in to see her. Got too close to her, I guess."

"Too close to a dragon. Goodness, that seems strange." She shook her head and pulled at the strap of her bag.

I gave her a nervous smile and ran my hands through my hair. I kicked at the vine stuck on my sagging pant leg. "So, uh, what do you do? In the city, I mean? Besides being a spy for your daughter's rebel gang?"

She laughed. "I'm just the wife of a general. Technically, I don't do a bit of anything. Except what I'm told."

"By the dragons?"

"No. By my husband." She shrugged. "But I'm able to get away when he's out. No one cares much about the wife of the general. I just have to make sure not to get caught."

I swallowed, following her around a large ditch. So far, I had not heard one good thing about my father. *But he's not your father*, I reminded myself. He was Tess's father. Just like the woman walking next to me was not my mother. She was Tess's. It went quiet between the two of us. The thought of what Tess had over me dampened my spirits considerably.

Vera must have noticed my change in demeanor. "Tell me about yourself," she said brightly. "All I know is that Tess hates you, Arik is falling for you, and you came through the link from a place where dragons are friendly. I have to admit, all that put together makes me curious."

"What would you like to know?"

"Okay, where are you from?"

I pressed my lips together. How I wanted to tell her everything. How I wanted to spill my life's dreams, goals, just—everything. But instead, I said, "Far away."

She studied me with curious eyes. "Why did you come here?"

I opened my mouth, ready to tell her everything. Who I really was, where I really came from, and why I was here. She knew enough anyway, didn't she? But that tiny voice of fear spoke to me from far away. What if she didn't believe me?

Sighing, I shook my head. "I . . . can't really tell you." I glanced up at her, hoping she wasn't put off by my answer. "I'm sorry," I added. She had no idea how sorry. I pulled at the waist of my large pants, hating myself for lying to her.

She stopped to lean against a tree, dropping her bag to the ground. Rolling her shoulders, she gave a little laugh. "It's funny, isn't it? You and Tess."

I kept my eyes down, wondering if she had the gift to read my thoughts. "What is?"

"How different you are, yet how similar."

I couldn't keep the surprise out of my voice. "What?"

She gave me a warm smile. "You are both so strong-willed. Fighting for what you need. Both so full of life." She stopped and cupped my chin with her smooth hand. "Both so beautiful," she murmured, looking into my eyes.

My heart hurt as we stood, almost like mother and daughter, talking and laughing in the woods. Together. How I wanted to tell her. I was her daughter. I was Tess. How I wanted her to take me in my arms in joyous surprise at finding out I belonged to her. And she belonged to me. That we were a family—even though we weren't.

I wiped my face and looked down. "I could never be as strong as Tess. Or as beautiful as you."

Vera grabbed my hands with both of hers. "No, Quinn, you are. You just don't know it. I see it in you. It's almost like—" She stopped and bit her lip. "I'm so sorry. I didn't mean to make you cry."

"No, no, it's not that." I gave a weak laugh. "I guess I just cry all the time these days."

She ran a hand through my hair, brushing it out of my face. "I cry, too, honey. I cry too." Then she pulled me into a hug I was not expecting and we stood. I have no idea for how long. Two strangers in the woods, holding each other like a mother would hold a daughter.

We sat, leaning up against a fallen tree, watching the sun fade behind the mountains. We had to wait until after dark to enter the city. I didn't care. My butt was asleep from my position on the dirt, but it didn't bother me at all. I could have sat here for hours with her, laughing and talking, smelling the lilacs every time a cool breeze blew in. At the moment, we were giggling at a squirrel who kept stopping in front of us and tilting its little head. We tossed it a nut and watched it munch away, right in front of us.

"Tell me about your parents," she said suddenly.

I looked up at her, wondering what she was thinking. "My father is Head Chairman over Port—uh, over our city."

"Is he a good man?"

I looked down at my hands. "Yes, he is. And a good father."

She smiled. "I'm glad to hear it. What about your mother?"

"I don't really remember her. She died when I was six." I swallowed thickly, thinking this was the most bizarre conversation I had ever had. I was sitting in a forest with my mother, discussing her death.

"Tell me about Tess." I changed the conversation. "When she was young. What was she like?"

Vera shrugged, tossing another nut down. "She and her father never got along, that was for sure. Arik was always by her side. Those two were just a pair."

"They have always just been friends?"

She glanced at me with a knowing smile. "Yes." She settled back on the ground. "Tess's father hated him. He lived outside the compound and wasn't supposed to be inside the gates. But since he was a Fighter, he got away with it."

"A Fighter?" I remembered the talk Arik and I had sitting in the empty Dragon Keep.

Vera nodded. "The Svaris loved their fighting matches. Blood, I suppose. Arik had been fighting since he was a teenager."

I played with a stick, running it through the dirt. Swirling it round and round. "Was he in love with Tess?"

She put her head back and stared at the sky. "I think it was the idea of Tess. What he wanted her to be. But she never felt the same." She elbowed me. "Maybe you are the only way he'll figure that out."

I blushed, smiling. I liked the sound of that, but . . . it would never matter anyway. At least, not to me. If all went right, I would leave and never come back. But maybe Arik could finally move on. I supposed that made it all worth it.

"What about her father?" Though I didn't want to hear any more horrible stories of the man, part of me was still curious. What if he was even worse than I imagined?

"Oh, just your usual lacking dad. The wars keep him busy. Too busy, I suppose."

"Are there a lot of wars?"

She sighed. "Yes. The Svaris want more land. More control. And that means more war. More times the general could not be there."

I waited, expecting to hear the bitterness and hate in her voice that Tess used when she spoke of him. But it never came.

She sat pleasantly, leaning against a tree, as if she had just told me the weather prediction for that night. Interesting. That didn't sound like the father Tess spoke of. The man who tortured humans to win the affection of dragons. I got the feeling that our father did much worse to Tess and my mother than just being a "lacking dad."

"I heard they had a mission tonight. Seemed important. Do you know what they are after?" she asked, staring up at the fading sunset.

I crunched up a dry leaf in my hand, letting the bits fall onto the forest floor. "Some shipment coming in, I think. Arik said he had to be ready for it tonight."

Vera sat up. "Shipment?" She shook her head. "No, that's impossible. This port has been declared off-limits. No shipments in or out."

"Oh. Guess they'll make the trip for nothing, then." Arik would be disappointed. He seemed very tense about this mission. Someone must have said something to make them think it was coming. Odd. "Who tells them about these shipments?"

"They have someone in town, I think. They contact them more often than me, or I would have told them." She looked thoughtful. "Strange," she muttered. "Everyone in town knows about the port."

My heart began beating faster. "You don't think—You don't think someone set them up, do you?"

She looked around nervously, making my stomach jump into my throat. "I'm not sure."

We both stood and stared at each other. Arik was going to be there. What if he was walking into a trap? What if the dragons found out?

Nighttime was approaching fast, fast enough to make the trip back toward the base difficult.

"We have to stop them!" I put my hands to my forehead, wondering what in the hell we could do from this far away.

Vera ran a hand through her hair, her beautiful face tense. She nodded. "Okay. We have to hurry. If I'm missed in town, someone might start looking."

"We'll hurry."

We turned and ran back through the wilderness, praying we weren't too late.

Chapter 20

Tess

I slammed my way into the back entrance of the building, hauling a bucket of small, dirty vegetables. I threw them under the counter in the kitchen and stood up, breathing hard. Setting my hands on the counter, I squeezed my eyes shut, forcing the colors to stop spinning in my head. Punching the counter, I took a deep breath, letting the colors lessen with the screaming pain in my fist.

While I was considering raising my fist to pound the counter again, I heard the deep voice behind me. "We're back. Arik said we'll leave soon."

I nodded, running my hand through my hair. I looked up at Loic. He stood with his arms crossed, leaning on the frame of the door. He was tall, with a muscular chest and broad shoulders. Attractive. Useful. I grabbed his shirt and pulled.

He stumbled out after me in the hallway. "Uh, what?"

I dragged him toward the closet where our ancient wood-burning stove sat, two metal chairs, and an old trash can.

Shoving him in, I slammed the door behind me. "Spare a minute for me?" I panted.

He narrowed his eyes. For one second, I thought he would turn me down, still angry from the first time I ran off. But he slipped his hands around my waist and yanked my slight frame to him. I let him run his hands inside my shirt as I bit at his neck and clawed at any open skin possible. I shakily worked at the buttons on the front of his shirt while he worked on the zipper of my pants, letting them drop to the floor.

We discarded each other's clothes and ended up on the cold floor of the storage room, knocking the dirty trash can from its place. I ignored the smell of rotten vegetables and dead animals, instead letting Loic run his hands all over me, squeezing my breast so hard I gasped. But I didn't care. I needed it more than I had ever needed it before.

I wasn't sure if I simply needed the distraction or if I needed to get back at Arik. His words had stung, had slapped me hard across the face. Was it because I was the one who was used to hurting him? Instead of the other way around? At the moment, all I needed was the release. I needed the headache to lessen, the colors to die away, and my hunger to be fed. While the sweaty man moved on top of me, I forced Arik out of my mind.

After we were done, my headache was down to a dull thud. I sat up and leaned against the wall, wiping the perspiration from my forehead. I pulled my shirt over my head and shoved my feet back in the boots, eager to get my bare ass off the stained concrete and away from what I had done. It always amazed me how much better my head felt, but how much worse I felt about myself. Every time.

Loic lay there next to me, pants around his ankles, hands behind his head. I rolled my eyes. *Yes, congratulations, Loic. You just scored. From a woman who didn't give a damn about you.* I sighed and stood, struggling to pull up and fasten my pants. The taste of Loic still lingered on my tongue—like a sour, sweaty man—making me want to guzzle pond water.

He reached down and grabbed his shirt, clearly impressed by my exhausted state. I let him hold on to that pride as he puffed his muscular chest out.

"Better?" he asked.

I nodded. "Yeah. Let's get going."

"Oh, come on. Mommy already left," he joked, sticking his hand up my pant leg.

"Very funny." Swatting his hand away, I crossed my arms and peeked out the door.

I exited the storage closet in a hurry, trying to put distance between the two of us. Casually, I tucked in my shirt and strolled to the war room. Shoulders back, head up. Nope, nothing to hide here.

Arik was speaking to the small group in front of him. Hash, Vic, and Finch looked over as the door opened, and we stepped in.

No one commented on our late arrival, and Arik remained fixated on the other three men standing in front of him. "As usual, we have one gauge weapon with us, and the other stays on base. Everybody carry a blade."

Vic shook his head. "Don't have one."

Arik ran his hand through his hair. "Right." He pulled the sheath from his belt that held the knife we had stolen years ago from my father's safe. "Take this."

I eyed Arik, noticing the sweat around his forehead and the way he kept running his hand through his hair. Arik being nervous usually made me nervous. We hadn't made a raid on a shipment in a year. Tensions ran high, being that close to the militia. It was a risky job, but a necessary one. We desperately needed just about everything.

"I have the tools to get in the lock," he said, patting his front pocket. "Do not engage the enemy unless absolutely necessary. Let's stay under the radar. Only take what you can shove in the bags."

I reached down and grabbed the three large sacks we had sewn together last year. It took months to gather enough torn and destroyed clothing to make this many bags, but they were worth it. From collecting food and plants to raiding shipments, they were well-used.

I handed one to Loic, who stood so close I could feel his breath on my neck. I shoved the bag in his hand and took a step forward, hoping he would take the hint.

"Let's go, guys. Through the woods only," I announced, eager to put some distance between myself and Loic.

Arik brushed past me to be the first one out of the room. The others followed him, leaving me alone in the room, holding a patchwork rucksack. I sighed and reached behind my back to feel my knife, making sure this time I was at least wearing my own pants.

The trip through the woods to the port was quiet. Well, as quiet as it could be with six adults traipsing through an overgrown forest. Dried leaves and trees coming at us from every angle made it impossible to be silent, as well as the occasional curse or mutter from someone catching a thorn from a briar bush.

Something nagged at me, and for the love of Vatra, I couldn't figure out what it was. Probably just Loic. Most likely my guilt, settling on top of my brain, torturing me. I did my best to steer clear of him, but apparently, he thought, because of our encounter in the storage room, he needed to place himself within groping distance. I walked next to Hash and forced myself to stop glancing in Loic's direction.

Arik's words still tugged at me. But I couldn't make myself say anything to him. I had to concentrate on what we were doing and what needed to be achieved.

This shipment was a big deal. It had been the farmer who informed us of the shipment. He had connections in the city, where he often went to trade and purchase goods. We didn't know exactly what was coming in, but dry goods could mean anything from food to weapons to gear. We hadn't made a raid in so long. I had become worried they were no longer using these storage units.

I came to a halt. "Anybody hear that?"

The six of us froze. All hands moved to their weapons.

"Hear what?" Hash whispered next to me.

I looked around carefully, trying to move as little as possible. The wind breezed around us, moving the scenery we stood in slightly, but nothing else. "Never mind, I guess." I took another glance around, watching for moving branches, rustling brush, anything. I pressed my lips together. Maybe that fight with Arik screwed me up more than I thought.

Just as soon as I thought his name, he glanced back at me. Was it an apologetic glance? Or a quick look to see if I was losing my mind? I couldn't be sure.

It took a couple hours, but we reached the clearing we always stop at, right where the woods thin, directly north of the storage area. The sailors keep the units right off the path for easy access. It was a straight shot down to the port from the containers, right where the ground leveled off.

Arik peered through the woods, stepping on the small perch of logs we built to get a better view of the port. "I don't see anybody yet. No lights. Could they already be gone?"

Of course, they could be. A ship could arrive early or late, or whenever the hell they wanted. But usually, they adhered to a pretty strict schedule. And it took a few hours to offload goods. We liked to watch what they put in, decide what to take, and wait until they were good and gone before we approached the containers. There were three storage units they used, and it would be a gigantic waste of time if we spent five minutes picking the lock, only to find it empty.

Arik stood looking out for a moment while I chewed on the inside of my cheek. I didn't like the idea of going at this blind. We needed to know which container to open. If we permanently damaged a lock, they would know a container had been tampered with. And if the container was empty, we risked time and damaging the lock.

So we stood and waited, paced, and continued to peek out through different vantage points. After nearly two hours of sitting in the dark, ignoring the heat from Loic's stare, I sighed. "We must have missed it. So either we take our pick or call this a failed mission. Anyone have an opinion?"

Loic spoke right up. Even in the dark, I could feel his eyes on me. "I say we go for it. We didn't come all this way for nothing."

Silence fell. This didn't feel like a good idea to me. Arik agreed with me without saying a word. We glanced at each other and locked eyes.

"I'm scrapping it," I announced, standing and stretching my back. "Let's get back to the base."

"What?" Loic exploded. "We come all this way, for all this stuff, and you're just going to walk away?"

"Yes," Arik said from behind him. "If we haven't seen anything, we have no idea what we're walking into. We're not chancing it. We'll make do with what we got."

"No way," Loic said. "I'm going. Anyone who has an actual pair of balls and wants to join me, feel free."

Hash, Vic and Finch looked at Loic and shrugged, then stepped toward the other side of the clearing where we entered, following Arik's lead.

"Sorry, man," Vic said. "Not worth it."

"Let's go," Arik said, throwing his thumb behind him. "Something isn't right here, and we're getting out. Now."

Loic glared at Arik, then at the rest of us. "Some damn rebellion, huh? Scared of your own damn shadow." He pushed past Arik, shoving branches aside, away from the port.

I shook my head, hoping this wasn't some big show for me. Trying to look tough and brave. Impress me, somehow. Mercy, I hoped not. And this was definitely going to be his last mission. I couldn't afford team members who were willing to take these kinds of risks.

Wait a minute.

I launched myself over to where Loic fought his way through the trees and grabbed the back of his shirt. The same shirt I ripped off him hours ago.

"Hey!"

I dragged him back into the dark clearing, fighting, though Vic and Hash were quickly at my side. I grabbed the front of him and slammed him against a tree, my worst fears seeping into my brain.

"What the hell?" he screeched, trying to shove me back.

"How did you know Vera was my mother?" I asked through clenched teeth.

"What?" Loic looked at me like I had two heads. "What the hell are you talking about?"

By now, Arik had walked up next to me. He shoved me aside and put his forearm up to Loic's neck. "How did you know Vera was her mother?"

Loic's eyes darted from side to side. My shoulders fell. Oh, no. I glanced at Arik with wide eyes. We couldn't kill him before we found out who he was.

"How?" I demanded, pushing Arik over so I could be front and center.

"Oh, shit," Hash muttered from behind me. "Oh shit, Tess. We gotta get out of here!"

I turned to face him as Arik held Loic in place.

"This raid. Shit! It was Loic who got the information from the farmer! He said it was the farmer who told him! This guy's a damn spy!" Hash ran his hands through his hair. "Son of a bitch, I left him by himself while I worked. It was my fault—"

"Hash!" I grabbed his arm. "Forget about it! Let's get the hell out of here!"

"Don't worry about it," Loic struggled to speak, Arik's arm still against his throat. "It's too late, anyway."

Chapter 21

Quinn

"Hurry!" Vera yelled over her shoulder. "We have to make sure they haven't been tricked!"

This woman could run. Through the forest, over logs, she even footed a tree and jumped over the damn ice-cold creek I fell face first in. I supposed living out here you'd have to know how to run in the woods.

But the direction we were moving in—didn't seem right. "Vera!" I called.

But she kept running. Fast. Shaking my head, I followed the sound of her trampling through the woods. With nowhere else to go out here, I felt completely stupefied. It would make sense that I had no sense of direction out here, I supposed. We must be nearing the containers they planned on raiding. I wished she would stop screaming. If they were really planning on capturing Tess, a couple of women stomping and screaming through the woods would help no one.

Vera finally stopped at the tree line, crouching down to look through the brush. I finally caught up and fell next to her.

"What is going on?" I panted. "Where are the containers?" As I peered out of the trees, I saw lights. Tall lights. A building.

Confusion flooded my brain as I gasped. "Where are we? I thought we were going to the containers?" I stepped back, shivering, looking around. What was going on?

She patted my arm. "Don't worry. First, we're going to see if the militia is still around. The bad guys. They will lead us right to them. I know these guys, remember?"

I looked around nervously, still panting. "But what if they already left? What if they are already there? Shouldn't we at least—"

Vera grabbed my hand and yanked me toward her. "Quinn. I know this place. Don't you trust me?"

Her eyes burned into mine, the green now almost a gray color. I blinked several times and nodded. "O-of course, I just—"

"Then we wait," she said firmly. "We will find out what the militia is planning and follow them wherever they go. I know these men, Quinn. Remember, I am his wife."

I nodded. "Okay. Yes." I trusted her. Of course, I trusted her.

Tess was her daughter, after all. And Arik. I had to help him. She would get us there. Even so, a fear gnawed at me. I tried not to bite my fingernails. I stared at the dark blue sky, feeling exposed in this open area overlooking the compound. Surely, we should be in the trees. Right? I pushed my hair back, glancing over my shoulder. The feeling of being watched hung over my head, almost like something breathing in my ear.

So we sat. I tried a few more questions, but she seemed out of the mood to talk. I pulled my knees up to my chest and hugged myself, trying to keep from shivering. Did it get this cold at night where I was from? Not that I remembered.

I gnawed on my fingers in silence. Vera sat staring at the twinkling lights surrounding Tarrith. As the silence continued, a fear slowly consumed me, something deep in my stomach telling me I needed to get out. Get away. Something bad was happening somewhere. And it was happening far from here.

I rubbed the heel of my hand against my forehead. "Vera . . ." I whispered. "I think I am going to go back. To the base." I stood, hoping she would realize I was serious. I grabbed her hand. "Please come with me."

She stood slowly, nodding. I breathed an immense sigh of relief, turning to leave.

"Wait!" she said. "Did you hear that?"

I stopped, only hearing the thumping of my heart. The look in her gray eyes showed a strange excitement, a sort of . . . glow. I disentangled my sweaty fingers from Vera's grasp. I glanced around, up and down, and slowly began backing away.

"Quinn! What are you doing?" She grabbed the front of my shirt and dragged me back toward her, nearly pulling me off my feet.

"Vera, please," I begged, tears stinging in my eyes. "What are you doing?" I tried to wriggle out of her firm grasp, shocked at how strong she was.

"You're not going anywhere, Quinn. This is where you belong. With me." Those gray eyes stared at me. My mother's eyes. My mother's eyes were not supposed to be gray.

"No!" It came out as a scream. I kicked out, not planning on hurting her, but desperate to get away from those eyes.

She stumbled backward but regained her balance much too fast. I turned and ran, dodging through the trees, slipping over dried leaves and tripping on upended roots in the quickly darkening forest. I had no idea what way I was even running. All I knew was I had to get away . . . from that woman. Whoever she was. But that was not my mother.

Dashing blindly through the dark trees, I slowed to look over my shoulder. Suddenly, it seemed too quiet. No one was running after me. What about the insects, the birds? The sound of the wind howling through the trees? This was worse than being chased. Before I could turn my eyes back forward, I ran smack into a body, screaming in fear and falling to the ground. The gray eyes. I had just enough time to see those horrible gray eyes.

Instead of standing, I scrambled away on all fours, too frightened to stand and fight back. The forest had gone silent again, waging war on my terrified mind. I crouched behind a tree in the dark, cold forest, wrapping my arms around myself, completely blind to the thing hunting me. I tensed when I heard the footsteps in front of me. The slow crunch . . . Crunch . . . I fell backward, trying to make it to my feet and failing. The footsteps seemed to come from all around me now.

Hugging the wide tree in front of me, I winced against the rough bark, praying whatever doom approached would just get it over with.

I gasped as the colors started, snapping my head up. The scrape along my cheek from the tree didn't even register as I froze, moving my eyes slowly in the dark. The grays moved in my brain, colors I had not seen for days. They moved slowly at first, like a small leak in my left temple. Drip. Drip. The gray and black pooled in my brain, bright as sunlight shining on my face. I put both hands to my face, rubbing my eyes like a crying child, trying to rid my eyes of the colors in front of me. This wasn't right. I must be dreaming, overreacting . . . No, not now . . . Not in the dark . . .

I put the heel of my hand to my forehead, willing the colors to stop. Without waiting, I turned and ran straight into a man's arms. I screamed and fell back, straight into the tree, feeling the heat from his body above mine.

I froze, my eyes squeezed shut, waiting for whatever pain I would experience. The scent of the sour ale I hated swam all around me, making my eyes flutter open in shock. Why, now, why was I doing this to myself? I put a hand to my forehead, trying to keep the nausea down. The horrid scent filled my lungs. A fake, loathsome smell. Oh, God. Without looking up, I turned to run, unsure where but knowing I needed to be far from this place. A woman's small arms stopped me.

"Quinn!" Vera's voice said, wrapping her arms around me, crushing my ribs. She stared at me with those gray eyes. "It's all right, Quinn. Everything will be okay." Her voice . . . I could hear Vera, but it couldn't be Vera.

"No!" I screamed. "Let me go! Let me go!"

My feet left the ground with muscular arms around my waist. My legs still kicked wildly through the air. How was this possible? How was this right . . . No! The grays danced in my vision, refusing to lessen. Only one man had ever made this tornado of color in my mind, making my skin crawl and pushing shivers up and down my body. Only one could make me break into a cold sweat and turn my stomach.

The arms around me clapped a cold, rough hand over my mouth. Her hot breath in my ear made my breath hitch. "I would like you to meet Tess's father, Quinn."

I stared into the cool blue eyes of Luther Grimbley.

He reached down and took my trembling hand, holding it in his. He stared into my eyes as I stared back, too confused to speak.

"My daughter," he murmured, his sandpaper finger brushing my chin, causing goosebumps to break out over my skin.

The arms holding me finally let go of my mouth. "No . . ." I coughed out. "He is not Tess's father! You know he's not!" I begged the stranger who had been chasing me through the forest to believe me. There was no one else to convince.

I kicked out wildly, finally being dropped on my rear end, making me gasp. Holding my bruised elbow to my side, I looked up, afraid of what I would see.

My mother smiled as the moonlight bounced off the glare in her eyes. "I think you'll find things are much different here, Quinn."

"No . . . please," I whispered from the ground, still shaking, desperate for someone to tell me something that made sense.

Luther towered over me. As fear took over my brain, I let the man stand me upright and pull me toward him. I winced as his calloused fingers found my chin, brushing my face the way he always loved to do.

"How I've missed you, Quintessa," he murmured. "Just as beautiful as always."

My stomach lurched, and I turned back to Vera.

Only Vera was gone.

In the moonlight, I could see the glow of the pale skin. Where I expected her lovely face, I saw a bony face with gray eyes too wide to be hers. Dark, greasy hair fell across his wide forehead. He gave me a toothy smile, and I stared, open-mouthed. Gray eyes. Glowing, gray eyes.

Not my mother. Not even close.

Luther Grimbley stepped up behind me, his scent overpowering my exhausted, confused brain. All I could do was close my eyes as his large hands squeezed my shoulders and he pulled me to him.

"Together, Quintessa, we will change everything. Forever."

Chapter 22

Tess

Loic stood against the concrete wall with his wrists bound hastily in the long sleeves of Hash's button-up shirt. The same room Loic and I had disrobed ourselves in so few hours ago. I tried to push that thought from my mind, pretending the smell of sex was not still floating in the air. Focus. I needed to focus on the anger instead. This prick was a spy. And what I had gotten myself into.

There had been a quick discussion on what to do while standing around the forest, with Vic holding the gauge weapon at Loic's chest. Was Vera in trouble? Was Quinn? Were they walking into some elaborate trap? We had more questions than answers, and we agreed the best choice was to return to base and figure out what the hell was going on.

My chest burned as I stared at his smirk. I knew exactly what he was thinking. He was thinking of the way I clawed at him or how he bit my skin hard enough to leave a mark. "Who are you?" I asked through gritted teeth.

Arik and I stood facing Loic. Hash stood behind me, literally breathing down my neck, as the oversized heating closet was not made for multiple adults and a gauge weapon. Arik stared at Loic, a thoughtful stare, which drove me insane. I wanted to beat the living crap out of this asshole. He had been on base for almost three weeks now. I had sent him off to the farmer several times during the last three weeks, sometimes even alone. We assumed this was when he was sending or receiving information.

"Doesn't matter who I am. They'll be here soon enough." He shrugged.

"Who?" I was doing my best to remain calm. But my insides were spinning, my head pounding, and it was taking every bit of woman I was not to rip this guy's head off his shoulders.

My father. My own father had sent him. I didn't need Loic to tell me that. What should humiliate me more? That I screwed with the spy who was spilling the location of my rebel base? Or that my father sent the spy, with whom I subsequently screwed?

I called for an immediate lockdown and placed Finch and Vic at either entrance. No one was to leave or enter this place without my say-so. No one. Was there anyone else? Were there other saboteurs lurking among us? We had no way to know.

All I knew of Loic was what he had told me over the last few weeks. He had appeared out of the forest one day, dirty and barely alive, as so many others had. Said he was in the militia. Snuck in on a shipment that came in months ago and had been living off the land. He came from a village called Merrigan. Never heard of it, but didn't care. There were villages all over the place, small, dying groups of people living under the constant threat of the Svaris. And I accepted it. Just like that. Instead of a two-faced spy, I saw a good-looking, muscular man who could contribute to my cause.

Hash had the weapon pointed at Loic, the barrel wedged between Arik and me. But so far, we had gotten him to say little that mattered.

Loic gave me a grin and raised one eyebrow. "Feeling a bit of regret, Tess? Wishing you hadn't begged for my services so many times?"

I balled my fists. "You son of a—"

"Tess." Arik rested his hand on my arm. I took a deep breath. I knew exactly what Loic was doing—trying to piss me off. And it was working.

I took the hint. Turning my head, I forced myself to study the cracks in the concrete wall, running up and down, trying to see around the red blocking my vision. Arik had a plan, and I would let Arik do what he did best. Get under your skin.

"I don't think he wants us to know that his plan failed, Tess," Arik said, putting his hands in his pockets.

Loic scoffed. "I didn't fail, man. It worked perfect."

"Really?" Arik leaned in close to him and stared for several seconds. "I think you were supposed to get us into those containers. And you didn't. Screwed up big time, didn't you?"

"No more than you did," he replied darkly. He glanced in my direction. "But at least I got to screw her a few times."

I took a deep breath in and grabbed for my knife, planning on shoving it up against his balls. Hash grabbed me around the waist and held me there. "Keep it together," he murmured so that only I could hear. "Let him mess up."

I swallowed thickly, my hand shaking. Hash kept a hand on my arm until the grip on my knife relaxed. I shook him off and stood with my arms crossed, my glare set upon the enemy. Let him say whatever he wanted. I could handle it.

Arik continued his staring match with Loic. "So, what was the plan? Get us in the containers, and they would be there waiting, I'm assuming?" Arik nodded to himself, agreeing with his own logic. "Couple big problems there, my friend." He ticked them off on his fingers. "One, we're not nearly as stupid as you think we are. And two, Quinn wasn't even with us. So he wouldn't have gotten her, anyway."

"Oh, yes, he would have," Loic countered. "She wasn't supposed to be there, anyway."

Arik raised his eyebrows. "So it is the general you're working for?"

Loic began to say something and stopped. Instead, he just scoffed and looked away. "Big deal."

"Oh, it actually is a big deal, man. A very big deal. It's not the dragons that are after us. It's the General that is after *her*." He pointed at me. "And Quinn."

Loic narrowed his eyes and said nothing.

Arik smiled and clapped him on the shoulder. "Thanks, man. You've been a wealth of information." He turned toward me. "Tess, let's go talk." He nodded to Hash. "If he moves, you have my express permission to shoot him," he said joyfully. Arik stepped around Hash to the door and held it open.

I shot one last look of hatred at Loic and followed Arik into the hall. He shut the door and walked down the hallway into the kitchen, running a hand through his hair.

"I assume you know what is going on?" I asked him. "Because that made no sense to me."

He shook his head. His cool demeanor and cocky grin were gone. Beads of perspiration started at his hairline. "Not really. Just kind of took a stab at it. I think we have a big problem."

He chewed on his upper lip while rubbing his elbow. This was not good. Oh, this was not good at all.

"Oh, really? 'Cause I thought this was just all part of the fun."

"No, no, Tess, I mean bigger than we thought. Think about the last few days. Quinn falling from the sky. All the Code Greens. Your mother being a week late. And Loic has only been with us for a couple of weeks."

I threw my hands up in the air. "Your damn point?"

"Luther has known about us. Our location, everything. He's had to. How else would Loic find us this deep in the mountain? So why the hell hasn't he taken us down yet?"

I shook my head, my brain trying to form a reason. " I don't know. To screw with us? To find out what we know?"

"The dragons wouldn't care, though. They would have just killed us. We're traitors, remember?"

I did. The penalty for treason had only one consequence. "What are you saying?"

"What if Luther is working against the dragons? Not for them anymore."

I shook my head. "No way. They would know. They would have known if . . . " I stopped and stared at Arik. "Oh, no."

Arik nodded. "Luther has the weapon."

I sat on the church steps, smoking the very last cigarette I could find. Half of a cigarette, actually. It had been lying in the corner of the hallway, a piece of trash meant to be stepped on and thrown away. I inhaled deeply, holding my breath for as long as I could, then exhaling it painfully slowly. My lungs were begging me to rid them of the horrible substance I filled them with. Like they wondered why I should cause them pain, the innocent lungs whose only mistake in life was to keep me breathing for the last twenty years.

The base was silent tonight. Early for it to be so quiet. Even the forest had quieted. As if the wind and krekels knew—things had changed. A traitor had made their way into our small little haven. I saw the looks. The strained smiles as I walked upon people in hushed conversations, trying to pretend they weren't speaking about what a failure I was. Not that I could blame them. I'd be saying the same things.

The reds lining my vision had lessened. Eased up a bit. Interesting—my self-hatred and guilt seemed to do the trick. Possibly the pain I was causing my lungs. Now if only it could punish me, smack me on the back of the head for being such an idiot. Whatever the reason, my vision of the night was clear. Yep, everything was perfectly clear now.

I heard his shuffling footsteps from the side, but I made no attempt to move. Right now, I wanted to sit and hate myself. Go over all the mistakes I had made.

Instead, Arik plopped down next to me, forcing me to move my ass over. I sighed and took another drag on the cigarette, looking away.

"He's stopped talking."

I nodded.

"Don't think we're going to get anything else out of him."

I nodded again.

"What do you want to do with him?"

I put the cigarette back to my lips, talking around it. "I was thinking about cutting his legs off at the kneecaps and letting him bleed out on the storage room floor."

"Sounds like a good idea to me." He leaned back on the next step, looking up at the stars. "Do you think Vera and Quinn made it to the city?"

I exhaled. "Nope."

This time, Arik nodded. A small part of me wondered what he was thinking of. Was he worried about Quinn? More concerned for her than Vera? Probably, knowing Arik.

"When do you want to leave?"

I tossed the cigarette butt out onto the dirt. "Let's get going."

We walked back to the base in silence. Determined silence. I didn't want to speak about Loic, and Arik didn't want to either. Most of the time, he knew when to keep his mouth shut. We hadn't spoken a word of our argument earlier. But it was over. Dead and buried.

"Meet us in the war room," I said to Hash as soon as we walked in the door. "Where's Loic?"

"Same place. I've got Vic on him."

I chewed my bottom lip. We still didn't know what to do with a traitor. A rather large, well-muscled traitor.

"Fine. We'll leave him there." Arik and I made our way to the back room where we kept the rucksacks. Without a word, we grabbed our bags and began filling them with what little supplies we had to make the journey. Dried food and our water containers, mostly. Hash stood there with his hands buried deep in his pockets.

"You're in charge," I told him. "Let everyone know the situation in the morning. I want you, Finch, or Vic to stay with Loic every damn second." I ran my hand through my hair, running through the list of a million things I could have instructed him to do to keep my operation running smoothly.

Instead, I squeezed his arm. "Just . . . keep everyone safe."

Hash gave me a tight-lipped smile. "You guys gonna take the gauge weapon?" Arik's favorite.

"No," Arik answered before I could. "The two weapons are going to stay here. You guys need them more than we do."

Hash opened his mouth to object, but I interrupted him. "You've got an entire base of people to keep safe. We'll be fine. We always are."

Hash didn't look convinced. "Okay," he muttered.

"Good luck, man." Arik clapped him on the shoulder, turned, and walked out of the room.

I followed, hesitating at the door. Gripping the door handle, I turned to look at the broad-shouldered rebel I had known for so long. "Just . . ."

He put a large hand on my shoulder. "I got this, Tess. Go get Vera."

I gripped the strap on my bag and nodded. Before leaving the room I stopped, dropped the bag, and wrapped my arms around his large frame. I let my arms fall before he could hug me back and turned to follow Arik down the silent hall. We shoved open the door and walked out, leaving our home of the past four years in the dark. I wanted to turn around to give Hash one last wave, one last reassuring look, but I stayed looking forward. Looking back never helped anyone. Instead, I focused on the sound of the creek in the distance and the scurrying of the krekels high in the trees. We would be back. We had to be back.

So why did this feel so final? So drastic? Was it because we were walking toward a fight we couldn't win? The two of us against a fleet of dragons and a whole militia?

I glanced up at the sky, thinking of praying to Vatra like when we were kids. We asked her to come and fight the dragons, chase them away in flames, and let us live our lives again. She never listened. But I closed my eyes anyway, speaking silently, asking for her blessing. If ever I needed her on my side, it was now.

Glancing over at Arik, I saw him doing the same thing. Reaching down, I grabbed his hand. He squeezed it, his lips moving but not making a sound.

Maybe this time, she would listen.

Chapter 23

Quinn

I stood with my arms tight across my chest, pressed to the corner of the white room. So far, no one had entered. But when I awoke, dizzy with fear, I was lying on a bed. A light blanket covered me with a cushy pillow beneath my head.

I could still smell him. It sprang me from the scratchy covers, practically making me scream in revulsion. I fell off the bed, tangled in the blue and white quilt, my body shaking from what I had been doing there. Why was I in this bed? Who put me here? My stomach turned as I stared around the sparsely decorated room, breathing in quick gasps, feeling the hotness already forming behind my eyes. Taking a deep breath, I held the tears in. I leaned against the wall to stare at my surroundings.

Not a single window existed in this room. Only a closed door. I stared at the table next to the door warily. A plate of biscuits sat on the table. My mouth watered at the sight of a light white and brown breakfast, still steaming. Food. A sparkling, clear glass of water sat next to the plate. I swallowed, trying not to imagine how wonderful it would feel to have clean water running down my parched throat. Hesitantly, I reached over and snagged a biscuit before I could change my mind. I chewed the crispy but soft biscuit fast, reveling in the taste of true oven-baked food. Then I drained the glass of water even faster than I had eaten the delightful biscuit. My stomach rejoiced at the soft, warm meal. I sagged against the wall, wondering how long it had been since I had an actual meal.

Wiping my mouth on my arm, I stared around the bland room. The bed, the small brown table by the door, and a chair were the only furniture. The blue quilt crumpled on the floor was the only sign of color in this lifeless room. A painting hung over the bed. A portrait I would never want perched over my head as I slept.

Tess stood in the middle, probably about eight years old. She wore the same scowl I'd seen on her face any time she looked at me. Vera had a light, easy smile on her face, with her arms resting on Tess's shoulders. Her soft face seemed to naturally hold a smile, imprinted there her whole life. A woman so lovely, so happy.

And Luther. Standing tall, with one arm around Tess and one around Vera. He stared at me from that picture. Laughed at me. Knew he was telling a lie and knew he was safe in it. Because I couldn't stop it.

I closed my eyes. Why, oh why, was Vera pretending to be married to Luther? Pretending Luther was Tess's father? How could she do this to my father? I stared at the painting, trying to read her smile, trying to understand her thoughts.

His face in the painting made me break into a cold sweat. I shook, standing there, staring at the man who Tess thought was her father. He couldn't get away with this. I didn't realize I had the Dragon Eye gripped in my palm in my pants pocket. The anger, the rage pressing against my palm when I held that stone. Powerful. Almost satisfying. Like I could rip Luther Grimbley's head off and put it on a platter for all people and dragons to laugh at.

I gasped and shoved the stone back into my pocket. I pulled my hand out and rubbed it, trying to rid my palm of the desire to rip a person's head off. Shaking my head, I turned away, rubbing my hands together.

I sat in the white chair, resting my hands on my knees. Rocking back and forth, I ran a hand through my hair and took a deep breath. Think nice things. Calm things. I leaned back and closed my eyes. Arik. Think about Arik. I breathed in slowly, imagining he was holding my hand now. How I wished he was sitting right next to me, holding me, protecting me. I would gladly accept his protection right now. Not like Tess. I remembered the way her eyes narrowed when she saw him speak to me. The heat of anger started in my mind, making me grind my teeth and narrow my already closed eyes. What would Tess say now? Years of brushing Arik aside . . . And this was what she got for it. He was mine. Not hers.

I opened my eyes, taking a quick breath. What was wrong with me? Was this jealousy speaking? I rubbed my forehead, wondering why these feelings would pop up now, of all times. I closed my eyes again, attempting again to calm myself, thinking of his smile. The way he held me close, sitting with him under the stars. I wrapped my arms around myself, pretending he was holding me like he had last night. His lips on mine were so soft—

"You look quite content, Quintessa."

I jumped up, falling right off the chair.

Luther sat on the other side of the bed in a chair I didn't remember being there. The tone of the voice led me to believe he read my thoughts and knew exactly what I had been daydreaming about.

"It's nice to see you, Quintessa."

I got up off the floor, fighting the color in my cheeks. I lifted my chin, glaring at the man who sat with his legs crossed. He looked like the Luther I remembered. Arrogant.

I wasn't sure what had changed in my brain since running around a dark forest. Instead of fear, I had a dark, angry feeling taking over, begging to be let loose on this horrible man.

I glared. "Where is my father?"

He cocked his head. "I am sitting right here, Quintessa."

"You are lying," I spat out. "Where is my real father?"

He smiled. "Ah. Arden, I presume? So, where you are from, Arden is playing the role of father?"

I paused. What was that supposed to mean? Playing the role? Luther was implying he was *actually* my father?

"You're lying," I repeated, for I could think of nothing else to say.

"Am I?" He raised his eyebrows. "How would you know that?"

"How did you know I was talking about Arden?" I shot back.

"The only man arrogant enough to assume the role."

I wanted to grasp the Dragon Eye. How I wanted to reach into my pocket and hold the round stone, shove it in the face of this liar, mussing his perfect mustache. Instead, I swallowed. "How do you know who I am?"

He laughed. "One would have to be blind not to, child. You are Quintessa, through and through. Though that scar down your cheek is something I never imagined."

I tried not to show my confusion. He knew who I was?

"Where is Vera?" I had to find her. The real Vera.

"Your mother, you mean? The traitor who put her daughter before her city? Who lied to the man who puts a roof over her head and lives only to protect her?"

This time, I smiled. "Yes. That Vera."

"I'm afraid she is indisposed at the moment."

I bit my lip, afraid of what that might mean. What had he done to her? Horrible images of Vera rushed through my mind. Her soft face twisted in agony, tears running down her light skin. I squared my shoulders, determined not to show the fear building in my mind. "Where is—"

"I'm afraid now, Quintessa, it is my turn. The location of the Axis. You will give it to me."

I looked at him, bewildered. I couldn't help it. "You know about the Axis?" Did he not realize he lived in the middle of the Axis?

"I'm afraid I do."

Trying to look confident, I searched my brain for a plausible answer. I had believed no human outside of my world would know of such things. Besides Corben Willoughby, that was. My eyes widened at the thought. What if Professor Willoughby . . .

He stood, smoothing out his tie like he always did. "The Axis, Quintessa."

"Why?"

He raised his eyebrows. "Why, indeed? I have been wondering why a beautiful girl like yourself would want to come into my world. Unless, of course, yours is worse. In that case, I am deeply sorry. You are welcome to stay, relax, and have dinner with me tonight." He walked over to me and stood close, forcing me to look up at him. "Now."

"Why?" I whispered, suddenly forgetting my tough girl act. What if he went into my world? The realization of what he could do . . . Especially to my father.

I knew how Luther felt about my father. Whenever the two of them shook hands or exchanged pleasantries, Father's voice would lower. Luther's chin would jut out, and they would smile at each other—for just a moment too long. The injustice of heading up the U.P.D was simply one more slap in the face to Luther. While Father spoke to the president over important matters, Luther wrote reports on the latest deliveries and how morale was among Flyers. To him, my father had everything. It made me worry to think that now things were in reverse.

"I'm afraid that is not your concern, dear. I need the location, and I need it now. Before something" —he paused— "drastic happens to someone you care for."

My chest rose automatically. Who was he threatening? Vera? My father? Arik? My mind spun, unsure of what to do, how to make things right, and what I was even doing anymore. "First, tell me why."

He only stared. Waited patiently, like I was about to spill my life's secrets.

"Why?" I repeated, trying to keep the shaking out of my voice.

"I need the book, Quintessa."

I blinked, unsure of whether I heard him correctly. A book? "What book?"

"Corben Willoughby wrote a book. I will be taking it."

My mouth dropped open. "*Dragons Among Us?* You want to go there for a book?"

"Yes. I believe Arden gave you this book?"

I frowned. Why would he think my father had given me the book? My father never even knew I *had* the book. Or did he?

"No, that makes no sense. Why would you—" I stopped, pressing my lips into a thin line. "No. You can't have it."

He narrowed his eyes. "One does not tell the High Commander of the militia no, Quintessa."

"Don't call me Quintessa, *Luther*." I don't know where the burst of sass came from, but I liked it. The look on his face told me I had struck a nerve. I tossed my hair behind my shoulders. "You will never get my book. Never."

He leaned down and put his face in mine. It took everything I had not to back away and turn my nose from his offensive scent. "I will get that book, Quintessa. You would be surprised at what I can do."

I stared back, having been told many times what he could do. My hand curled around the Eye, letting the smooth surface sink into my mind. "I think you'd be surprised at what I can do, Luther."

The chill of my voice surprised me. Apparently, it surprised him as well. His eyebrows raised, just a touch, and then he straightened, tugging at his jacket.

He smiled at me again. "I see a bit of her in you, Quintessa," he murmured, gazing down at me. That same voice that made me shudder, the voice he used whenever my father was not around. The look in his eyes matched it. A longing. A hunger.

I wanted to stand up straight, to spit in his face, to laugh and toss my hair. But his eyes. A flutter ran through me, and the bravery, the sass that I had been so proud to use a few moments ago, flickered just out of reach. Finally, I stepped back, turning my head.

"Oh, no, Quintessa." He grabbed my arms and pulled me forward, close enough to smell the cigarette on his breath. "You would like to play the rebel? The strong, fierce female who spoke back to her father?" His fingers dug into my biceps, but I refused to pull away. This man could not frighten me.

"You are not my father," I whispered, trying to keep my breathing normal.

"Oh, but I am, dear. And you will behave like a daughter should."

I followed his eyes as they left my face and ran down the length of my body. I went stiff as the courage melted out of me, and drained far, far away.

"You're hurting me," I said, struggling under his grasp. "Please."

"Tell me the location of the Axis. Tell me how to get through."

"I . . . I don't know," I protested. "A dragon took me there! You would never find it."

He paused and lightened his grip on my upper arms.

I wrenched out of his grasp, just to get his rancid breath out of my face. I made my eyes meet his, rubbing my upper arms. "It's the weapon, isn't it? The book tells you how to work the weapon, doesn't it? That's why you want my book!"

He adjusted his suit. "It's really none of your concern, Quintessa."

The book . . . The weapon . . . The Axis . . . What was he planning?

Luther smiled, clasping his hands down in front of him. "Everything is falling into place perfectly, dear. Your arrival here only made things happen faster."

"What?" I asked, still holding my right arm.

"I have been waiting for you, Quintessa. The arrival of something amazing, the solution to my problems. You are my solution. The one who can make everything happen."

I swallowed. "No. No, I'm not. You can't have my book!"

He nodded. "Yes, actually I can. And I will, Quintessa. All that has been accomplished, we have accomplished together. Like father and daughter should. Together, we can do so much more."

My heart was thumping so loudly I was sure it was vibrating my body. Or perhaps I was simply shaking. What was he going to do? What was going to happen to my world? Why did he think we had worked together? Me, coming through the link—it had been a mistake. A mistake I couldn't take back.

Luther turned and headed for the door. "Dinner is one hour. I expect you there."

Chapter 24

Tess

"Careful!" I smacked Arik in the arm.

He elbowed me back. "Just hold still. It's hard to see your hair in the dark. You know, I recall you warning the team not to get caught in this junk."

I rolled my eyes and winced as the tugging of my scalp continued. Yeah, yeah, I had warned everyone to stay out of this vine or shrub or whatever the hell it was. But the vine rarely hung from trees. Or so I thought.

"Can't you move any faster?"

"No. Whenever I move faster, you hit me and tell me to go slower."

I sighed, letting Arik tug at my hair, strand by strand. I wasn't sure how long we had been standing in this grove of trees, but we were wasting time. In five minutes, I planned to cut this tree in half and drag it with us. The plan to make it to the city was quickly failing. I became very grumpy when plans didn't go as they were supposed to.

At least this happened in front of Arik. Had it been any other member of my team, it would have been embarrassing.

"Okay. Hair's free. But it's still wrapped up in your shirt. It's caught in all the buttons."

"Oh, for the love of kings. This is ridiculous." Shoving his hand away, I began ripping the shirt off, fighting my way out of the long sleeves.

He shook his head. "You'll regret that."

I tried not to shiver as I threw the warm shirt, still attached to the vine, down on the ground and kicked it away.

"Good riddance." I stood in the white sleeveless, low-cut top, the one holding my flat chest close to my body. I rubbed my upper arms, the goose bumps already covering my bare skin. "Move the eyes there, pervert."

He laughed and followed behind me. Arik knew better than to offer me his shirt, even if he wanted to. He knew I wouldn't take it.

I stomped ahead, occasionally rubbing at my arms, feeling the shivering all the way to my bones. For mercy's sake, it was cold out here. By now, I could see the lights of the city, occasionally glimmering through the trees. My stomping turned to a creeping, lifting branches more slowly and murmuring instead of talking.

The forest thinned and brightened the closer we got to Tarrith. Our occasional whispers came to a stop, and our eyes darted around, paranoid at every branch cracking or rustling in the leaves. This close, it wasn't hard to imagine a member of the militia or a hunter poking around.

We stopped at the edge of the forest, staring at a paved road lined with lights. Paved?

"Things look different," he murmured.

I had been thinking the same thing. Four years ago, when we left Tarrith in the dead of the night, we climbed over the gate and followed the dirt road out of the city. Now, bricks lined the dirt, making a precise route I assumed led straight to the port, as the dirt one had. I frowned at the tall light posts, brightening the road below.

I scratched at my throat, my eyes following the tall balls of light leading into the city. It had to have been the Svari's idea. Svaris couldn't see well in the dark. But the way this place was lit up . . .

I scratched my bare arm. "This might be a little more difficult than last time." Hopefully, we were still professionals at sneaking around the compound.

As kids, Arik and I could navigate the streets of the city after curfew with ease. Prats would be posted at their usual stations, but we outran them easily. Militia were more skilled at their jobs and much faster. Luckily, they weren't often in the city, depending on the battles and wars that went on around the country. Fewer and fewer returned after each battle. The draft would stretch outside of the compound, taking any man or woman tall enough. Another reason to live far from the gate.

"Let's follow this until we get closer to the gate. No one guards these side roads. There's nothing on them."

That was four years ago. I chewed on the inside of my cheek. It would make up lost time jogging along a paved road rather than trying to stay silent, trekking through the forest. We'd been standing here for five minutes, and the only disturbance I noted was the strained squawking of a krekel. "Yeah. Okay. Let's go."

We stepped out onto the paved road, putting ourselves in the spotlight. There was simply no getting around it. The lights were serving their purpose.

We hurried west, staying to the side of the road and making our way toward the compound. From this distance, I could see the lights that ran across the tops of the capitol building. They stuck out just over the tops of the trees to our left. My home, in a previous life. Arik and I knew every nook, every cranny in that building.

Only the military lived in the compound. Being the daughter of the general, my family had the capitol building to ourselves. The rest of the military was not so lucky. They lived in the Jeklos, all cramped together, lining the edge of the city. Cheap, heat-resistant steel made the strangely semi-circled huts fast and easy to produce. I'd never stepped foot in one, and I hoped I never had to. Small spaces didn't really bother me, per se, but something about sleeping in a fireproof metal container gave me the shivers.

I always envied Arik's freedom outside the gates—no militia, none of my father's Praetorian guards. He envied my freedom—freedom from hunger, sickness, and the constant threat of being a dragon's meal. We always complained someone switched us at birth. Ended up in the wrong place.

I looked down at my feet as we jogged silently along the road, doing our best to dodge the pools of light. "What are these roads made of?" I whispered as we ran.

I might have been crazy, but I would swear the bottoms of my feet were getting warmer. At first, it felt like a nice massage to my tired and battered feet. But it seemed to be getting warmer. I stopped, panting, and lifted my foot to stare at the bottom of the black boot. The heat was beginning to prickle uncomfortably at my heel. I sniffed. Was I crazy, or was something burning?

Arik stopped, looking down at his feet. "Maybe we should get back off this road. Something's not right."

At the same moment, sirens went off all around us, ringing louder than a dragon could roar.

"What in the—" I stopped, staring around, grabbing at Arik's arm.

"Go, go!" Arik yelled.

Before I could make my feet run, red lights shot up all around us. We jumped back as the red beams shot upward, as high and bright as the streetlights, encasing Arik and me together. We stood, chest to chest, looking around wildly. Before I could stop myself, I reached my hand out to the rays of color.

White-hot pain sizzled through my fingertip, radiating up my arm like fire. "Damn!" I swore at the lights, clenching my throbbing hand.

"Don't touch it!" Arik yelled, grabbing my arm.

"You think?" I yelled back over the alarm, rubbing the red welts appearing on my fingertips. "What the hell are they?"

"Some kind of damn trap!"

We stood helpless with the burning lights holding us in a circular prison much too small for the two of us.

The sirens of the militia vehicles started, shrieking that horrible sound I hadn't heard in four years. Headed our way, ready to take us prisoner. The alarm we somehow tripped grew louder by the second. The miserable wailing of these lights had surely awoken every damn Prat and soldier in Tarrith.

I threw my hands over my ears. "How the hell do we get out of here?"

"Tess! Arik!"

In the confusion, I could barely hear my name being screamed. But Arik stared over my shoulder, his mouth hanging open. I whipped around, wincing as my arm ran through the red light again.

A dirty man in a large brown overcoat fell out of the woods and ran to us, stopping on the side of the road.

His wide eyes followed the flashing red lights up toward the sky. "I don't believe it," he said. "They did it."

I held my throbbing arm to my chest. "Get us out of here!" I had no idea who this man was, but dammit, we needed his help.

His head spun back and forth, then he dove to the ground. He began punching the ground near the light post, beating at the paved road with his fists.

I looked at Arik, then back at the man on his knees. "What are you doing?" I cried at the man flinging dirt all over the road.

We stared as he stomped on the road with his heel, his long hair flying all over. He let out a guttural cry and gave one more kick, and a section of the stone road swung open. He kicked again, this time down in the hole that was produced. Dropping to his knees, he yanked something out as his long coat flapped behind him.

The red lights around us fell back to the ground, disappearing under the stone road. The screaming alarm came to a halt. Arik and I glanced at each other. Then we dove off the road.

The wailing of the militia's siren grew louder. Flashing lights bounced off the forest, getting larger by the second. The militia was on its way to apprehend the enemy.

Without a word, we fell into the woods, shoving aside branches and dashing through the foliage. We ran toward the flapping overcoat of our stranger savior.

Arik shoved him forward as the man turned to look at us. "Go!"

We scrambled and climbed through the forest until we were out of breath, and the woods behind us had turned quiet. We continued, unable to stop checking over our shoulder. What I would have given to have the Eye in my pocket now. I wiped at my forehead as the man pointed further into the woods. "This way," he panted, holding a hand to his side.

Arik and I shared a quick glance and a nod. We had no better option at the moment, and I thought we could afford to trust the man who saved our lives. We followed him in the moonlight, his jog quickly turning to a hurried walk. Finally, he stopped, leaning on a tree. The stranger fell to his hands and knees and gave a strangled cough, then another.

Arik and I stood over him, trying to keep our gasping breaths quiet. I put my hands down on my knees, letting the breeze blow against my sweaty back. That was close. Too close.

I kneeled down across from him, studying the long brown and gray hair falling over his face. He looked so familiar, yet I couldn't place this old man, his chest rising and falling so heavily I was worried he would pass out from exhaustion.

Wait—the jacket. That long brown overcoat. The man reached into a pocket and grabbed a handkerchief, mopping his forehead. I stared at the handkerchief. It had probably started out white many years ago. Now, it was a soppy tan color with splotches of dark. My eyes moved to nicks and cuts all along the man's pale face—like he had sloppily shaved himself with a dull knife. Shaved away a beard. A long, gray beard . . .

I clapped a hand over my mouth. "Benny?"

Arik's eyes snapped to mine, then back to the old thin man. "Benny? What . . . Why are you here?"

The man sighed, tucking the rag back in his pocket. "I followed you."

I stood, my eyes wide. "You talked."

He spoke. Clearly. In the years I knew the man, I had never heard him utter anything more than a mumble. And usually, he was mumbling to himself.

He looked up at me dully. "Yes, I speak." He reached into his other pocket and took out a flask, swigged a drink out of it, then offered it to me.

I took it after a moment, taking a quick sniff. My dry throat welcomed the warm water. Wiping my mouth, I handed it to Arik. "Why did you follow us?"

Benny stood, leaning on a tree. "Because you are in danger. Everyone is."

I raised my eyebrows. "I think we all know we are in danger."

He shook his head, pushing his shaggy hair out of his eyes. "No, you are in more danger than you think. We all are. It's Luther."

I narrowed my eyes. The use of my father's first name made me uneasy. People did not refer to the High Commander as Luther. Only my mother and I had ever used his first name that I knew of. And rarely, at that.

"You know my father?"

Benny looked at the ground. "I'm sorry to say I do."

I nodded slowly. "Yes, I'm sorry too."

"How did you disable those lights?" Arik asked, looking over his shoulder.

"They use a power source that comes from underground. They have probably connected every road in the city now. A special covering runs the roads, and specific spots trigger them. Specifically designed to catch anyone out when they don't want them to be. I had no idea these had been implemented. They were designed for use only around the Dragon Landing."

Arik and I shared another look.

"And how do you know all this?" I asked.

He sighed again. "I developed them."

Chapter 25

Quinn

I sat stiffly at the table, refusing to return the stare of the plate of food in front of me. The aroma of a roast chicken smothered in gravy continued to linger directly under my nose, practically tugging the drool from the corner of my mouth.

The room I sat in was too small for the overly large wooden table, and the walls contained far too many paintings of old people wearing fancy clothes and scowls. I wondered if every High Commander had lived here. Did Luther rule the city? Or just the militia? Arik had also mentioned someone called Prats. Who were they? I had so many questions and so much confusion, but I didn't dare act interested. I would sit here silently and brood.

So I sat, pretending not to hear the rumble of my stomach as Luther took hefty bites of chicken dripping in smooth gravy, reading over a document in front of him. The scraping of his fork and knife on the plate contributed to the pounding in my forehead.

He had more food on his plate than one man could eat. Glaring at him from the corner of my eye, I wondered how the rest of Tarrith fared during dinner hour.

The door behind me opened, and Luther looked up. "Finally." He set down his pen and paper and took a sip out of his wineglass. "Please, join us."

I sat with my arms crossed, glaring at the painting of the old man in military attire. The curly brown hair on top of his head made the pompous look on his face almost comical. Gold fringe decorated the shoulders of his costume, enough to make me roll my eyes at the still man. These people sure liked their outfits.

The newcomer walked around the table, a tall man in blue leading the way. His pleated pants looked far more uncomfortable than the baggy ones sitting around my waist. And the hat perched on top of his combed hair looked ridiculous. What use could that tiny hat be for?

They stopped at the seat across from me, and I finally let myself look at the woman standing in front of me. I took a deep breath and froze in my seat.

The white, poofy dress required a second pair of hands to maneuver. The man struggled to tame the skirt, forcing the fluff under the table. He helped her to sit, fussing with the poof, and stood with his hands behind his back. The woman stared over my shoulder with vacant eyes and a limp expression.

"Vera?" I whispered.

She did nothing and gave me no expression of surprise or even a hint of a smile. Just sat, staring past me.

I glanced over my shoulder, feeling the panic rise in my chest. "Vera?"

I looked at Luther, cutting his chicken and sipping on his wine, acting as if this was an everyday occurrence. I looked back to Vera and back to Luther again. Her point of vision had not changed, nor the dead look in her eyes.

I turned to Luther with my mouth hanging open. "What have you done to her?"

He was busy cutting the meat on his plate. He took a large bite and washed it down with another drink from his glass.

Finally, he sat back in his chair, patting his mouth with a delicate white cloth napkin. "I saved her, Quintessa." He gave me an icy stare. "Just like I saved this entire city. According to the Svari/Tarrith treaty, she should have been put to death for her crimes against the city. Now, she will live a long, full life. All she had to do was agree to let a modifier take possession of her mind."

"Possession . . ." I couldn't even finish the sentence. "You *what*?"

Luther sighed, rolling his eyes upward. "Don't be so dramatic, Quintessa. She is perfectly fine. Alive and well." He continued his meal, buttering a roll. "Watch." He nodded at her. "Vera, eat."

Vera looked down at the plate of food automatically, picked up a fork, and put a length of broccoli in her mouth. She chewed slowly, staring at the plate. Then she took another bite. Chewed. Swallowed. Then another.

Bile burned at the back of my throat. Her movements were so . . . emotionless. So pointless. I stared at the man sitting to my right, enjoying a warm biscuit with butter dripping off the sides. The desire to rip his head off burned deep in my gut again, and this time, I didn't shake it away.

"What did you do to her mind?" I stood up so fast my chair flipped backward to the floor. "What did you do to her?"

He shook his head and continued eating. "I suggest you sit down and finish your dinner, young lady."

To hell with this. I ran around the long table, grabbing her bare shoulders. "Vera? Vera?"

She continued to stare blankly at the plate in front of her. I grabbed her chin and pulled it toward me. "Please! Talk to me, Vera! I know you are in there!"

Her lame eyes stared at me, lost in her mind.

I wrapped my arms around her, tears welling in my eyes. "How could you do this? How could you do this to her?" I glared at him over her head, wishing words strong enough existed to describe my rage. She was in there. She had to be in there.

Luther wiped his face with his napkin and set it in his lap, a strange smile on his face. "It was actually because of you, Quintessa. Thanks to your falling from the sky, I had no choice." He swirled his cup, the last of the red liquid moving in his glass.

"What are you talking about?" My arms still wrapped around Vera's neck as she picked up a fork and began eating again.

"You think I didn't know who saved you that day? I knew you had to be with my daughter." He drained the last of his glass. "And I knew your mother would lead me right to her."

There it was again. My fault. What hadn't gone wrong since I had appeared? What hadn't I made worse by showing up here?

Tears spilled onto the top of Vera's light hair. This poor woman. What had he done to her? What had I done to her? I squeezed my eyes shut and held her. My mother. My true mother. He would pay. He would pay for everything.

I lay in the dark, watching Vera sleep. I had insisted. Fought. Screamed some pretty impressive curse words that I wasn't actually sure were words, but in my mind, they made sense. I needed to be with her, watch over her. And I would not leave her side. Finally, Luther had conceded, probably just to make me shut up.

I helped her into her frilly, ridiculous nightgown before she lay down, even though I was sure if Luther instructed her to, she could have done it herself. But I would rather her be a vegetable of a woman than taking orders from that man.

My face burned in anger as I thought of the way he had addressed her. Ordered her to eat. And how sickening it was to watch her do it. Like she was some sort of puppet, and he was pulling the strings. Oh, God, what else had he ordered her to do? I closed my eyes and shoved my face into the pillow, trying not to imagine the horrible things he could order her to do behind closed doors.

I gripped her hand, praying she would open her eyes and smile. Or just squeeze back. Anything to show me she was still there and not hanging as a puppet for Luther's enjoyment.

"Mom?" I whispered to the sleeping woman in the dark.

She lay perfectly, covers pulled up across her chest, her arms perfectly at her sides. Like a doll. She even had a slight smile on her face, as if Luther had instructed her to have pleasant dreams.

She remained silent.

I let my tears soak the pillow beneath my cheek. "Father would be furious if he knew what was going on—if he knew what Luther was doing to you. He would never treat you like this. Never." I ran my finger over her soft palm. "He still loves you, you know. Your portrait hangs over his desk in the office. You know how he stays in there most of the time." I rolled my eyes, imagining her doing the same.

I reached up and smoothed her light hair, running my hand down her smooth cheek. Was she really sleeping? Or just closing her eyes because Luther had told her to? Could she hear me somewhere in there?

"Do you remember how I would sneak into his office and stare at your painting at night? For a few weeks, I would take a blanket and just curl up on the floor right underneath. Be as close to you as I could." I sighed. "I think he knew. He would just let me sleep in there all night. I never imagined that one day I'd be holding your hand while you slept. So if you can hear me, Mom, I need you to fight. I need you to fight Luther. For Dad. For me," I whispered.

She took a deep breath in.

My heart leaped into my throat. She had heard me. I know she had. "Mom?" She let her breath out slowly, her heartbeat regular.

Giving her a teary smile, I nodded. "I heard you, Mom. I heard you."

Inching closer, I snuggled up against her and slung an arm over her middle, remembering how many times I wished I could do this very thing. Like when I had a nightmare. Like the nightmare we were living in now.

"I wish Dad was here now, Mom. He would fix everything. Since he's not here, it's up to me, I guess. So, I'll take care of everything."

I whispered to her for the rest of the night, telling her stories I'd always wanted to tell my mother and asking her questions I had always wanted to know.

We talked for hours, a one-sided conversation until the door opened.

I hugged the sleeping woman to me, closing my eyes to feign sleep. Wishing we could just stay here forever.

"The High Commander has requested your presence at the breakfast table."

Vera sat up, pulling away from me and throwing her legs out the other side of the bed. The same man in the blue uniform entered the room. He walked to the armoire and pulled open the doors, removing another one of those stupid frilly dresses from a hanger and setting it next to her on the bed.

"Stand," he said.

Vera stood automatically as the man grabbed at the waist of her nightgown and pulled it up over her head.

"What do you think you are doing?" I swung around to her side of the bed, wedging myself between Vera and the stranger. "Don't touch her!"

"I am dressing her," he replied in a bored voice. "She can't attend breakfast in a nightgown."

"Why not?" I snapped, pushing him back. "Get out. I will dress her."

"Fine. I'll wait outside."

I gave him my best dirty look. What a pervert. I held up the dress he had laid next to her on the bed, rolling my eyes. Throwing it on the ground, I flung open the armoire myself. I dug through the dozens of ridiculous dresses and outfits, each one making me more and more angry. My mother would never want to wear this filth. These low-cut, froofy things displayed cleavage and made her look like some high-class, snooty whore.

I dug through the closet until I found a simple black dress, hidden in the back, that I figured would cover her enough so Luther wouldn't be able to ogle her curves and breasts.

I turned toward her with a brave smile. "Can I help you get dressed?" I asked her quietly.

She simply stared over my shoulder. I reached down and squeezed her hand. "Remember, Mom. I'll fix everything. Just think of Dad. Think of Arden."

Her hand closed around mine, ever so slightly. My eyes widened. "Yes, yes, think of Arden, Mom. Dad."

Had I imagined it? Or had she responded? "Mom? Are you thinking of Arden?" Another light squeeze filled me with the hope I so desperately needed. I threw my arms around her. Everything was going to be okay. I would fix her. I would fix everything.

Chapter 26

Tess

We pushed through the brush, ducking under the branches. By now, the sun was rising, the much-needed heat warming my bare arms. The tall lights lining the paved road had died away, and we had already seen one military vehicle rolling down the road. Probably looking for the intruders who sabotaged their funky light traps.

"How far are we going?" I called to Benny, who was suddenly limber and in quite good shape.

"Not much farther. We need to be behind the capitol building. There's a way in."

The more we talked to Benny, the more shocked I became. The things this man knew, the way he spoke—everything out of his mouth surprised me.

We stopped at the edge of the trees when the tall gate surrounding the compound and the Dragon Landing was finally within view. We stood on the side of the Landing, in the trees directly behind my old home.

"Look." Benny pointed in front of us, ducking under a branch. "A Svari is landing."

I grabbed Arik's shirt. Oh, kings. A Svari was landing, not a hundred feet from where we stood.

"No militia. Let's go." Benny left my side, leaving the safety of the trees.

"What are you doing?" I hissed, grabbing the tail end of his jacket. "Get down! If that thing smells us or senses our presence—"

"Ha!" Benny shook his head. "False. Svaris cannot sense or smell anything that is not lying two feet in front of them and covered in blood." He grimaced. "Trust me on that."

Arik and I shared another nervous look. Strangely enough, I believed this new Benny, the Benny who had slept next to my base for the last four years. And I had no desire to learn why he knew so much about a dragon's blood-smelling abilities.

We followed him to the tall fence running around the compound, encompassing the rest of the military compound. Arik and I had become professionals scaling this fence at a young age. We spent time back here in the woods, usually after curfew, when the chance of seeing a dragon was minimal. Doing nothing more than climbing trees or building forts under which we would lie and imagine living on our own, by our own rules.

I looked warily at the blinking red lights on the top of the posts placed along the fence. Another recent addition to the compound. The humming coming from the iron was barely noticeable. But it was there.

Arik came to stand next to me, looking up. "Electric fence."

I grimaced and glanced back at Benny. "So, how do we get in?" I looked over his shoulder at the dragon sucking water from the watering station. He was facing away from us for the moment.

"We use the tunnels." He turned and headed down the fence, toward the Landing.

"What tunnels?" Arik and I asked in one voice.

"We designed a tunnel system long ago after the Blood Wars without the Svaris knowledge." Benny stared up at the building as she walked. "For a situation exactly like this."

"Situations like this? How many times have you been in a situation just like this?" I asked, hurrying behind him.

"Not once." He motioned to us over his shoulder. "Hurry. We have to find Quinn and Vera."

I opened my mouth to ask how he knew about Quinn and Vera, but a look from Arik shut me up. Clearly, this man knew a lot more than I gave him credit for. Why bother?

I chewed on my cheek as we neared the Landing. We were getting close. Too close. The Svari made an awful snuffling racket while he groomed himself, apparently unaware of the three strangers who approached. If he even looked up . . . we were done for. I glanced at Arik, silently asking if he agreed that maybe Benny simply had a death wish.

As we neared, Benny dropped to his knees, then his stomach. We followed suit, snaking away through the weeds on our stomachs. It was a difficult way to travel, at least at any decent speed. Groaning silently, I followed Benny's feet through a muddy section, wrinkling my nose at the squishing between my fingers. Finally, he stopped. He got up on his knees and began digging in the leaves and dirt furiously.

"Here," he said breathlessly, wiping his forehead, leaving a streak of mud across his face.

I crawled over and peeked down. Sure enough, I could see the beginnings of something metal buried just outside the compound, apparently untouched for years.

I jumped forward and copied Benny's movements, pulling away soil and leaves, letting chunks of debris fly wildly, acutely aware the dragon noise had stopped. I didn't have time to stop and look, but prayed he wasn't watching the three humans digging in the dirt.

After several minutes, I took a relieved breath. Enough ground was gone to display the round metal hatch, sitting in the ground innocently. Benny lifted the metal lid with a grunt, the rusted hinges moaning so loud I clapped my hands to my ears. I winced and glanced around, doubting the Svari *hadn't* heard that.

"Give me a hand," he gasped, still holding the metal hatch. "Hurry."

Arik bent over and grasped the thick metal, the two men finally easing the manhole cover back. They both leaned over and coughed. Benny threw a hand over his nose. The smell of dank, decayed earth leaked out, about forty years' worth.

Covering my nose, I leaned over, staring down into the hole. "Wow," I muttered. "How did you make these?"

Benny stood and wrapped his long overcoat tighter around him. "Right after the treaty with the dragons was put into effect, we decided one day we might need to escape out of our own city." He stepped down onto the first rung of a ladder. "Hurry. Arik, you go last and pull the cover back."

After more grunts and cursing, Arik got the cover back over the top of us, leaving us in pitch black. We stood in the tunnel, listening to the deafening silence all around us. I waved a hand in front of my face, trying to mask the stench of rotting, damp soil.

"How do we get through here in the pitch black?" I whispered though I wasn't sure why I was whispering. "Benny? Benny?"

"I know it's somewhere . . . Hold on a minute . . . There!"

I gasped as tiny lights blinked and glowed above us. "Wow. You guys really did all this?" The lights flickered, then came back bright again.

"Let's go. Not sure how long these lights are going to last."

I hurried after, my teeth chattering. The temperature must have dropped twenty degrees on the climb down.

"Do these go to Luther's house?" I asked as I wrapped my arms around myself.

"Yes. That's where they start. The only reason we could construct them since they go right to"—he cleared his throat—"Luther's basement."

"G-good," I stuttered. My whole body shook from the cold. My teeth chattered loudly in this silent hole, but I really did not want to admit that I shouldn't have left my button-up shirt in the woods.

Arik draped his shirt over my shoulders as we hurried through the tunnel, bumping into the wall as he did.

I started to object, but Arik gave me a light shove. "I don't want to hear it, Tess. Just wear the damn shirt."

I was too cold to argue. "Thanks," I said. I took a deep breath of his scent, like pine trees and sweat. I missed that scent.

The lights flickered. I sighed, wrapping the shirt around me. "Well, that's going—"

"Run!" Benny screamed, turning and sprinting down the tunnel. "We can't be down here without lights!"

With that, the lights went out.

I jerked to a stop, Arik running into the back of me.

"Oh, no." Benny's voice came from somewhere in front of me.

I didn't like the sound of his voice. Arik's grip on my waist tightened.

I reached out, looking for something to hold. "Uh, what's the problem? Can't we just feel our way through?"

"Don't touch the walls!"

The urgency in Benny's voice made me gasp and snap my hand back. I grabbed Arik's hand, and he squeezed it back. Swallowing thickly, I gazed around the nothingness, the surrounding blackness suddenly feeling so much heavier. I looked back and forth, leaning into Arik's powerful body, feeling that something terrible was about to happen. And then I heard it.

The scrambling, all around us. But this time loud enough to grab Arik in fright and let him wrap his arms around me.

"What is going on? Benny?"

The flapping of his coat sounded in front of me, as though he was trying desperately to rip it off his body. He swore loudly, then stomped several times, cracking something. "Run!"

I needed no explanation. Holding a hand out and feeling Benny's shirt, I ran behind him. The three of us made a sort of train as we ran, trying not to trip over each other. Arik cried out from behind me and his grasp on my shirt disappeared.

"Arik?" I yelled as we ran blindly. Things were dropping over our heads, brushing against my face and shoulders.

"Go, go!" he yelled back.

I ran behind Benny, ducking my head and doing my best not to trip over his heels in the pitch black. I cried out as something sliced my shoulder, screaming pain down through my fingers. "Damn!" I smacked at my shoulder as I ran, feeling the squishing of something hairy between my fingers.

I wiped my fingers on my pants as I ran, scrubbing them against my upper leg in hopes I never found out what I just smashed. Arik struggled behind me, and the grip on my shirt returned.

"You okay?" I called behind me.

"I'm fine," he gasped. "Just go!"

I reached for him, desperate to know he was okay, needing him to be close to me. Without thinking, I ripped the shirt off my shoulders and threw it over his head.

"Come on!" I grabbed what I hoped was his arm and pulled him toward me. I ran clumsily through the dark, gasping and slapping at the crawling on my chest.

"Benny?" I yelled, having absolutely no idea where the mercy we were, which direction we were running in, or if we were going to die in this miserable tunnel.

I ran smack into him, feeling Benny's arms around me.

"Here! It's here! Climb!"

I let go of Arik's hand to climb, praying he was still behind me. I gasped in relief when light shone above me. Pulling myself up, I rolled out into a dark room. Arik leaped out behind me. I lay gasping on the floor, still feeling the creepy crawling all over me.

I jumped up as Benny cried out. A monstrous brown insect followed us out of the tunnel, making the most awful yowl I had ever heard. It was easily the size of a raccoon or a huge ketrie, but with dripping, oddly shaped fangs. I stumbled and kicked, aiming for the hairy black legs. It rolled and smacked the wall, still yowling.

"Close the tunnel!" Arik yelled.

As Benny struggled with the enormous steel door, Arik and I dashed after the bug with our knives out. We cornered it at the wall, stomping, kicking, and beating the shit out of the murderous creature. The *crunches* and *cracks* on the concrete floor disgusted me almost as much as the crumpling of its shell under my boot. We stomped on the body again and again, stopping only when the sizzling white goo spread underneath the insect. After three more stomps, I let myself believe it was sufficiently dead.

I fell back against the wall next to Arik, panting. He reached over and pulled something out of my hair, throwing it down and slamming his boot down on top of it. Again. And again. I looked away as the faint smell of dead, malicious creature filled the room.

The steel lid fell in place, shaking the floor. I breathed a sigh of relief, hoping I never again had to see one of those things.

Benny fell over the lid, gasping for breath. He pushed himself back up slowly, sitting back against a box.

"What"—I stared at Benny—"in the *hell* was that?"

Benny wiped his forehead with his sleeve. "Stygivar." He dropped his hand, closing his eyes. "They are sensitive to light. Carnivorous."

I stood shakily, wiping my face, wincing as I felt the warm liquid on my face. Blood. I wiped my fingers with my shirt, sighing. "Yeah, got that." I looked around the room, rubbing my arms, trying to get those red and black eyes out of my mind. None of this looked familiar. Stacks of pallets, boxes, and more wooden containers filled the small room. "I thought you said this would come out in Luther's house."

Benny stood, inspecting a gash on his leg. "We are in the High Commander's home. You have just never seen this part of it."

"Guess not," I muttered, staring at the low ceiling. We must have been in a bunker of some sort. "Wait a minute. You know who I am?"

Benny nodded, straightening his long coat. "Yes, I do."

I sighed. "Who are you? Really?" This was becoming tiresome.

He looked down. "I was someone of authority during the wars. Someone of importance. But that all changed."

"Why?" I demanded.

He shook his head. "Later. We don't have time for this. We have to find Quinn and Vera. If we want to change anything of our future, we need Quinn."

I crossed my arms. "Why?"

Benny stood and stared at us. "Haven't you realized it yet? Who she really is?"

I glanced at Arik. He shrugged, but the look in his eyes led me to believe he knew what Benny was talking about.

"She is from another dimension. Quinn is our only chance at defeating Luther. It's why she is here. Why she fell through the sky."

I paused, confused. "Wait, what? Luther? What about the dragons? I thought we were trying to defeat the Svaris."

Benny shook his head. "Luther is much more dangerous than the dragons. What he possesses could destroy us all."

My heart leaped. "The weapon? You know about the weapon?" Of course he did, I told myself. "Well, what is it?"

"After we find them. Soon it will be too late."

He turned and walked toward the opposite wall of the concrete room. He jumped, reaching for something. Once, twice, until finally, a piece of the ceiling swung down, flapping back and forth.

"Come on," he said. "Give me a leg up."

When all three of us had made it up through the ceiling, I stood and looked around. This room I recognized. We were in the storage room of my home. I looked at the stacks of boxes, old furniture, and there was the radio with the missing knob. Arik and I had broken it many years ago.

My eyes narrowed as I gazed around.

I was home.

CHAPTER 27

Quinn

I slouched in the wooden chair, ignoring the ache that spread through my lower back. I stared at Vera, wearing a horrendous white dress Luther ordered her changed into. She stared at the wall with her hands resting in her lap, a dazed, far-off, dreamy look in her eyes.

For the last hour, I sat in front of her in this wooden seat, trying to get her to listen, repeating Father's name, and squeezing her hand. I had even grabbed her chin and yelled at her. I wanted her to yell back. Slap me. Anything. But she only stared.

It seemed any progress we made this morning evaporated. Was it progress? Or had it been my imagination, my ridiculous hope to see any sign of the mother I didn't even know? I would not entertain the possibility she was gone. Not an option. I just had to find a way to reach her.

Putting my face in my hands, I took a deep breath. I ran a hand through my tangled hair, trying not to regret my refusal to eat at breakfast. When Luther hadn't been looking, I snagged a sip of water and shoved another biscuit in my pocket. But that was it. I wondered if my pride could outlast my starvation.

He wanted my book. What had Corben written that could be so important to him? I knew that book back to front. I could think of nothing to do with a weapon or secret codes that could mean anything here. Sighing, I rubbed my forehead, willing away the pain threatening to take over my brain.

I hadn't seen a single window in this building, or house, or wherever in God's sake I was. The lack of daylight in this place frustrated the hell out of me. I couldn't tell if it was day or night, raining or shining, or a damn volcano was erupting in the front lawn. Where the hell was I? Small rooms, sparse furniture, and no windows. What I would give for a chair with a cushion on it.

I picked at a loose string on my pants, twirling it around my finger. What would Selyse tell me to do at this very moment? *Head up, my friend. It is always darkest before the light.* Smiling sadly, I let myself remember sitting with her in the Keep, watching the sunset. Talking about real things. Life. The reason we were here. What we were meant to do with ourselves. Probably not things other nineteen-year-olds talked about with their friends. I wouldn't know. Selyse was the only true friend I had ever had. And she was gone. A tear dripped down my face. I didn't have the strength to wipe it away.

—of the human?

I sat up straight, gripping the sides of my seat. Barely daring to breathe, I looked around slowly, worried whatever else was being said would slip away. Vera sat as still and calm as a statue, staring at the same spot on the wall she had been staring at for hours.

After a quiet moment, I leaned back in my chair, keeping my mind open. Perhaps my overactive imagination, thinking about Selyse and life's purpose made me hallucinate. When no other voices came through, I let my spur of excitement fade. Just my imagination. I plopped my chin on my hand and sighed.

—is being held. We do not know . . .

I jumped out of the chair, freezing in position, straining my ears. It was a dragon. I heard a dragon.

As slowly as possible, I crept around the room, taking deep breaths. I had to control myself. Selyse taught me that a calm mind is necessary to hear a dragon speak. Well, usually it was. After a while, things just came—

You promised the weapon . . .

I jumped as the roar sounded between my ears. *Geez,* I thought, as I rubbed my temple. That was a pissed-off dragon. But angry at who? And what was he talking about?

You took a vow to . . .

Holding my breath, I prayed for a full sentence. Nothing. Breathing deeply, I reached out with my mind, struggling to relax. A Svari must be speaking to Luther. But why would he be roaring? I chewed on my bottom lip. A dragon mad at Luther. This could help.

A window. I needed a window. I needed to see what was going on. To hear a dragon, I need to see the dragon. This time, at least. Glancing at Vera, I made my decision.

Crouching beside her, I took her chin in my hand. "I'll be back, I swear. I need to find a window. Everything will be fine." Kissing her on the forehead, I squeezed her hand. I waited briefly, hoping for any hint of a squeeze back. When I got nothing, I turned and hurried for the door.

Turning the knob carefully, I peered into the narrow hallway. To my relief, it was empty, except for the pile of dirty rags in the corner. I quietly closed the door behind me and ran to the left. I had no idea why.

I tried the first door I came to. Locked. The next door contained nothing but boxes and a small cracked table. No window. Slamming the door, I stepped across the hallway and tried the other door. It creaked open. A room with four white walls and a bed. But no view of the outside world.

The last door of the hall led to the stairwell. Without thinking, I went up, thinking the higher I could get, the better. The closer I could be to flying dragons, the better I could hear them. Metal stairs echoed and shook as I climbed, but I didn't have time to care. I reached the door marked *Five* and peeked out, whipping my head back as I saw at least four guards walking down the hall. No, thank you.

I ran up to the next floor, taking the wobbling stairs two at a time, and cracked the door open, carefully this time. Quiet. Empty. I hurried down the hall, grabbing at doorknobs as I went. After four locked knobs and my frustration mounting, I stopped. A picture hung in the empty hall, the only picture in this hallway.

Men lined the bottom, standing proud, in front of a tall building. There were at least twenty of them in their suits, standing on the steps, broad smiles on all their faces. A special day, I could tell. I searched the men, their faces, until I saw him. I gasped out loud, my hand flying to cover my mouth. My father. My real father. His dark hair sat combed over like it always was, with a pleasant smile on his face.

It brought a teary smile to my face as I reached out to run my thumb over his face—my father's face. The first time I had seen my father in days. He had been here. Proof. Wasn't it proof? That he was actually my father? That he was here, somewhere, married to my mother, and Luther's status in this horrible place was all a lie. My arm dropped to my side. Or maybe it proved nothing.

I stepped closer to the frame. That building—I knew that building. Tall, maybe six floors. I chewed on my bottom lip, trying to imagine it with shrubs planted around the entrance and windows on every level. I had been in that building. It was the headquarters. In Tarrith. My Tarrith. Father's office had been on the sixth floor . . .

I looked around, realization hitting me hard in the face. I was in headquarters. Where headquarters should have been. This hallway, right now. Where Tess had grown up.

Disbelieving it could be true, I turned and stepped down the hall, running my left hand along the wall. This was how I found Father's office when I was younger. The chair rail, which should run all the way down this hallway, would guide me to his office. I would wait for the tiny crack, the break in the molding, and know Father's office door was next.

I found the third to last door on the right. Father's office. I remember standing in his office when I was young, staring out the window at the bustling city. *The window.*

I came to the door and closed my eyes. The knob turned easily in my hand. Freezing, my mind reminded me of the possibility of Luther sitting right inside this room, behind a desk. Deciding I didn't care, and part of me hoping to catch the man off guard, I threw the door back. It slammed against the wall, blowing papers off the brown desk. They fluttered to the ground, and I took pleasure in stepping on each one.

The desk looked eerily similar to my father's. Perhaps it was the same one. Part of me longed to sit there and pretend I was back with my fat in his office, on a normal day. But the window behind the desk won my attention. The maroon drapes hung to the floor. I threw them back, putting my hands to the window. My mouth practically hit the floor.

Svaris flew in all directions, in what looked like some sort of special formation. Oh, God. Something was happening. Something bad. I had to speak to them. Now.

I tugged at the window, shoving it all the way up and leaning out, shivering in the sudden chill. I opened my mouth and closed it. Took a breath, then let my chest fall. Should I just yell out? To which one? If only I knew a name, a designation, anything. The same second I opened my mouth to scream, the door behind me *whooshed* open.

I froze, half my body hanging out the window.

"I said I don't care—get it taken care of." Luther's voice boomed from the hallway.

Without thinking, I stepped out of the window onto the ledge, fighting silently with the drapes wrapped around my leg.

"There isn't time. You concentrate on what you are supposed to do."

As quietly as possible, I closed the window, leaving it open just enough to hear more of his yelling. Then I made the mistake of looking down.

Oh, shit.

I plastered myself against the brick wall, wondering what the hell I was thinking, climbing out a window on the sixth story of a building. My heart pounded in my ears as the sky and dragons in front of me began to blur. I shoved my head back against the building, flattening myself and jamming my entire being into a brick wall. I blinked rapidly, forcing my brain to remain conscious.

"Signal the dragons. Get me a Redwing here tonight."

My eyes closed. Oh, God. He wanted a Redwing here. Tonight. The lurch of my gut nearly made me puke right there on the side of the building. As tears gathered at the corner of my eyes, I pressed my lips together, holding myself against the rough stone. If a Redwing came, we wouldn't be able to . . . My eyes popped open. That didn't make sense. I curled my fingers against the rough brick with my muddled brain, trying to make sense of this conversation.

Why would the dragons want a Redwing here? Dragons from different factions didn't intermix . . . Did they? Things were not making sense. Breathe in, breathe out. I could not pass out six stories above the ground. Breathe in, breathe out. I took another trembling breath, squeezing my eyes shut.

A door slammed. Luther. He left the room. Or did he enter the room? Grinding my teeth, I inched my way back toward the open window.

My hand grasped the edge, feeling the warmth of the room. *Okay,* I thought, *you're just fine. Now, you just have to turn carefully and climb right back in. That's all.* I spoke to myself as I moved, inch by inch, with my back scraping the brick as I went.

Panting, I slid my foot until it was right in front of the opening. Now all I had to do was lift the window and climb back in. My hand tugged at the window. It didn't move. By now, my heart beat so fast I was positive I was having a heart attack. I tugged at the window, gasping. *Please, oh God, please open.* It didn't listen. The window stayed where it was. Stuck, open just enough for a damn bug to crawl out of. No, please, please. This could not be happening. Tears streamed down my face as I pulled at the window blindly, begging the piece of glass with my entire soul. The window refused to budge. It wasn't going to work. I was going to fall, die here, with absolutely no one to scream to. My body shook violently as I stood on the side of the building, ready to crumble. Alone.

No. I could not do this. I put my shoulders back and squeezed my eyes shut. I blinked several times, trying to clear my vision. Deep breaths. *Stop acting like a child and think.* After a few more breaths, I stared at the dragons in the distance. What would happen if I screamed to one of them? *Not a good idea,* I thought with my head shaking. No. Do not call over hungry, angry dragons that breathe fire.

Wait. My fingers brushed the side of my pants. The Dragon Eye. I had the Dragon Eye. What if . . . Somehow . . . I could get their attention, get them close enough with that? Bargain with them for the Eye. Save my life in exchange for their precious relic. Maybe, I thought, trying not to let the tears leak out again. Surely they wouldn't eat me or tear me limb from limb. Surely.

Achingly slowly, I reached into my pocket and felt the stone. Wrapping my fingers around it and letting the cool stone calm my stomach, I took another breath. Then another. I closed my eyes and pulled it out, holding it down by my side. Now what?

My eyes followed the flying dragons while I steadied the hand holding the Eye. They didn't change formation, look over, or give a damn that a woman was hanging off a building near her death. They would wait to care until I fell and broke my neck, then feast on my mangled carcass.

Wincing, I held the stone out with a shaking arm. I closed my eyes and tried to relax my body, the first step to calming your brain. I imagined walking down to the Keep in the evening, Selyse lying peacefully at the pond, looking up at me with warm colors moving around her.

Breathing deeply, I called to them. I asked for their assistance in return for their relic, speaking silently, as respectfully as possible. My eyes were still squeezed shut, and my extended arm began to ache.

Be strong. Shoulders up. Do not show fear. Words Selyse had told me many times.

Then I opened my eyes.

CHAPTER 28

Tess

I glanced back at Arik and Benny and nodded. "Go," I whispered.

We slid out the door from the stairwell and crept down the empty hallway. Something felt wrong. I had been gone four years. Things looked different, as if the place had kind of been . . . let go. Forgotten about. Which, I guess it had. The walls had a brownish tinge, the composite flooring stained and dirty. Crumpled towels lie in piles in the corner, probably a temporary solution to some type of leak.

The wars continued. Luther was still in control. The dirty floors and lack of guards led me to believe the capitol building was not nearly as important as it once was. Vera had been concentrating on our rebellion, being our spy, and getting us information. Who knows what Luther had been concentrating on. According to Benny, it was more than I had thought.

We crept along the wall silently, even though I knew there was little chance of a guard being on this floor. Four years ago, the fourth floor contained only my family's sleeping rooms and a bath. A sitting room my mother sometimes used. Not much excitement up here, especially midday, when soldiers would be posted at their stations around the compound. The Prats would be around somewhere, but that could mean anything from cleaning toilets to finding the dragons a human to consume—when times were especially bad.

Vera's sleeping room was empty, along with the bath. Only one more room on this floor she would be in. I stopped at the door and turned the handle, praying to the kings in my mind. I almost cried in relief. My mother sat in her favorite chair in a ridiculous white gown.

"Mom." I ran to give her a hug, waiting for her to stand and greet me, hug me back, or acknowledge me in some way.

But she sat, with her hands in her lap, staring at the wall.

"Mom?" I grabbed her elbow and shook her, then turned to look at the wall. "What are you looking at?"

I turned back to Benny. "What's wrong with her?"

Benny moved to stand in front of Vera, his forehead creased.

I crouched down to be eye level and grabbed her chin, pulling her face to mine. "Mom? Talk to me. Say something."

But she sat dazed and silent. Her eyes looked far off, half closed. Something was very, very wrong here.

I stood slowly, dropping my hand from her face. She slowly turned to stare back at the same location on the wall.

I took a step back, shaking my head. "What did he do to you?" I whispered, feeling the knot forming in my stomach. "Oh, that bastard, he did something to you, didn't he?"

She stared.

I turned to the two men behind me with my hands clenched into fists at my sides. "You guys stay here. I need to have a word with my father."

Arik grabbed my arm. "No, Tess, don't. We have to find Quinn. If Benny's right, and she's the way to stop this whole thing, we need her."

Little Quinn, his new lover girl. He could have cared less about stopping anything as long as he had her by his side. I took a deep breath, shrugging out of his grasp. I didn't want to admit it, but she might come in handy later.

"Fine." I didn't want to leave Vera. But Arik was right, as much as I didn't want him to be. "Benny, you wait here with Vera." I stopped. "My mom." By now, of course, he would know who she was. Granted, he'd probably known for a long time.

I grasped Vera's hand and squeezed. Pulling her face toward mine, I stared into her light eyes. "I'll be back, I swear." I kissed the top of her head, praying she was still in there somewhere.

"I will guard her with my life," Benny murmured, putting a hand on her shoulder. He looked me straight in the eyes.

I believed him.

We turned to walk out the door, as I heard her murmur something.

"What? Mom?" I dove back to the ground to kneel next to her in the chair. "Say it again." I grabbed her hand.

"Window."

I looked up at Arik. Had I heard her right? "Window?"

"Win . . . dow," she murmured, still staring at the wall.

Benny bent down to look at her. "What window?"

"Quinn . . . tessa . . ."

"Did Quinn go to look for a window, Vera?" Arik stepped up to her chair and leaned in. "Is that where Quinn is?"

We all stared at her, waiting. But she closed her eyes in a sleepy sort of trance. "Window."

I stood. "Why the hell did she want a window? Gonna climb out of here?" I chewed on my lip, rubbing my forehead. "There's only one window in this building."

Benny stood, nodding. "Luther's office."

I would have asked him how he knew, but there was little point anymore.

Arik turned, already heading out the door. "Let's go." He knew the building just as well as I did. We had dared each other to climb out of that window many times.

He headed for the stairwell without checking to see if I was following. I kept my comment to myself. There would be plenty of time to fight later.

We dashed up the stairs, stopping at the wooden door with the shining *Six* on it. He went to pull it open as I put my palm against it.

"Wait." I put my finger to my lips, leaning against the door. "Shit, go, go!" We took off up the stairs, opening the last door marked *Roof*. We slipped out just as several men in blue slammed out door six and thundered down the stairs.

We were on the roof, an unnatural breeze running through the air. Wings flapped all around, making whooshing noises from all angles and throwing my hair in all different directions. Svaris swarmed over the compound in some type of circular fashion, making an intimidating parade directly over the city.

"What the hell is going on?" Arik called over the noise.

I only shook my head, for the wind up here was too strong to talk against. As I gripped the door handle to go back inside, Arik dashed over to the edge of the roof.

"What are you doing?" I yelled. Svaris were circling our heads, and he was running around on the roof of the capitol building. Had he lost his mind?

"Quinn!" he yelled, practically hanging off the side of the building.

I ducked out of the cover of the door frame and hurried to where he bent, looking over the side of the building.

"Oh, shit," I said, putting my hand to my face. A hungry-looking Svari hovered in front of the building. And there was Quinn, her arm out, standing on the ledge.

Stumbling back, I grabbed Arik by the arm. "Get back here!"

He let me drag him back a few feet. Then he pulled out of my grasp to run back to the side of the building, apparently eager to get another look at the Svari hovering in front of Luther's office. I stayed back, wondering if he was going to get his head bitten off. Or worse.

"Look!" he said back over his shoulder. "Look!"

I winced and stepped forward, peeking over the roof of the building. Yes, there was a dragon staring at the side of the building. Just staring. At a dark-haired girl with impressive boots. Quinn balanced on the ledge of the building, face-to-face with a damn Svari. They were having some sort of bizarre staring contest, Quinn appearing the size of a tree frog in front of a green monster. I could see the smoke blowing in her face. She could reach out and shine the dragon's teeth if she so desired.

"What is she doing?" I called to Arik over the wind.

I had seen dragons eat people, but never up close. Never close enough to see the fear in the dinner's eyes. Close enough to stroke his monstrous green scales. Why was the dragon not attacking? Was it possible? Could she speak to a damn dragon? My vision locked on the row of white dragon teeth, glistening in the sunlight.

Arik grasped my forearm. "How do we save her?"

"We get the hell out of here." I turned to leave, tugging at his shirt. "You can't defeat a damn dragon, Arik. Look at her. What the hell is she thinking?"

"The Dragon's Eye." His eyes widened. "What will they do if they find it?"

"What?" What did the Dragon's Eye have to do with anything? For a split second, I went to reach into my pocket, where I would have carried it if I had it. But I didn't have it.

My eyes narrowed. Betrayal. The only word that came to mind. I stared at Arik, the look on his face telling me everything I needed to know. "You took it."

He closed his eyes briefly and nodded. "Yes, but for a good reason."

"Then why didn't you *say* something? You stole it for her, didn't you?" I shoved him backward so hard he actually fell. I no longer cared that there was a dragon standing face to face with a woman below us anymore. Arik, my best friend, who I *thought* was my best friend, stealing. From me. For her.

"Oh, shit, Arik, do you realize what you did? She could tell them everything. Everything. What if the Dragon Eye is the damn weapon, and they have wanted it all along?"

"No, Benny said—"

"Screw what Benny said! We have no idea what is going on while she stands there telling them everything!" I shook my head and turned away. "I'm done with her, Arik. With it all. I'm going to get my mother, and we're going to get out of this place." I turned toward the door, part of me hoping he followed. But he stood at the edge of the roof, refusing to let Quinn out of his sight.

I stood at the door with my arms crossed. My chest burned. "So, this is how it is, then? *Her*?"

"Of course not!" He threw his arms out to the sides. "It's not a damn competition, Tess!"

I strode to him and stared him in the face, despite my short hair blowing in my eyes. "If you care about me, you will walk off this roof with me. You will walk down those stairs, get my mother, and we will get the hell out of here."

He rubbed his face, shaking his head. "Why does everything have to be a competition, Tess? Why can't I be your best friend and care about another woman? I watch you screw another meaningless man every day and still stand by your side! Maybe it's my turn to be selfish and not give a shit how it makes you feel!"

I gasped as if he struck me. I opened my mouth to say something hurtful, something awful back. But I could think of nothing.

"Get away from me," I yelled, shoving him away. Finally, it all came pouring out, right here on the roof of the building we spent so much time in. Where we had grown up. Together.

He pulled me close. I could see his jaw clenching. "No. Tell me why." His hair blew in the wind, and his eyes glistened. "Why did you have to do it to me? Why was I never enough?"

We stood on the roof, so close I could feel his breath on my face. His hands trembled against my body, holding my shirt in his grasp. For a moment, I thought of pressing my lips to his. Letting him wrap his arms around me. Hold me. I let the tears well up as my shoulders sagged.

"It wasn't you," I choked out. "It was me."

I pulled my shirt out of his grasp and left him there. I slammed the door behind me, wiping my face furiously. No. I did not cry. I did not let myself cry. Crying was a waste of time. I leaned back against the door for only a second before I remembered the whole reason I was here.

"Vera!" I called to the empty staircase. I ran down the stairs, tears clouding my damn vision, needing my mother by my side. I needed to hear her voice.

Bursting out of the door marked *Four,* not giving a damn how much attention I was drawing, I ran for her. I would get to my mother. She needed me as much as I needed her.

I threw open the door to the dark sitting room. "Mom!" I sobbed into the darkness, tears still streaming down my face as I squinted through the darkness.

"No, Quintessa."

The voice in the dark room filled my chest with rage, all tears forgotten. I knew that voice. Only one voice could bring about the anger, the contempt, and the hatred that threatened to overflow my very soul. Only one man.

Light filled the room. Luther sat in Vera's chair, legs crossed, in his crisp, clean suit. "I think it's time you and I had a little chat."

I nodded slowly, narrowing my eyes. "Yes, I think it is, Luther."

CHAPTER 29

Quinn

I stared into the Svari's eyes. Ignoring my pounding temples, I concentrated on the blues and purples intermixed in his left pupil. For some reason, my gut told me to avoid looking directly into the gold slit in the center of his eye. Was it a sign of disrespect? Could he read my mind? Or was it simply the yellow and black colors swirling around his left ear making me uneasy?

The Dragon Eye scalded my fist, but I didn't dare open the palm of my hand. To a dragon, strength was everything. Having strength meant you were worthy of their time. Maybe even worth their interest. Weakness was a sign of an individual that was nothing more than scum underneath their claws.

Looking into those gigantic eyes, close enough to smell the blood on its breath, I opened my mind. Connected it. Let the same pulsing of my mind run down my face, through the length of my scar.

But the colors. His emotions. The mix of yellow and black confused me and made it difficult to hold the connection. I must hold it. He must know I am strong.

I nearly jumped out of my skin when I heard him in my head.

Why do you contact a dragon, human?

I swallowed and stared, shoving my body back against the stone wall. His deep and hollow voice was in stark contrast to Selyse's sing-song rhythm.

Taking a deep breath, I let my mind take over. *I have been trying to contact you. I have been sent by the one with a spotted underbelly.*

Selyse did not actually have a spotted underbelly. I had learned long ago how a queen should be referred to. A sort of code among dragons. A way to protect their beloved queens.

His eyes penetrated mine. I grimaced as my skull slammed the brick wall, but immediately relaxed my face. The Dragon Eye cooled in my hand, making my palm sing in relief. A strange sort of vibration started around the Eye, echoing in the scar down my face.

You carry something that does not belong to you. You have stolen from a dragon?

I tried not to wince as his breath steamed my face. *No, I have not stolen. I discovered your relic and am returning it to you.*

Humans do not possess the power to use a Dragon Eye.

I paused. *How do you know this?*

He bared his teeth, making my heart jump into my throat. My scar pulsed harder, making me want to squeeze my eyes shut and rub the scar furiously. But I did neither.

Are you suggesting you are as powerful as a Svari, human?

I could feel my pulse pounding in my ears. My plan was failing. He perceived me as a braggart, a showoff. I could tell by the swirling colors around his face darkening. *No. But I have powers above other humans, powers that I used to get to this place.*

He said nothing. At least nothing I could hear. For a moment, I thought I lost the connection. But as long as I was standing on the edge of this building, with a Svari in my face, I would stand and stare back.

You are in need of my assistance.

I swallowed. *I simply require your power to move me to the top of this building.*

And why should I help a small human?

I paused, not sure I wanted to continue down this road. Before I could stop myself, I blurted it out. *I have a message from your queen.*

His enormous eyes narrowed. *Lies. My queen is no more.*

Your queen risked her life to get me here. She is a beautiful, wonderful dragon named Selyse. I blinked back the tears that formed as I said her name. Crying would not help my situation.

We partook in another long-winded staring contest. My arm sagged with the Dragon Eye feeling heavier and heavier. Sweat dripped down the side of my face, and I prayed the dragon didn't sense or see my exhaustion. My shoulder screamed in pain from the awkward position of my arm, making me breathe in hard gasps I tried to conceal.

The scene in front of me changed. I no longer felt the warm, sticky air of dragon breath on my face. Suddenly, I smacked my head on a hard surface, flat underneath me. I lay there, staring at the blue sky above me, my scar still throbbing.

"Quinn!"

Before Arik could lift me, hold me, or do anything else, I grabbed his arm.

"Don't say anything," I whispered fiercely. The pulsing of my scar told me Svaris were near. And waiting.

I stood shakily, pulling away from him. He let me go. I let my arm drop to my side, ignoring the feeling of a knife spiking through my shoulder.

Three Svaris stood on the edge of the building, staring down at me.

Tossing my hair, I stood tall. I kept my mind silent, waiting for them to establish communication. I could not appear to be in charge. Completely submissive, bowing to them at all costs. Strong, but weak.

I no longer held the Dragon Eye in my fist. But I could feel where it had burned my palm. I stared at the Svaris carefully, hoping Arik was staring at the ground. Part of me wondered if I should stare at the ground as well. But it was too late to change my mind now. Indecisiveness was as bad as weakness. I think.

I swallowed, feeling the tension in the air. Something was not right. I opened my mouth to address them when the white-hot pain started in my neck. I gasped and collapsed to my knees, unable to explain why I could not lift my head. Tears stung at my eyes as the nails stabbed at every joint in my body. I wanted to cry out, to beg them to stop, but I could think of nothing but the pain.

Why do you not bow before us, human?

I squeezed my eyes shut. I tried to think. But my mind would not connect. I clamped my teeth down and tried to think it again, with all of my might, but could not make my brain speak.

"I'm sorry," I gasped finally, staring at the ground. "Please!"

The nails sank deeper into my skin, causing a pain deep within me—parts of my body I did not know could feel pain. The nails twisted and bent, tearing my muscles and stabbing at my inner organs. But I couldn't scream. I couldn't move. It hurt to breathe. To think. They were going to kill me. The taste of dirty metal filled my tongue, pressed down my throat, filling my brain with the heavy stank. They tore tearing achingly slowly through every part of me, jamming through my bones as if the dragon himself was swinging the hammer.

Suddenly, it stopped. I fell in a heap onto the dirty roof, coughing and gasping for air. Even in the breeze, the sweat dripped down my forehead, pooling at my lips. The aches and pain were a distant memory. I wiggled my fingers and bent my elbow in slow relief. What the hell just happened?

Let that be a warning to you, small one. You do not disrespect your saviors.

I nodded miserably, breathing in the dirt I lay in. The tears started, cool against my sweaty face.

Now stand.

I swallowed, still tasting metal, and climbed to my feet. My skin still felt the echoes of the imaginary spikes being shoved through my body. I winced as I pulled my head up to look at them.

"Look down," Arik whispered from behind.

I dropped my head automatically, squeezing my eyes shut. I braced myself, waiting for another massive wave of pain for angering them, but nothing came. After a moment, I let myself breathe and peeked at my feet. Okay. Lesson learned. Do not look at male dragons.

Why do you dare speak of our queen, human?

I paused, staring at the ground. Was I supposed to speak now? I opened my mouth to answer, but snapped it shut. I tried to glance back at Arik for permission.

What is the message from our queen?

"Sh-she requires your fire! She would like to produce an egg," I said to the ground. What would happen if they didn't believe me?

How do you know of our queen, human?

"She is my friend," I sobbed to the pebbled roof. "The one who told me of the Axis and brought me to the link."

I was also the one responsible for her death. I closed my eyes. Yet I was promising them their queen wanted an egg. I bit my lower lip, wishing I had never called these assholes over.

The silence was overwhelming. I squeezed my eyes shut. Their voices had gone quiet. My heart began ramming in my chest. Would we still have time to escape? Would we still—

I gasped my face jerked upward so hard my neck popped. What could only be the point of a dragon claw held my chin in the air, forcing me to look up.

The Svari stood in my face, the air he breathed blowing my hair back. I waited. He was going to eat me. Rip me limb from limb.

You bear the mark of our queen.

I would have looked down if possible. But he still had a hard grip on my chin, pulling my face closer. So close I could see the yellowing of his teeth.

"I was injured by a dragon," I squeaked.

Why would our queen show you mercy?

I cried out as I felt the needle in my spine. "No! Please! I-I was injured when I was young. By your queen." I resisted the urge to crumble again. "Please! I am not from this world." The hot tears streamed down my face as my neck cried out in agony.

What world do you come from, human? Where is our queen?

"I came through the link," I sobbed. Pain radiated through my neck as he held my face to his, practically lifting me off the ground by my chin.

They went silent. The dragon dropped me hard on my feet, causing me to stumble backward. The pain faded as quickly as it had started. The tears were coming in what felt like waterfalls. I had been wrong. About everything. I thought I was some kind of expert on dragons. And I was standing here being tortured by one.

You come from the link?

"Yes," I whispered, staring at the ground.

How do you know of this byway?

I opened my mouth to speak and stopped. The book. That Luther wanted. Oh, no. Should I tell them? Should I lie? Would they be able to sense I was lying? "I-I—"

Speak!

"Selyse told me!" I screamed downward. "She told me and then took me there. She really did," I added pathetically.

My brain told me not to say a word about the book. I had no idea why. But for now, the book had to remain a secret.

We will decide if you are being truthful, human. For now, you are to remain.

I nodded, at a complete loss for words. Was this a good thing? A bad one? More torture? Before I could wonder further, the whoosh of air blew all around me.

More pain shot up my back as I landed on something hard. I cried out and put my hand to the back of my head, rolling over on my side. A damp darkness replaced the sunlight we had been standing in. My eyes moved through the silent area as I turned on my knees, waiting for something horrible to arrive.

"Quinn?" I jumped as I felt Arik's hand on my shoulder. "It's okay. They're not here." He grabbed me under the armpit and lifted me to my feet. "Are you all right?"

I sniffed, wiping at my nose. "No. I'm not."

"Guess you've never had a dragon interrogate you, huh?"

I looked at him in surprise. "You have?"

"No. But I've seen it." He put an arm around me. "You're okay. It could've been a lot worse, you know."

I let out a shaky laugh. "Worse, huh? I came here for their help, for God's sake. I came here to save my world, I-I was so completely wrong. What the hell do I do now?"

My desperation was turning to anger—an anger with myself. For being so unbelievably stupid, so arrogant, so naive. Thinking I could fix an entire world, that I could do something as ridiculous as save a race of dragons. Now what? I had made things worse for Arik, for Vera, and for everyone they were trying to protect. Fenwick and Selyse. For what?

I wrapped my arms around myself, the cool air nipping at my neck. "What will they do to us?" I took a step forward, slipping on the stone underneath us.

"Don't know. I've never had the joy of being in the pit." He shoved his hands in his pockets and leaned back against the dark rock. "Smells terrible," he muttered.

I turned to face him. Even in the darkness, I could see his expression. Despair. Maybe regret mixed with despair, for catching me from the sky that cursed day, for ever asking my name. Or sharing a moonlight kiss with me. My regret turned to anger. Anger that made no sense. Arik was going to die because of me. Just like Fenwick. Again.

My hands balled into fists. "What the hell were you thinking?"

He looked up at me. "What?"

"Why were you there?" My fists went to my face, wishing I had the courage to beat myself to death. "You should have been with Tess, not me. What were you thinking?"

I put my fists on his chest and hit him, nearly falling on my ass.

He stepped to the side, then leaned against the rock, my pathetic attempt to damage him failing. "I was thinking maybe you could use a hand. You're welcome, by the way."

I gritted my teeth. "I didn't need your help. You shouldn't have come after me. You should have been protecting Tess, not me. All you are doing is driving her away!"

My words echoed off the slick black walls. I was being unfair, and I knew it. But I couldn't stop. I had never been so furious in my life.

He stood up straight, slowly. I could see him narrow his eyes in the dark, making me take an uneven step back. "You know nothing about me and Tess."

"Just what she told me," I snapped. "It's why you lost her, isn't it? You can't stop every bad thing that's going to happen." I took a deep breath in and crossed my arms, trying to hide the trembling of my arms.

He stared at me. "And why the hell are you so concerned about me and Tess? I did drive her away—for you." He jabbed a finger at my chest. "I don't know why I stayed. Next time I won't."

I could hear the anger in his words. The hurt. A part of me longed to grab him and hold him, cry into his chest. Let him put his arms around me, and breathe softly into my ear. But I couldn't stop. "There won't be a next time! We are as good as dead and if you had just stayed where you were supposed to, none of this would have happened!"

"Where I was supposed to be? With Tess?"

"Yes!"

He shook his head and turned away. "You're so damn screwed up you can't even think straight. You're blaming everyone but the one person responsible for every damn thing. Why don't you even have the guts to blame yourself?"

I stood there, letting my act of bravery come to a bitter end. My shoulders sagged as I leaned against the hard wall and put my face in my hands. "You're right. About everything. I—"

A scratching sound made me stop. My hands dropped from my face at the same time Arik's eyes swung to the side. His hand moved silently down to his waistband. He put a finger to his lips, and I nodded, holding the sweaty wall for support, too afraid to do anything else.

I put a hand on my cheek. The pulsing. Running down the length of my scar. Since we'd been down here, I felt it, but didn't think to care. The same throbbing I had standing on the window ledge with a Svari in my face. Or sitting in the Keep with Selyse. The same feeling I had whenever a dragon was close.

Very close.

Chapter 30

Tess

My fists curled down at my sides. The rage I felt for this man burned through my chest like dragon fire. I wanted to rip that sardonic smile off his face.

"Where is my mother?" I asked slowly. I would need to hold my temper until I found. Then I would let all hell break loose.

"She is being taken care of, Quintessa." He smoothed down his tie. That same blue faded tie. His suit was drab and worn, but he wore it like a prized possession. Every day. The only man I had ever seen wear such a ridiculous outfit. As if it made him better than all the rest. It only made him more pathetic.

"Don't call me Quintessa, Luther." It was a name I despised, a ridiculous one I only put up with because my mother must have had something to do with it.

He surprised me by nodding. "Agreed. But in return, you will call me Father."

I let out a sarcastic laugh. Oh, how he lived for these games. If only I could take that tie and knot it around his throat. Something I had dreamed about many times. "Fine. Now, where is my mother?"

He stood up, straightening his faded jacket. "She is fine, Quintessa. But we have important matters to discuss."

I scoffed, rolling my eyes. "Oh, of course. My mother is of very little importance around here. Isn't that right, Luther?"

He narrowed his eyes. "If you continue to speak to me with this tone, my daughter, your mother may bear the brunt."

I bristled at his last comment. It was the same every time. If I disobeyed, Vera would take the fall. I hated to even think about what he put her through when I disappeared. And I never would have gone if she hadn't told me to. She refused to back down. I refused as well. We had agreed a long time ago not to let this man use us against each other. And I wouldn't start now.

I crossed my arms. "Go to hell."

He nodded. "I was afraid you would say that. So I will have to take more drastic measures." He paused. "I'm afraid I will have to burn your little base and all of your friends to the ground."

My heart skipped a beat. "I have no idea what you are talking about."

"Don't you? Your little base across from the church? Population twenty-eight?"

Loic. That bastard.

I swallowed, my heart pounding against my rib cage. My team. My base. "Fine," I seethed, trying to ignore the reds that planted themselves in the dead center of my right eye. If I tilted my head just right, it looked like his chest exploded. A calming sight.

"Fine, *Father*."

"Fine, Father," I snapped.

"Good. Isn't that better?" He strode to me with a smile that made my stomach clench.

When he placed his hands on my shoulders, it was all I could do not kick him in the balls.

"Father and daughter back together again. Finally." He pulled me close.

I closed my eyes to hold in the reds bursting from every inch of my brain. My body trembled as he wrapped his arms around me. He was enjoying this. That much I knew. The feeling of wanting to cause him physical pain, to watch the man crumble . . . I closed my eyes and tried to pretend I was somewhere else. But his fake scent kept my brain fully aware of being completely vulnerable in this horrible man's embrace. The red. The pain. They swirled together as one, making my head pound in a violent, colorful misery.

After what seemed like an eternity, he released me. "Now." He clapped his hands and turned. "Onto your duties."

I said nothing. I had nothing to say.

"You will retrieve something for me, Daughter. I need you to get your friend Quinn's book."

I stared at him, trying to see around the blood-red spots. A book? My base for a damn book? "And what is in this book, exactly? Something about a weapon, perhaps? Having a little trouble?"

He smiled. "You will need Quinn's help to do this. So I suggest you find her and get started."

This was too much. Threatening everything I knew and loved for a book. I couldn't take it anymore. He should know me better. I did not respond well to ultimatums. Everyone on my base knew that, and we all knew what could happen one day. What did they say? Keep feeding a tyrant, and they will be hungry forever?

Luther snapped his fingers in the air, and the door behind me flew open. As much as I wanted to, I did not turn but kept my eyes on the man who had ruined my life.

A tall, thin man came and stood next to Luther, rubbing his nose and wiping his long blond hair out of his eyes. The stranger gave me a sly smile and looked up at Luther as if waiting for him to pet his head and congratulate him. He couldn't have been older than sixteen.

I made up my mind. The reds settled. Slowly, I walked to Luther, feeling a strange calmness in my chest. I waited until I was within a breath. "May the dragons eat you alive, Luther. Get your own damn book."

"I hoped it wouldn't come to this, my dear." Luther stood in front of the bars with his hands in his pockets. "But if you insist on being difficult, there's not much I can do."

"Oh, there is plenty I would like you to do," I muttered, leaning back against the brick wall. The only light came from a torch hanging near the door. In all my years in this building, I had only been down here once, on a dare from Arik, of course. And I hadn't even come in. All I did was peek in through a crack in the wall, just long enough to see the crusty steel bars. Then I ran back, boasting I had danced in the middle of the empty jail cell.

Getting me down here this time had been simple. One moment, Luther and I stood, glaring at each other, close to clawing out eyeballs. Next, I was stuck behind bars in this dingy place, standing as far as possible from the dark stains taking up most of the floor.

It seemed Luther had new friends. The boy he summoned to his side had powers I had never seen before. All it had taken was his clammy hand on my forehead. A whoosh of cold air surrounded me, and I landed on my ass in the middle of this disgusting cage that reeked of blood and bodily fluids.

Luther smiled. "Since you refuse to help me, Quintessa, I thought it was time for a little incentive." He turned toward his thin friend. "Bring them in."

I closed my eyes. He had Vera. I took a deep breath, swearing I would remain calm. I had no idea what this book was Luther wanted so badly, but the fact Luther wanted it meant he should not get it. Ever. Vera knew that. She would never want me to do this. Never give in.

The door creaked open. I looked up, head held high. He could hold me in this cell forever. I refused to budge. Nothing could change my mind.

And then I crumbled.

I watched the young couple enter, hands held tightly, faces matching in terrified expressions. Pale-Face goaded them with a stick, and his bright eyes and toothy smile told me he enjoyed it.

Luther turned to them with all the charm of a tyrannical dictator. Liv held her stomach as Sawyer put an arm around her shoulders. Oh, shit. I had sent them to Tarrith two days ago to find Forster.

I grabbed the bars. "No, Luther, you can't. They are completely innocent."

"Innocent, you say?" He put his hand on Liv's shoulder and walked behind her slowly.

Despite Sawyer's best attempts to stay by her side, Pale-Face restrained him, with nothing more than a hand on his shoulder.

The look of sheer dread on Liv's face made me want to rip the bars from the wall. She whimpered as Luther pulled her long hair behind her neck. He leaned forward into her neck and breathed in her scent. "Quite lovely, isn't she, Quintessa?" he murmured, running a hand down her shoulder.

Liv's entire body trembled. Her hands grasped the bottom of the long shirt she wore, pulling it tighter around herself. The shirt was one of mine. I had given it to her because it was larger than her own.

I held my breath as Luther ran his hand down her side, stopping right at her waist.

"Hmm. Feel a bit full here, don't you, my love?"

"Luther . . ." I warned, gritting my teeth so hard it blurred my vision.

He moved around her to face away from me. He leaned in and whispered something, to which Liv's eyes went full and round. She shook her head furiously, her brown eyes shining with tears.

By now, Sawyer was red in the face and sweating, with Pale-Face's hand on his shoulder. He gave a yawn while Sawyer struggled. He was no match for Pale-Face's strength.

Luther smiled back at me, running a finger down the side of Liv's quivering chin. "It would seem your friend is not so innocent, Quintessa. Procreation? Pregnancy? Rebellion? The Svaris would love to get their claws into this one."

I stared at the man threatening my pregnant friend. "She doesn't live under the Rule anymore, Luther."

His eyes brightened in an evil joy. "Ah, but she is under the Rule now, isn't she?"

I stared into Liv's eyes, trying to tell her everything was going to be all right. I would save her, and this horrible man would do nothing to harm their unborn child. But the tears running down her cheeks masked any thoughts I tried to get to her.

"What am I thinking?" Luther said. He reached into the corner and pulled out a rusted metal stool. "Please, dear, have a seat."

Liv swallowed and sat right on the edge, surely hoping she would have a split second to escape. She wrapped her arms around herself and cried silently, her tears hurting my insides.

"Now that I have everyone's attention, I shall ask your leader again, dear." He turned to me with a bright smile. "Quintessa? Would you like to listen to my proposition now?"

I glared at Luther as I gripped the grimy metal bars. I tried to murder him with my eyes. Cause him some sort of physical pain with my thoughts. Finally, I let my defeated shoulders sink.

"What do you want?" It seemed my pledge to never give into this man's torture had fallen flat. But I couldn't fail Liv and Sawyer. Images of Harlen flashed through my mind. Red, blistered skin. For hours, the smell of charred flesh had remained trapped in my nostrils. I couldn't let it happen again.

He reached into his jacket pocket and handed me a small vial. I stared at the green liquid, then looked at him. What the hell was this?

"You will need to take this, Quintessa."

I sighed and took the glass tube, dropping my hand down by my side.

"And I would be careful with that, dear. You never know what could happen with dragon's blood."

My body went rigid. I glanced down at the vial in my hand. "Why are you giving me this?"

"To retrieve the object I require, you will need dragon's blood. Quinn can tell you the rest, I'm sure. There is a book she owns, and you will get it for me."

I glanced down at the vial in my hand, giving a shudder. I hoped the glass would keep it in place. "What book?" I stared at the dirt ground.

"It is titled *Dragons Among Us*, and she has it stored in her home." He clapped his hands. "Get me the book. I will release your friends, and leave your little rebel base alone. Fail, and there will be consequences."

"Tess." Liv stared at me with watery eyes. "Don't." Her small voice shook. I had to admire her strength. To be tough, to never give in, just as I had taught her. But I looked at her young, tear-stained face. I couldn't lose another one. I just couldn't. Some rebel I was.

I pocketed the vial carefully. "Fine. Let's do this." I stood back with my arms crossed.

Luther smiled. "Orvus!"

In a whoosh of cold air, I had traded places with Liv. She was on the ground, looking confused. Sawyer was in the cell next to hers, separated from his love by more metal bars. He reached through desperately, trying to comfort his wife.

I ran to the bars. "Luther! Put them in the same cell! Now!"

"I'm sorry, Quintessa, but I thought this would help speed you along a bit."

Liv sat up and wiped her face, moving to the bars to hug Sawyer through the metal.

I gave my friends what I hoped was my most reassuring smile. "I'll be back for you."

They both nodded, holding each other awkwardly.

I gripped the bars. "This isn't over. Remember that," I whispered.

CHAPTER 31

Quinn

The beads of perspiration gave off a sort of glow on Arik's brow. He grabbed my wrist and pulled me to him, keeping his movements slow and easy. His eyes stayed connected to mine, as if trying to instruct me on every move he made.

I swallowed thickly as we stepped slowly to the other side of the cave, moving only our feet. Once there, I looked at him in the face and nodded. *It'll be okay*, I told him silently. He nodded.

Holding my breath, I turned. Yellow eyes stared at us from across the cave. Eyes that did not blink. Did not move. For a moment, I wondered if the eyes were even real or my overtired mind was playing games. Then something moved in the darkness, and the yellow eyes closed. It lay on the far side of the cave we stood in, underneath a rocky ledge. No wonder we hadn't noticed it.

A Redwing. It had to be. No other dragon could fit in this cave. The grip Arik's hand had on mine tightened. Why hadn't it attacked? What was it waiting for? By now, he should have feasted on our organs, drained our bodily fluids, or used our skin to polish his fangs. They were man hunters. Hungry for human flesh.

The silence stretched on. Fear turned to uncertainty, and uncertainty turned to curiosity.

Finally, I spoke. "What are you doing here?"

The yellow eyes opened. I took that as a reply.

I tried again. "Are you a Redwing?"

The eyes disappeared into the darkness. "I was." The words came out low and raspy, like the voice of a creature who hadn't spoken in years.

Arik grabbed my hand. "H-he talked. I heard him."

Well, of course, he heard him. He spoke his words aloud, as easily as Arik and I did.

I dropped Arik's hand and stepped toward the dark figure. "You were?"

He turned his scaled head away and rested it on the rock. "I no longer see myself fit to hold that title."

I stepped closer. "Why?"

"Quinn! What are you doing?" Arik hissed.

I ignored him and continued toward him. "You are a prisoner." A thick chain hung around his large neck and a rusted padlock on the ground.

"Quite," he muttered. "As are you."

"Quite," I agreed. "How long have you been down here?"

"Long enough."

This Redwing was not the forthcoming type. I tried a more direct approach. "How were you captured?"

"A despicable method."

I held back a sigh. "Can you tell me how?"

He turned and snuffed, blowing dust out at me. "You think I need your help? A human?"

"Yes," I said, narrowing my eyes. "My friend here could get that damn chain off. But you have to tell me something. Or I can just leave you here until Luther sends for you."

He glared at me through glowing eyes. I folded my arms and tilted my head, unimpressed. This dragon was about as menacing as an alley cat.

He spoke to the wall. "A man posed as a Redwing deceived me. A man who can shape himself at will. Pretended to be injured. A cowardly attack. I do not know how many of my brothers have fallen at the hands of your leader."

"He is not my leader. I don't listen to a damn thing he says."

"He is still a member of your faction." He turned to me and gave a low growl. "Humans cannot be trusted."

This time, I did sigh. "Well, seeing as this human is offering to free you, I say you give them a chance, hmm?"

"Your leader experiments on the members of my faction. Holds something deadly in his hand that causes great pain."

A weapon. I looked up at Arik. His eyes locked on mine. Tess had spoken of a weapon.

Arik finally spoke up. "Why would the Svaris let him use the weapon? Are they under his control?"

The Redwing glared up at him. "Hardly. They could squash him if they so desired. But without a queen, a Svari would take orders from anyone appearing to be smarter than themselves. "

I frowned. That didn't make sense. A Svari was a fierce warrior, a dragon who fought for honor. Would trade their lives for their brother. I had thought. I had read. It seems Corben may have gotten a few things wrong.

"Would you like to get out of those chains?" I asked, glancing up at Arik.

"And do what? I am hardly worthy of the scales that cover my back."

I rolled my eyes. "Oh, for God's sake, enough of that. Would you grow up? How about you go find Luther and bite his head off?"

"He has the protection of the Svaris. One pathetic Redwing is hardly a match for a fleet of Svaris. Though dim as they are," he growled.

I stood up. "Take the thing off," I ordered Arik.

Arik crossed his arms and gave me an *Are you crazy* sort of look.

"Please? We need him."

Arik sighed and reached into his pocket, pulling out something silver and slim. He stepped toward the dragon hesitantly, then kneeled down and went to work on the lock resting against his wing.

"Okay, here's the deal," I said, kneeling back down. "We're gonna get you out of here, then we rescue the rest of your faction."

His yellow eyes looked at me dully. "A human rescue Redwings? Impossible."

"Would you instead like us to sit here and rot?" I had never wanted to smack a dragon as much as I did at that moment. Even when being tortured by one.

With a click, Arik stood back up, dropping the metal lock on the ground. "Done."

The Redwing said nothing but lay there, putting his head back on the floor.

I shook my head and put my hand to my forehead. "Oh, get up. They could come for you any minute. Is it so honorable as a dragon to be used as a science experiment? Let's get the hell out of here."

He raised his head and looked at me. "Dragon Code says I deserve to die. It is without honor to be used to a lesser creature's benefit."

I rolled my eyes. This pity party was getting old. Time for a new strategy. "Okay." I nodded. "You are not worthy to live. Wouldn't it be more beneficial to die in a place of your choosing? A place where you can be laid to rest peacefully? Save your damn dignity and die on your own terms."

He looked thoughtful for a minute. "I suppose ending my life in a place of my choosing would not be against the code. On one condition." His bright eyes zeroed in on mine.

"What?" I asked, rubbing my forehead.

"You must be the one to kill me."

I dropped my hand and stared. "Excuse me?"

He stood slowly, standing on his back two legs. The spikes on the top of his head scraped harshly against the rock above our heads. I swallowed as he lurched toward me, trying not to wince at the screeching. I was determined not to appear frightened in front of a suicidal dragon. A smaller dragon, but still larger than me.

"You must be the one to kill me." He released a large breath in my face, hot enough to make me jump back.

I hacked into my arm, my dry throat feeling the effects. He might as well have shoved my face into a fire pit. Glaring up at him, I cleared my throat, wondering if the nose hair was just singed out of my nostrils. He did that on purpose.

I crossed my arms and tossed my hair back. "Why me?"

"Because it will be a challenge for you." He nodded as if this explained everything.

I paused. "You'll get us out of here if I promise to kill you?"

"Yes."

I bit the inside of my cheek, feeling Arik's eyes on me. "Fine."

Arik grabbed my hand. "No. She does not agree."

"What?" The Redwing and I spoke at the same time.

"She does not agree. I will be the one to kill you," Arik said, pulling me behind him. "Or no deal."

I opened my mouth to speak when the dragon spoke over me. "It would seem the deal has already been made. I will die with dignity by her hand, no other."

"Then she refuses."

"*She* has a name, thank you very much," I said, shoving my way in between the two males. "And yes, I agree. I will be the one to kill you. *If* you get us out of here."

"You don't know what you're agreeing to," Arik murmured. "You don't want to do this."

"I know perfectly well what it means to kill someone."

"To kill a dragon? What about the others? What if they take revenge on you? You want to piss off the Redwings?" Arik's eyes burned into mine.

I opened my mouth and shut it. I swallowed. Arik didn't know it, but I wasn't planning on actually killing this dragon. I would talk him out of it. Somehow. If only Arik would shut up.

I nodded to the dragon. "I accept."

The Redwing nodded back. "We require your dagger," he said to Arik.

My eyes widened, and I held my hands up. "Whoa, whoa, I said after you saved us, I would kill you. Remember?"

He held his claw out to Arik. "This is for our oath. You will join me in a blood oath."

Oh, dear. I looked nervously at Arik, wondering if I should have listened to him. "What is a blood oath?"

"The joining of our bloods. An unbreakable bond. Only when the oath has been fulfilled will you be free of me."

"Oh." My heart began thumping. I pushed my hair behind my ear. "What, uh, happens if you break a blood oath?"

He glared at Arik, holding his claw out to him. I nodded to Arik as I held back the gasping breaths my lungs wanted me to take. Calm. I was perfectly calm. "It's okay," I said to him. "Please."

Arik unsheathed his blade, holding it by the handle. The dragon snatched the blade out of his grip and, without a word, sliced open the scales on his arm. My stomach dropped as the bright green blood oozed from his leathery skin.

"If you break an oath with a Redwing, your soul will be forever damned to the Golorn," he said conversationally, inspecting the knife's handiwork. "And I then have the right to kill you."

He looked up and handed me the knife. I stared at it with the glowing green blood dripping from the sharp edge.

Trying to keep my body upright, I pressed my lips together. The bright green substance dripped slowly from his arm. I stared at the knife while listening to the *plunk* of droplets as they hit the stone floor. He waited with the knife in the air. I took a shaking breath, then another. The large blade shined in the dim cave, with its tip coming to a fine point. Pointing directly at me.

"Quinn," Arik muttered. "Don't do this."

I looked at him, then back at the Redwing. Before I could think further, I grabbed the knife. Squeezing my eyes shut, I ran the slick blade across my forearm. It took a full second to actually feel the pain—to feel my arm split open and the warm blood spreading down my arm. Crying out, I let the knife drop to the floor and grabbed my arm, bile rising in my throat. My head spun as the cold air mixed with the wound, filling my body with a strange, light feeling. Ripples passed through my veins as I held my bloody arm to my chest, soaking my shirt. My head spun as the sickeningly sweet smell floated up, invading my nostrils with the scent of my blood.

Arik grabbed my shoulders to steady me. I took a breath, swallowing hard as the dragon in front of me spun. Arik dropped his hands. Wiping my face with a bloody arm, I put my chin up.

"Now what?" I said weakly, gritting my teeth as I let my bleeding arm drop.

The Redwing reached forward and grabbed my injured arm with his own. He pushed his oozing green scales onto my wound and squeezed. His claws cut into my already bleeding skin. We stood for what felt like hours, wound to wound, as I tried not to focus on the repercussions of green dragon blood leaking into human skin.

Finally, Arik stepped in. "That's enough!" he boomed. "Let her go so I can wrap her damn arm!"

The Redwing stepped back, apparently satisfied. "Yes, I see humans do not cauterize their own blood."

By now, his arm had healed. He wiped at it easily, flicking the green and red dust away.

I stood with green and red blood running down my arm, panting, looking anywhere but my arm. I blinked several times, sweat burning my eyes. But I stood tall, determined not to look like a coward in front of this Redwing. Arik ripped the sleeve off his shirt and went to work, tying it around my arm, his back to the dragon.

"Why did you do it?" he whispered, his hands shaking. "You didn't have to do that."

I flinched as he knotted the shirt over my wound. The knot was turning a dark color, spreading all over the material, giving off a strange shine. I put my arm down, wishing I hadn't looked.

I took a shaky breath. "Yes, I did. It will be all right. I promise." Giving what I hoped was a smile, I patted him on the back. I looked at the Redwing. "So, what do we call—"

I stopped and looked back down at my arm. That strange tingling returned, but stronger. Up and down the wound. Slowly, I untied Arik's tourniquet. The cut on my arm was healed. Gone. I flicked at the green and red dust covering my forearm. The sight should have been welcoming. But it sent chills down my spine.

Dragon blood. In my blood. A Redwing's blood.

"My name is Rhesh."

Chapter 32

Tess

Running through the hall, I tried not to think of the vial I carried in my pocket. Strangely, no one stopped me. I passed two guards on the way out, but they looked on, not caring that Luther Grimbley's daughter, a known traitor, ran wildly through the halls.

I slowed to a hurried walk, the vial of green murder-goo in my pocket feeling heavier and heavier. Dammit. Luther had a plan. These guards were under orders to let me go. I scrambled down the stairs, racking my brain for ideas.

Dragon blood was dangerous. But the funny thing was, no one really knew why. Rarely did a person actually see dragon blood, and only an idiot would carry it on their person. I had heard stories about it for years, some saying to never touch it, others saying just smelling it would create disastrous effects. Dragon blood could remove your soul from your body, leaving you an empty sack, or speed up the beating of your heart until it explodes out of your chest. There were supposedly lands, desolate wastelands under the skies where Redwings and Svaris fought. People said blood rained down as dragons fought, killing all plant and animal life. Dried up the rivers for 112 days. Did I believe any of these things? Well, no, not really. But I didn't care to test out any theories, either.

My mother still sat somewhere in this building, staring at an empty wall. It tore at my insides to realize I would have to leave her in this place again and come back for her later. *But she's tough,* I reminded myself. She had put up with Luther for longer than I had. She could do it. But I knew the guilt of escaping this place while leaving my mother trapped would leave a permanent stamp on my brain.

I had to go back into the tunnels. I reached the last door in the hallway and peeked in. Empty. Well, of course, it was empty. It was a damn storage room. My head swung all around the room, trying to clear my brain. Where was that damn trap door? I bit my lip, trying to remember where we had come up from the bug-infested tunnels. The mirror. There.

I hurried to the corner and dropped to my knees. There had to be some sort of latch, catch, or something. But the stone floor was smooth, or as smooth as a dusty basement floor could be. Dammit. Dammit. How the hell had Benny done it? I sat back on my haunches, running my hand through my hair. I hated being out of ideas—stuck. And I hated it even more that I was in this position because of my father. I rubbed my face until it hurt and tried not to think of Liv's round eyes as Luther touched her belly or Sawyer fighting to get to the woman he loved while some punk kid held him back.

"Argh!" I screamed, running my fingernails down my face. The reds were starting. They entered my brain without permission, laughing maniacally and jabbing at my pupils.

I punched a wooden crate stacked next to the wall. My throbbing knuckles split, and a drop of red seeped out. I pinched the bridge of my nose, telling myself to get my shit together. There wasn't time for this.

I put my bloodied knuckles back to the floor. Ran my fingers along the dusty floorboard, gasping when I felt it. A button or a switch or something—I didn't care. It wouldn't move. Stuck, probably from years of no one needing to escape a well-lit, bug-free room. I got down on my belly and rubbed the area free of dirt, hair, and rodent droppings. It clicked.

Throwing my legs in, I let my body fall to the floor of the bunker, landing on my feet. I looked around at the boxes and pallets, shivers moving up my spine as the sound of crunching Stygivar replayed in my brain. Ignoring the splats on the concrete and partial remains of the insect, I headed for the corner of the room, right where Benny had struggled with the cover of the tunnel. I got on my hands and knees, running my hands along the cold stone floor.

There. The floor, slightly raised. I grabbed the lip on the floor, not even budging it. I tried again, groaning, standing up, and bending. Finally, I wedged my foot under. After what seemed like hours and murder on my lower back, it sat back against the wall. I took a moment to roll my neck, apologizing silently to my upper back.

Squatting down, I felt blindly for the ladder with my boot, missing the top rung. Instead of stepping down gracefully, I tumbled into the dark pit, crying out as my arm met the edge of the opening in the floor. Panting, I rolled to my knees, spitting out dirt and whatever else had rotted on this floor for forty years. I stood, holding my arm, looking down at the pitch-black hole. The bugs. The dark. I needed a light.

I climbed back up the ladder and glanced around the basement. There had to be something in this room of junk . . . There. Lying next to the door was a lantern on its side, the glass spiderweb cracked. It would do. I reached for it, grunting, and snagged the ring on the top. The ring dropped innocently on the floor, far, far away from the lamp itself. Screaming again, I lunged for it, shoving back the hatch above me, finally touching the glass.

This time, I tugged the wooden hatch back down over the top of me. It took some groaning, some grunting, and almost squashing myself, but the door finally shut above me. I wasn't counting on the smack on my head as it fell, but at least, I was fairly used to head pain. I stood up again, this time in complete and utter darkness, fumbling for the lantern. Running my fingers over the broken glass, I found the switch, clicking it to the right. Nothing happened. Shit. Clicking it again, the skittering sounds of insects began above me. Or was I imagining it? I slammed the lamp against my fist. It flickered and glowed for a split second, and went dark. Screaming in frustration, I punched it again, then again.

I stood there, beating the lantern to a glass pulp, when my fist froze in midair. The tiny crawling legs on either side of my neck moved slowly, one toward my chest, the other down my back. I screamed out and spun, slapping at myself until my chest hurt. The other bug crawled down my back, underneath Arik's mangled shirt, out of my reach. I slapped at my backside helplessly, finally shoving myself into the dirt wall. Again and again, I shoved my backside into the grainy wall, still rubbing at my shoulders furiously. Finally, I peeled myself away from the wall, gasping for breath. I squinted up in the darkness carefully, holding a hand over my eyes. Something dropped on my hand.

To hell with this. I slapped my hand on my pants and ran. I ran with my arms out in front of me, then moved them to the side, trying not to hear the sounds of thunderous scrambling all around me. The air became thick and warm as I ran blindly through the tunnel, the burns and claws of insects all over my body. I smacked at my body and tugged at my hair, crunching the bug legs in my own hands, trying to ignore the grimy sludge left between my fingers.

By now, I was running with my arms slapping, not caring if I ran face-first into a wall. I just wanted out. Kings help me, I wanted out. I tripped over something on the dirt floor and stumbled until my chin landed hard in the dirt.

Coughing and smacking, I picked myself up on my knees, wondering what the hell could have tripped me in this underground hell. I reached back and felt it. Someone's hair. Oh, shit.

"Vera?" I screamed through the scattering and scampering noises. I ran my hands down her back until I found a shoulder and began dragging her through the tunnel with me.

Tripping again, I fell to the ground, smacking at my arm, grabbing at the dirt for my mother. I found a wrist and began tugging it toward me, moving inch by inch through the bug-infested tunnel.

"Vera!" I screamed again. Was she alive? Deciding I did not care, I continued my backward descent, dragging a body with me by the wrists while carnivorous bugs continued to fall from overhead.

"Tess," the voice coughed. "Tess."

I nearly screamed in relief when I felt resistance on the arm I was dragging. I fell to my knees. "Get up! We have to get out of here!"

"Go, Tess. You have to get out," the voice said weakly.

My brain clicked on. It was a male's voice. "Benny! Where is Vera?"

"I don't know," he coughed. "Go! Leave me!"

"Shut up!" I screamed. Grabbing his wrist again, I tugged him down a pitch-black dirt tunnel, trying to ignore the crawling and burning all over my body.

I tripped and fell hard on my side, sitting up when I felt the crunch. "You have to get up!" I screamed. "Get up!"

I gasped as I went to stand. My hand sat in the warm liquid, now spreading through my fingers. I looked down, more confused than ever, and moaned when I saw the bright green glow dripping from my hand.

The dragon's blood.

"Oh, shit." I watched my hand shake in the dark, covered in the neon substance. I was sitting in dragon's blood . . .

"Come on!"

I jerked my head to the voice in surprise. Benny was standing, this time tugging me to my feet. He was there suddenly, in view. I let him pick me up, and we stumbled forward. I held my hand out in front of me as we ran, trying to keep the drips away—far, far away. The soft glow bounced as we ran, illuminating the tunnel.

Benny stopped and grabbed my green hand, smearing the dragon's blood through his own fingers. I nearly doubled over in surprise when he smeared the green all over his face.

"W-what are you—"

"Let's get out of here."

Benny pushed me from behind, shoving me forward. The blood was acting as a light, a soft glow to navigate our way out of this horrible place. I kept my green hand out, holding it out as a guide, ignoring the faint scent of burned toast.

Silence. Only the thudding of our feet and our gasping breaths echoed around us. The tunnel had gone silent. Dragon's blood . . . The bugs were afraid of it . . . But so was I . . .

"Vera!" I gasped.

She lay crumpled by the metal ladder we had climbed down earlier that day. One hand still held a metal rung while she lay in a heap on the dirt floor.

I made it to her, keeping my soiled hand away from her.

Benny stood behind me. "She needs the blood."

I gaped at his glowing face and hair. "What?"

"Rub the blood on her. Now."

When I did not respond, Benny grabbed my hand and smeared it on her cheek. I gasped and yanked my hand back.

Benny took her chin in his hand. "Vera?" he murmured into the quiet. "Vera?"

When her eyelids fluttered open, I cried out in relief. I dropped to my knees and wrapped her in a fierce hug.

"Tess?" Her voice sounded foggy and filled with sleep.

"Can you stand?" I asked.

"I-I don't know . . ."

Benny reached down and picked her up easily under the arms. She put her arms out for a second, putting a hand to her head.

"What . . . Where . . ." She squinted, gazing up and down the small tunnel until her eyes landed on me. "What is going on?"

"Oh, there is plenty going on. But first, we're getting the hell out of here." I reached around her to grab the metal rungs and made my way up the ladder, using my shoulder to shove at the hatch. It took a couple of tries, but with Benny's help, we managed to shove the cover back, letting in the blissful evening air.

I helped Vera climb out, and she looked around shakily. She brushed the hair from her face, running her hand through the green blood. "What . . ." She looked down at her hand and gasped. "It's . . ."

"Never mind that," I said, grabbing her hand. "It just saved our lives." We rushed for the tree line, Vera's arms over our shoulders.

We collapsed as soon as we made it into the trees. I lay in a puddle, holding my shaking hands to my face. The forest smelled wonderfully normal, full of pine and mountain air. Wonderfully normal. I took a deep breath and ran my hands down each of my arms, feeling the rips and burns on Arik's shirt. But my skin was clean. Uninjured. The pain from the claws and insect fangs had faded.

I looked at Benny, who had his head leaning against a tree. He had the green glow on his shirt and face, in his hair, and on the backs of his hands.

I stared at my own hands. Put two fingers together. The blood came off easily, almost a fine green dust by now. The burned toast smell faded as the dried blood flaked to the ground. "Did you know?" I asked him.

Benny opened his eyes. "What"

"The dragon blood. It heals? Why the hell were we afraid of it?"

He closed his eyes. "I suspected. But I never tested it. Until now. Luther didn't want anyone to think for a second that these dragons might have a higher purpose. He needs us all afraid."

My eyes widened in surprise. "Luther?"

He reached down and slid off a shoe, shaking out the dirt. "Who told everyone dragon blood was fatal? Who told the people everything there is to know about dragons?"

Realization slipped over me. "Luther. But what does that mean? That dragons want to heal us?"

He kicked the ground and shook his head. "No, I doubt it would go that far. They are still in control. Or at least they think they are."

"The weapon. He's using it on the Svaris."

Benny sighed and ran a hand through his matted hair. "Well, no."

I waited for him to elaborate. "That's it? Just *no*?"

He shook out his coat, keeping his eyes on the ground. "If he was using the weapon . . . More things would be happening. He doesn't know how to operate it correctly. Yet," he added.

I narrowed my eyes. I did not like the sound of this. And I especially did not like how purposefully evasive he was being.

"You know—"

"Who are you?" Vera interrupted.

Oh, kings, we had completely forgotten she was there. She stared intently at Benny, studying him, looking even more confused than I was.

He cleared his throat and looked down. "Just a failed citizen, ma'am."

"You know Luther?"

He nodded, still looking at the ground. "Yes, ma'am. I was one of his researchers. You might recognize me from years ago."

She nodded but did not look convinced. I looked between the two of them. And then again. Benny still stared at the ground, and Vera still stared at Benny. Anyway.

"What do you remember?" I asked Vera. She still seemed a bit off, a bit out of it.

She bit her lip. "I . . . remember Orvus coming to get me from the sitting room . . . then nothing."

"Orvus? You mean Pale-Face," I muttered. "Creepy thin guy. Rubs his nose when he's excited."

"That's him. Luther's new toy," she said, rubbing her forehead. "He has gifts I've never even seen before." She put her head against a tree, closing her eyes.

"Wait, do you remember coming to the base?"

"The base? When?" She looked in the distance, her eyebrows crinkled in thought.

"That wasn't Vera," Benny said quietly. "It couldn't have been."

My head snapped in his direction. "Why?"

He shook his head. "It wasn't her. Probably Orvus. It's why her memory has been altered. He blended with her."

"He what?" I asked, scrunching my face. "Pale-Face can *blend*?"

We heard stories of such gifts when we were young. But that was all they were. Stories. Beings of a higher authority that could take our place, blend into our own, fill our shoes. I never even considered where the term came from.

Benny nodded slowly. "It would seem so." He sighed. "Things just keep getting better and better," he said, staring at Vera, who was still staring off into space, twirling her long hair.

It occurred to me I had never seen her twirl her hair before. My mouth immediately turned down, just the sight of her hair on her finger irritating me. I couldn't stand it. I had seen someone do it more than once in the last couple of days.

And something bad always came soon after.

CHAPTER 33

Quinn

"Hold my arms. Each of you," Rhesh instructed.

I grabbed his scales without hesitation. Arik looked warily at the dragon holding out his red, leathery front arm, claws at the ready. I gave him a look, and he reluctantly reached for the Redwing.

"What are we—"

Before I could finish my sentence, we were standing in a small field, still grasping arms. I gaped at the night sky above us, fading away to morning. Shaking my head, I shivered in the morning breeze.

"That was easy," I muttered. "Why hadn't you done that already?"

The dragon glared at me. "I am unable to use my power while being restrained."

I looked away in a hurry. "We have to find Vera. And Tess. Then we have to stop Luther."

In the distance, what looked like small, rounded huts filled a field. Maybe they were huts. It looked as though each had one small window.

Arik put a hand to his forehead and looked toward the rounded gray shacks. "Better not wait here too long. Soldiers live in those Jeklos." He nodded at the camp of silver huts.

I nodded, wiping my palms on my pants. "How do we get to Luther?"

Arik sighed. "You think the three of us can stop a flock of Svaris?"

"Us?" Rhesh interjected.

"Luther wants my book," I said, ignoring Rhesh. "There is something in that book that he needs, and I want to know what it is."

"What book?" Arik asked back. He joined me in ignoring the Redwing as long as possible, therefore pushing back his ultimate murder.

"A book by Corben Willoughby. Luther wants it. Badly. I've had it since I was a kid."

Arik scrunched up his eyes. "How would he know about a book from"—he motioned toward me—"there?"

"Excuse me," Rhesh said.

"I don't know. I've been going over it in my mind, and I can't think of a single reason—"

"Excuse me!" the dragon thundered.

Arik and I jumped back, looking nervously toward the huts, then at the dragon standing before us with smoke coming out of his nostrils. He stood towering over us on his back legs, his yellow eyes narrowed and glowing, giving me a stare that made me wince and look away. I clenched Arik's hand, my nose twitching at the scent of singed leaves. Perhaps I had gone too far with this unspoken plan.

"Do not think I do not know exactly what you are doing," Rhesh growled. "It is time for you to uphold the agreement. Right. Now."

I gulped, my brain scrambling for an excuse to keep Arik's knife out of my hand.

"Give her the dagger," Rhesh said. "Now!"

My heart jumped into my throat as his yell echoed through the area, practically blowing leaves off the trees. "Okay, okay," I said, putting my hands in the air. "We were just talking. There is plenty of time to kill you. Plenty of time for you to leave your brothers to suffer at the hands of Svaris, who outsmarted an entire faction of Redwings."

Rhesh stepped forward, breathing hot smoke into my face. For a split second, I was sure he was going to breathe flames into my already burning eyeballs.

He lowered his massive head to mine. Those yellow eyes were bright, too bright to look into. "No Svari could outthink a Redwing. A Redwing has more thought in their minds than a Svari has air in their lungs," he spat.

I struck a nerve. Perfect. I chanced looking up at him. "Then why are you willing to have someone kill you without at least trying to free your brothers? Why would you leave others to suffer when you could help?"

The Redwing went silent. His chest fell from the pompous posture it had taken. He stared into the distance.

"What would your queen want?" I asked quietly. "Would she want you to kill yourself without trying to save your faction? If Luther succeeds, the Redwings will be gone. Forever." A queen's relationship with her dragons was incredibly meaningful, at least with Svaris, and I had no reason to believe it would be any different from Redwings.

He stared at me in a stony silence. "You have quite a way about you, small one." He gave another large puff of air. "Fine. I will assist you in saving my brothers. They are being held all over this area."

I let out the breath I had been holding. "Thank you. I promise we will save your brothers."

"But."

My shoulders fell, already knowing what he was about to say.

He leaned in so close to my face that I could count the tiny spikes on his forehead. "You will still uphold your part of the deal. Dragon Code is not altered when a new goal is set. It is most important in times like these." His eyes hardened, and his nostrils flared. "Do you understand?"

I swallowed. "Okay." I swallowed again. "Okay."

"Fine." He nodded, stalking off, still walking tall on two legs. "We shall continue."

"Wait! Where are you going?" I hurried after him down the paved road. "We need a plan!"

"The plan is to save my faction."

"How are you going to do that?" I asked, jogging next to him. He was at least double my height and a great deal faster, even on only two legs. I glanced up at the lights lining the road, hoping the dark morning helped conceal us a little. He didn't seem to care about being stealthy.

"I am going to kill every Svari in this city. Then I will kill their leader by ripping his throat out and showing it to him before I burn him to a crisp."

I glanced back at Arik nervously. "Uh, shouldn't we talk about this first? Make a plan? We don't even know where the Svaris are—"

"I know."

"Where?" I ran after him as he turned off the road. I followed him into some sort of junk field, having a hard time keeping a conversation with him while tripping over trash and crawling over large hunks of metal. "Where? How?"

"They give off a terrible scent. It fills my nostrils with a stank of repugnance."

I wanted to point out he was most likely smelling the stank of this disgusting field as my feet slipped out from under me, and I fell forward into a hole in the ground, splattering myself with muddy water. I cringed, pulling away torn remnants and pieces of filth from my face.

Groaning, I stood in a hurry, scrubbing my face and running after Rhesh. "So we're going to the dragons?"

"Yes. They are gathered. It is the perfect time for attack."

"Whoa, whoa, whoa!" I stopped, hoping he would stop as well. But he marched forward, shoving aside half a vehicle missing both front doors. A dragon with a vendetta.

Oh, crap. I had turned a suicidal dragon into a murderous one. Ironic.

"So you're going to attack an entire fleet of Svaris? How?" I gave Arik a desperate look, though his eyes were moving up and down the field, searching for an enemy. Realizing I would get no help from him, I continued running after, toward the only tall building in the city. Two rebel humans and a Redwing, traipsing loudly through a military compound. This just kept getting better.

"I will not do it alone. You will assist me."

"Me? How?" I panted. "Could you just stop for one minute?"

"You have the blood of a Redwing. You have inherited my powers until you take my life."

I stopped in my tracks. "I *what?*"

"You have the power of the wing. We will attack together and then free my faction." He reached down and grabbed my hand, his sharp claw scraping my inner arm. "Here."

My eyes widened, and I pulled away from Rhesh, staring down at my hands. They looked like normal, human hands. Didn't they?

I looked up at Arik, standing next to me. He wiped at his face and stared back. "Can you?"

"I-I don't know." I turned my hands over again, holding them up for him to see.

Rhesh finally stopped ahead of us and turned back. He stomped back to me with a grim face and bent down until his breath blew my hair back.

"Use your powers," he said.

"What powers?" I asked desperately.

"Your powers."

I looked sideways at Arik as he stared at my hands. Biting my lip, I took a deep breath and twirled my fingers. Nothing. I could feel their eyes boring holes into my brain, which was not helping my concentration. I focused my thoughts on what was between my fingers and closed my eyes. Power. The power of a dragon.

I didn't jump or scream when I felt it. A tiny spark that disappeared as soon as I opened my eyes. I furrowed my brow and stared at my fingers, feeling the warmth spread through my hands.

A flame. Steady and growing, until I had a small fire growing between my hands.

The flame of a male dragon.

"Are you sure about this?" I asked as we crept toward the tall building, walking along the black fence.

"Quite."

I swallowed, beginning to feel overwhelmed by what I held between my fingers. What did he think I was capable of? *I* didn't even know what I was capable of. He thought I could assist him in taking down a fleet of Svaris? Small beads of regret were inching their way into my brain as I followed him. And I was keenly aware of my hands hanging down at my sides. They felt warm. Hot, even. Or was that just my imagination?

Arik's head darted back and forth as he kept a hand on my elbow. It seemed he thought it a mistake to hold my hand now.

"Go, now," Arik said quietly. We hurried toward the back of the building, flattening ourselves against the wall.

Rhesh crawled on all fours to peek around the building to the field Arik called the Landing. I watched Rhesh's spikes move up and down as he stared, chewing on my bottom lip.

"How long . . . uh, how long will I have your . . . powers?"

"As long as I draw air," he murmured over his shoulder.

"Oh. Okay." A deep feeling settled in my stomach. I had the fire of a dragon in my hands. All I needed was dragon blood . . . I glanced down at Arik's knife. Just as quickly, I snapped my head back up. My face warmed at the thought, even though neither male so much as glanced at me. No one could hear my thoughts. Could they?

I looked at Rhesh, but his mind was clearly on the Svaris. Arik continued to look left and right, and even up to the sky, that familiar bead of sweat appearing on his forehead.

I let out a silent breath of relief. No one could hear my thoughts. No one was aware of the tiny thought that crept into my mind. If only for a second.

We stood and waited while Rhesh stared at the Landing. I looked up at the building we leaned against, gnawing at my fingernail. Was Vera in there? Was Tess? I opened my mouth to suggest an alternate plan when Rhesh turned and stood on his back legs, knocking me back into Arik.

"You. Remain here."

Arik and I looked at each other.

"Who?" I asked, praying he would say both of us.

"The male. He remains. He will only interfere."

Arik glared at him and raised his eyebrows. But it gave me what I needed. I grabbed Arik's hand before he could object. "Get to Vera. And Tess. Please."

I could see his jaw clenching. But he sighed and gave me a quick nod, sending another glare in Rhesh's direction.

He turned back, walking low in the same direction we had just come. I took a deep breath. He would find her. Both of them. He would save them both.

I rubbed my sweaty palms against my pants. "What now? We just climb over the fence and start blowing fire at everyone?"

"Don't be foolish," he growled. "We will first attack their weakness, then take them out one by one."

My fingernail found its way to my teeth. And the nausea found its way back to my stomach. "What weakness?"

"They have many. A Svari has poor reflexes and needs to be led in battle. As a group, they are foolish and clumsy." He marched toward the Landing, leaving the safety of the back of the building.

"Wait! You don't expect me to fly, do you?" I asked, horrified. Could I actually fly?

"You cannot fly. Flying requires wings, human." I could literally *hear* him rolling his eyes.

"So we fight them on the ground?"

"Yes. They are most clumsy on the ground."

"Fight them? How do we fight a Svari on the ground?" The nausea that had started in my stomach was growing, spreading up my chest. What had I gotten myself into?

We stopped at the corner of the building, the Svaris now in plain view. The black gate stood several yards away, encasing the entire Landing. It was similar to the Dragon Keep back home. Six or seven Svari lay in a group, facing away from us. If I hadn't been more terrified, I would have tried to hear what they were saying. Or maybe just study them for color swirling out of their body. Not this time. I stood on my tiptoes to see toward the gate entrance. Two men in green stood with rifles.

"Follow my lead."

My mouth dropped open as he marched through the black fence. Just walked through it. His red body became hazy for one second as the vertical bars passed through his scales, and he simply appeared on the inside of the Dragon Landing.

I watched helplessly as his body disappeared. He was camouflaging himself somehow, turning the same color as the landscape he was walking on. Disappeared.

"Wait, wait, I don't get it—"

"Use your power." He growled, sounding much further away than I would have liked.

I leaned against the building, wringing my hands, ready to vomit what little stomach contents I had. *Concentrate, concentrate. Think of things that are invisible.* I opened my eyes and glanced down at my hands. Was I invisible? Hesitantly, I stepped away from the building, walking slowly toward the gate.

"Are you mad?"

I nearly wet myself as Rhesh's voice appeared in my face. Luckily, I slapped my non-invisible hand over my face before I could scream out. He dragged me back behind the building, away from the eyes of the guards.

"Sorry," I snapped back at him. "You can't expect me to use dragon powers without knowing how. Maybe it is you who is mad. How about some damn direction here?"

He was silent for a moment. Good. I hoped he realized what a complete idiot he was. But I still stood around a Dragon Landing pad in between two rifles, guards, and a fleet of Svaris.

"You are using your mind," he said in a low voice. "Think with your power."

I wanted to scream. "If I don't know how to use my damn power, how am I supposed—"

"Like this."

A small flame appeared in front of me. I stared at it. Flame. Think with my power. I took his advice. Stopped thinking. Just stopped, staring at the fleet of dragons. I let my fingers warm. The tingling in my fingers started moving through my hands, then up my arms.

"Find your power," the voice growled again, much closer.

I jumped, looking all around, then nodded. Invisible. Camouflage. Protect me. Stepping away from the building, I closed my eyes and stepped forward. Again. By now I was in view of the soldiers, but they had yet to react. I reached the bars and glanced back, my breath hitching when I saw the man in uniform standing at the entrance of the building, just on the other side of the grass. I froze, looking back and forth, wondering if I should run or hide.

The guard leaned against the front of the building lazily. A rifle leaned up against his shoulder, and he put a finger up his nose. I let out a breath as I watched the tall man pick his nose, unaware that a young invisible woman watched from twenty feet away.

I did it. Nodding to myself, I put my hands to my sides and stepped to the fence, eyes squeezed shut. The cold steel passed through my body, like freezing wisps of a cloud slicing through my skin. I gasped when I opened my eyes, putting a hand to my chest. I glanced behind me, then down at my hands.

"Weird," I said to no one. I cleared my throat, blowing a large gust of air out.

In the distance, the group of Svaris still huddled in a large but tight group. Rhesh and I had yet to be noticed. I let my shoulders relax and looked up to see Rhesh standing right next to me.

He nodded. "Well done." And he turned and walked off, a dragon with a purpose.

So, I could see him. And he could see me. I held my hands up again, this time shocked to see them in front of me. But with a strange red glow following wherever they moved.

Shoulders back, I marched after Rhesh. I stopped thinking with my mind.

I would think like a dragon.

Chapter 34

Tess

"I need you to get Vera away from here." I stood up, putting my hands on my hips.

Benny nodded. "All right. And what do you plan on doing?"

"He has my friends. A pregnant friend. I have to get them out of there."

"Why did he take your friends?"

I shook my head. "He wants me to find Quinn to get some damn book."

Benny grabbed my arm. "What book?"

I shrugged. "Who cares? I'm not going to let him torture my friends because Quinn started some horrible disaster."

"No, the book. What book?" His eyes were wide and confused.

"Some dragon book Quinn has. I don't know and don't really care."

Benny dropped my arm and put a hand to his forehead. He closed his eyes. "He thinks the book . . . That must be why . . ." And then he laughed. He actually laughed. Even Vera looked up at him questioningly.

"Can I ask what is funny at a time like this?" I stood with my hands on my hips, glowering at the man. "My friends could die for that book."

"No, it's not that," he gasped, standing upright, wiping tears from his eyes. "He thinks the book is important. He thinks the book tells him how to work the weapon."

I threw my hands in the air. "So what the hell does it do?" I did not have time for this.

"It was Corben's dying wish to protect that book. His memoir. I took it back to keep it from being destroyed. That's all. Nothing more."

"Took it where?"

He wiped at his nose, staring at the ground. "Through the link."

I gritted my teeth. "*You* took it back?" I threw my hands in the air. "Well, hell, I guess everyone has been through this damn portal. Why don't we just all go through and get the hell out of this place?"

"No, no, it's not that easy. You have to be on the right surface, in the right place, with the blood of a dragon." He sighed. "Apparently, in Quinn's world, she found these things."

"So Quinn actually took this link? Why?"

He shook his head. "I don't know. But somehow she had the blood of a dragon. And an ample supply of staphonite."

Dragon blood. The vial Luther gave me. "What is staphonite?"

"A kind of rock. Black, sort of magnetic. Crumbles easily. Combining it with the blood has a . . . unique effect." He shrugged, sitting down hard on the forest floor.

I took a silent breath. "Are you saying Quinn needs this rock to go back through the link?" I demanded.

He nodded. "But I don't know where she would find any."

I raised my eyebrows. "I do."

As I jogged, I thought about everything that had happened in the last few days. Quinn fell through the sky. Harlen died. Arik fell head over heels in love with the twig. Loic. Vera's brain nearly turned to mush. A thick layer of anger settled throughout my body, and by the time I made it up the steep hill toward the base, it was nearly boiling over.

She had lied. Again and again. She was the reason everything had happened, from Harlen dying to Liv and Sawyer being kidnapped. Because of her, my friends had been hurt and killed, my base compromised, and my best friend stolen.

After struggling up the cliff, nearly breaking my neck, and fighting my way through the thick of the forest, I stopped dead in my tracks. That smell. I knew that smell. A smell that wasn't uncommon to smell growing up in the compound, living next to the Svaris who breathed flames. But I hadn't smelled it so strong in four years. Fire. But it was more than that. It was like the burning of an entire building, the burning of supplies, of bunks, blankets.

The burning of my base.

I ran faster than I had ever run in my life. The closer I got, the more smoke I inhaled, the fumes assaulting my lungs. I climbed through the forest, my chest on fire, but I couldn't stop to cover my face. Limping up the hill, holding my side, I saw the very thing I feared.

The base was gone.

I fell onto the grass, staring at the place I left not a day ago. The very place I intended to return, the place I called home. Now, I stared at a smoldering pile of rubble. Bits of ash flaked through the air as I gasped, shaking my head, arguing with my brain about what I was seeing.

Random bricks still stood, outlining the building Arik and I found so many years ago. Charred, black bricks scattered across the scalded terrain. Where there had been tall grass and piles of firewood, a shed, proof of life, was now only . . . black. A small section of brick still stood upright, possibly big enough for a person to cower behind, praying they were not scorched to death. Benny's tree was gone with no evidence of the dirty white sheet that fluttered in the wind for years.

Even the krekels were silent. Perhaps they were in mourning for the food they would never be able to steal or the small tree they would never again shriek from.

Gear, backpacks, and a pile of blankets and sheets were piled off to the side, sitting out in the open, unprotected, waiting to be stolen or breathed fire upon.

I put both hands to my face. The church that I would have held base meetings in was now missing—the only evidence was a few benches turned on their sides and still-smoldering pieces of lumber.

I opened my mouth. But no sound came out. Gone. Everything . . . just gone.

"Tess!"

I turned toward the familiar voice. "Hash!" I coughed, stumbling toward him. I twisted my ankle on a small piece of my base and fell into his arms.

"What happened?" I asked into his shoulder, gripping his large frame. Never so badly had I needed someone to hold me together. Never so badly had I felt I was falling apart.

"The Svaris attacked," he said into my hair. "I tried to get everyone out, Tess. I tried, I swear." His voice was thick with tears. His words shook with the thoughts of a man who shouldered the responsibility for a disaster. For lost lives. But he was not the one responsible. Not even one bit.

I dropped my arms, using the sleeve of Arik's shirt to wipe my face. "Where is everyone?" I whispered, too afraid to turn back toward the scene.

He swallowed. The dark circles under his eyes shone against his red face. "I got the survivors down into the woods." He stared at what was once our home, what we had given everything to protect. "I'm sorry, Tess," he croaked, his head hanging.

"No." I grabbed his upper arms. "You did everything right. You never could have prevented this, Hash. Thank you for saving them." The look on his face made my eyes fill with tears. I pulled him into another hug, and he wrapped his arms around me tightly. "It wasn't your fault," I whispered into his trembling chest.

He shook his head into my shoulder. "It just happened. They surprised us. The lookout didn't even see it coming, there was no chance . . ." His voice cracked.

I squeezed him around the middle.

I didn't ask how many survived. I didn't want to know how many burned to death trying to escape the flames. How many dead bodies Hash had to sort through to find survivors. Instead, we stood there, arms around each other, letting each other fall apart.

I put my hand down on the dirt as I climbed up the steep hill. The sweat dripping down my forehead seeped into my eyes, blurring my vision. But I didn't stop to wipe it away. No, my pain and discomfort were well deserved. The scent of burned lives still hung heavy in the air. Destroyed hope. It smelled bitter.

I wanted that woman. The one who destroyed everything, demolished my base, killed my friends, and put everything I knew and loved in jeopardy. The girl had destroyed everything. Now, I would destroy her.

Then I wanted Luther. He sent those dragons—I had no doubt. He went back on our deal and set the dragons on my base when I followed his despicable orders. Why?

I wasn't sure. But I knew one thing. I was going to find that book, and I was going to burn it in his face. Then I would laugh.

Hash insisted on coming, wanting to help. But I told him to go be with the others who needed him now more than anything. They needed a real leader. I failed as that leader. Hash would do well for them. I knew that. I could not be the leader they deserved, the leader who could get them through times like this. Only because of my failure were they in the position they were in now, defenseless, homeless, and in danger. But it would not be without revenge.

I made it to the grassy landing, the large house in view. The same place where Arik and Quinn had sat and smiled. I had listened to them talk and watched him nudge her with his shoulder. Like he had done with me for the last eleven years. And it was in those few moments I knew Arik had moved on. He let me go, finally. After so many years of me flaunting men in his face, hurting him in a way I could never take back, he fell for my mirror image, with a huge scar across her face. Someone who would eventually get us all killed.

I remembered seeing the bulge in her shirt that morning at the meeting. I had wondered what she carried underneath the shirt Arik had dressed her in, probably one of his own. But at that moment, my mind immediately fluttered to the idea of Arik giving her something of his own, forgetting the bulge temporarily. Whatever it was, she didn't have it when she returned. That much I knew. I searched her myself that night while she slept.

This house remained a mystery. So much space. The extra furniture in every room that had probably never been used. The house smelled empty and unused. Forgotten. Without the essence of human beings, taken over by inanimate objects that would remain for the rest of years. Small, fragile things made of pottery and glass sat on shelves and dusty end tables as if their only purpose in life was to be beautiful. Who in the world could live like this? Pretty, breakable things lying about, covered in dust, things that had no real purpose?

We had taken the sheets and blankets from the house years ago, the ones that covered all the flowery chairs and sofas, and even the ones off the beds. Now the furniture sat caked in thick layers of dust and spiderwebs. Forgotten.

I ran a hand through my hair, wondering why she would have picked this place to hide a book. Why this house? I chewed on my bottom lip, remembering the first day we carried her to the base. She had crawled up the same hill I just did to stare at this house. But why?

I started looking under dust-covered furniture and between cushions. Pulled a wooden ladder away from the wall and searched behind the cobwebs. Nothing. Searched what was left of the kitchen and two other bedrooms. Pulled closets open, looking for any sign that the wench had been there. Not a fingerprint, a boot print, or any sign that the woman had set foot in this place.

I slammed the bedroom door shut, prepared to scream to the kings curse words, when it occurred to me. Only one door in this hall remained closed. The very last one. In four large strides, I was there, kicking the door in so hard I heard the tiny scurrying feet of rodents underneath me. She couldn't hide from me. I knew her better than she thought.

It was an office. Not that different from my father's office. A large desk and chairs. But where a bookshelf sat in my father's a padded bench sat here. I studied my surroundings, trying to think as The Twig would have. Yes, this room. It was here. I could feel it. I peeked under the desk and opened all the drawers, finding nothing but mice droppings. The painting on the wall showed a calm, flowery place with a glittering lake and a vibrant sunset. Where in the world could life be so peaceful? Turning in a slow circle, I examined the walls from top to bottom. Could this house have some secret tunnel running underneath? That would make things infinitely more difficult.

I put my hands on my hips, not enjoying the idea of searching on my hands and knees like I had done at my building. My eyes zeroed in on the flowery bench near the window. I took a step forward and picked up the top, not surprised to find out it was hollow.

A beaten-up, tattered copy of a book sat in the empty space, all alone. *Dragons Among Us*. Such an innocent-sounding phrase for murderous beasts. I bent slowly to pick up the thick, tattered text. The book everyone was willing to die for. My fingers gripped the edge of the book tightly, my anger growing as I stared at the drawing on the front cover. A Svari, with swirls of color stretching out from behind it, a beautiful rainbow of colors behind such a hideous beast. I stared at its arched neck and spread wings, my anger growing at the sight of it. It was being portrayed as some sort of beautiful, gentle creature. How could anyone write a book like this?

I flipped through the pages madly, practically ripping them from the spine. This? This was what Luther was willing to torture and imprison my friends for? I wanted to rip each one out and crumble it into little bits. Right in Quinn's face. Then I wanted to take her face and shove it into the ground over those pages. She thought she could come in, destroy my base, kill my friends and just breeze back through her little portal. *Nope*, I thought, shaking my head. She made this mess. She was damn well gonna stay here until she cleaned it up.

The yellowed pages crinkled as I flipped through them, obviously pages that had been read thousands of times. Scribbling and pen marks filled the sides of nearly every page. She had filled a book full of her own notes, written on the sides of pages, with random arrows, circles, and question marks. Why? I flipped through the pages faster, faster, gritting my teeth as more of her scribble appeared as if she had written her own damn book inside this book. A dragon lover. I gripped the book until my knuckles turned white, feeling that I could rip it in half this very second if I really wanted to. But I made myself take a deep breath. I would wait. I would destroy it in front of Luther and Quinn, and enjoy it. Thinking of the looks on their faces as the precious pages fluttered to the ground gave me a small bit of satisfaction. Yes. I would wait.

I turned to leave and stopped. Flipped open the front cover. I ran my fingers down the front cover, over the black ink, the curly, fancy writing—barely legible. My finger stopped over the short line of scrawl in the bottom corner. The last word was the only thing I could make out as I stared at the faded ink.

Quintessa.

Chapter 35

Quinn

"We will draw them into the woods," Rhesh said as we strode toward the cluster of green giants. They were completely unaware of the marching Redwing with the human who ran to keep up.

"Right." I nodded, panting. Shouldn't be too difficult. I was invisible. But for how long?

A gate stood in the fence behind the grouped giants, leading right into the forest. Seemed like an odd place to have a gate, but whatever the reason, its position in this field today would prove useful. Using my newly conceived powers while hiding in the trees seemed like a much better idea than using them in a wide-open field.

The closer we got to the Svaris, the faster my heart pounded. My self-confidence in these newly gifted powers waned, and my determined jogging slowed. The dragons could not see me, no, but would they hear me? Rhesh wasn't bothering to keep his voice down, but that didn't surprise me. He was a dragon on the edge, put there by my words of encouragement.

The Svaris were enormous. Not as large as their queens, of course, but giant in a more menacing sort of way. Longer horns, more spikes, and their claws sharper. All a shade of green, similar to Selyse, but could not look more different. I sniffed as I hurried behind Rhesh, then blew out the air I had sucked into my nose, trying not to cough. Apparently, males smell more of overcooked meat than they did ambrosia, like Selyse.

Compared to them, Rhesh looked about the size of a house cat. I looked over at him as we neared the Svaris, but all I saw in his eyes was fury. Perhaps he was missing the big picture here . . . There were at least six Svaris in the herd, and we were two. A jittery human and a dragon as big as one of their claws.

I froze to the spot as a Svari roared at another, no actual fire coming out of his mouth, but black smoke curling out of his nostrils. My hands flew to my ears as another roared back, again with only the aftermath of a true flame, but making the ground we stood on tremble. Panting, I watched with wide eyes as they all crawled around each other, low to the ground, acting as if they were ready to strike. Great wings stretched wide, making me gasp.

When Rhesh didn't slow, I cleared my throat. "Maybe we should just let them fight? Maybe they'll attack each other?"

He scoffed. "What a pity. Fighting Svaris only assists in our plan. It could not be more perfect."

I opened my mouth to protest, but my shoulders sagged. He could not be stopped. If I had known how easily this dragon's anger and pride fluctuated, I would not have gone so far in my speech over his queen.

He finally stopped right outside the group of angry Svaris. I stopped further back, looking around wildly, positive I was feeling the beginnings of a heart attack. What if my powers stopped right here, leaving my powerless body for dragons to feed on? What in God's name had I been thinking when I walked through the fence of the resting place of evil, limb-ripping dragons?

Rhesh turned and looked at me. "They are completely occupied," he called to me, his voice dripping with annoyance. "Look."

At least, that looked true. For the moment. "You're invisible," I gasped to myself, with my hand to my chest. "You're invisible."

It took me at least a minute to reach Rhesh ten feet away. He reached back and grabbed my arm, pulling me the rest of the way. I stood with my shoulders back, too frightened to breathe, so close to a roaring dragon I had to turn my head so as not to inhale the black smoke.

Gaping up at the Svari next to me, I realized with a start I had forgotten how to make fire. I stared down at my hands as Rhesh spoke to me in a low voice. My heart fluttered. I couldn't do this. Whatever he wanted me to do, I couldn't do it. I couldn't fight a dragon. I was a young woman who couldn't even throw a punch. Why the hell did I think I could take on a fleet of Svari?

"Are you listening?" Rhesh snapped beside me.

"W-what?" I stuttered, gazing at him stupidly.

He glowered at me, maybe for the first time realizing how stupid his plan was. But he adjusted quickly. "We will run through the center of the group, leaving a trail of flames. Through the gate, into the forest, where we will attack. Is that clear?"

"What? No," I cried hysterically. "I can't attack a dragon. I'm barely five feet tall! I can't—"

"Size has nothing to do with it," he interrupted. "Redwings have fought Svaris in battle numerous times and left victorious. It's about remaining in motion and confusing them. In the trees, they will be forced to stay on the ground to search for us. They are clumsy fools, and being small will only work to your advantage. You will stay hidden nicely and can attack from anywhere you please."

"R-right." I took a deep breath, nodding. "Right." Small, invisible, and fire. I could be in a damn tree the whole time. Right.

He nodded at me, then clapped the talons on his hands together. "To begin."

Without another word, Rhesh took off, running on two legs through the middle of the herd. I yelped and stumbled after him, refusing to get stuck alone in this smoke-filled field.

As I trailed behind him, I saw the flames draw out of his back. Then he turned, running right back to where we had come from, his flames glowing even brighter. He turned again, and again, a fireball running in an odd-shaped pattern between the bellowing dragons.

Finally, I stopped since running after him seemed useless. The dragon fight around us stilled. I expected Rhesh to head for the gate, but instead, the fireball turned and headed for the largest Svari—and did not stop.

I watched in horror as Rhesh collided with the Svari's underbelly. The dragon launched backward on his two legs, letting out a howl that made me clap a hand over my mouth. Enough was enough. I ran for the gate into the woods, waiting for the scalding flames or the teeth of a Svari to pick me off and swallow me whole.

I fumbled with the black gate, pulling at the hot metal with sweaty hands. The latch was on the top of the fence, far too high for my reach. I tugged at the metal desperately, clanking it back and forth. Shit, if I could not even get the gate open—

"What are you doing?" Rhesh yelled.

Before I could answer, my feet were lifted off the ground. I felt the alien sensation of metal bars passing through my body, and less than a second later, my butt met the hard ground.

"Go!" Rhesh yelled again, from somewhere already far away.

My brain snapped to attention as I struggled to my feet and ran for my life. I fell into the woods and grabbed a large tree around the trunk, cowering behind it. The snap of a metallic gate and the rumbling of the earth followed as Svaris crowded into the forest.

The oversized dragons clashed, causing the trees to crack and be trampled underfoot. Rhesh was right about one thing—they acted quite clumsy and disoriented, running into one another, trees smacking them on the scales. A few gave up the attack position and leaped into the air to stretch their wings, hovering far above us.

Rhesh wasted no time. He had the Svaris on the ground surrounded in flames within seconds. They fell toward each other, trampling each other and roaring. I watched from the safety of my tree as they scrambled around on their rear ends and fell on top of each other to get up.

"Now!"

I looked around wildly for Rhesh, hearing my instructions but not understanding them.

"Fire!" he yelled after a moment.

Right. Right. I looked at my hands, trying desperately to focus my brain. *Fire,* I tried to think. *Fire.* I squeezed my eyes shut as I felt the rumble of the surrounding ground. My hands warmed slowly, much too slowly. I squeezed my teeth together, begging my brain to work. Tears of frustration, confusion, and pure terror began leaking out as I bent and screamed at my hands.

There! A spark! I gritted my teeth and closed my eyes again, taking a deep breath. I could do it. There was no choice. I had to do it.

"Get down!"

I turned toward Rhesh's voice when I was shoved to the ground. I cried out as the small of my back burned, throwing my arms over my head.

"Shit!" I crawled on all fours as I heard the cracking above me.

Claws grabbed at my wrist and dragged me across the dirt, filling my mouth with dirt. The cracking sounded right above me. I tried to scream but only choked on dirt, coughing and retching. As the tree came down, sounding as if it was bringing the rest of the forest with it, I could only curl into a ball and scream. The thunderous boom and rush of wind came not two feet from my face.

Crawling again, I found a tree trunk and held on, trying to look at my hands and conjure fire power I knew I did not have while ducking flames and covering my head. The heat flying in all directions was intense, burning my lungs and making my eyes sting. What was I doing? Where was Rhesh?

Everywhere I looked, fire swarmed—high in the trees and all over the ground. I hugged my cheek to the tree, whispering words only I could hear in this scene of mass destruction. I wanted it over. Done. *Take me back, let me go home, just let it be over.* I repeated my silent prayer over and over again, hoping maybe somewhere someone would hear me. Anyone.

It took me a few minutes to realize the rumbling and trampling of dragons had ceased. Except for the crackling of the flames, it was quiet.

Turning my head slowly, but unwilling to let go of my tree, I gulped. A circle of Svaris crouched, huddled around something. Something smaller than them. Oh, no.

Forcing myself to stand, I crept through the flames and falling ash. Glancing up at the dragon, I peeked under a wing, trying not to get too close to the sweating scales. Was Rhesh alive? Did he die because I could not help him? Biting my lower lip, I forced myself to take a deep breath. Then another. Clear my mind.

—think one Redwing can defeat an entire fleet of Svaris?

Yes. I heard Rhesh's low growl back at them. *It has been done before. Clumsy fools are not difficult to overcome.*

Is that so, Redwing? Why is it you stand at the center of our flock, useless and near death?

Better than part of your pathetic warrior faction, Rhesh growled.

What shall his punishment be, Brothers? Beheading? Burn him alive? Or shall we divide him up for an evening meal?

My eyes widened as I crept between two snorting Svaris as they blew dust and dried leaves with their laughter. Oh, God. They were going to eat him alive. Swallowing hard, I glanced up. They were quite preoccupied.

The largest of the group had Rhesh by his wings, down on his knees. Another was holding Rhesh's head down on the ground, probably so he couldn't spit fire.

I took a deep breath and readied myself, trying to calm my shaking hands. Oh, God, what could I do? I could feel the beads of sweat inching their way down my back, which had nothing to do with the heat and flames still filling the area.

The Svaris began shoving Rhesh back and forth, then using their feet to smash him into the ground. I clapped a hand over my mouth as a Svari picked him up by the neck and slashed him across the chest with razor-sharp claws, making a large *X* on his chest and spurting green blood all over the forest floor.

Rhesh did not cry out or even flinch as blood poured from his chest. They snorted more and threw him on the ground, one still holding a clawed foot in his back. He didn't move as he lay in the dirt, and I watched in horror as the green blood began leaking out from underneath him.

I couldn't take it any longer. I wouldn't watch this dragon die after I had failed to help him. Without thinking, I jumped between the two Svaris and landed over Rhesh. The snorting immediately ceased.

"What are you doing?" Rhesh coughed into the ground.

"They can't see me, remember? Now let's go!" I panted, grabbing his arm and pulling. I stopped and glanced up at the enormous green giant staring back at me. Something was not right.

Rhesh rolled over on his back to display the neon green blood. The forest had gone silent. Even the crackling of the flames seemed to be in some strange, awed silence. "Of course they can see you. We are not camouflaged," he said through gritted teeth.

With a sinking heart, I looked at the blood. Of course, we weren't camouflaged. They were holding Rhesh by the wings. Knocking him around. If they could see him . . .

They could see me.

"Just close your eyes," Rhesh muttered next to me, barely audible.

So I did.

CHAPTER 36

Tess

My hands shook as I stared inside the cover. I took a deep breath and closed my eyes, trying not to care what I had just read. I had the stupid book. The book that Luther wanted. I could easily take it back to him, free Liv and Sawyer, and get them the hell out of Port Tarrith.

I didn't care what name was written inside the cover. So we had the same name, so what? All that meant was our parents had equally poor taste in names. That was all.

A loud thump outside startled me. My hand automatically reached for my blade.

I strode out of the room, hackles raised. Someone was outside. Even in the hallway, I could hear the shrill voices. Angry voices. Narrowing my eyes, I tucked the book in my waistband, and stepped into the front room. Two voices, shouting at each other. Sounded like someone was about to get their ass kicked. I rubbed my fist on the dusty window to get a view of the front yard.

And I could not believe what I saw.

Quinn. The matted brown curls were a dead giveaway. She was covered in a green metallic liquid. Dragon blood. The same blood Benny and I stood covered in so few hours ago. And she looked pissed. But who was she yelling at? Cursing myself for not having grown taller, I grabbed a dusty chair and dragged it to the window. I hopped up, getting a full view of the front yard of the house. I gasped, nearly falling right out of the damned chair.

A Redwing. It had to be a Redwing. First, well, it was red. Much smaller than a Svari. My mind went back to the rolled-up drawings in the file cabinet. The long back legs. Standing upright, on two legs, similar to a human. The claws that protruded from the heels of their feet. I breathed in a huff of dusty air, my mouth resting on the dirty window. Something didn't make sense.

For one thing, Quinn was yelling at it. For another, it roared back, leaning down to get in her face. Why didn't she run away? Where were the tears streaming down her face, and why weren't her skinny legs pumping to get away from a monster? That was what I expected from The Twig. I raised my eyebrows as I watched the screaming match, wondering what could possess the woman to set loose on a Redwing.

Hopping off my chair, I threw open the door, blade still in hand. The human and dragon screaming at each other under the tree didn't notice me standing on the porch, arms crossed, watching their tantrum from a safe distance.

The Redwing held her in the air by the arm, her black boots dangling as she struggled against him. "You are weak and could never handle the powers of a Redwing. To think, I traded an *oath* with you," he roared.

Quinn's face went crimson. Her face moved toward his, the spit landing on the dragon's face as she screamed back. "If I am so damn weak, why did you insist that I be the one to kill you? Why? Why not Arik? Why me?"

The dragon finally dropped her to the ground, tossing her easily. She landed in the grass with a thud, but she clambered back to her feet, running to be within grasp of the dragon.

I gave a little gasp as she planted her hands on his scales and shoved. The Redwing remained still.

"Why? Huh? Are your spooky dragon senses so horrible that you could not sense the weak little girl two feet in front of you?"

I raised my eyebrows. I hated to admit it, but I was slightly impressed. And confused. My heart jumped a bit when she mentioned Arik's name but dropped back into place. And who had to kill who? If I was hearing things right, it sounded like the Redwing wanted Quinn to kill him. The Twig, of all people.

I shook my head. Apparently, I had missed a long conversation. I leaned against the porch as Quinn used her fists on the giant, not even making a scratch on his scales.

"It would seem my senses misguided me. All the more reason you should have killed me when you agreed to," he said, the white of his teeth glistening in the afternoon sun.

Quinn put her head back and laughed. "You know, for a Redwing, you are not much of a dragon. More like an indignant, impulsive, whining child! No wonder the Svaris foiled our plan."

My eyes widened as I saw the smoke coming out of his nostrils. No flames yet, but they would be soon. A plan? With the Redwing? That the Svaris foiled?

I cleared my throat as I stepped into the yard. "What's going on here?"

The Redwing leaned in to be in her face. "The Svaris foiled our plan because you failed as a warrior. Because you couldn't follow simple instructions. You are a more pathetic warrior than they are. You could not even make *fire*."

"I never *claimed* to be a warrior who could make fire. And thanks to your great warrior plan, we ended up all the way back here, too far from Vera and Arik to get them back. Why the hell did you bring us here?"

The Redwing looked positively murderous. "I reached for the first place in your mind. I brought you here so you were not filleted and eaten." He put his claws in the air as if he was praying to a dragon god. "To think, I disappeared in the middle of a battle. If one of my brothers were to hear I chose to save a *human* instead of staying to face punishment, I would be scorned for all time. I might as well kill myself now."

"Then go ahead!" Quinn screamed back.

I did not appreciate being ignored. Sighing, I grabbed my blade and took aim. I flung the knife straight for the tree they were standing under. It hit the bark straight on, right in front of Quinn's nose, flicking scraps of wood into the dragon's face.

Both stopped screaming and jumped back, looking around wildly. The Redwing's enormous head swung toward me, and his eyes glowered. The look on his face almost made me take a step back. But if little Quinn could handle this Redwing, then by divine, I could.

"Tess?" Quinn looked at me with a green and black-streaked face. "What are you doing here?"

I crossed my arms. "Just trying to clean up the mess you created. And I got here just in time to see my base destroyed."

"What?" A hand flew to her mouth. "Destroyed? Why?"

Reaching behind me, I pulled out the book from my waistband. I threw it at her feet. "Because of you."

Quinn looked down at the book, then back at me. She closed her eyes. "Oh, no."

"Oh, yes." I stepped toward her. "And Luther is holding two of my team members hostage until I get that stupid book for him. Who knows what the hell he could do to a pregnant woman and her husband?"

She closed her eyes. "Oh, no, no, no . . . I'm so sorry," she whispered, shaking her head. "What do we do?"

I put my nose even with hers. "You have done enough."

Then I punched her in the face.

She cried out and fell back, landing in the weeds, green blood spurting from her face. She wiped her nose and looked at the green smeared on her hand. "What—what the hell was that for?"

"For Harlen. For Vera." I jumped on her as she tried to stand up, shoving her back down in the grass. "For Liv and Sawyer. " With every name I yelled, I hit her again. "For my base."

She struggled underneath me, reaching for my face. But I wouldn't let her go. I held her by the neck, enjoying the feel of my fingers tightening around her throat.

"For Arik!" I screamed before I could stop myself.

She rolled underneath me, shoving me sideways. Before I could right myself, I felt her knuckles on my jaw. My head snapped back at the sudden and unexpected blow.

She let out a scream and dove on top of me. "You never cared about Arik! Never!" She threw her fist at me again, hitting me square in the forehead.

I swung my fist at her, hitting nothing but air. The Twig had more muscle than I gave her credit for. I brought up a knee in her stomach and we rolled through the weeds, running smack into the large tree.

"Quintessa!"

The voice echoed through the field we lay tangled in. I gripped Quinn's shirt in my fist while both her hands yanked at my hair. For a moment, our eyes met. We both knew that voice. Shoving her off me, I looked around, still on my knees in the scratchy weeds. Luther. He was near. I started to stand, ready to beat the living shit out of the man.

"Get down!"

Quinn grabbed my wrist and yanked me behind the tree. "He's in the Keep," she murmured, glancing around the trunk.

"In the what?" I followed her gaze down and to the side, where the large fenced-off area was.

"I have something you would be interested in, Quintessa!"

"He is joined by the Svaris," the Redwing breathed into my ear.

I jumped and had my hand on my blade when Quinn put a hand on my arm.

"It's okay," she muttered, staring down at the "keep." "He's not, uh," she shook her head, "your typical Redwing."

She received a low growl from behind but only rolled her eyes.

I glanced back at the Redwing, then back at Quinn, my heart still thumping. I cleared my throat and tossed my hair back.

"He has Vera," Quinn moaned, her cheek pressed against the side of the massive tree. "Oh, shit, he has Vera."

"Answer me, Quintessa! Or would you rather your mother bear the weight of your insolence?"

"What do we do?" Quinn's voice shook.

The last thing I needed right now was tears. "Will you shut up a minute? I'm trying to think."

Quinn gasped beside me. "Wait! Do you know if these Svaris have an excess of iron in their blood?"

I looked at her as if she had just sprouted another head. "Are you insane?"

She shook her head. "No, no, it's important, I swear! Do you know if they have excessive iron in their blood?"

"How in the hell would I know?" I asked through gritted teeth.

Quinn ran her hands through her hair. "No, no, um . . . food! What do they eat?"

I stared at her through narrow eyes. "Why?"

"Could you just trust me this once? Please?" She glanced back down at the gated field and then turned to me. "Think. What do they eat besides humans?"

"Anything. Everything They're total pricks." I ran a hand through my hair, my frustration and anger quickening my headache.

Quinn grabbed my face in her hands and pulled me to her. "Tess. Think."

I fought to keep my face away from hers. "I don't know, cattle? That's the only thing we have enough of around here—"

"Yes!" she cried, grabbing my hands. "Cattle! I think I have a plan! But"—she swallowed—"we'll all have to work together."

I stood outside the gate, holding the book in my hands. Luther stood behind Vera, on the other side of the field, staring at me. A gleaming blade pressed against her throat, but even in the face of death, her shoulders were back and her eyes were still. She did not look afraid. Pale-Face stood at Luther's side, and four Svaris crowded around him. Not the biggest Svaris I had seen, but still bigger than I was.

I lifted the latch and entered the "keep." I pulled it shut tightly behind me, waiting until I heard the soft click.

Throwing my hair back, I marched toward Luther. The look on his face made my insides burn. Satisfaction. He thought by threatening my mother and bringing a couple of dragons, I would beg at his feet. How wrong he was. My glare settled on him as I walked through the brush. He didn't scare me. Neither did his fleet of dragons. Fine. Eat me alive, you horrid beasts. But I had no intention of bowing down to *him*.

Quinn swore this plan would work. Something about iron in their blood, something about a fail-safe? I had absolutely no clue what she was talking about. And did not know how she would know about this magnetic fail-safe. But it was the only plan we had at the moment. I had to trust her. I had no choice. But at least her plan involved me taking down my father. That was the one part of this plan I agreed on.

Pushing through the overgrown grass, I stopped at what I imagined a dozen yards to be.

Luther smiled at me. "I'm glad to see you, Quintessa."

Vera stood in front of him, jaw tight. A bruise was forming around her left eye. That son of a bitch. I took a deep breath. I had to keep it together. For just a little longer.

"Not glad to see you, Luther." He never liked that I called him Luther, and I liked that.

"Give me the book."

I crossed my arms. "Let go of Vera."

Pale-Face's hand lifted from his side, leaning toward me. Luther turned his head, glancing back toward him. His little errand boy stepped back.

"A brave young girl you are, Quintessa. Either you give me the book now, or I let my flock of Svari go, and they can take you and your mother. And then I will take the book."

I tried not to squirm. I needed to waste more time. Quinn said she needed at least ten minutes to get where she was going.

"You never could face anyone alone, could you, Luther? Always had to have a fleet of dragons on your side. Scared of your own daughter."

I tried to keep down the revulsion I felt when I used the word. Calling myself his daughter made me nauseous.

"Fortunately, Quintessa, your opinion has never been of high value to me. Perhaps it is the father in me, willing to give into your childish games."

"Games? Like the burning of my base? That kind of game?" My voice shook at the thought. For a moment, I completely forgot our plan. "We had a deal, Luther. You lied. You went back on your word."

"Our deal was your friends for the book. I never said you could take your mother."

I swallowed. I should have known. Dealing with tyrants never ended well. I let him have the control.

"I could simply kill you and your mother. But I will trade. Now give me the book."

This was going much too fast. Maybe I should have walked slower.

"What do you not understand, Quintessa?" he asked slowly. "Give me the damn book." He pressed the blade of the steel into Vera's throat.

I took a breath in when I saw the red drip onto the blade. Damn. I hated it when he won.

Chapter 37

Quinn

I dashed through the weeds next to the wrought-iron fence, trying to keep up with Rhesh. He ran ahead of me on all fours, making a god-awful racket. I prayed Tess could keep Luther and the Svaris on edge long enough so that they wouldn't notice the disturbance in the field behind them.

It was a snap decision. We needed to get to the far south side of the Keep for my plan to work. And we could go camouflaged, as my newly found dragon power allowed.

But there was a flaw to this plan I hadn't expected. It was a much farther trip around the backside of the barrier than I thought. From our previous position up on the hill, everything had appeared doable, but now? Ten minutes. I had told Tess to give me ten minutes. That might have been a bit of an understatement on my part.

We made it to the back of the Keep, right behind the pond they would have drank out of in my world. Where Luther stood with a knife pointed at Vera, surrounded by his flock.

Up ahead, I saw Rhesh slow and glance to the left—inside the Keep. I could only imagine the vivid thoughts running through that deranged mind of his. Dreams of stretching his arm twenty feet to grab a Svari by the throat and roast their private parts. What was I thinking? He could just walk through the damn bars.

Miraculously, he kept it together. I dashed after him, pushing up the sleeves of my shirt as I ran. The late afternoon sun beat down on me, even invisible, and I would've given the boots on my feet for something to hold my ridiculously wild hair back.

As we passed behind the scene playing out in the Keep, Tess's voice played through the air at a condescending level. I gave her one look through the bars and could tell she was struggling. I tried to send her good thoughts as I tripped through the tall grass and weeds. Just be a bitch, Tess. For a little while longer.

By the time we made it to the south side, I was holding a hand to my side. My lungs hinged on the brink of collapse, and I could hear my heart beating in my ears. I needed a second to stop and breathe but had no extra seconds to give.

Rhesh was already combing the ground, searching for something that I couldn't even describe. "What am I searching for?" he asked as I fell to the ground in front of him.

"I don't know," I wheezed. "Some kind of lever . . . or something." I stood up, leaning on the fence. "I've never actually seen it."

He rolled his large dragon eyes up into his head. "Humans."

I opened my mouth to snap back, but changed my mind. Later. Hopefully. I began crawling on my hands and knees, combing through the underbrush, searching for anything that could create a force throughout the Keep that would render a Svari unconscious.

I had done extensive research on the thing only a few weeks ago. The fail-safe method, if the tower wasn't responsive. To use in the Dragon Keep in case of emergency. There should be a manual switch on this side that would start the deadly, magnetic current if the need ever arose. You would think I would have some idea of what the damn thing looked like. It could be the size of a damn fly or as big as the Svari I was trying to defeat.

Solar-powered. Powered by the sun. I had been terribly impressed with that idea when I read it, in a sick kind of way. It ran under the Keep and stayed connected to the solar-powered fence. Too powerful and too dangerous to just remove. Luther had made that clear the many times I had questioned him about it. *No wonder they fed them those kinds of cattle*, I thought to myself as I scrambled through the weeds. They needed more iron in their bodies. It made so much sense now. Those collars weren't connected to the fail-safe. It was the dragons themselves.

"It is not here," Rhesh growled.

"No, no, it has to be," I said, sweeping through the weeds frantically. "It has to be!" Thoughts of what could happen, what *would* happen, if I screwed this up, filled my mind. More pain, death, and heartache. Because of me. I mentally shoved the thoughts down, the same way Tess had shoved my face in the dirt. It only made sense that it was here. It would be here. I knew it was. *God, tell me I know it is.*

"And you said this lever would do what?"

"It sends a magnetic current through the Keep that is aimed at the Svari. It will render them unconscious," I gasped, shoving the hair out of my face. "Are you going to help me or just stand there?" I said through gritted teeth.

But for the first time, he looked thoughtful. He tapped a claw against his chin and studied the fence next to us.

Shaking my head, I went back to the weeds. I didn't have time for this. I didn't want to admit it. But what little hope I had was dwindling, turning from that great big flame I should have been able to make into a tiny, pathetic spark too far out of my reach. But I swallowed my tears. Tess was still in there, with a flock of angry male Svari and Vera. I couldn't give up on them now.

Rhesh had given up on our search and was leaning against the fence. I forced myself to take deep breaths. Turn my anger into fuel. Energy. If that piece of filth Redwing didn't want to help, well then—

"What do you gather this is?"

I looked up, clambered to my feet, and fell against the fence, letting myself close my eyes in relief for less than a microsecond.

Rhesh was staring at the black fence, his claw scraping against a flat black piece that stuck out. He had found the lever. It was on the damn fence, not sticking up out of the ground.

We both stared at it for just a moment, then looked at each other. Suddenly, the urge to vomit came hurtling back. I bit down on my lip, thinking of all the things that could go wrong. What if this was one more time I screwed everything up? I put my palm on my forehead. I had the chance to save the day. Kill Svaris, save my mother, and save Tess. But what if I could do none of those things?

"What are you waiting for?" he asked me crossly.

I nodded, putting a piece of hair behind my ear. "Right." I gripped the flat black metal in my hand, squeezed my eyes shut, and flipped it downward.

Nothing. After a moment, I opened my eyes.

Rhesh stood staring at me, arms crossed, eyes ablaze. "Well?"

I turned to stare at the scene playing out in the Keep. By now, Tess's condescending tone was turning to one of desperation. Vera lay on the ground in front of Luther, not moving. And every single Svari still stood, completely unharmed and poised to attack.

"It . . . didn't work," I said, my head feeling light. I closed my eyes. What had I done?

"Why did you think it would?" Rhesh asked.

"I-I don't know. It's controlled by the sun. Why wouldn't it?" I put a hand on my forehead.

"In a world where dragons are prisoners, correct? Dragons are not prisoners here."

I let that sink in a moment. But that meant . . . What did that mean?

It meant we were screwed. I had sent Tess on a suicide mission. I would almost welcome her to punch me at the moment. God knew I deserved it. I shook my head, forcing away the heat behind my eyes. I could not leave her to die alone. Not without at least trying.

"Fly me over there."

His nostrils flared as he glowered at me.

"Please. I have to do something!"

"And what do you plan on doing?"

"Well, I won't know 'til I get there, now will I?" I moved to stand behind him. "Please, Rhesh. Please. I need your help." I didn't want to beg. But I would.

He stilled for a moment, then sighed. "Fine," he muttered. He crouched down for me to jump on his back. I climbed on awkwardly, grabbing at him around the thick neck. "If you tell any of my brethren I let a human on my back, you will be sorry."

"Deal," I said breathlessly. "Now go!"

He jumped up so fast I nearly throttled him. We adjusted quickly, and he soared up and over the black fence, flying low and fast toward the group of Svari.

Dragon heads began to turn. The Svari crouched in attack position, ready to take out a flying predator and his rider.

"They can see us!" I yelled, my only advantage in this situation fluttering away like a feather in the wind.

"Camouflage only works with claws on the ground!" he yelled back.

I gritted my teeth as we flew. That would have been nice to know.

Almost immediately, the Svaris reared back, and fire shot toward us like flaming arrows flew through the air. Rhesh dove as I screamed, covering my head with my hands. The heat burned my side as I had been hanging over a fire myself. The smell of burned hair was near, next to me, maybe on top of me. I began smacking at my head wildly, my mind temporarily forgetting what flew between my legs. I lost my grip and fell to the ground, landing on my back.

"Quinn!" a voice called out to me as I lay in the field. I opened and closed my breath, trying to grasp hold of the air I knew was floating all around me. Finally, in a choking cough, I drew in a gulp of precious air, holding my hands to my throat. I rolled to stand on my knees, prepared to throw up on any approaching dragon.

Vera was on her knees with Luther's hand on her neck. It was her voice that had called to me. The Svaris stood around Luther, protecting him from the two five-foot-nine young women. I had never been growled at this many Svaris before. Well, at least not in the last half hour. It was enough to make anyone weak in the knees.

I tried to look brave and purposeful as I made my way toward the pond where the Svaris stood. I stopped next to Tess, holding my chin high. At least I would die with dignity.

"I guess your plan didn't work," she muttered.

"Not exactly," I coughed.

Rhesh had limped to join us, standing next to me. Smoke curled out of his nose as he huffed. I glanced at him, wincing as I saw the blackened scales down his back leg. The wound glistened with glowing green but was apparently not healing fast enough. The three of us stared at the crowd in front of us, the air thick and tense, as if someone was going to lunge at the other at any moment. Quite a possibility.

"My, my," Luther said with that horrible smile. "Quite the rebel group."

Three of us versus an entire fleet of Svari. Four hungry Svaris stared us down, practically licking their chops in delight.

A spark caught my eye, far behind the group of dragons. The fence. It was sparking. Coming to life. I glanced at Rhesh, but his eyes were locked on the Svaris in front of us.

If only I could—What? Use my special tools to fix an electric fence capable of destroying Svaris? My knees wobbled. The fence. I needed it to work. Now.

"Drop the blades, Quintessa. Now."

Silence. With a sigh, Tess grabbed the two blades around her back and threw them into the ground.

"Now, give me the book."

Glaring, she bent and picked up the book from the ground. She threw it at him, and I tried not to wince at the sound of pages flapping in the wind. My most prized possession landed at his feet, lying wide open.

Luther bent to grab the book. At the same moment, I snatched Tess's blade out of the soil and threw it as hard as I could toward the black fence.

Miraculously, the blade flew right through the group of dragons and hit the black steel with another spark. Everyone looked up as a loud creaking happened all around us.

It was at that second I wished I could take back throwing that damn knife.

The black gate shook and began to hum with a terrible screeching noise running through each post.

"Get down!" I shrieked, falling on top of Tess.

Even Luther took my advice, and we fell to the ground as lightning shot out of each post, aiming for the four Svari gathered around Luther.

The screeches they made as the current connected with their scales made my eyes water. I threw my hands over my ears to block out the sound of dragons being electrocuted. The ground shook as each Svari fell in a heap, a heap of Svaris, all around Luther.

I looked up as the dust settled, confused and guilty. My body was jerked back down to the ground as heat spread on top of us, warming the air like only a dragon's fire could. The fence. It had not been strong enough.

The Svaris lay on the ground, unable to flap their wings or stand, but could still produce flames.

"Run!" Rhesh roared, jumping in front of me and Tess and blowing fire back toward the Svaris.

"Vera!" Tess and I both yelled. I leaped toward what I hoped was Vera, keeping my hands over my eyes and my body bent. "Vera!"

I grabbed her wrist at the same time Luther tackled me to the ground, pinning my shoulders down. My face met the ground again, and I tried to cry out as Luther shoved my face into the weeds, the familiar taste being forced down my throat.

Jamming my elbow back, I connected with Luther's gut with a satisfying thud. The weight on top of me lightened as another thud and grunt happened behind me. I spun to see him fall backward as Tess kicked him in the face. I reached to snatch the book off the ground, but jerked back as a flame nearly incinerated me.

"Come on!" Tess yelled from somewhere behind me.

I turned and ran awkwardly toward her voice, falling on my knees as I reached Vera, shaking her shoulders. Tess grabbed her under one arm, and I grabbed her other. We ran at an uncomfortable angle, dragging Vera and occasionally falling to the ground. I felt the heat die away as we made our way toward the front gate.

Something wasn't right. Had Rhesh defeated them all? Wiped out a fleet of Svari all alone?

While Tess yanked at the gate, I turned back toward the fighting. "Tess!" I yelled as she pulled at the gate. "Look!"

She stopped long enough to look over her shoulder. This time, it was her mouth that dropped open. The Svaris backed into the pond, a circle of fire holding them in. Rhesh was there, on all fours, but there was more. Fire was being blown toward the Svari from every direction. And Arik was standing right behind them.

I wanted to jump with joy. "The Redwings!"

"The book!" Vera coughed.

Vera turned, leaving my grasp, and stumbled back toward the Svaris—back toward Luther. My book still lay on the charred grass in the middle of the firefight. Tess and I ran after her, jumping around, dodging the orange flames still alive on the ground. I dashed past Rhesh, despite his protests. I grabbed the book on my knees as another hand grabbed it as well.

The cold blue eyes met mine. "You haven't won, Quintessa," he said hoarsely, blood running from his nose.

Before I could answer, he sliced the top of my hand. Green blood sprayed out directly into his eyes. He fell back, crying out and rubbing furiously at his eyes. I shoved him in the stomach with every ounce of remaining strength I had.

He fell back into the pond, his fancy suit nearly incinerated by the flames circling the Svaris. Before I could stop myself, I picked up the knife and ran it across my forearm, spraying bright green all over the rock.

"The weapon!" Vera coughed, reaching out and grabbing Luther's blue jacket as he fell.

"No!" Tess screamed next to me. Or was it me that was screaming?

I reached for her as Luther screamed. The earth shook as light struck out of the ground, all around the empty pond. Tess and I dove to the ground, hands over our heads as multiple claps of thunder reverberated in my ears, over and over, until I was sure the ground I crouched on had to be split into pieces.

I held my hands to my ears as the thunder quieted, the shaking calmed, and the smell of burned earth filled the quiet air.

After a moment, a cool breeze wafted through the area, lifting my matted hair off my sweating neck. Still shaking, I lowered my hands and dared to open my eyes. Taking in a strangled breath, I looked around with my mouth hanging open.

The flames around the pond had disappeared, sucked into the earth. Even the mad flames around us had vanished, leaving behind a trail of scorched earth. It was gone. Not just the empty pond. Luther had disappeared, along with all the Svaris around him. Where the black, empty pond had once filled the ground, now crispy land, burned to the soil, stretched all the way back to the fence.

"Mom?" Tess yelled. "Vera?"

I looked around, fear gripping my insides.

Vera was gone, too.

"Mom!" Tess screamed, her hands on the side of her face. "Mom!"

I stared at my hands. The green blood that dripped from my hands shone brightly, almost sparkling.

The link. Dragon's blood. On the Dead Rock . . . Dead Rock . . . The pond. It had taken him through the link. But he hadn't gone alone.

"Quinn!" Arik yelled, falling next to me. "Are you all right?"

"I'm fine," I whispered, still staring at my hands. "Vera . . . she's gone."

Tess was standing, staring at the charred earth where her mother had stood only moments ago. I closed my eyes and fell into Arik, wondering what in the world I had just done.

Redwings began appearing all around us. Rhesh offered me his hand. When I didn't take it, he grabbed my wrist and pulled me to my feet.

"You have defeated him," he said. "Perhaps you are better in battle than I once thought."

I swallowed thickly, looking up at him. "Ready for me to kill you?" I asked shakily.

He cocked his head. For the first time, I noticed the colors. Warm, sunset-like colors swirled around his head, floating lazily through the air as he stood tall and looked around at all his brethren.

"I think that can wait."

Chapter 38

Tess

I stood at the black fence, my hands shoved deep in my empty pockets. Scorched, black earth filled the area, and now and then, a whiff of burnt toast would ride out on the breeze. Redwings still strode up and down the field, marching in a strange sort of dragon fashion, all on their back legs. What they were searching for, or why they felt the need to trample over the dead and crispy ground, I wasn't sure. Though they helped save the day, I still had not attempted to introduce myself. It would take me a little longer to feel up to that.

The tight feeling in my chest refused to dissolve. Almost a heaviness. Why did I feel the dread, deep down, at the base of my gut? Luther was gone. But so was my mother. And I still stared into a black field filled with dragons. Was it possible this was only the beginning? That despite what we accomplished today, things were only going to get worse?

I turned and trudged back up toward the house. The rest of my team had moved to the house for now, and those we had left stood in tight groups, arms around each other, speaking in quiet voices. There weren't many of us. Liv and Sawyer had made it back, praise the kings. Benny and Arik had gotten them out. Then they had run around with Sawyer, freeing all the Redwings they could find. Of course, Benny knew all the locations of dragon pits around the border of the city. Apparently, hearing of Quinn's Redwing bravery had sparked a little something in them as well.

At the top of the hill, I stopped to give Liv and Sawyer a hug. I smiled as she held a hand over her swollen belly. Soon, we would have a new addition. We would have to prepare for that.

I glanced over toward the porch, where Quinn and Arik sat practically in each other's laps. Quinn had been the first person he ran to. The way he held her in his arms around her shoulders, as she buried her head in his chest. Then it was my turn. A brief hug, a firm nod, and he was gone.

I guess we would all have to move on sometime. He just moved on faster than I did.

Benny was sitting under the same tree Quinn and I had argued at, at the top of the hill that overlooked the Keep. I wandered over, wondering what was going through his head at the moment.

Sighing, I plopped down on the grass next to him.

"Everybody okay?" He spoke toward the Keep, his eyes following the Red-wings.

I shrugged. "As okay as they could be, I guess." I stared down at Hash, who stood overlooking the empty field where the base would have been. He hadn't spoken a word since we pulled them from the woods.

"It's strange," I murmured.

"What is?"

"The Svaris are gone. Luther is gone. So why do I have this feeling? That things are only going to get worse?" I ran a hand through my hair, wishing I could convey these horrible feelings I had. I shook my head. "Why do I feel like we only made everything worse?" I whispered.

Benny leaned back. "We paid a heavy price for freedom. Lives were lost." He glanced over to the Keep. "And in all honesty, we're still under a dragon's control." He looked down. "I dreamed about a day I could have my family together, having picnics on the bay, going sailing together on the ocean. But it's too late for that."

"You have a family?" I asked in surprise, all dread momentarily forgotten.

He shook his head, looking down. "Had a family. It was taken away from me. By someone I trusted. Because I thought I was making things better." He gave a deep sigh. "How's that for irony?"

My heart tightened at the look in his eyes. A man who had given up everything. A man who had everything taken away. Now, he sat on a grassy hill next to me, of all people, as alone as I was.

Benny looked over at me. "What are you going to do now?"

I looked back at him, then out at the landscape. "There's no one who needs me now, I guess. Guess we try to get back to our lives."

He shook his head. "No, Tess, they all need you. Look at them. Without you, they are nothing. You must keep them fighting."

"Them? What about you?"

He looked off, a ghost of a smile on his lips. "I'm just a broken old man. Useless."

"Useless? Ha! I doubt there are few people who could disable traps in the roads and navigate the secret tunnels of Tarrith."

"I have the knowledge, but you can motivate them. To start over. We're not done, you know. Not by a long shot."

I felt the heaviness inside me shift. "What does that mean?"

He shifted where he sat. "Luther has Vera. There are more Svaris. Far away, but once they learn of what happened here . . .We have to destroy the weapon." He put his head in his hands. "We have to destroy the weapon."

"Why?" I wanted to throw my hands in the air. "It's in another universe, on the other side of a portal. Who cares?"

"What about Vera?"

I swallowed, looking down at the grass. "You think she's still alive?"

He put a hand on my knee. "I know she is."

"Why?"

"Because she is a fighter. Never forget that."

I nodded, pressing my lips together. "Okay," I said, with more bravery than I felt. "What are you going to do now? Your problems are finally over."

He shook his head sadly. "No, my problems have only begun. And it's only a matter of time until Luther realizes it."

"Realizes what?"

"The weapon. It's unstable. I fear traveling through the portal caused the rift in the atmosphere it needed to activate." His face was set in a grim line. "Somewhere out there, the weapon is alive."

I swallowed. "In the other universe. How can it hurt us?"

"It's not just us. Every universe, every being on the face of this miserable planet. I fear we've started something we can't take back."

The weight on my chest increased. "What is the weapon?" I whispered.

He looked down at the ground. Shook his head. "I don't know. It could be the pen in his pocket or the size of a Svari. All I know is what is on the inside. The parts it's made up of."

I looked at him through narrow eyes. "How do you know so much about this thing?"

He sighed. "Because I helped make it."

That much I had figured out. I nodded slowly, staring out. We sat in silence for a long time.

"Your name's not really Benny, is it?" I asked the fading sun.

He smiled. "No." He stuck a tired hand out. "Arden. Good to meet you."

About the Author

Michelle Massie is author of *The Mirri Series*, her first fantasy novels. She has a love of reading, quilts, outdoors, Star Gate, and any DIY out there. She is a wife to a wonderful, handsome husband and mother to a beautiful seven-year-old daughter, without both of whom she could never have completed three novels. (With more to come!) You can follow her at www.michellemassiewrites.com!

Reviews Matter!

If you enjoyed this book, please consider
leaving a review to help this author spread her
story to the world! Every opinion counts!